CODE
CENTAURUS

CODE CENTAURUS

FRANK LENTZ

ISBN: 978-1-63732-240-6   (Paperback Edition)
ISBN: 978-1-63732-241-3   (Hardcover Edition)
ISBN: 978-1-63732-239-0   (E-book Edition)

Some characters and events in this book are fictitious. Any similarity to real persons, living or dead, is coincidental and not intended by the author.

Book Ordering Information

Phone Number: 315 288-7939 ext. 1000 or 347-901-4920
Email: info@globalsummithouse.com
Global Summit House
www.globalsummithouse.com

Printed in the United States of America

Confirmation

OUTSIDE OF THE cave, the dense humid air of Northern New Guinea lay oppressively on the rainforest canopy. It was getting on to ten-thirty in the morning and Doctor Konrad Volger knew that even with the coolant working to capacity in his micro-stat suit, the cloying heat would soon make his work unbearable.

The dig site was at the rear of a deep cave about two hundred winding yards from the entrance. Prying out a jawbone section from concrete hard rock was delicate enough work under normal circumstances. Manipulating precision dental tools through gloved fingers was an exercise in frustration. Still, Konrad was determined to free the mandible today.

The perimeter of the pit, measured some twenty five by thirty feet. It had been excavated down to a depth of twelve. If not for his daughter's newfound powers Konrad reckoned the chances of finding the site would have been one in a thousand. Two years ago when Margo's visions had guided him here, the cave entrance had been covered by jungle growth so thick it would probably never have been uncovered by chance.

The tip off that the cave had once been inhabited was the finding of the ash. Carbon dating had shown it to be two and a half million years old. Almost certainly it was the remains of an ancient meal cooked up by a family of Homo erecti.

Dr. Konrad Volger had made it emphatically clear that the excavation was to be known solely to his immediate staff. Only when he had all his palentological ducks in a row was the media to be notified. His find would shake the scientific community. Konrad looked forward, with delicious anticipation, to the monograph that "Science" or "Nature" would shortly publish. Blinking away the sting of salt sweat in his eyes, Dr. Volger focused on a section of the masseter bone directly behind the last molar. His fingers trembled as he chipped the last of the binding rock away. He swept the bone gently with a fine horsehair brush, then carefully pried almost the entire left lower jar from the pit wall.

From a velcro-closed packet in his protective suit he removed a second fossilized jawbone. He walked a few steps to a folding table in the pit center and laid the two sections on it side by side. He nodded knowingly to himself. It was as he'd suspected, yet barely believed possible. There was no mistaking the differences between the sections. The first he had excavated only days before. With its angular chin and deep-notched ear hinge, there was no doubt it belonged to Homo sapiens. This new one with it's thicker rounded chin and shallow notch came almost certainly from a two million year old member of the species Homo erectus.

Dr. Volger anticipated what the critics would say. Like a pack of jealous jeering kids they would say that yes, we predicted all along that human remains would be found intermingled with those of near man. They would gleefully point out it was only logical that the caves used by ancestral Australopithecus or erectus would have later been taken over by modern Cro Magnon types. And yes, it was true what they would say, except for one thing.

Konrad picked up a meter stick from the table. He placed it horizontally across the little depression left from the excision of the sapiens mandible. With a child's sidewalk chalk marker he drew a line left to the spot of the erectus jaw. The line was level, nearly perfectly horizontal. That could mean only one thing. The bones in the identical stratum had come from individuals living in the cave at the same time. Modern man and his predecessor shared this very spot together. Thinking about it sent a frisson of excitement through Dr.Volger. So often he'd been the overseer of the newest scientific discoveries of others. This time it would be his turn to step into the glow of adulation. Explaining exactly how sapiens could have co-existed would be a problem he would leave to the theorists to hash out. The important thing was that he had proof that they did.

Dr. Volger wrapped the mandibles in soft cotton gauze, secured them with masking tape, then started up a wooden ladder to the top of the pit.

He walked briskly toward the glaring high noon sun outside and in two minutes was at the cave entrance.

If he hadn't been quite so anxious to get back to his ship, or had walked a little slower, he would have been close enough to hear the soft hum begin. The sound originated from just a few feet below the place in the pit where he had been working. Subsequent events might have taken a decidedly different turn had he heard the sound that day. How often it is that trivial happenings open the door to the most significant consequences.

Chapter 1

COLIN GRIER WAVED his pass at the United Nations guard, patted the snow from his overcoat, then headed for the elevator that would take him up to the offices of the World Health Organization. He was in a foul mood. His badly needed vacation was to have started tomorrow and here he was being called in for some damn "emergency". Colin strolled off the elevator, down a hall past double glass doors with their silver frosted UN symbols. He nodded politely to the secretary, Ms. Van Wyck as he passed by. She had been behind her keyboard so long Colin thought she might have laid the cornerstone of the founders East River building.

He made a left at the end of the hall then a right to a dead end. A door marked Electrical Room-No entry faced him. Colin inserted a pass card into a nearly invisible slot and waited. After a moment the door swung open. Colin stepped into a suite of spartan rooms furnished at little cost to the tax payer. His friend and mentor, Dr. George Trimble sat behind a desk smiling benignly, his folded hands resting on his paunch.

"You could have at least waited until I got unpacked," Colin said, a note of irritation in his voice. "It's not my fault sir," George answered with a shrug. "Orders from on high." Doctor Trimble thumbed toward a large cubicle off to his right. "Edwin wants to see you. The other investigators who might have taken this thing on are tied up on their own cases." George leaned forward.

"Please keep in mind Colin we can't be operating like a regular agency." Colin grunted. He moved a chair closer to George's desk and flopped. "What's on the menu this time? Ebola? No, let me guess. Mad cow." Dr. Trimble frowned. "Alright George I shouldn't

1

make light of stuff that kills like that. I'm just pissed from spending three weeks chasing down the meningitis blowup in the Sahara and not getting to catch my breath before I have to go out again. My sense of proper protocol is out of kilter."

Dr. Trimble filled his yellowing meerschaum with dark tobacco from a large crystal container. "McClure says you're to get an extra two weeks off after this. That should be some recompense."

Colin brightened.

"Great. Maybe I'll use the extra time to dash off an autobiographical screenplay. Single, thirty something M.D. chases down bugs no other agency wants to deal with. I could call it Who's The Secret who at W.H.O." Trimble winced. "Could bring seven figures," Colin kept up. George suppressed a laugh with a cough.

"Watch the levity. McClure will be out here in a second," he said with a furtive over the shoulder glance toward the chief's cubicle.

If George Trimble had been born another member of the animal kingdom Colin figured it would have been a cow. A pair of droop lidded watery blue eyes reflected the inner contentment George enjoyed as a gift of genetic predisposition. With his ruddy jowls and bushy white eyebrows he reminded Colin of a Tudor-time lord of the manor.

In earlier days he might as easily been belching and tossing stray scraps to the hounds as assisting the head of a secret epidemiology unit. Colin had liked him instinctively.

"Dr. Grier, have you been filled in yet?" a piping voice called out from the corner of the suite. "No Dr. McClure, George was just beginning."

"Fine. There's more that's come in just in the last few minutes." Colin heard Dr. McClure's door click shut. After a few jerky bounds he moved behind the desk hovering over Georges' shoulder. His anatomy was nearly opposite to Georges'. Tall and thin, he conjured up a picture of a reedy-legged heron always on high alert, missing nothing.

Edwin scrutinized both men, placed his hand authoritatively on the back of Georges chair as an unspoken signal that he wanted to sit there. George scooted around to a chair, next to Colin. Edwin smiled his tight thin smile, then plopped a file folder on the desk.

"I won't belabor you two with the origins of this office" Dr. McClure began. His fingertips ran a slow circle around the point of a letter opener. "Just let me remind you that we serve at the pleasure of the Security Council. In their deliberations they have deemed it prudent to have this auxiliary epidemiological unit on standby in cases where political tact dictates open disease investigation is unwise."

George and Colin nodded with due solemnity. McClure removed a thick volume of the U.N. bylaws from his desk drawer, and flipped pages with the opener. "Here it is." He began to read in an official tone. "There shall, from time to time, be established an epidemiological office whose duty it shall be to give appropriate aid to States whose peoples suffer from microbial outbreaks, but who, due to disputes among States may be denied access to prompt and thorough relief."

"Quite a mouthful," Colin quipped. McClure's brow tightened.

"With due respect sir, I believe Colin and I are fully aware of the bylaws," George interjected. "Colin's Sahara mission was authorized because the authorities there would only agree to help for their people from a non-sovereign agency."

Dr. McClure replaced the bylaws in the drawer. He leaned forward catching Colin's and George's eyes with his own.

"I took the trouble to explicitly read that text for a reason. You'll notice there is no *written* stipulation that our work be open or closed. However, that being the case it's important that you continue to regard the mandate's intent as being as it has evolved....closed." Dr. McClure pushed back his chair and stood. "I want to reinforce to you that our office is to do its job out of the glare of publicity. There have been leaks to the media about minor outbreaks the public is better off not knowing about. That is until the information can be parceled out in an orderly manner." McClure sat down again. "Enough then. George, let Colin look these over." Dr. McClure pushed the folder toward George. George selected several four by six color prints and handed them to Colin. "We received these last night Colin. Give me your diagnoses," Dr. McClure ordered. The photos hadn't been taken in the best light but there was little doubt about what they showed.

"Human livers right?", Colin asked.

"Obviously, What disease?" Colin noted that each organ was swollen almost to bursting. There were small capillary hemorrhages uniformly speckling the liver's surface. Instead of a healthy brown red these organs were sewer water green. "Hepatitis," Colin said.

"Correct," Dr. McClure confirmed.

"This is why you're sending me out again", Colin queried. "Just hepatitis? Can't somebody else take care of this?"

"No, they can't," George interrupted. "The lab reports show the livers are loaded with hepatitis B. These photos are of the livers of a group of isolated fishing people. Natives of New Guinea. Some twenty-five villagers are dead in the space of ten days. Hepatitis B has no business being there."

"There haven't been transfusions or blood products given within miles of their village," McClure added.

"No dirty needles of course," Colin said. George shook his head.

"Hardly. These people wouldn't know smack from half and half. They're innocent types......at least as innocent as are left now a days. You see a lot of bad teeth and jungle itch. No way they came in contact with this virus." Dr. McClure cracked his knuckles repeatedly. Not a good sign Colin knew.

"Show him the rest George."

"Here's why it's got to be us," George said. He laid a second spread of pictures in front of Colin.

Colin's face tightened.

The photographs showed three naked bodies. Two males and a female lying on thatched mats. The males were about 40 years old Colin guessed. With the woman there was just no way to tell. The men's skin was covered with smallpox pustules. That was alarming enough. But the woman; Colin had never seen anything like it. Her skin was brown and wrinkled. Not old age wrinkled but more..... crinkled was the word that came to mind. It looked as if it had been subjected to deep frying. The skin's outer layer was separated from the dermis underneath. There were a multitude of pus filled blisters between the skin layers.

"Jesus", Colin muttered. George drew his chair closer into Colin.

4

"There's a possibility the cause is an environmental toxin" he said. "I'm looking into that, but Dr. McClure thinks it's probably caused by a bug we've never seen before." McClure began to pace slowly, his hands clasped behind his back.

"You should know Colin, that shortly before you signed on here there was another outbreak in this exact area. Basically the same scenario. Rampant hepatitis B and a crop up of small pox. The skin horror hadn't shown up then. This was in '09 when Fratelli held George's post."

"Naturally, I looked over Dr. Fratelli's papers when I replaced him Colin", George offered. "Fratelli made a note about getting a call from Port Moresby's Health department late in 2009. As you can imagine they're a pretty small outfit. They hadn't seen a flare up of anything worse than the flu in years."

"Scared to death and I don't blame them.", McClure added. "Dr. Fratelli and I flew down to Moresby ourselves", McClure went on.

"A charter took us over The Owen Stanley's up to the North Coast. The village is called Barubi by the local tribe. It's not on the map."

"Find an index case?", Colin asked.

"No clue at all. The dying stopped as suddenly as it began." Dr. McClure ran his fingers through his sparse hair. "Ever heard of ERSEV?", McClure asked. Colin shook his head. "I didn't think so. Not many people have." McClure exhaled deeply. "When I was a graduate student I had a summer foundation grant to study at the University in Zurich. The money only covered my tuition. So I looked around and picked up a part time job as a lab tech. The lab was affiliated with the ERSEV society. I learned their headquarters was up in the mountains near Ulringen."

"ERSEV, odd name," Colin opined.

"Acronym for Erforschen Vereingung. Roughly translates to explorer's association." "What's it have to do with the Barubi outbreak?", Colin asked.

"Don't know. Maybe nothing." McClure tapped the tip of the letter opener with his finger. "ERSEV has a reputation for avoiding the spotlight. They take pains to fix it so their research is done privately. They were working at Barubi during the first outbreak".

"Doing what?" Colin's eyes opened in surprise. "They had discovered a twelfth century Hindu temple near the village. Neither Fratelli or I saw it, but excavating had been going on a few months. The dig was headed up by a lovely young woman archeologist."

"That's their field of expertise? Archeology?", Colin asked.

"That and pretty much anything else you care to mention.", McClure continued. "They have people on their staff with first rate minds in any number of scientific fields. Noble Prize candidates. From what I've been able to find out, the ERSEV Society had it's start in Germany way back in the seventeen hundreds. It began as an informal club of what were then called Natural Philosophers. They liked to think of themselves as particularly enlightened and independent."

"How about their funding?", George broke in.

"Over the years they're said to have built up a portfolio running into the billions," McClure answered.

"You mentioned they've been helpful. How?", Colin asked.

"It's hard to find out what they're up to just now," McClure said. "But I've learned that a generation ago their research had a lot to do with development of the tiles on the space shuttle and the workup of cyclosporine, the anti rejection drug. It's even rumored that early evidence for plate tectonic theory was funded by ERSEV money."

"And their price for all this," Colin asked.

"None. Just the freedom to follow their theoretical pathways without government red tape."

"Any instances where they've locked horns with the bureaucrats?", George asked. McClure held Georges' eyes with his own for a moment. "Yes, with me."

Mc Clure puckered his lips obviously pondering the smartest way to go on with his explanation. "I had to get them away from Barubi, no doubt about it. I had the area quarantined in Autumn of '09, including the Temple site. Chased them home then left Dr. Fratelli there to oversee that the evacuation was carried out." McClure looked away recollecting ERSEV's expulsion. "I had a hell of a row with their chief of staff, a Doctor Volger I think the name was. They wanted to take their chances with the outbreak, sign a waiver releasing me of any responsibility, but I forbade it. Naturally it was for their own good."

"What about the villagers?", George asked.

"Had them medevaced out along with some ERSEV staff." Dr. McClure turned to a small safe behind his desk. He dialed a combination, then took out a small accordion file. He handed it to Colin.

"Tickets to Barubi?", Colin asked as he untied the string. McClure nodded. "You have to get down there as soon as possible Colin. You're the only one I want to handle this. Wish I could give you some help but it's best you go alone."

Colin fingered through the file. "Everything you should need is in there," McClure said. "You'll see I'm having you pick up a private charter out of Darwin. I don't want you using public transport."

"Questions from customs? Since the Twin Towers they're a lot nosier," Colin said. "It's taken care of."

"Don't forget about Lippincott," George politely interjected. He'd been taking in the interchange with a bemused smile.

"I was just getting to that George. Thank you," McClure said. Colin looked back and forth between the two men.

"Who's Lippincott?"

"You won't be totally in the dark when you get down there Colin," McClure went on.

"Ed Lippincott is one of Morsby's two fulltime Health Department people. You should find him at Barubi village by the time you get there."

"I'll have the initial doses ready for you before you go," George added. "Doses for what?", Colin asked. There was an awkward silence.

"I meant whatever medications we have that are appropriate," George replied, somewhat defensively. With a wave of his hand Dr. McClure cut the developing line of conversation short.

"You're first priority is to be an analysis of the situation Colin. Find the index case or cases first, but I want causes to take precedence over therapeutics. Help those you can, if you can of course, but you need to focus first on locating the source of this mess."

Worry lines deepened on Georges face.

"If this skin thing is some new mutation and it should spread south toward Sidney..." he said, his voice trailing off.

"Or North to Indonesia and up the Asian Coast", Dr. McClure added.

"I was thinking", Colin said. "Roughly the probability of smallpox popping up in Northern New Guinea is about five thousand to one. Same thing for hepatitis B and the skin business....." Colin let out his breath in a silent whistle. "Let's hope it comes from some chemical and not a mutated microbe."

"Let's hope," Dr. McClure repeated heading toward the office door.

"George and I should be in contact with Lippincott before you get to the village. I'll want updates from you every few hours."

"Will do." Colin shook hands with Dr. McClure and George and pulled the door closed behind him. He started down the hall then stopped halfway. Colin leaned back against the wall. A lot of information had passed through his brain in the last fifteen minutes and he needed a quick mental breath to catch up.

He hadn't watched McClure in action very much but he knew that underneath the brusque efficient façade a reservoir of anxiety was brewing. Actually there was more than that. Colin smelled fear. That McClure was alarmed that a second edition of a mysterious collection of diseases was breaking out again shouldn't be surprising.

It was any one's guess why the disease popped up so suddenly and then disappeared as quickly. This time the diseases might continue their infectious spread for many miles. But Colin suspected that the threat of multitudes dying wasn't what McClure feared.

The scuttlebutt was that McClure was in line for the next opening on the Presidents Science Advisory Council. If word got out among the insiders that McClure botched the containment of the '09 outbreak, that would put paid to his hopes for a seat at the President's table. Colin felt sure that the apprehension he'd seen in McClure's eyes was not so much for the outbreak's victims, but rather for his obsessive ambitions. Colin pushed himself away from the wall then turned into Ms. Van Wyks office. The old woman was busy on the phone. She held up her hand for Colin to wait. When the call was over she handed over a money envelope with a sincere "Be careful." A good lady Colin thought. He gave he a wave goodbye, assuming he's be back in perhaps a week to ten days. He might have made a more heartfelt farewell had he known he'd never return.

CHAPTER 2

IN A CRAMPED cockpit behind the pilot Colin stretched out his legs as far as he could.

"How long before we get to Barubi?", Colin shouted over the noise of the old seaplane's engine."

"We're doing a hundred and four knots now," Buz Ryan, the pilot hollered back. "If I push her to one twenty five we should be there in two hours. She'll burn a little more oil than's good for her, if I crank it up anymore than that."

"Okay, why don't we keep her at one hundred and four. Wouldn't want to have you throw a bearing." Ryan laughed. He was wearing an antique leather-flying jacket that looked like it was new when Chennault was flying his P-40's. Tobacco juice stains from years of chewing added a certain nostalgic patina.

"No need to worry Mr. Grier. As long as I stay under six thousand feet Betsy here will run just fine.

If she should have a little spell she always starts up again."

"Great," Colin yelled not bothering to query Ryan about what might happen should the old crate have it's "spell" with the peaks of the Owen Stanley's within feet dragging distance. Colin had taken off in Ryan's charter from Darwin only fifteen minutes earlier. Already the last vestiges of Australia's Northern most peninsula were fading behind the plane. The open cockpit gave Colin a panoramic view. Great piles of pink and white cumulus clouds rolled gently to his right. Below, the turquoise Arafura Sea separating Australia from New Guinea, flowed peacefully under the late noonday sun.

"You one of those anthropology people?", Ryan asked.

"Doing another other kind or research. Bird wing studies," Colin lied. "Bird wing?"

"Giant butterflies. The biggest specimens in the world live in New Guinea. I work for an organization interested in saving rare species."

"I figured you were a scientist or something." Ryan spat a stream of tobacco juice into the prop wash. "We get these anthropology people hiring the charters a couple times a year. There are still some Stone Age tribes up in the mountains. They go up to live with them. You married?"

Blindsided by the question, Colin felt a little catch in his breathing. "No, no I'm not."

"I can understand that," Ryan said. "Must be hard when your job takes you all over the world." "It is that," Colin agreed, without much conviction.

Married was something Colin had figured on being by now. It was something he'd always wanted, assuming he could find the right woman. But after doing the club scene for awhile he'd come to the conclusion that his soul mate wasn't to be found in the bars, upscale or down. He'd tried internet dating but wasn't satisfied with the women there either. He was beginning to think it was him. Not that he wasn't a fair catch. He was reasonably good looking, witty when in the mood and basically what most considered a nice guy. He guessed it must be that he was just too picky. Looking for Ms. Perfect. Anyhow, Ryan had put his finger on a part of it. He was away from his cozy condo so much it was hard to run a string of dates with the same woman together. A cough from the plane's engine jolted Colin back to the present. Ryan turned his head back toward Colin.

"Nothing to be alarmed about Dr. Grier. We've just passed by the highest peak in the Finisteree Range. Up this high the engine gets a bit quirky. I always expect it. Just complaining about the thinner air."

"Much longer?", Colin shouted.

"We're starting down now. Keep an eye out to your left. When the north coast shows up on the horizon Barubi will be at about ten o'clock. Hard to see though. Just a little hollow in the jungle."

"You've been there?", Colin asked.

"I was supposed to drop some people off there a couple of years ago. Never got there. Some kind of quarantine going on. I never did find out what the fuss was all about."

"Did you ask around?"

"Stuff like that gives me the jitters. There's two things get on the nerves. Snakes and breathing in germs I can't see."

"Don't care much for either one myself," Colin replied with a grin. Under the biplanes wings the jungle was a deep verdant green. A mist hung, gossamer like, just above the slowly darkening valley. Colin sensed an air of sleepy brooding rising up from the wild land.

Far off in the west the veiled sun was just beginning to edge below the horizon. Colin closed his eyes and leaned his head back. How much of his appetite for field work was stimulated by the threat of danger he wasn't sure of. At bottom nobody knew the real reasons for their attraction to this job or that. Certainly the element of the unknown was an enticement. Colin pictured his research lab back at Sanofi and was glad he wasn't still wearing a white coat.

After spending three years there wearing the silly plastic hats and gloves, he'd had enough.

Research and Development had its place. A vitally important one in fact. After all, where would the newer medicine come from if it weren't for the plodding efforts of the guinea pig gang. Still, he was aware of a sense of superiority to those who preferred the comfort of their stainless steel and glass boxes to the adventure of medicine in the raw. Running around in their crisp white coats, they sometimes seemed just a more intelligent version of the pink eyed rats they tracked through their mazes. It was a prejudice and Colin knew it. Still, it was hard for him to totally respect the M.D.'s who had chosen to keep their hands clean of the pus and scabs of the sick.

A crackle of the seaplane's radio focused back Colin's attention. Ryan picked up a pair of ancient ceramic earphones from the instrument panel and strained to hear over the noise.

"Yep this is Ryan's charter. How did you get my call letters?........ Oh." Ryan bent forward over the stick pressing the earphones tighter to his ear. "Yes he's right behind me.....Say again?......That's right Barubi."

"Who is it," Colin shouted. Ryan waved him to be quiet.

"How far off the beach?.....Got it....Hold on one second." Ryan pulled back the stick picking up the hundred feet he dropped when his eyes were off the altimeter. "There's this ship off the coast near Barubi Dr. Grier. They want to pick you up before you get to the beach. The communication officer says they've been in contact with a Dr. Lippincott. They say they have vital information for you. What should I say?"

"What kind of ship?", Colin yelled.

"They said to tell you it's an ERSEV vessel." Colin's eyes widened with surprise. "Tell them I will be coming aboard."

"Roger." Ryan relayed Colin's answer and hung up the headset. "I don't mean to pry Dr. Grier but this seems to be a lot of fuss over butterflies. I know how to keep my mouth shut. Mind telling me what's really going on?" Colin's first impulse was to lie some more. But his gut told him Ryan was a man who could be trusted.

"Germs you can't see," Colin answered. "I work for a disease control unit that steps in when the Boards of Health like Port Moresby's have too much to handle."

"Like a temporary help company in disease prevention", Ryan offered.

"That's the gist of it. Since you're already in the know about the last quarantine I guess I can tell you the truth." Colin made a quick mental calculation about how much truth would be safe to parcel out.

"There's been a smallpox outbreak at Barubi. We thought we had it wiped out years ago, but it looks like the last fugitives have been hiding out down here. About a dozen villagers have died." That was enough. Colin sure as hell wasn't about to mention the hepatitis or the skin horror.

"I appreciate the straight scoop," Ryan said. "Happy to be doing a little part in clearing up the last of it."

"Just keep it to yourself", Colin said. "The last thing I need are media people underfoot."

"Mums the word Dr. Grier." And what were ERSEV people doing with a ship off Barubi? Colin wondered. What kind of information could they have that would possibly help? Colin was sure the quarantine Dr. McClure slapped on them was still in effect.

"Did they tell you where the ship was exactly?", Colin shouted.

"They're anchored fifteen, twenty miles off the beach." International waters then, just barely. The quarantine wouldn't be in effect out that far. The only reason for an ERSEV ship to be parked off Barubi had to be the twelfth century temple McClure mentioned. Why else would they be hanging around?, Colin wondered. Maybe they'd been shuttling out to sea and back to the coast since McClure's order. But McClure had left Fratelli behind to make sure nobody returned and not much got by Fratelli. Then there was this fellow Lippincott. How had ERSEV gotten hooked up with him? Well, I'll be finding out soon enough Colin thought. Not a lot of profit in hypothesizing. A little knowledge is a dangerous thing so they said.

"Hold on", Ryan suddenly shouted back. "There are a few peaks that can jump up out of the coastal fog here. I'm going to run a couple of miles out of our way to slide around them." Colin braced his legs. Ryan was at four thousand feet. He banked the plane in a steep dive that took the seaplane down to treetop level in a few seconds. Colin swallowed hard trying to negate the elevator rise in his stomach. The engine hummed happily now that it had its fill of oxygen. Ryan sped down a steep valley. Then turned left around the base of a long loaf shaped mountain. And there just a few miles in front of it was the north coast beach. "Straight ahead. You see it?", Ryan asked.

"Couldn't miss it". Colin had expected to see a ship the size of a coast guard cutter, maybe two hundred fifty, three hundred feet. In the creamy glow of a low rising full moon what looked like the largest cruise ship ever built sat glowing radiantly out beyond the breakers. ERSEV had doubled back to the no go zone.

"They're not lying low are they?", Ryan asked.

"Looks like an ad agency photo. Half the beach is lit up from their wattage," Colin replied. Ryan took the seaplane down close enough for Colin to smell the sea salt. A series of signals flashed out from mid-ship.

"What's that about?"

"They flashed Welcome Dr. Grier," Ryan answered. "They want me to come up on starboard." Ryan set the plane down gently on the easy swells, but the pontoons still sent a spray of water into the cockpit. Ryan cut the engine and skillfully let the plane drift slowly to within a hundred yards of the ship. Gently rocking on the waves, the little plane was a speck below the towering thrust of the bow. On the ship's side ERSEV was painted in large blue initials. Colin saw no one on the decks. In a moment a twin hull 30 foot sea-cat came throbbing around the bow. It's big 150HP engines threw up a trail of hazy gray exhaust. A smiling indistinct figure at the wheel waved as the boat approached. Colin waved back. "You should take off your shoes Dr. Grier," Ryan said. "You're liable to get wet in the transfer."

"Thanks. I only have one pair." Colin tied his laces together then hung his well worn Timberlands around his neck. With a grunting tug he managed to wedge his duffle and himself out of the cockpit. Somehow he lowered himself onto the rocking pontoon.

"Dr. Grier, greeting," a cheery voice called out from the approaching cat. With one hand on the pontoon strut and the other holding the duffle Colin nodded an awkward reply. The boats pilot, a clean cut olive skinned young man, drew up next to the plane and held out his hand for Colin to jump over.

Colin timed the roll of the sea-cat and the plane as best he could and managed to jump over without a swim. The young man steadied Colin with an arm clasp. "On behalf of the ERSEV foundation I'd like to welcome you. I'm Roberto Valdes, Dr. Volgers assistant."

"Thank you. This isn't quite what I'd expected."

"I understand entirely." Roberto motioned for Colin to sit. Colin put his shoes back on, then signaled Ryan that it was okay to take off. In a few seconds the seaplane was airborne and winding back toward Darwin. "I hope you will forgive this unusual interruption of your work Dr. Grier, but by a serendipitous accident I believe we've found the cause of the outbreak."

"Really?" Colin felt shocked. This wasn't at all what he thought Roberto was going to say. Before he could question Roberto the pleasant young man stopped him.

"Your finding us here is a real surprise for you I know."

"Well, I know your foundation was doing archeological work near Barubi when the initial outbreak occurred."

"And you're concerned. I fully understand." Roberto started the launch back toward the ship. "Dr. Volger wants me to be sure to let you know that we've followed Dr. McClure's quarantine order to the letter," Roberto said. He docked the sea-cat under a ladder stairway at the ERSEV's stern.

"Your archeology work is connected with this outbreak?", Colin asked.

The back of his brain was lining up more pointed questions, but better to be polite first he thought. "You know of course about the Temple find."

"I got a bit of background from Dr. McClure on the way out the door, yes." "Well let me give you the fuller story then," Roberto said, while tying up the cat.

"As we cleared the Temple ruins we found writings showing that in the 12th Century Hindu pilgrims had come here by ship to the Temple site. The writings tell of a storm that killed most aboard one of the ships. The writings contain a prayer to Vishnu in memory of the lost pilgrims. I won't bother you with the details but in short we transferred much of our exploration from the Temple to these waters offshore. We were fortunate to find the remains of the ship." Colin began to speak but Roberto held up his palm. "And what does all this have to do with the outbreak you're thinking."

"Quite."

"Well, by sheer accident we've found the answer to both outbreaks down there also ." "Underwater?", Colin asked incredulously.

"Yes. If you'll accept our hospitality and stay aboard this evening, then first thing tomorrow Dr. Volger will layout all the findings for you."

"How about Lippincott? I was to meet him at Barubi." "Dr. Lippincott has been briefed fully on our discovery. He's on his way back to Port Moresby now."

"And the sick have been medevaced out?"

"Along with most of our researchers on board, the sick have been transported to a private facility near Darwin. Believe me everything is under control. We know how much your office is concerned with helping all this, under the radar, as they say. We at ERSEV have had much practice in doing science out of the media's glare. You can depend on our discretion."

"Sounds like there's little left for me to do," Colin said.

One damn efficient bunch, but almost too good to be true Colin thought. "What have you found out about the skin syndrome?"

"It's from a synthetic toxin. Thank God we don't have some horrible new microbe to deal with." "I'll want to examine everything you've found myself", Colin admonished. "Absolutely. All the data will be at your complete disposal.", Roberto answered. "As soon as daybreak if you wish." Colin thought about it. Lippincott certainly wouldn't have gone back to Moresby if there was still any disease spreading. And if ERSEV's labs were as up to date as advertised there would be little to worry about. No doubt they'd been meticulous in analyzing the outbreak's origins.

"Okay. You've got yourself an overnight guest. I can't say that sleeping in a bed will bother me.

Much nicer than a sleeping bag in Barubi."

"We'll do all we can to make you comfortable Colin." Roberto headed up the stern ladder with Colin following. "Your stateroom is amid ships Colin on deck C. Almost all the decks below us are fitted out as research labs." Colin dutifully tagged behind Roberto until they came to stateroom C-47. Roberto unlocked the door to reveal a stunning interior.

"Beautiful" Colin said stepping inside.

"Are all your live-in rooms this nice.", Roberto laughed.

"Until a few days ago this was Margo's room...Dr. Volger's daughter. She's the one who discovered the Temple."

"Not good enough for her?", Colin wisecracked. Roberto's face took on a serious cast. "She's been rather ill unfortunately."

"I hope it's not serious", Colin said. The polite words came automatically but he made a sincere effort to imagine the woman who'd occupied this exquisite room.

"I'm afraid it is Colin. It may possibly be related to the outbreak ashore. Margo is being tested in the infirmary now. We don't want to speculate until the tests are completed."

"I'm sorry", Colin said regretting his flip remark.

"Well if there is anything at all that you need just pick up the phone" Roberto said, dropping the subject. "I'm sure you must be hungry. In the kitchenette you'll find a tray of hors d'oeuvres and some more substantial foods laid out for you."

Roberto crossed to a chest of drawers. "If my directions were followed there should be sleepwear here. Ah yes". He took out a thick terry robe, slippers and pajamas and laid them on the bed.

"I think your toiletries are in the bathroom. Let me check a moment". Roberto headed around a corner toward the bathroom. Colin plopped down on the bed and took in the details of the stateroom. The furnishings were exquisite. Colin wasn't an art expert by any stretch, but would have bet that the chest and couches were antiques from somewhere between the sixteenth and eighteenth centuries. The end tables were ornamental with gold leaf and pearl inlay. His stocking feet felt soothed in a thick oriental.

All together Colin guessed he was looking at about a quarter million dollars worth of stuff.

Obviously, McClure was right on the money about ERSEV being worth a fortune.

With a contented sigh he laid back on the thick down mattress. The frantic bustling to make his connection hadn't left much time for relaxation. He began to drift off when his eye caught a painting he hadn't noticed on the deck side of the stateroom wall. Colin sat up. The sleepiness suddenly gone from his head. "Is something wrong?", Roberto asked reappearing with a stack of thick white towels.

"No everything's fine", Colin replied. Something about the painting galvanized him. "It's wonderfully done," Colin said, letting his eyes roam over the vibrant colors.

"Margo painted it. The oils are still not completely dry." Roberto put the towels down, walked to a dimmer and turned up the light. "It's titled "The Ceremony." Margo has become enamored of Ancient Greek Rites lately."

"Was she in Greece when she began this?"

"No, no. Done totally from her imagination." The painting, about 3x5, was of the entrance of a Parthenon like Temple except that the friezes above the fluted columns were brilliantly colored. Probably the way the iconic monument on the Acropolis once looked, Colin thought. In a semicircle at the Temple steps there was a gathering of women, most with double flutes or other musical instruments Colin didn't know the name of. In the center of the women was a scarlet robed man with his back to the viewer ascending the marble steps. The little bit of technique Colin did know about told him the brushwork was first rate, somewhere between realism and impressionism.

The whole painting was suffused with an inner luminescence that seemed to emanate from a source beside the pigments themselves. Just why it drew him in so much Colin couldn't say. He had a hard time taking his eyes away. "So you believe in Omens?", Roberto asked unexpectedly. Colin paused to reorient his thinking.

"Omens? I don't know. I don't discount them totally I suppose. I try to keep an open mind. Why?" "A good thing an open mind," Roberto said with a thoughtful smile. "Much research is in progress on this ship in a myriad of disciplines. We pride ourselves on not excluding any area of inquiry." Roberto's warm gaze moved between the painting and Colin. "Rest well. See you in the morning," Roberto said as he opened the stateroom door. Colin turned the lights off. A soft shaded bulb kept the painting lit so that it seemed to float its dazzling colors in the air. Colin laid back taking it in.

Exactly where was Roberto heading with the Omen query?, Colin wondered. Did some connection with the painting trigger his question? Colin wished he'd asked him outright. The result of being too brain weary he thought. He closed his eyes half way and with a minimum of effort played with his focus, letting the paintings colors dissolve and sharpen by tiny changes in eye pressure. He made a game of it for a minute then the urge to sleep finally won out. After a while he had a dream. It was of the Temple painting. Only he was inside now standing before an altar. A young woman appeared who greeted him with a kiss. Abruptly he woke. He tried by force of will to fall back into the same dream again. The feeling was wonderful. But to enter it again was impossible. Colin grumbled to himself, rolled over and fell into a restful, but ordinary slumber.

CHAPTER 3

AT ABOUT 9 a.m. a quiet knock on the cabin door woke Colin. In a gravely voice he called for his visitor to come in. When his eyes focused Colin saw a pleasant looking youth of about eighteen holding a tray with delicious smells wafting from it.

"Good morning Dr. Grier, I'm Tony. We thought you'd be wanting breakfast." Colin usually skipped breakfast preferring to grab a piece of fruit around ten, but when food was prepared for you and under your nose it would be rude to refuse. Bacon, eggs, cereal, coffee and orange juice were on the tray.

"Thanks I am hungry," Colin said. He propped himself into a sitting position. Tony placed the tray before him.

"Dr. Grier, I'll be your steward while you're aboard." The young man handed a cell phone to Colin. "Whatever you need anytime just dial 555. It will be my pleasure to act as your valet."

The young man grinned seeming slightly embarrassed. "I'll be leaving now to let you have your breakfast in private. Just ring when you're finished." With a half bow Tony turned and shut the door quietly. "Whatever you need anytime," Colin mused. If only it were as easy as that. Colin started in on the food which tasted as good as it smelled. He was surprised at how hungry he'd become. He even ate the stewed prunes which he normally passed over. After a satisfying belch he went to the bathroom turned on the shower and luxuriated under the steaming water. He shaved and in fifteen minutes felt fully refreshed. It was good to know he could still bounce back with just a few hours rest. Colin stepped out on deck and took his first good look at the north coast beach. An early morning haze still lingered over the tropical greenery. It was hard to believe that behind the towering coconut palms diseased villagers had been suffering. There wasn't the slightest indication that the lush quiet rainforest had so recently harbored killer viruses. About a mile inland a thin wisp of smoke, probably from a cooking fire, gave the only hint that Barubi village was there.

Colin had learned that a few of the north coast tribes were descendants of highlanders and still preserved their head hunting ways. Hopefully the Barubi people were not among them.

The stillness was broken by the insistent chiming of the cell phone in his cabin. He hurried in.

Roberto was on the line.

"Good morning Colin. I hope you slept well." "Very well thank you. Listen Roberto, I'd like to see the dope on the diseases as soon as I can."

"Of course. That's exactly why I'm calling. Dr. Volger wondered if you could meet him on the bridge. By the way have you done any scuba diving?" Roberto seemed to have a habit of changing subjects abruptly.

"I did a little off the Keys. Just tourist level stuff. Maybe down to fifty feet for a half hour. That's all."

"That's fine", Roberto enthused. What we have to show you is only down about four fathoms. Dr. Volger and I will meet you in the wheelhouse." Colin turned off the cell, trying to imagine what was below the surface. He found his way to the bridge where Roberto was already wearing a wetsuit.

Next to Roberto stood a tanned vigorously looking man of about sixty shouldering his air tanks. He grasped Colin's hand with both of his own.

"Dr. Grier, I'm Konrad Volger. I must apologize for not greeting you personally last evening. As both captain and ERSEV administrator, I was compelled to sit through a rather boring meeting with my supply people. You are most welcome aboard." Colin had envisioned Dr. Volger to be a small acerbic looking man although for no good reason other than some mental picture was better than none. The man zipping up his wet suit emanated energy and personality. There was a definite charisma Colin's conjecture hadn't accounted for. "I know how anxious you are to get to the source of the outbreak Colin," Konrad said, pushing a shock of pure white hair under the wetsuit's hood. "As they say seeing is believing. I hope you don't think me too presumptuous," he went on. "I thought this little dive would provide the fullest answer to your concerns." Colin nodded amiably.

"You go ahead and run the show for now. I'm ready whenever you are." Colin dressed quickly in a wetsuit Dr. Volger had at hand. Roberto checked the fittings. Konrad led Colin and Roberto down a port gangway to an eight-man rubber boat. A fifty horse Mercury outboard was attached. Colin sat next to Konrad at the throttle with Roberto in front. Within a few seconds the bright yellow boat was skipping over the water like a thrown stone. In a couple of minutes they arrived at a spot about a third of a mile off the beach. Konrad cut the noisy Mercury.

"I'll wager you're the first physician to search for a disease source under the waves," Konrad said. "At least in a wetsuit," Colin answered going along with Dr. Volger's lighthearted banter. Konrad threw his head back and laughed heartedly. In spite of the serious purpose of his mission Colin found Dr. Volger's not to worry mood contagious. The ERSEV chief projected an easy sense of light heartedness that Colin felt rubbing off onto himself. Probably Volger was one of those rare creatures who couldn't wait to hop out of a bed in the morning. The thrive on any challenge type. God bless them. Colin wished he'd had a bit more of that joie de vive himself. Konrad stood and pointed down to a barely discernable sandbar about twenty feet below.

"We go down there Colin. Look closely. You can just see a reddish brown object sticking out of the sandbar." Colin cupped his eyes to cut down on the reflected light. After a few seconds searching he saw what Konrad was pointing to. There was a faint rusty form just visible along the sandbars centered section.

"What is it?", Colin asked.

"The wreckage of a Russian transport. Your index case," Konrad said. "We'll go down and you can see for yourself." Colin put his flippers on, adjusted his mask and at Konrad's signal all three men flipped backward into the warm sea. Colin tested his air supply.

When he was satisfied all was normal he swam down toward Roberto and Konrad. The ocean floor was patched with clusters of purple staghorn interwoven with golden etched brain coral. Schools of red and white stripped clownfish darted in and out among them. At another time Colin would have wanted to leisurely wander through the mazes of the reef. The coral stretched out in a wide beautifully colored carpet toward the deep. Regretfully, he reminded himself he wasn't on vacation, and that serious business was at hand. Some distance away Konrad hovered over the far end of the rusty hull. He signaled for Roberto to swim toward him. Then gave a definite stay back sign to Colin. Colin nodded. He watched as both men dove down to the sunken vessel. Roberto used a portable air hose to blow silt and sand from the sideways hull. In a few moments he had blown away enough of the covering for three letters of the ships name to become exposed. Konrad pointed emphatically at the script, YAH. Colin signaled that he saw them. Konrad beckoned to Colin to follow him.

He trailed dutifully along behind the two into deeper water wondering what was up. When they got to seven fathoms, Konrad again waved Colin off. From a hundred feet away he watched as the two men removed small rakes from their belts. They began to gently scratch at the bottom's sand. After the silt clouds settled Colin could see the men had uncovered two olive green thermos sized canisters. There was iridescent orange lettering on them two small for Colin to read. Konrad pointed to the two buried objects, then swept his arm around in a wide arc indicating, Colin understood, that more of the canisters were buried in a wide area around the hull.

In a cutting gesture, Konrad drew his hand across his neck. There was no doubt about his meaning. Roberto pointed to his watch. Konrad nodded and pointed to the surface. Colin followed the two men up to the yellow boat. Roberto helped Colin roll inside. Konrad stayed in the water holding onto the side. He tossed his mask into the boat.

"The name of the ship was the YAHKA" Konrad said, a bit breathlessly. "It's Russian for seagull. We came across it while looking for the 12th Century wrecks. A little research turned up the information that the YAHKA was headed for North Vietnam

23

in '67. The canisters are biological warfare pieces. Experimental germ warfare containers the Soviets were sending to Ho and his troops in case your country decided not to bail out. Fortunately they signed the cease fire before they were ever used." Colin unbuckled his tanks.

"How did the YAHKA go down?"

"A series of typhoons blew by here in the sixties", Roberto spoke up. "Best guess is that she foundered in one of them. The Soviets would have had little interest in claiming her." Colin made a grunt of comprehension. The Russians would have wanted the United States to believe the canisters were the doings of the Viet Cong should they ever be used. Best for the Soviets to let sleeping dogs lie he considered.

"So the canisters broke open then," Colin said following the logical line.

"Exactly," Roberto said. "They should have been impregnable for years," he continued. "Our labs took a few apart...very carefully I might add. The canisters were well insulated, but in machining the cases a small gap was left at the top seal. Enough to let the viruses escape." "*And* the toxin, that's the cause of the skin ailment.", Konrad added.

"They put the concoction in a chamber at the base of the canister. Altogether a treacherous little package." Konrad pulled himself into the boat. "We have the canisters ready for you to examine whenever you wish," Konrad said. "I think you'll agree that there's little profit in letting a post Glasnost world know about this."

"I see your point. It would only serve to stir up old animosities," Colin agreed. Not much of positive value would come from letting the media hordes know the Soviets had been prodding Ho to let loose a plague on American service men. "Dr. Lippincott knows all about this. I told him a full report about his findings with us would be going out to his office in Port Moresby today.", Konrad said. "They'll know the whole story of the sinking and the canisters." Konrad pursed his lips thoughtfully. "There's the question of compensation to the villagers naturally. The lawyers in Moresby can hash that out with the Russians I suppose. It's not a question my foundation or your people need to deal with. Colin, if you want to sign off on this

I can fax a report to New York this evening," Konrad encouraged. Colin thought it over. The whole business had mostly transpired between Lippincott's agency and ERSEV. In a sense he'd come in as a fifth wheel. If Lippincott had seen fit to share the trauma with ERSEV first, there wasn't much sense in his holding things up.

"Fine. Send it," Colin said contentedly. He realized his job was for all intents finished. Really, the only thing left for him to do would be to write up a summary to go along with Konrad's report and hand it over to McClure when he got back to New York. McClure should be delighted. No media. No panic. No threat to McClure's ambition.

Konrad started up the Mercury, then steered the craft back to the ship. Colin stretched out his legs letting the smell of the ocean breeze refresh him. There was an urge to help Konrad, to say he'd be happy to do this or that but there was nothing he could think of that needed doing. He was like the guy who walks into the kitchen to help with the dishes only to find the last plate dried and put in the cupboard.

"If it's okay with you we'll finish up the paperwork first thing. Then I'll have our chef whip up one of his splendid dinners. If you wish you may want to take a short tour of our ships labs." Konrads eyebrows rose hopefully. "Do you drink wine?"

"Only if I can pick it up for less than fifteen bucks." Konrad laughed good naturedly.

"Well then, this evening I'll open one of my prizes. I have a bottle of Haut Brion '61 I've been waiting for a special occasion to uncork. I think the discovery of the canisters is reason enough."

"Sounds great", Colin said. In a few moments they were aboard the ERSEV again. Back in his stateroom Colin undressed. He looked forward to getting the sweat and ocean salt off his skin. He hopped into the shower and adjusted the knob to just the right temperature. He let the steamy water wash over him for an indulgent long time. As the soapy water drained away he felt the last residue of the tensions he'd been holding flow away. Instead of the open ended time he might have spent in Barubi Village, it looked like he would be back in Manhattan in another twenty four hours. Thanks to ERSEV's interest, this would be the shortest mission he ever went out on. And an extra week's vacation waiting for him when he did get back. A very satisfactory situation. Colin wrapped himself in the thick terry cloth robe Roberto had left for him, threw off the comforter and flopped on the bed. A delicious drowsiness quickly overcame him. He shut his eyes and in seconds was deep asleep. He had a dream, unusually vivid and colorful for one of the afternoon types. It was of the scene depicted in the painting.

It would leave him with the strangest feeling after he woke. And it would never fade as dreams are meant to do.

CHAPTER 4

WHEN DR. MCCLURE mentioned the big money ERSEV had accumulated over the centuries he'd probably underestimated their wealth if anything. Colin strolled down one of the research decks looking right and left with Roberto at his side. He counted twenty four labs on each side of the gleaming hallway. And this was only on one deck. He was amazed at the level of technology operating inside the labs.

He paused briefly at each lab door. Roberto gave a snapshot explanation of what research was going on. While Roberto described the goings on, Colin quickly added up the cost of the equipment he knew about. He figured the average lab had somewhere between three and five million dollars worth of hardware and that didn't account for the price tag on the stuff he was unfamiliar with.

"Very impressive," Colin said. "How much of the ship is devoted to research Roberto?" "Around eighty percent of the space has been turned into labs."

"A lot of it is beyond me," Colin said. "I know what's under way in some of the bio labs but the activity I see in the physical science labs is a puzzle."

"Well the research is so specialized nowadays nobody knows it all. Don't feel badly about it." Colin grunted. "If we had more time I'd take you into some of the labs where the latest in stem cell research and nano-technology is progressing," Roberto said as they neared the end of the hallway. "There are eleven more floors like this" Roberto said, a note of pride in his voice.

"I'd like to go into them all", Colin replied appreciatively. "With more time to chat with your researchers I could get a hell of an education." Roberto looked at his watch.

"Dinner is in fifteen minutes. Perhaps before you leave us tomorrow we can see some more." Roberto gestured toward an elevator at the end of the long hall. "Shall we head up to dinner?"

"Sounds good," Colin said. A buffet had been laid out in his room but the call to go exploring had come before he'd had a chance to get at it. He was looking forward to what would be going along with Konrads' '61 Grand Cru. The elevator doors opened to take them up, but before they could step in a nasal sounding voice called out from behind them. Colin turned to see a short white-coated man with a shiny baldhead approaching. Roberto hit the hold button. The little man was hurriedly pushing a stainless steel cart.

"Roberto, I'm glad I caught up with you. I have something I think you should see."

"Colin this is Dr. Boka. He's doing work in our neurological lab these days." Dr. Boka looked quizzically at Colin squinting through thick coke bottle glasses Colin thought they'd stop making.

"Nice to meet you sir. They did tell me a guest was being shown around. I hope your enjoying your tour," Boka said.

"Very much so," Colin replied.

"Dr. Grier was sent here to help Dr. Lippincott with the disease situation," Roberto explained.

Boka's nose wrinkled rabbit-like.

"Then you too will want to hear about what I've discovered about the villagers who died," Boka said.

"Really?", Colin replied with heightened attention.

"Yes. I came up from my lab to get some gold stain for my glial cells. Fortunate to run into you." Dr. Boka pushed his glasses up on his nose. "Look at this." Boka pulled back a white sheet covering the cart. There were three halves of human brains cut sagittally down their middle from forehead to cerebellum. They were nestled in porcelain white bowls surrounded with crushed ice like so many supermarket fish. Their transparent membranes still glistened with freshness.

"Colin, Dr. Boka is completing a neurological examination of the autopsied villagers. Lippincott wanted the work done right away. With the facilities on board here he thought it best not to ship the cadavers all the way to Port Moresby."

"Makes sense," Colin agreed. "The sooner post mortems are done the better of course. I am amazed that you have the autopsy facilities on the ship," Colin said. Roberto put his arm around Colin's shoulder.

"If we had the room Dr. Volger would have Fermi lab brought aboard." The joke brought a nervous titter from Dr. Boka. "Well Sandor, show us what you've found" Roberto said, as if indulging a child excited with an insect brought in from play. The little man cleared his throat before speaking.

"Well there's a couple interesting things. The whole body autopsies turned up what we expected. Both microscopic and gross indicators consistent with hepatitis and small pox viruses. Chemistry tells me they've yet to analyze the blister toxin. My work in particular was a complete examination of the brains." Dr. Boka took a ballpoint from his pocket. "Look here. You'll see a big difference between these specimens." Boka pointed to the centers of the halved brains. Two of them showed a normal morphology and color around the pituitary. The third, however, had a walnut sized orange colored tumor just above and behind the gland.

"Cancer?", Colin asked.

"No these cells are benign.", Boka said. "Very odd. I've never seen neurons quite like them. Nearly the whole hypothalamic area is infiltrated with the cells. They have axons that extend all the way into the cerebrum."

"And what would be the effect of such a growth?", Roberto questioned.

"It's hard to say exactly," Boka answered. "I know the histology of the hypothalamic area very well. You understand it contains a nucleus of cells that are at the very center of a mammals most primitive emotions. A growth like this might cause severe psychic anomalies in humans."

"Such as what?", Colin asked.

"Uncontrollable anger and rage. Things of that sort," Boka replied. "A man made toxin could do this?" Colin continued.

"Hard to say what the cause of the growth is," Boka shrugged. "But there are a couple of other things that are peculiar."

Dr. Boka tapped the afflicted brain with his pen. "Of all the Barubi villagers who died this brain is the only one with this growth. And the man who's brain this was, was a murderer."

"I don't follow," Colin said, wondering what the connection could be.

"Well, it makes me wonder if there isn't some direct casual relationship between this man's horrible behavior and the tumor." Colin and Roberto exchanged quizzical glances. "I'm just hypothesizing here," Boka went on. "Rutledge, that's my assistant, helped with the transfer of the sick villagers. He told me this man was believed by the villagers to be possessed by evil spirits. He'd murdered his wife and three children."

"So you're saying you think the stuff in the canisters caused the manic behavior? In some way made this hypothalamus active?", Roberto asked.

Boka scratched his shiny head.

"It's a possibility. Maybe I'm just pointing out a coincidence. It's very curious don't you think? The one villager who was a societal pariah being the one whose hypothalamus has grown wild?"

"And what's the other interesting thing you mentioned," Roberto asked.

"I found some growths around the eyes of this same individual. White pustules about two centimeters across. He was the only one with them. Strange."

"You're finished with your examination?", Colin asked.

"No, no. I still have some microscopic studies to finish. As I said. I ran out of stain."

"When you're able, Dr. Boka, get an analysis of your findings to Dr. Volger and myself as soon as you can. Colin will want to study your results too. And thank you for sharing your discoveries with us." Boka made an old world bow of his head and shook Colin's hand. "It was pleasant to make your acquaintance doctor. I hope the remainder of your visit with us is happy." Boka smiled shyly, turned his cart around and disappeared down the hallway.

"What do you make of that?", Colin asked.

"Has to be a coincidence of course. The toxins only effect was the skin desiccation. Nasty enough certainly, but if there was a real link with the chemical and the brain center growth there would be more than one individual with it."

"I suppose so," Colin said, 'but do you think.....? Roberto shook his head no, stopping Colin in mid thought.

"Colin, you should know something about our Dr. Boka. He's a terrific micro-bio man. But." Roberto drew in a deep breath. "When it comes to theorizing his head is in the clouds. He's made up some pretty bizarre scenarios based on nothing before. Had us all turned upside down taking time and spending money needlessly. The whole thing will probably turn out to be from a metabolic reaction peculiar to that one man," Roberto smiled reassuringly. "If there's anything significant in Boka's findings we'll know about it when Rutledge has had a chance to add his data." Roberto thumbed toward the elevator at the end of the long hall. "Meanwhile your dinner is getting cold."

"Oh dinner. I almost forgot." Roberto pushed the patio deck elevator button. "This is the floor you want Colin. I'd join you but I have to check on a couple of things first. You go ahead. Enjoy. I'll be seeing you later." Colin stepped inside and flicked a nonchalant wave to Roberto legging down the long hall. The elevator took Colin up to the patio deck. A second pair of elevator doors surprised him by opening at his back. Colin turned around to see a breathtaking garden. The sterns upper deck patio had been transformed into the loveliest display of flowers and greenery Colin had ever seen. The semicircular deck was covered with luxuriant grass as manicured as any one of Augusta's greens. The air was peacefully still. The only sound came from the occasional rustle of the red and white Swiss flag standing at the stern end rail. Colin let his eyes roam over the lush garden. Roses, orchids, calla lilies abounded, scenting the air with subtle fragrances. The retreat had obviously been laid out to be Konrad's little piece of Arcadia. Colin stepped lightly into the garden unconsciously not wanting to crush the grass. Tiny creatures darted and dipped among a cluster of tropical plants. At first Colin thought they were damsel flies but a closer look revealed them to be hummingbirds with spectacular colors glinting off their rapidly beating wings.

"Hello," a voice called out. Colin turned to see Konrad step out of the elevator. He was dressed in a white jacketed summer tux. He was followed by a pair of crisply starched and smiling waiters. They rolled their serving carts to a crystal topped dining table in the center of the garden. "My apologies for being late. Do you like my hideaway?" Konrad spread his arms proudly.

"It's wonderful. You forget you're aboard a ship."

"Quite so," Konrad nodded. He gestured toward the dining table. "I wanted a spot to read and refresh myself. A place where I could let my mind retreat from the world's inane chatter." A waiter pulled out a chair for Colin and indicated for him to sit. "A bit of champagne?", Konrad asked.

"Thank you" Colin said. Two glasses were quickly filled with a bubbling vintage whose label Colin didn't recognize but suspected was a bit more expensive than Great Western. "I hope you don't think me ostentatious," Konrad said, watching the bubbles dance in the glasses. "I detest the vulgarity of so much in our society today. Sadly, there is no escaping the Philistines. The graciousness that was part of my generation I'm afraid is lost. At least here I like to think I've preserved a little island of good taste." Dr. Volger raised his glass to toast. "To civility." "Civility," Colin echoed rising to touch Konrad's glass. Konrad signaled one of the waiters who quickly placed gold plates before the two.

"John will you tell Paul we're ready," Konrad called to the closest of the attending waiters. In a moment a red cheeked stereotype of a chef appeared. His white tocque sat jauntily at an angle on his head. He seemed to beam with pride. "Who is it we have today Paul? Escoffier?", Konrad asked, touching a gold plated fork to his lower lip.

"A good guess sir but no. Today it is Careme."

"Wonderful. Just as well," Konrad replied. "Escoffier. Careme. They were all marvelous." Konrad gestured to Colin. "This is Dr. Colin Grier. He has come to take charge of the unpleasantness on shore. I promised him a first rate dining experience after the toils of our business. I'm sure he won't be disappointed by what you have planned for us."

"I've done my best sir. I'm sure dinner will be up to your usual standards," Paul assuredly replied. "If you will Paul, Dr. Grier and I will have a taste of the Haute Brion. Then we'll be ready to dine momentarily. Thank you Paul." The rotund chef retreated to the far end of the garden to busy himself with his trays of culinary treasures.

A white gloved hand reached unobtrusively across the table to pour the great vintage. "My friends tell me it is gauche to drink champagne before a good grave or burgundy. I pay them no mind. Their taste is in their ass." Konrad threw back his head, laughed and half choked at once.

"Excuse me Colin. I am in a particularly frivolous mood this evening. The champagne is doing her work. One of her most appreciated benefits." Konrad replenished their glasses. "I must explain the little game I like to play for my guests," Konrad said holding up an index finger. "I have selected twelve of the great chefs of the past, each one born in a different month." Konrad looked searchingly skyward. "For the life of me I can never remember which is which. But Paul keeps track." Konrad pursed his lips. "This is January. Careme was born in January. That's right isn't it Paul?", Konrad called over his shoulder to the busy chef. "Careme is January?"

"Yes sir," Paul replied not looking up from his culinary creation.

"So then," Konrad continued, "we will be dining on the cuisine the marvelous Careme prepared for his guests years ago." Colin's mouth watered. Tantalizing aromas drifted through the garden. "It is interesting that Careme was chef for the Baroness Rothschild and earlier for Talleyrand himself," Konrad said. "The Baroness was a confidential supporter of the ERSEV society in it's formative years."

"That is impressive Konrad. I suppose if you could look at the behind the scenes efforts of many of our historical personalities you'd find them working quietly for all sorts of good causes," Colin added.

"It's true Colin. The efforts of many influential personalities often go unnoticed." Konrad nodded to Paul and the feast began, one course more appetizing than the last. Colin had been to his share of Michelin four stars but his taste buds confirmed this was the finest food he had ever eaten.

There were truffles as large as apples, a great variety of quenelles, pheasant pate en croute, canard a l'orange and other delicacies too numerous to count. By the time the strawberries romanoff was served a swollen luminous moon had settled over the ink blue horizon. Colin felt mildly embarrassed at the fullness of his satiation. Lucky for Konrad that he didn't have guests aboard too often he thought. He'd be twice the size of Paul. As Konrad sipped the last of his coffee a waiter appeared with a box of Cuban Cohibas. "Care for a cigar Colin?", Konrad asked. Colin did smoke a cigar now and then, mostly on family occasions like a birthday or confirmation, if it was offered. He'd never fired up a real Cuban.

"Thank you I will," Colin said. Konrad deftly clipped the ends from two fat chocolate brown Havana's. He reached across the table to light up Colin's. Then stared cross-eyed at the end of his own cigar while he slowly watched it flame. "Excellent," Konrad said. "Delicious," Colin agreed.

As the blue gray cigar smoke drifted over the ships rails Colin felt his stress go with it. Worry, disease, the streets of Manhattan seemed a universe away. Konrad poured the last of the Haute Brion. When the dishes were cleared away Konrad gestured toward a pair of lounge chairs under the now still stern flag.

"I'm afraid I may nod off after a meal like this," Colin warned.

"A capital idea. I may very well join you. Let's toddle over." Both men settled in the cabana chairs sipping cognac, content as old friends on a back porch. Colin had a pleasant buzz. Judging from the color that had risen in Konrad's cheeks so did the ERSEV chief. Colin laid his head back and closed his eyes, reviewing the goings on he'd seen in the ships labs. Clearly the research on the ship was twenty five to fifty years ahead of what anyone else was doing. A sizeable number of hallmark discoveries could easily yet come from the work that was going on below his feet.

He was curious to find out just how far a lead the ERSEV researchers had, but how to ask without seeming to step on proprietary toes could be touchy. He was a guest and it would be crass to appear too inquiring. While he was weighing various approaches a musical feminine voice unexpectedly drifted his way. He opened his eyes to see Tony pushing a wheel chair. In the chair sat a young woman with a radiant smile. She was extraordinarily beautiful.

"Father you've been keeping secrets from me," she called out. Her voice had the sound of a youngster who has stumbled on hidden Christmas gifts. "You should have told me you were growing these father......but then they wouldn't have been such a nice surprise." As Tony wheeled her closer Colin could see her hands held a small clay pot. Growing from it was an extraordinary flower. Tony halted the chair between Konrad and Colin, but a bit too abruptly. The flower began to tumble from the young lady's hands. Colin reflexively reached out to catch the pot. He got his hand underneath just before it hit the ground. "Thank you," she said. Her expressive eyes searched Colin's face. Colin wondered for a moment why the lady made no effort to rescue the falling flower. Then he realized. She couldn't. She was paralyzed. Colin settled the flower securely back in her lap.

"Colin this is my daughter Margo," Konrad said. He squeezed her hand in his own. "My pleasure," Colin mumbled. He was feeling an amazing twinge of embarrassment. Margo wore a long diaphanous white camisole that fluttered softly around her ankles in the light breeze.

In every way, except for the paralysis, Margo seemed to be in perfect health. Her hair was a thick glossy brown framing a classically proportioned face. Her skin seemed luminous. Large doe like eyes had flecks of emerald green that perfectly complimented her lustrous hair. Colin couldn't help but stare.

"As you have seen Colin food is one of my passions," Konrad said. He paused momentarily while Colin reluctantly withdrew his attention from Margo. "Flowers are the other." Konrad wagged a playful finger at Margo. "I have Margo here to blame for drawing me into that other addiction." Konrad drew a long smoke stream from his Havana. "Margo and I carry on a little contest you see. We wager small amounts on who can create the loveliest hybrids. It seems my daughter must have her spies poking around my corner of the hot house. She has uncovered my secret prize." Margo giggled at her father's sham accusation.

"Really dad I don't need spies when your assistants leave your newest plants in full view. The greenhouse *is* made of glass you know."

"Quite so," Konrad grumped. "As I was saying Colin, I really must keep a closer eye on the staff," Konrad said with a mischievous wink.

Colin fingered the flower petals lightly. They had an almost sensual velvet like surface.

"I've never seen a flower quite like this. Was it developed from a plant here in New Guinea?"

"It really is a blend of varieties cultivated from all over the world," Konrad replied. "I've spent much more time on it than I should have. I brought it to the bud stage many times only to have it wither and die. This is the only one that I could get to bloom."

"Well, it's beautiful and I'm green with envy" Margo said, then flashed a beguiling smile.

"And I have you to thank," Konrad replied. "Before I had Margo's help plants would cringe at the sight of me. Now I'm a candidate for florist of the year." Margo gestured with her eyes for Colin to take the flower. As he turned the blossom slowly he tried to imagine what other flowers could have been hybridized to develop it. It was unlike any other flower he'd ever seen. Large triangular petals at the base were midnight black, streaked with pinks and yellows. Then a second tier of pure white petals folded gracefully over the black. "You know Colin, nature abhors black pigment in flowers,." Konrad said. "Geneticists have been trying for years to grow black roses. Absolute black that is. They've come close with a deep blue but that's all. It's as if some flower goddess has ordained any color but black."

"Like Henry Ford," Colin said. Konrad chuckled. "Yes but Mr. Ford was hardly a goddess."

"Well, you've snuck one by her," Colin said with admiration.

"Well I thank you. But really the expertise to do it was not so great. My horticultural accomplishments are nothing compared to Margo's." Konrad gestured to Tony who was at the food cart stuffing himself with leftover canapés. "Tony will you take the flower back please? And if you would bring the sketches?" Tony mumbled an "of course" through bulging cheeks. He carried the blossom carefully to the elevator and disappeared behind it's closed doors. "I'm going to name the hybrid after you Margo," Konrad grinned. "As soon as I can figure out how to translate your name into Latin. What do you think?"

"Delightful and pompous," Margo replied. She threw her head back with a laugh. Colin noticed a tremor in her arms, probably the result of a spontaneous effort to clap her hands in applause. A surge of adoration and compassion swept through him. She was clearly at peace with whatever affliction had crippled her motor skills. And what about yourself? Colin wondered. What would his reaction be should he suddenly find himself in a wheelchair only able to move his neck and head? Like most people he took his ability to do day to day activities for granted. Like they said you don't miss it unless you don't have it anymore. It would be nice to think he'd adjust. But he was afraid he might not have the guts to deal with an independence robbing paralysis. Becoming as effervescently vibrant as this young beauty before him would be beyond his reach.

"The sketches I've asked Tony to bring are of the Temple Margo discovered two years ago," Konrad said with prejudicial pride.

"Now that the source of the disease has been found I'm hoping our teams can finish the excavation," Margo said excitedly. "Of course I won't be able to take part but as my co-workers uncover more of the Temple I should be able to piece together what it looked like in the twelve hundreds."

"I see no reason why your teams can't resume the dig right away. The dangers gone now," Colin said, pleased to be able to offer something to Margo. Colin turned to Konrad. "Do you know when the last of the canisters will be accounted for?"

"All numbered and plotted. We haven't pulled them all out of the bottom as you've seen, but we know the remainder are safely sealed." Colin pondered for a moment.

"Well then I see no reason why Margo can't send her team back to the Temple tomorrow." Margo looked expectantly at her father.

"Tomorrow it is then. We'll have the job finished in what do you think Margo? Two, three more weeks?"

"We've excavated about two thirds father. Three weeks more and it should be done." "You're training was in archeology?", Colin asked Margo.

"Archeology and the fine arts. Father wanted me to grow up well rounded. I'm glad I followed his advice. I think the mental challenge of science with the creativity one finds in the arts is a wonderful combination."

"Aristotle thought so too," Konrad quipped. "Along with her archeological studies Margo pursued painting and dance at the Sorbonne. Top ten percent of her class," Konrad bragged.

"Well I don't dance much anymore," Margo said with the slightest hint of regret. "But my Temple find at Barubi makes up for my not doing any more Giselles."

"I'd like very much to hear the circumstances of your find," Colin said, accepting another refill of cognac.

"Well I'm not certain yet but I think I've uncovered proof that the Khmer people of modern Cambodia migrated to this locale late in the twelfth century." Margo's eyes flashed with excitement as she began to explain. "As a grad student I became convinced that the Khmers who built Angkor Wat and Angkor Thom filtered down to New Guinea and Northern Australia in about twelve hundred fifty." The Angkor Temples Colin thought. The thought of them in his minds eye was fuzzy. He wasn't sure whether the massive brooding structures had ever been completely examined even now.

"The Temples were discovered by the French. Am I right?", Colin asked.

"By Henri Mahout in the eighteen sixties," Margo replied. "The site was so obscured by jungle growth he nearly missed it."

"If you give the jungle seven centuries it will cover most anything I suppose," Colin opined. "Don't forget about the Buddhists," Konrad volunteered, lazily swirling his snifter.

"I'm getting to that father," Margo said shaking her head. "He's so impatient Colin." Margo took a deep breath. "I found evidence of a major revolution among the Khmers at around eleven hundred ninety. We know that the Buddhist influence from the north reached Angkor at this time. The Khmers were descendants of Indian Hindus. The Temples were dedicated to Siva the Hindu god. A clash with the Buddhists was almost certain to occur."

"So the Khmers migrated here to New Guinea then," Colin said. "We know they migrated. The question is where," Margo answered. "I was lucky to come across the writings of Chou Pakuan during my studies. Chou was a Chinese traveler who was a witness to the religious fighting around twelve hundred ninety six. He says that thousands of Khmer's abandoned Angkor and traveled to the southern lands. What he meant by this has been in dispute for years. I guess my woman's intuition helped me out. I suspected the lands were New Guinea and hit the jackpot."

"Don't belittle your achievement Margo." Konrad crushed out the stub of his Havana. "It was hard work and study that led you to your find. Luck comes to those who have laid the groundwork for it. Narrowing the Khmer's settlement to this area was a splendid piece of deduction." Konrad folded his arms across his chest. "Please understand Colin, Margo is too ladylike to brag. She deserves recognition from the archeological community. I've designated myself her official horn tooter whether it embarrasses her or not." Momentarily, Tony returned carrying a folded artists easel under one arm and a pack of sketch boards under the other. He set the easel up close to Margo's wheelchair, then placed one of the charcoal drawings on the tripod.

"This is the first one you worked on Margo. The sketch of the whole Temple." Tony said. Colin got the clear impression the young man idolized Margo. He was no doubt one of the rare species of valet- aides who took real pleasure in working for their employer. "Did you want me to stand by Margo?", he asked.

"No, no, Tony, thank you. You did have your dinner?" "Yes ma'am," Tony replied with an appreciative smile. "Then I won't be needing you until bedtime. Thank you again." Tony nodded a goodbye and turned to the elevator.

"Charming fellow," Colin said.

"My nephew," Konrad winked. "He'd better be." Konrad moved the sketch closer to Colin. "Before my illness I drew these sketches of what I thought the Temple once looked like. What is standing there now is the ruin left after an earthquake around 1290," Margo said.

"About half of the Temple is still standing," Konrad added. Margo shot him a just sit still and be quiet look. Margo had sketched a graceful curved roof stone Temple that once measured sixty by eighty feet. To Colin it looked similar to one of the smaller Greek Temples. Instead of the round columns of the ancient Greek structures the columns on this one were square. Margo had filled in the swirling intertwined images typical of Hindu stonework. Looking between the columns, an altar in the Temples center had been water colored in. A figure of a blue hued four-headed Indian God sat on a triangle carved on the altar's face.

"This is my best guess as to what the intact Temple looked like Colin," Margo said. "I've puzzled the arrangement of the broken roof beams and pillars together with most of the altar. The carving of Brahma was luckily found in great shape."

"And Brahma was who?", Colin asked.

"Brahma the creator. But he's rarely represented like this in stone. Could we look at the next one dad?" Konrad placed the second sketch on the easel. This one was a close up of strange writing below the altar face triangle. "What language is that?", Colin asked.

"Ancient Khmer. Margo reads it fluently," Konrad interjected.

"Not fluently enough father," Margo confessed. "For the life of me I don't know what this particular script says. It seems to be simple unconnected Khmer letters. It's as if in English you have written BXCDYJ or some such meaningless string of letters across the altar face. There isn't any other writing we've found among the debris to give a hint."

"Could the letters be a simple abbreviation of some sort?", Colin timidly offered.

"I thought of that possibility, but the concept of abbreviating was unknown to the ancient Khmers," Margo replied.

"Maybe in a culture that didn't do much writing, there was no need to abbreviate," Konrad suggested.

"Maybe so. But it annoys me that I haven't been able to figure it out. The altar was a sacred object.

What looks like gobbledygook to us must have said something with deep meaning to the Khmers." "You still have time to mull it over honey," Konrad said. "You'll decipher it I'm sure." Margo stared at the mysterious writing for some seconds then shook her head. "Well anyhow, there's one more sketch you should see Colin. The long plinth that the alter rested on." Konrad plucked out Margo's sketch. The sketch showed the right hand end of the plinth broken off. On the left was carved a large circle with a lotus blossom in the center. "This is harder to decipher than the crazy lettering," Margo said. "I've never seen a circle like this carved in any other Khmer art. Why it should appear here is another thing I need to work out."

"When you think of it, what do we really know about the beliefs of the Khmers?", Konrad speculated. "We like to think we stand above the ancient cultures in so many ways," he went on. "I'm convinced their inner life was much richer than ours. I think they were in touch with a part of existence the noise of modern life has made us deaf to."

"Really there's no way to know," Colin said. "I take it you're one of those who believe some ancient civilizations possessed wisdom that's been lost to us," Colin continued.

"I think it probable. That may sound odd coming from the chief of a ship devoted to scientific research. But a number of our ongoing projects in neurobiology are indicating that non-sensory knowledge may be reality."

"You mean ESP?", Colin queried. The conversation had taken a turn Colin hadn't anticipated. "You could call it that," Konrad answered. "But non-sensory perception I think is a better term."

"Do you think ESP or NSP as dad likes to call it, is nonsense Colin?", Margo asked. Her eyes took on a coquettish glint.

"No, not nonsense," Colin replied with a slight taken aback feeling. "Just like so many others I haven't seen much evidence for it."

"You must get in touch with your intuitions. Everyone has them you know. Like forgotten dreams they evaporate away unless we take the trouble to open up to them." Colin hesitated not sure just how seriously to take Margo's statement.

"Are you involved in this NSP research too?", Colin asked. Margo started to speak, then stopped while she weighed her answer.

"Yes I've participated in some aspects. But I haven't quite gotten to the oracle stage yet."

"We don't want you to leave us with the wrong idea Colin," Konrad broke in. "The ship is dedicated to the hard sciences for the most part. It's just that we have the time and finances to explore certain mind and matter interfaces others haven't the luxury to pursue. It would be a mistake to think our experimental progress lacks rigor."

"Oh no. It's just that it's unusual to find the scientific minded giving much credence to the reality of the paranormal," Colin said. Since Margo arrived, a feeling had been growing in him that something was going on below deck that had little to do with his work for McClure. Colin's habit was to give his more amphorous feelings short shrift. He'd found that dealing with maybes and mightbes was best left to the philosophers. He usually got into trouble whenever he started spinning edgy hypotheses. Cold logic applied to the stuff he could lay his hands was always the best problem solver. Right now however he was finding it difficult to push his fascination with Margo aside or ignore his odd feeling about the significance of her find.

"Well it's getting rather late for you Margo," Konrad said glancing at his watch. "Perhaps Colin will get to see the newer sketches before he leaves us tomorrow."

"Definitely," Colin said, not needing the helpful hint to convince him to delay his departure a few hours longer. He welcomed the chance to get to know Margo better.

"If Margo expects to get back to her work tomorrow it's important that she save her energy," Konrad said.

"Father's right," Margo sighed. "It wouldn't do for me to start the day off in a cranky mood." Colin found it difficult to imagine this beautiful young woman blemished with any mood close to crankiness.

"I'm very glad to have met you," Colin said.

He started to offer an automatic hand to her, then awkwardly drew his hand back remembering Margo's paralysis. "And thank you for the use of your suite." "You're very welcome. And thank you for dreaming of my painting." "Yes of course," Colin half blurted. Did he mention the dream to Roberto? He was sure he hadn't but must have. He ran the events since he left Margo's room quickly through his head. No, he was sure he hadn't spoken to anyone about the intriguing dream. Colin felt a warm flush creep up his neck. How could Margo know he'd done any more than glance at it? Suddenly he felt the need to talk to her, to open up to her in a way totally out of keeping with this evening's brief encounter. Before he left he'd make sure to talk to her alone.

As if on schedule Tony returned to wheel Margo back into the elevator.

"Good night father. Good night Colin," she said as the young man briskly pushed her chair away. "Good night," Colin called with an abstracted wave of his hand. After the elevator doors had closed Colin turned to Konrad. "She knew. About the painting I mean." Konrad raised an eyebrow. "I spent a lot of time looking at it. That's not unusual I guess. But I'm sure I didn't mention it to anyone. Somehow she knew." For a moment a brief look of indecision crossed Konrad's face. Then he nodded his head to himself as if settling on the right thing to say.

"I'm surprised Margo demonstrated her ability to you. Until now she's been reluctant to allow anyone but those closest to her to observe her new found powers."

"Then she herself has the NSP ability we were just speaking of?", Colin asked.

"Yes." Konrad walked over to a food cart and spent a pensive moment fingering the strawberries. "It was just at the time of her Temple discovery that her psychic insights began to develop. Not steadily by any means. There have been weeks on end where her growing paranormal abilities faded to nothing. There seems to be a flow to the phenomenon. Sometimes strong and then at times gone."

"And the paralysis? This also settled in when she found the Temple?"

"Three days afterward," Konrad said. He gave a little unhappy sigh. "She was perfectly healthy.

Then hour by hour we watched her motor functions deteriorate."

"Could there be a connection between the paralysis and her psychic power?"

"All I can say for now Colin is possibly. The psychic researches we spoke of are an attempt to get to the cause of her illness and find out if there is a link with her gifts." Konrad caught Colin's eyes in a heartfelt gaze. "I love my daughter very much as you can no doubt tell. I hesitated bringing her back to Barubi knowing she might get worse here. But she's adamant about finishing her Temple work." Konrad drew in a deep breath. "Beside Roberto and one or two others, you're the only one I've talked to about this." Konrad looked off beyond the garden's edge into the deep night. "You should know that were it not for an experimental drug we've developed Margo would not be alive. She's totally dependent on the medication."

"I didn't realize the seriousness..." Colin started but Konrad cut him off.

"That's good. It gives me a bit of hope that a physician such as yourself should not detect how ill she really is."

"Have you been able to make a definite diagnosis?"

"No. In some ways the paralysis has developed as expected. Yet there is something happening on the molecular level that evades us," Konrad said with a note of frustration. "Colin you should have seen her glide across the stage. Like a sylph carried by a breeze." Colin could see that Konrad was looking back in memory to the sight of his daughter dancing once again. "She was to dance Giselle only days after the paralysis began."

"I'm sorry." Konrad drew himself up straight.

"My daughter is a fighter Dr. Grier. She is as determined to recover as I am to restore her to health. The affliction came on suddenly. It is possible it could evaporate just as easily." Was this a case of wishful thinking or did Konrad have real hopes for Margo's dramatic recovery?,Colin wondered.

"Is there any chance that her condition may have been caused by something overlooked in the canisters?" It seemed the obvious question to ask. Surely that would have been Konrad's first suspicion.

"I wish it were that," Konrad answered. "Then we would have something concrete at least to work on. We went over the canisters in detail. As you'll see tomorrow when you look at our data. The viruses were embedded in a chemical base that encouraged absorption through the skin. A nice technological trick by the

Soviets. The skin toxin was set up to evaporate quickly from a liquid to a gas, but we found nothing that could have had any strictly paralytic effect."

"Could the paralysis be a latent body response?", Colin offered. "We thought of that. The natives that recovered at our dispensary show no indication of paralysis. Why wouldn't the paralysis have shown up by now in at least one of them?" Konrad thrust his hands in his pockets and began to pace. "I don't speak of Margo's illness or of her psychic insights very much. We have well paid researchers looking into every aspect of her situation, so what I speculate about isn't worth much. But seeing how I've gone on to you it seems I must have a need to review my thoughts out loud."

"We all know it's not good to bury unpleasant feelings inside," Colin sympathized. Konrad's lips began to quiver. "I'm glad you're here to listen."

"Your daughter is a fascinating woman. I'd be only too glad to hear whatever you might choose to tell me about her. If there is any way I can help with her recovery don't hesitate to ask."

"I thank you for your concern," Konrad said turning away so as not to let Colin see his watery eyes. He began to clear away the empty glasses softly humming an old tune Colin vaguely recognized as from an operetta by Friml or perhaps Lehar. Konrad was an appealing man. A nineteenth century sensibility linked with a twenty first century intelligence. Colin realized it had been an effort for Konrad to confess the depth of his love for Margo. Much easier for him to appear cool and in control. As much as Colin would have liked to explore the backgrounds of Konrad and Margo, he knew he'd be making better use of his time finding out all he could about the experimental drug Konrad had invented. Had it been tailored specifically to Margo's condition or might it have broader application? Were there plans to license it and could there be a real link between Margo's psychic episodes and her illness? There were a lot of questions to be answered. Colin wished he had more time to nose around the ship, but he should be leaving by noon tomorrow. McClure would be anxious for a face to face report. Maybe if he got started early enough he'd be able to see the Temple and still get away on time. Margo's find was probably only minutes into the interior. Her enthusiasm for the Temple ruin had him fired with a curious urge to see it first hand. Colin decided to squeeze himself into the party going back to the Temple.

"Would it be convenient for you to show me your records early tomorrow?", Colin asked. "I'd enjoy seeing the Temple. Even more, I'd actually enjoy watching Margo's pleasure when she returns." "But of course," Konrad beamed. "She'll be delighted to know you want to join us." Konrad wagged a finger in the air. "You see I was right. Margo was afraid the sketches and her Temple talk would bore you. "No," I said. "If I read Dr. Grier correctly he has a curiosity that expands far beyond his field of medicine."

"Let's say I can't resist sticking my nose into other people's business," Colin quipped. Dr. McClure had mentioned ERSEV's passion for privacy. There was little evidence of it here, Colin thought. Konrad seemed perfectly willing to open up the organizations business to outsiders. Of course it was Margo's find Dr. Volger was revealing and not a techy research project. Colin wondered just how forth coming Konrad would be should he ferret into matters concerning the hard science that had to have been part of the experimental drug development or even the stranger psychic research. Maybe I am too nosey Colin thought. All in all he'd accomplished what he left Manhattan to do, even if it was in an unexpected way. He'd found the source of the outbreak. Literally seen it bottled up. Instead of a couple of weeks sweating in the rainforest he'd leave tomorrow afternoon largely still unpacked with ERSEV'S disease data under his arm. McClure would be happy. At least as happy as it was possible for that man to get.

McClure's paranoia that TV cameras would descend on Barubi to tell the world that he'd screwed up two years ago could be put to rest. Once the canisters were destroyed, any chance of blame falling on McClure's head would be gone.

"Tell me Colin. Do you know where your next assignment will find you?" Konrad asked, stacking the last of the dinnerware.

"No. I'm not anxious to take on another assignment right away. I'm long overdue for a couple of weeks off."

"So, perhaps then you would care to be my guest at our headquarters. I have an old chalet near Ulringen high up in the mountains. A world away from the atmosphere here of course. You could stretch out by a roaring fireplace. Margo will be going back with me for treatment." "Oh?" That *did* have possibilities Colin thought. He'd save some money and get to know Margo better. Maybe even putter about ERSEV'S Swiss labs.

"I really hadn't thought about a real vacation. That's very generous. May I give you a tentative yes?"

"Of course. I sincerely hope you can come." Konrad offered a hearty hand shake. After all it was a most satisfactory day.

CHAPTER 5

D R. TRIMBLE NODDED as he tipped his snowflake spattered hat to Ms. Van Wyck and entered the office. The Nor'easter had intensified overnight leaving just the subway to carry whatever brave souls dared to venture out. He was over an hour late. It wasn't as if he was accountable to anyone but McClure, but still he prided himself on his punctuality as much as on his stubbornness in wearing bowties in the face of voguish fashion. George strained against his midriff paunch as he tried to pull off his totes. The phone rang in the midst of a grunt. "Yes Ms. Van Wyck," he answered with more pleasantness than he felt.

"It's a Dr. Channer from the Port Moresby Health Department. He says it's urgent. Line four."

"I'll take it now. Thank you Ms. Van Wyck." Odd that Moresby should be calling now. George glanced at the wall clock. It was 10:30 am, so it had to be long past office hours Moresby time. Maybe Dr. Channer was piling up overtime. " Dr. Channer, hello. This is Dr. Trimble," George said in that efficient way he always had when speaking long distance. A holdover from pre cell phone days. "Thank you for calling. We're anxious here for news from your Dr. Lippincott. I hope Dr. Grier has been able to be of assistance."

"Dr. Trimble, I'm not calling from Port Moresby." Channer's voice quivered. "I'm in a small fourteen bed hospital in Kokoori, a village nine hours north of Moresby. Something terrible is happening here. I have patients in the most God awful condition you ever saw."

"Smallpox?", George inquired.

"I wish it were just that. Lippincott briefed me about the outbreak before he left for Barubi. I got a call from a local G.P..

48

A Dr. Hudson. He sounded pretty upset. He told me three people came to his office this morning with symptoms of smallpox. What's incredible is that in the middle of examining them these crusty patches began breaking out on their skin. So I drove up here to Kokoori right away. You have to see these growths to believe them. They get larger as you watch."

"Where are these patients now?"

"I have two of them isolated upstairs and a woman on a cot down here in the operating room where I'm calling from."

"Could it be...?" George started but Channer interrupted him.

"Wait a minute. That's not all. I have a prisoner down here too. A Carl Jenkins. He was upstairs under sheriffs guard waiting to be shipped to Moresby for trial after his pneumonia cleared up. I have him here taped to a chair."

"Taped?", George stuttered. "What for?"

"For a couple of damn good reasons," Channer spit out. "First, he was howling and thrashing like a madman upstairs. Bloody canker's are breaking out over his entire body and what look like blisters are growing over his eyes. It disgusts me to go near him. I had to sedate him to get him taped." There was no mistaking the panic in Channer's voice. George could sense the fear reaching across the miles.

"Why was he under guard?"

"He raped a kid. Not for the first time either."

"I can understand you must be under a great deal of stress," George empathized. "No shit. I really need some help here. I've never seen anything like this."

"Would you consider the possibility that these lesions could be caused by some local toxin?"

"Hell yes. If you have any rationale for what's going on here I'm all for it. I'm not ashamed to tell you I'm pretty shook up." George held his hand over the phone as if doing so would shield Dr. Channer from his own apprehension.

"I suppose you haven't been able to run any tests."

"You suppose right. This isn't the Mayo Clinic. There's only me here."

"Sorry." George knew it was a dumb question as soon as he asked it. "Dr. Trimble, did Lippincott see anything like this at Barubi that maybe he didn't tell me about? I know he was suppose to hook up with a man from your office."

"Colin Grier left here to contact your Dr. Lippincott yesterday. Obviously you haven't heard from either of them."

"No I haven't. Look Dr. Trimble. This outbreak obviously has to be tied in with what's happening at Barubi. How it got from the north Coast down here so fast God knows. The bottom line is we have to find out what we're up against and fast."

"Of course. We'll get help to you as soon as possible. For now I think it's necessary that you not leave the hospital."

"I understand.", Dr. Channer said. He knew he might be infected already and couldn't take the chance of contacting others. "Word went around Moresby's staff that we were not to cooperate with the news people.", Channer said. "Now I understand why."

"It's critical that until we get a lead on this that the media be kept at bay," George said, with all the authority he could muster. "What other hospitals are close to you?", George asked.

"This is it, except for an army facility about sixty miles away."

"Good. Call the commandant. Have him call me. I'll see to it that your patients are transferred there. If anyone gets nosey say you have a couple of cases of highly infectious meningitis. We'll be getting help to you as soon as we can."

"I just hope we're not dealing with some new mutation Dr. Trimble." "I doubt it very much. I'll be back to you as soon as possible."

George hung up the phone and slumped back in his chair. He wasn't so confident as he let on to Channer that the skin problems were caused by toxins. But he couldn't recall any microbial agent ever having such minute-by-minute effect. He prayed his hunch was right.

Of course Dr. McClure had forbidden anyone but himself and Fratelli to follow up on the outbreak of two years ago. If he hadn't been so worried about looking bad in the press maybe a little follow up could have gotten to the root of the outbreak back then. But there was little time for blame laying, George considered. He swiveled his chair around to the computer screen and keyed in a data base on industrial toxins. He took some comfort in the orderly list that came up thinking that somewhere among them he'd find the agents responsible for the skin anomalies Channer had described.

Of all the newer chemicals synthesized in the past couple of years, thirty one were considered toxic enough to be highlighted. George noticed that all except for three of them were derivations of poisons already documented. He typed in molecular configuration and the structure of the three newer compounds appeared along with short blurbs on their uses and side effects. Headache, nausea and vomiting were listed for the three but no mention of possible skin problems. What George was hoping to find was a compound related to T.C.D.D. with some manganese or mercury bonded in. T.C.D.D. was notorious for it's ability to cause choloracne, a corrosive and persistent skin eroder. Mercury or manganese could well be the added elements that caused the hyperactivity Channer had mentioned. The two metals often were present when emotional disturbance was a toxic symptom. There was one other on the list that looked promising. It was a new configuration of the active molecule in Leptophos. It had a mercury atom in the 2 position of the benzene ring. It had been years ago but George remembered vividly reading a journal article about a leak of the modified Leptophos putting a group of Bay Port Texas workers on their backs for six months. George scrolled down to the side effects. There it was. "It has been reported that this molecule may cause severe acne-type skin lesions, especially in persons with compromised immune systems. Absorption by the C.N.S. may induce manic behavior along with hallucinatory episodes." What had probably happened was that Channer's patients had come in contact with minute amounts of the toxin over a number of months building up enough to finally overwhelm their immune defenses. George suspected that if Dr. Hudson had questioned the patients in more detail he would have discovered that they all worked close to a common industrial site. It was all very understandable. Both Channer and Hudson had probably never seen a choloracne case. The few that popped up now and then like the Texas incident ones were byproducts of heavy industry. Not much of that close to an outpost like Port Moresby.

George turned his computer off and allowed himself a satisfied sign. Channer would be glad to know he hadn't stumbled on Black Plague III. All it took was the right computer program and a little common sense. George dialed the Kokoori hospital.

He let it ring a dozen times then hung up. Channer was probably in the men's room. He'd call back in five minutes and give Channer the good news.

From the O.R. floor Dr. Channer looked up at the jangling wall phone only ten feet away. It might as well have been ten thousand. With a despairing shock Channer realized he was paralyzed. The strength in his limbs had seeped from his muscles as quickly as the air from a punctured tire.

Before the paralysis was complete he'd at least managed to prop himself up in a sitting position on the floor, his back against the tiled wall. As he looked unbelievingly at his useless legs his mind raced with confusion and fear. He realized he was in that peculiar shock state so often seen in combat where it takes awhile for the bad news to settle in. Channer would be needing all the self control he could muster.

If the paralysis could overtake him in minutes was it unreasonable to think it could dissipate just as quickly? Maybe that's what was going to happen. The movement would be coming back anytime now. Fifteen minutes, a half hour maybe.

Dr. Channer closed his eyes. Forced himself to breath long in and out breaths. What were the chances what had clobbered him had anything to do with what had hit the woman and the oozing prisoner taped in his chair? Maybe nothing, but probably a hell of a lot he thought. Channer entertained the idea that a sudden vascular accident had afflicted his spinal chord. A kind of non- cerebral stroke. That was a somewhat comforting self diagnosis. If that was what had happened to him then there was hope for recovery. As Channer began to mull over the possibilities, the rapist Jenkins screamed,an earsplitting inhuman wail, painful to Channer's ears. The prisoner's chancres had grown to six centimeters or so, nearly doubling in size since early afternoon. They dripped a foul dull green exudate down the felon's body. Dr. Channer stared disbelieving at Jenkins's face. The white cancerous puffs had fulminated explosively from his eye sockets. Sticky net like tentacles of slime ran down his face. Jenkins screamed again.

With a loud pop he snapped the tape binding him as if it were cotton thread. Jenkins stood and took a few tentative steps. He sniffed the air, wolf like, using his olfactory senses in place of his unseeing eyes. Jenkins, or what had once been a human who went by the name of Jenkins, took a few steps toward Dr. Channer, then caught his foot in the fallen tape. He pitched forward too fast to get his hands in front of him. His head hit the marble floor with a brutal thud. Channer clearly heard the crack of facial bone as Jenkins' chin smashed down. Roaring with rage, Jenkins groped for the object that had caused the terrible pain. He wrapped his hand around the tangled chair leg and groggily got to his feet. Dr. Channer watched him sniff and lick the pus from his lips.

A sense of implacable evil reached out to Dr. Channer from the swaying once human being. With both hands, Jenkins raised the chair over his head. He swung it in a wide circle pounding and punishing all the O.R. equipment within reach of his arc. Jenkins' screams were lost in the terrible clanging of metal on metal. He swung the chair upward into the old style kettle drum O.R. lights overhead. They broke from their connections tumbling in a jumble of metal and broken glass shards around the room. The floor was a mosaic of razor sharp slivers. Jenkins let out a maniacal laugh as if delighted with the chaos of the destruction he couldn't see. So far, Channer had escaped the rain of pinging and dancing splinters. Instinctively he'd shut his eyes when the mayhem began. Now he opened them to see a scalpel embedded in the shoulder of the woman on the cot. She'd been given a hypnotic earlier and was just coming out of a deep sleep. Her mouth opened in astonished surprise, the pain only partly penetrating her groggy haze. She never got the chance to feel the full ache of the scalpels lacerating blade. Jenkins seemed mindless of the shards. Blood ran from multiple cuts piercing the soles of his feet. Channer could hear the glass grind. Jenkins seemed oblivious. He planted his leg then took a looping swing across his body. The chair edge cracked with a sickening thud under the woman's nose. She stiffened as if hit by a high voltage charge, toes and fingers splaying out, quivering as the shock wave raced along her spine. A pathetic squeak escaped her vocal cords. She went limp, her head dangling unnaturally over the edge of the bloody cot. Jenkins groped the air. His hands contacted the dead woman's face. Channer's eyes were riveted on the pair. A mix of morbid fascination and horror rolled around in his mind. He watched Jenkins hold the woman's battered head by the hair then rotate it left to right, right to left. Each time it turned, the sound of broken neck vertebrae grinding stimulated a diabolical laugh. Jenkins seemed to take a peculiar delight in the grinding, whooping each time he succeeded in finding the right motions that would reward him with the grisly scrape. Whatever had invaded Jenkins, it was clear to Dr. Channer that it had degenerated his mind down to it's primal core. What was working now was a brain with the capacity only for the most base emotions. Basically a reptilian brain, functioning on it's most ancient and uninhibited centers. Tired of toying with the woman's head, Jenkins brought the chair down savagely on the dead body. Long whoops of pleasure echoed off the O.R. walls. He continued to batter the corpse mercilessly seemingly determined to reduce it to an unrecognizable pulp. Channer had shut his eyes again not wanting to be witness to more of the unholy degradations, when he felt a spray of viscous wetness hit him on the forearm. Automatically he blinked his eyes open only to see what had been part of the woman's eye dribble down his forearm to his wrist. He fought hard to squelch an urge to retch. Any sound would signal his location to the rabid like Jenkins. Channer hoped that in his orgy of rage Jenkins had forgotten him. The grotesque oozing hulk hovered closely over the woman's body sniffing. He was relying on his primitive olfactory center to give him the information he wanted. Jenkins held his nose inches from the smashed cadaver. Channer watched repulsed as Jenkins flicked his tongue snake like, grunted, then dipped his forefinger into the socket where the woman's eye had been. Half giddy with fear Channer saw Jenkins run his finger around in the mess then lick the gore like a kid finishing off icing in a frosting bowl. Channer tried to fight it off but the urge to retch was too insistent. Noisily he vomited on himself cursing that the paralysis wouldn't let him get out of his own puddle. Jenkins head snapped around furiously alert.

A challenger to the possession of his prize was hidden somewhere in the room. So this is how it ends Channer thought. Not with a bang but a ...what?...a bite? In spite of his fear, Dr. Channer began to chuckle softly at his silly whimsy. His laughing steadily grew louder until it became a full ravenous belly laugh.

Like a maddened grizzly Jenkins was about to sniff him out, and when he found him propped up powerless against the wall, mangle him. But suddenly Channer had run out of fear. What's the matter with me he wondered. He had little doubt but that he was about to meet the grim reaper. It was appropriate that he feel a modicum of panic. Or at least take his dire situation seriously. Yet for some strange reason he felt reassured. As if a part of him believed Jenkins could do him no harm. For a fleeting moment Dr. Channer entertained the notion that he too had been rendered insane. There was no Jenkins. No visit to Kokoori hospital. He was hallucinating. But he felt a confidence growing in him. A composure that convinced him that this was all quite real. The in control sureness he felt defied explaining, but it was rock solid.

Jenkins sniffed again. He licked his swollen lips and lowered his sightless eyes directly onto Channer. In a few bloody footed steps he stood at the doctor's feet clenching and unclenching his big boned hands. Jenkins snarled a low feline like growl. Channer stared at the diabolical face swollen as much with hatred as trauma. He waited for the fear of what seemed inevitable to engulf him. Yet again it didn't come. Instead a sense of mastery began to grow stronger replacing his simmering terror. Channer felt confused, not sure what to make of the sensations. A reawaking of some kind was filling him.

Whatever was happening or why, Dr. Channer welcomed the bracing sensation. A soothing wave of contentment washed through his mind. Jenkins was close enough to touch if Channers arm had been working. His foul breath filled Dr. Channer's nostrils bringing the urge to vomit again. Channer fought it off. Then the thought, clear cut and powerful, struck him like a bolt. Jenkins could be stopped simply by using his own thoughts. Some instinct, long hidden in the labyrinth of his mind had burst up into consciousness. Without knowing why he knew, Dr. Channer realized he could fire the shaft of his own will into the miasma of impulses that had become Jenkins' brain and stop him cold. How the power had risen up Channer couldn't say, didn't have time to muse about.

But it was his to use. Channer concentrated on the bulging tumors that had been Jenkins eyes. He imagined he could look behind them centering his mental forces into the primitive machinery of the man's brain. Jenkins planted his left foot between Channer's splayed useless legs. He pressed a knee hard into Channers chest. Foul smelling pus dripped generously down. With a lightening quick thrust he grabbed Channer by the throat. His sticky fingers dug painfully into the doctors windpipe. Channer grimaced. Held his breath. The oxygen in his lungs now would be the last he would get. He dare not waste a molecule giving into anxiety. Channer bore his stare into the bulbous growth covering Jenkins eyes. He visualized Jenkins stepping back in obedience to his mental command. Channer strained to summon every bit of his willpower. An exhilarating rush of mastery he'd never experienced before overtook him. Back. Retreat. Stop. Channer savored every wave of potency he felt as his dominance penetrated Jenkins degenerate brain. There were only seconds before Channer's own gray matter would be shutting down. Channer pushed his new found telekinetic power to it's limit. He gritted his teeth praying he wouldn't pass out. Ever so slightly, the constricting grip of Jenkins fingers began to weaken. A small whimper began to mix with Jenkins deep-throated growl, the sound a scolded pup would make. He felt Jenkins' knee pressure ease from his chest. Then with a fearful yelp Jenkins jerked his hand away from Channer's throat as if letting go of a red hot pan. Dr. Channer opened his mouth wide. He savored the fresh air rushing into his aching throat. Channer considered what he'd just accomplished. He'd used a mental operation he'd long been convinced was a hoax. ESP in any of its permutations he'd always regarded as pure hokum. Jenkins had backed away to the center of the O.R.

He stood trembling, his hands palms out across his blinded eyes as if anticipating another psychic blow. Dr. Channer stuffed the emergency overload signals that still were brewing back down in the motherland of his mind. Again he gathered his waning energy to shine an arrowhead of concentration on an image of Jenkins backing further off. Immediately Jenkins took another step back. Channer kept his gaze glued to the cancerous eyes. He knew he mustn't dare interrupt the flow of energy going out to Jenkins. There was another animal cry and Jenkins retreated, bent at the waist, shivering and trembling to the far wall. Channer allowed himself a contented sigh. It was true. He'd really been able to tap into a power speculated about for centuries but never scientifically demonstrated. Jenkins was completely still now, rolled up in an armadillo make the world go away ball. The contrast with his earlier demeanor of rage was stunning. Dr. Channer felt content that at least for now the retrograde man was no longer a threat. He looked down at the puddle on his lap that had been his lunch.

The contrast between the ridiculous situation his body was in and the new found power in his head made him laugh aloud. Actually his physical situations had worsened. Twenty minutes ago he'd been able at least to move his head freely. Now he had difficulty rotating it more than thirty degrees. At this rate Dr. Channer figured on being stone stiff in maybe another hour. Still his usual sensory pathways seemed to be working just fine. His sense of smell sure as hell hadn't gotten worse. The stench from Jenkins drippings threatened to bring on another round of puking. He tried to move his fingers and toes. It was futile. Could it be that his organ's smooth muscles would be freezing up too,? he wondered. The gut maybe and then the diaphragm. Channer chuckled lightly. He might be able to track his entire musculature seizing up. Should be panic time by now he thought. Dying has a way of bringing that on. But there was no fear. No dread in the face of his death he was sure hovered near by. Dr. Channer pondered Jenkins, still circled up in a fetal position and the unfortunate woman he'd mutilated. One afflicted by some corrosive skin-blistering agent who probably had never had an evil thought for anyone. The other a chancred malignant embodiment of depravity. "And myself?", Channer mused. A paralytic gifted with new found powers content to be dying. Dr. Trimble had to be mistaken. Maybe he was right that a man-made chemical was the cause of the skin dehydration. But what underlined Jenkins demonic rage was a thing unique. Protean enough to stimulate both satanic psychosis and wondrous psychic power. Without doubt whatever has invaded all three of us is not your garden variety of microbe Channer knew. It had to be some unknown vector that could stimulate the brains primal core and a part that led to the road of what?...enlightenment?

Dr. Channer quickly paged through old memories. The decision to go to med school, to give up his lucrative Los Angeles practice, to come here to Australia, to accept food or thanks in lieu of cash from the aborigines. It had all worked out the way it was supposed to. It had all pointed to this moment dying on a cold marble floor. Channer didn't know how he knew all this but he surely did.

There was one regret though that marred his new found tranquility. Dr. Channer knew he'd never be able to watch Alicia or the boys grow up. He'd surprised himself by growing so attached to the kids. He never thought he would feel sentimental about having to leave them. The twins, Juan and Pedro, would be eight next month. Either the twenty third or twenty fourth. He never could remember. They'd grow up just fine. And little Alicia with the ready grin would recover completely from her surgery. Juanita and the three kids would miss him he knew but in time their unhappiness at his leaving would mellow as it always does in the very young. Their regret would fade quickly to a distant memory as it should. But there was little time left for reminiscing Dr. Channer understood. A visitor would be coming soon. In his mind's eye a fair image of the visitor drew itself together. A rather pudgy middle aged pleasant tempered man he would be. It was to him that the critical directions were to be given. The power that had been growing in him, that had been strong enough to dominate the will of Carl Jenkins, was not yet potent enough to divine all the circumstances surrounding his visitor to come. But in broken flashes he foresaw the visitor arrive at the hospital. He saw the struggle there must be and he saw himself transformed. Other visions passed before him. A young man and woman standing before an altar. When or where they might have stood there Channer's imperfect vision was too faint to tell. Still he knew they all would play their part in what was to come. Dr. Channer felt his breathing become more shallow as the seconds passed by but he was content to observe his decline without a struggle. His chest muscles were faltering but it wasn't at all uncomfortable.

His vision was going too. Gradually the O.R. became a fusion of thrown together colors. Channer no longer could make out Jenkins or the woman or even distinguish them from other objects in the room. The operating table blurred into a block of silver against a smear of pale green wall. The glass shards stood out like prisms glinting and winking their reflected hues. With the room so murkily out of focus the slivers shone like a field of shimmering fireflies against the dark tile of the O.R. floor. Dr. channer found the array strangely hypnotic. Again that curious tingling sweep of energy he'd felt earlier scuttled through his head. The random pattern of glittering glare magnetized his attention. He felt a gentle compulsion to keep his out of focus gaze fixed on the glass pieces. Then suddenly he remembered the stars. It would be imperative that the young couple have knowledge of the stars. Dr. Channer was sleepy now. He let his eyes slowly close. He understood darkly, but knew that he'd been chosen this time to be at the privot point of a new possibility. Dr. Channer tried to move his head but his muscles were completely locked now. It was all right. He was satisfied. The O.R. darkened to a pitch blackness. The glass shards began to shine with diamond like brilliance. There seemed to be countless billions of them, receding far away into the void.

CHAPTER 6

"**O**H MARGO, HELLO. I didn't expect to find anyone in the garden." Colin stood at the patio's edge happily surprised to find Margo sitting before her easel. The garden was aglow with the soft creamy light of the large low moon.

"Couldn't sleep?", Margo asked with a mischievous grin. Colin shook his head. "Too much food too late."

"Well then it's indigestion that's brought us together," she laughed. "I'd love to have some company." Margo nodded hopefully to a large chair at her side.

"The garden is even more beautiful at night," Colin said, edging his chair close to Margo.

"I couldn't resist asking Tony to bring me out here. Dad would be displeased that I'm skimping on my rest, but the evening is too perfect to stay indoors. Besides I think better out here." Margo turned her eyes to the charcoal and ink sketch.

"This is an enlargement of the triangle carving you saw on the altar face earlier Colin. I suppose I thought if I made it bigger my ideas about it's meaning might expand along with it."

"I see part is done in blue ink and part in black." Colin said.

"Roberto did it for me. The black, is of what's actually carved and the blue is my best guess of what was eroded."

A pixyish glint came into Margo's eyes. "Tell me Dr. Grier, what would be your take on the carving? Just for the fun of it naturally."

"You don't think I know much about Khmer art then?", Colin asked in mock indignation. Margo shook her head. "Well you'd be right," Colin said with a wry expression. Without thinking he put his hand on Margo's knee. Normally he was cautious with attractive women, not wanting to offend their various and hard to read sensitivities, but this was different somehow. His instinct told him this particular lady would find his gesture perfectly understood.

"I get insights sometime from those who can look at the art of antiquity with non-specialist eyes," Margo said. "Tell me just at a glance what you think the carving might mean."

"Okay." Colin got up and stood behind Margo's wheelchair to view the sketch head on. This enlarged version showed three small human figures on each of the two sides of the triangle. Their arms were outstretched toward Brahma at the apex. Colin stared at the sketch looked at Margo then back at the drawing. "I haven't the foggiest," Colin said scratching his chin. "Maybe the figures are holding out some offering?"

"Very good," Margo enthused. "That's close to my reading of the sculpture too. Except I'm also inclined to think the triangle represents a mountain and the figures are climbers. I'm pretty sure they're hoping to receive a gift from Brahma. If you look closely at Brahma's forehand you'll see he holds three books. They're the Vedas, the Hindu sacred books. The fourth hand is holding a potion of some kind. I think the climbers have come to drink of the potion."

"What would the potion do?" "Well in Hindu belief these climbers are known as Muktas. The Rare Ones they're called."

"Rare. How?", Colin asked, his interest rising.

"According to the Vedic legends the Muktas can reenter or re-begin any life at will. They're free from the confines of time and space."

"You mean they have a choice about what or where they're next life will be?"

"Yes. Of course most of us have no choice. We go where our Karma sends us. That is if you believe in all that. The potion will give them Mukta status." "Fascinating." Colin stood staring preoccupied with the sketch. Margo broke his train of thought.

"Colin would you mind putting the last drawing up?"

"Oh yes of course, Colin blurted a bit startled. He exchanged the sketches quickly on the easel. This one was another enlargement of the broken lintel beam he'd been shown after dinner, but with much more detail. "The last one was easy. Maybe I should turn in my medical bag for an archeologist's spade," Colin joked.

"Not so fast Dr. Grier. This one is harder. You notice we have that large circle carved on one end of the beam. The other end was broken off in the quake."

"I think it's a pretty good guess that the other end would have a similar circle for balance. Right?", Colin said.

"Right. I'm convinced of that too. But then if you look close you'll see the tiny blue and black dots drawn in around the one circle."

"The dots wouldn't be just decorative?", Colin asked.

"Not for a carving that stood over the temple entrance. Would you care to give me a snap judgment?"

"Keep in mind I'm just a beginner. Give me a couple of seconds." Colin cocked his head thoughtfully. "What pops into my head is the sun. Or suns I guess I should say. If it's right that there was a duplicate circle on the broken end you'd have a pair of suns."

"The Khmers usually didn't portray the sun as plainly as this," Margo said.

"Well you asked me and that's what I come up with," Colin said mildly miffed. Margo smiled. "Really, thank you Colin. I was just looking for something to bounce my thoughts off of. Roberto is stumped too. And then there is the series of meaningless letters under the mountain. At least I'm convinced Brahma's triangle is a mountain and the climbers are Muktas."

"What about the lotus blossoms?"

"Always a symbol of reincarnation," Margo said with a deep sigh. "The altar carving and the lintel beams are all related somehow. I can feel it. Maybe a good nights sleep will bring matters together for me." Margo held Colins eyes with her own. "I know dad mentioned that I've been involved with psychic investigations lately. Mostly we've focused on the meaning of these carvings." Margo paused a moment weighing her words carefully. "You have been part of the psychic process."

"Me? But you hardly know me." Margo watched puzzlement furrow Colins brow.

"I know about the best part of you Colin. I knew you would be coming aboard today. I saw you arrive in my dreams."

"Really?", Colin said matter of factly. There was no hint of the ridicule he'd usually have for such a startling statement in his voice.

"I don't mean to be evasive Colin. I really should explain more about what's happened to me since the temple was first discovered." Colin edged forward in his chair. "Growing up, I showed no signs of having extra sensory powers or NSP. as dad calls it. The ability grew hand in hand with the onset of the paralysis. The more immobile I became the more insights I had. Except that the paralysis has been nearly total and the ESP episodes fragmentary. I enter into those mental states that seem half dream, half true sometimes. I knew of course you'd be skeptical. That's why I mentioned earlier I knew you're feelings about my painting." Colin studied Margo's face intently.

"Would you be able to tell what I'm thinking now?", Colin asked.

"Not at all. That's what I mean about the episodes being fragmentary. The ability comes to me quite at random. I'm afraid I wouldn't be a very dependable employee for a psychic hotline."

"But you're sure it's me you saw in your dream or trance state?" Margo nodded. "I recognized you as soon as I saw you sitting there with dad at dinner. You know, in a way I can't understand, I'm convinced you're coming here is meant to help me find the meanings of these carvings."

"Well that's very interesting Margo. A bit spooky too if you don't mind."

"I know. I have no rationale for these feelings. Things come to me in kaleidoscope like pieces that just pop into my head. It's all very unsettling. I do have someone to help me though."

"Roberto?", Colin quizzed.

"No, his name is Jhanda. A very elderly man from India. I would like for you to meet him. He is trying to help me make some sense of the psychic episodes."

"He's here on board?"

"Yes in the infirmary just now, sick with the flu. It was said in his village that he had attained divyadrishti, a kind of ability to see some past and future." Colin's face disclosed more than a hint of puzzlement. "Colin, I know how strange this all must seem to you."

"It's true I've always given this psychic stuff little respect. I'm a bit off balance." Margo looked into Colin's eyes with a kind of shy intensity.

"There's something else I know." Margo paused as if thinking of just what to say. "I might as well just out with it. I know you feel attracted to me. As I do to you. There it is plain and simple." Margo leaned her head to one side. "I'm right aren't I?" Colin felt a shock of pleasure. Margo certainly didn't mince words. No tiptoeing around the issue for this lady he thought. And she was right. Maybe it was the combination of the garden and the balmy moonlit night that had made him vulnerable to her beauty, but whatever was the cause of the delightful feeling that had stolen over him, there was no doubt that he was totally enchanted. Colin touched her hand lightly. That warm electric spark was there again. "Some people are meant to be together Colin." Margo gazed thoughtfully at the lintel sketch. "You know it might be that the legends are right. Given enough time kindred souls *can* come together and repeat lives. Did you ever consider that?" Margo asked.

"That might be rather boring don't you think?"

"Not really," Margo said with a touch of whimsy. "Not if each time they forgot their earlier lives.

Each recurring adventure would seem brand new to them." "An intriguing but pretty farfetched notion," Colin said.

"It is that," Margo acknowledged. "But maybe like the legendary Muktas, someday we'll be able to choose some life adventure all over again. It would seem as new and fresh as this moment right now is for us." Margo's eyes rested searchingly on Colin's. He turned away from her gaze a bit overwhelmed. He needed to clear his head, to get away from this woman so provocative, yet so unsettling. Suddenly, Manhattan and his meeting with McClure seemed ages ago. Colin prided himself on expecting the unexpected whenever he went out on a case. Surprises came, as they said, with the territory. But the combination of Margo's clairvoyant after dinner episode, along with the theorizing she was doing now, lay outside the bounds of your garden variety of surprises.

Somewhere inside Colin felt a deep urge toward helping Margo find the answers to her temple puzzle. Still there was his usual common sense caution urging him to be wary of the ESP stuff. Maybe Margo *was* just a sweet space cadet after all. And then there was Dr. McClure and George to consider. Colin could just imagine their reaction when he told them he was staying on the ship to see where he fit in with an archeologist's fancies. This was no time to get sucked into a situation that was over his head. When he agreed to board the ERSEV he hadn't bargained for a trip through never-never-land. At bottom, allowing himself to enter Margo's world might open up vistas he wasn't sure he had the courage to explore.

"Margo, it's past midnight," Tony's voice called out from the open doors of the patio elevator. "You said for me to remind you."

"Oh Tony we got so caught up in conversation I completely lost track of time. Colin if you'll excuse me I'd better get some rest. Otherwise I'll be useless tomorrow."

"Of course. I'd better get to bed too. It's been a stimulating conversation." "You'll think about the things we talked about?"

"I'm afraid I won't be able to stop thinking about them," Colin replied thoughtfully. "Margo, Jhanda is still up," Tony put in. "He asked me if I'd bring over the last sketches."

"Allow me to do the favor," Colin volunteered. "I noticed the infirmary is just down from my room.

I'd like to say hello to the old gentleman before I leave."

"Thank you Colin," Margo said. "Just be careful you don't catch his flu." Tony turned Margo's wheelchair toward the elevator.

"I'll hold my breath," Colin wise cracked. "Goodnight Margo. See you in about ten hours." "Goodnight and sleep well Colin." After the elevator doors had closed Colin walked over to a beverage cart left next to the stern rail. He plopped three ice cubes into an old fashioned glass and poured himself a healthy slug of Hennessey. Colin twirled the glass for a few seconds while he looked out absentmindedly into the deep night. Maybe the smart thing would be to forget the coming morning trek to the temple ruin. He'd already dipped one toe into an unexpected slice of bizarreness. It probably was not wise to jump in any further. Now might be just the time to quit the scene, Colin thought, his fascination with Margo not withstanding. Whatever psycho-biological experiments had been going on with Margo and this fellow Jhanda was really none of his business. It would be easy enough to just pack up, call Ryan's charter and in a few hours fly out. Later on he could look back on this strange interlude and see it in perspective. Just a quirky day that was an exception to the usual rule. "I think you've come here to help me decipher the temple carvings" is what Margo had said. On that score she might or might not be right. On the other hand about his attraction to her, of that there was no doubt. Logically the temple deciphering part was pure bullshit. He knew as much about Khmer artwork as he did about ballet. Just about zero. Colin gulped down the remains of the booze and threw the cubes over the railing. He was surprised to feel a surge of anger well up. He wasn't sure exactly why he should feel this way, but one reason might be that Margo brought up possibilities that weren't possibilities at all. Just the imaginings of some long ago Hindus who'd had nothing better to do than carve their religious fantasies into stone. Colin set the tumbler on the cart and walked over to the sketches. He found the one of the triangle mountain and put it back up on the easel. He ran his finger slowly over the mountain edge. It came to him why, after a most pleasant evening he should be feeling so odd. He hated being confused or undecided. Now he was both. A part of him felt like tossing the sketches after the ice cubes and writing off all that had happened since meeting Margo. And yet there was an instinct fetching him, telling him he could rely on this woman. That he should trust the urge to stay aboard and pursue the horizons Margo's broken dreams might uncover. Colin lifted the sketch from the easel. Where exactly did this Jhanda fellow fit into the picture? He wondered. He decided abruptly that it might be a good idea to talk to the old man right away. There would be no worry about being intellectually seduced by a wrinkled senior. An old fellow with the flu wouldn't mix much charm with the cold hard facts. Sizing up whether this Jhanda was the real thing or a phony shouldn't be difficult. The question Colin needed answered was what exactly was the nature of the Indians's relationship to Margo's trances. He poured himself another splash of cognac then strode purposefully to the elevator.

With the altar sketch tucked under his arm he pushed the elevator button with his one free finger.

When the doors opened he stepped in and hit deck eighteen, the floor for his stateroom. He'd stop in the stateroom first to wash up then make up his mind about this Jhanda.

CHAPTER 7

J HANDA SAT CROSSED-LEGGED in the middle of his stateroom floor. A small bronze Siva sat on his left. Patiently he waited for the arrival of Pandit Konrad. With his hand trembling from a combination of flu and old age, Jhanda adjusted his saffron colored robe. On a small table before him he silently counted the implements he would need for puja, the traditional ceremony for invoking the Hindu deities. All seemed satisfactory. The flu, added to his longstanding emphysema, had left Jhanda uncomfortably wheezing, but still he was glad to be out of the sterile infirmary. Jhanda disliked sick places intensely, especially the sick rooms of the West with their cold bright steel and tiled walls. Jhanda was a small man with limbs that had little muscle left between skin and bone. At ninety seven he knew there was little time left. Still, it would not be fitting to perform the puja ceremony in the bleak surroundings of a sick room.

That is why he'd insisted on returning to his own familiar room. Jhanda took comfort that Brahma had not altogether extinguished his powers. In intense meditation his inner visions had shown him vaguely, but surely, the outlines of a metal structure that had long ago been buried on the temple grounds. He had advised Pandit Konrad to search for the artifact. His powers had told him the object would be critical to Margo's quest to find her way to the meaning of her dreams. Jhanda prayed that the puja ceremony would help guide him toward those things still hidden. A soft knock sounded at his door. "Come in Pandit Konrad. The vessels are prepared," he called out. Konrad entered with a respectful bow. He carried with him a balsa wood model of the temple and it's surrounding grounds. Konrad held the model out for Jhanda's inspection.

"Roberto and I have just finished the last of this," Konrad said.

"Thank you Pandit Konrad. Please sit." Jhanda indicated that Konrad should take his place on the rug opposite. Jhanda took a jade necklace from around his neck and offered it. "Wear it please. For puja." Konrad put the necklace on. He began to speak but Jhanda shook his head. "In a moment you may speak Pandit Konrad. The gods wish silence now." Jhanda smiled and with a weakened solemnity set a small cube of camphor alight. Then slowly he mixed it in a bowl with a pinch of turmeric. Lastly he dropped in four fresh rose petals. Jhanda then dipped his fingers into another bowl of rose water and sprinkled the droplets over all. "You do same now Pandit Konrad," Jhanda instructed. He pointed a scrawny finger toward an already smoking incense burner on the low table. Konrad rose, then slowly walked around the rug until Jhanda was satisfied the purification was complete. "Please sit Pandit Konrad. We say a prayer now." Konrad mirrored Jhanda's crossed legged posture. "Don't forget shoes," Jhanda admonished with a twinkle in his eye. Konrad removed them. Jhanda folded his hands in prayer. "Now to the Lord Savitir," Jhanda intoned. His voice was weak with age but the ancient words were still clear. "TAT SAVITUR VARENIAM BHARGODEVASYA DHIMAHI. DHIYO YO NAH PRACODAYAT."

Jhanda drew in as much breath as his ailing lungs would allow, held it, then blew across the offering bowl. "You say after me Pandit Konrad. Fold hands please." Konrad obeyed. "Let us consider the shining brilliance of Lord Savitir that he may inspire our hearts." With closed eyes Konrad respectfully repeated the prayer. Jhanda reached out for a small bell, rang it, waited, then looked to the ceiling. "What is it you wish Pandit Konrad?"

"To enter with you Maharsi Jhanda into the way of mystical knowledge." Jhanda acknowledged Konrad's request with a forward leaning from the waist.

"Now we may talk one to the other Pandit Konrad. You have been able to find the hidden things?" Jhanda eyed the wooden model next to Konrad.

"No Jhanda. We have searched below the ground as you advised. The things you say are buried there may be too deep. I hope that today your powers can direct me to the place more precisely. There is little time. The new medicine we have for Margo is slowly losing it's strength and I'm afraid......."

"Unhappily I understand this too well Pandit Konrad. Perhaps the Gods will grant me their graces to further help you in your search. I will ask of them redoubled power and their compassion on young lady Margo." Jhanda let his eyes rove slowly over the wooden model. Roberto had fashioned the ruined temple and it's close perimeter as exactly as possible using a scale of one inch to ten feet. In front of the temple he had extended a triangular shaped platform. Shallow excavation had indicated continued use of the temple portico area even earlier than the fifteenth century. With a delicate but steady pressure Jhanda placed his palms on the model. Konrad watched him rock gently, allowing his breathing to become deep and long. Jhanda's cheeks, so shallow and dull in color, began to take on the bronzed color of a man younger by fifty years. The signs of his age and illness miraculously seemed temporarily suspended. Jhanda continued his rocking, brought his fingers to his forehead, then with a sudden start blinked open his eyes. Slowly the healthy color that had infused his face retreated. He was again the old Jhanda he'd been moments before. Jhanda covered his hands over his heart. "Very difficult Pandit Konrad. Those who made the hidden things died here. Quickly. Suddenly. This feeling is very strong in me. The earth was once in great turmoil here."

"Who might they have been Jhanda that were here so long ago? Can you see this?" Jhanda shook his head.

"This, Lord Vishnu does not allow." Jhanda lowered his eyes as if in embarrassment. "To piece through so many years is hard Pandit Konrad."

"Looking at the things of so many years ago strains your powers sorely Jhanda. I know that and esteem you for your effort."

Jhanda held a finger to his lips then dipped a wooden spoon into the puja bowl. With the turmeric paste he painted a crude circle in the middle of the models triangular foreground.

"Here the object I dimly see once stood. That I can say." Konrad could hardly contain his excitement. Still he knew how Jhanda abhorred any show of emotion during the puja ritual. He fought to keep his emotions under control.

"If I may be so bold Jhanda. Perhaps you can tell me something of the size or shape of the object buried here?"

"Yes I can tell this little something. It is round. Not unlike the wheel of Dharma." Konrad pressed on.

"Why Jhanda? Why would there be something buried there? Whoever left this object must have been here many years before the temple was constructed..." Jhanda cut Dr. Volger short with a flick of his hand.

"The Gods speak to us in many ways Pandit Konrad. To eyes and ears surely but also to the heart. Those who placed this ages ago were waiting for the Gods to speak to them." Reverently Jhanda replaced the puja implements exactly as they had been arranged at the ritual's start. With a tilt of the rosewater bowl he doused the incense embers. "My apologies to you Pandit Konrad. Unclear visions are all that Vishnu offers now. But it is something. There at the triangle at the center of the temple front you must search."

"Maharsi you have given me more than I could hope for." Jhanda shook his head.

"When I was younger I could have seen much more. But I am old now and this remnant was laid down so very long ago."

Konrad grasped Jhanda's hand.

"A thousand thanks to you Maharsi Jhanda. You have drawn back the veil of many years. With the help of the gods we will yet learn the meaning of this secret thing." Konrad started to remove Jhanda's necklace.

"No Pandit. You keep please. Give these beads to your daughter. Now her turn has come. She has been blessed with the powers of a mighty guru-diva. These beads will aid her efforts. It is she, not I, who will open the door to the answer of the many mysteries here." A worried frown turned down the corners of Konrads lips.

"And her sickness Maharsi? Can you say that she will recover?"

"That I cannot tell you Pandit Konrad. But you should not chastise yourself as you do. You think the fault lies with you that

Margo has become ill. It could not be prevented. The unhappiness of her sickness is a necessary part of what will be discovered here."

"But how Maharsi? Can you not tell me in what way her illness *must* be?" Jhanda smoothed the folds in his robe searching for a way to express to his Western friend the inexpressible.

"If Brahma would but give me more power perhaps I could tell you this. I dare not put demands upon his gifts. Think on this Pandit. That in returning to the temple you did what was right. In time all that should be revealed shall be." Konrad reached across the table and touched Jhanda's wrinkled hand with affection.

"I *have* been worried Jhanda. Guilt haunts me daily. I'm afraid I have not let myself admit how ill Margo really is. I ask myself do I do right in risking my daughter's life for a wisdom that has been long guarded by the Gods."

"There is no other way Pandit Konrad. Margo's power increases as my own ebbs. As I have said, within her memories are the answers to the questions we seek. Within her mind are many answers to the temple mysteries. The images she has so far seen are but parts of a larger vision that can be hers." Jhanda rang a small puja bell ending the formal part of the ritual. "Before we rise Pandit, let us take a silent moment to ask Vishnu for his blessing on our noble purpose." With some discomfort Konrad shifted his position on the puja rug. Of course he didn't really believe as Jhanda did that Vishnu, Siva and the rest of the Hindu menagerie of Gods really existed. Yet in a nebulous way he could open his mind far enough to at least entertain the possibility that belief might somehow bring him in contact with an unseen realm. In the years since Jhanda had become attached to the Society he'd been converted at least to the reality of paranormal phenomenon. Before the Maharsi had joined him it would have been out of the question for him to weigh seriously, the counsel of what he had once regarded as a circus swami. Still it was Jhanda who had predicted the source of the psychotropic proteins that had stimulated Margo's remembrances. And purer proteins would be ready for injection soon. The thought of putting the chemicals in Margo's body both worried and excited Konrad. There was the risk that Margo might die if the memory proteins pulled her down too deeply into her trance state. Each descent into the trance inevitably made the paralysis that much harder to hold in check. Yet her magical reveries, so deftly guided by Jhanda, had led him to the cave. That was marvelous enough. And then just days ago, the discovery of the elllipse. A machine he'd kept secret from all except his trusted inner circle. Thankfully his labs analysis of the ellipse's timing mechanism predicted no new disease particle outbursts for sometime to come. The machine, by all accounts should stay dormant for at least a few more days. Konrad prayed that the analysis was correct. For if the machine should come to life again then the plague it would unleash would be on his head alone. Jhanda, finished with his post puja prayer, indicated for Konrad to stand.

"One more thing Pandit Konrad. The young man you entertained at dinner. He must be told the truth.

Our destiny and his are allied. I have seen that he will be the one to lead Margo to the fulfillment of her vision." Konrad turned back from the doorway. He sat down again on the puja rug.

"But Maharsi the pains we have taken to keep outsiders away." Jhanda dismissed the protest with another wave of his finger.

"Now is the time for boldness Pandit Konrad. It is necessary that you bring this young man into your confidence. I know that you are concerned that entanglements with certain authorities will disrupt our work here. That the temple site itself may be taken over by others. This you must risk. You must have faith that this young man will choose the correct path among those that are open to him." Konrad nodded acquiescence. Up to now he had believed it would be folly to allow any, but the need to know, knowledge of the cave's secrets. Since the discovery of the jaw bones two years ago, he had taken stringent steps to keep the find clandestinely disguised, even going so far as to hold the knowledge of the ellipse from Margo. To Konrad it seemed axiomatic that if there was to be only one person who should *not* know about the buried machine it was Dr. Grier. It was obvious that Colin's mission was a direct threat to his own research.

"Pandit Konrad please," Jhanda said interrupting Konrads musing. "May I say I believe you worry too much. Be done with this way. Trust my words."

"I want to do so Maharsi. But I also must be sure." Konrad stood staring down at the puja table, hands thrust in his pockets not wanting to meet the old man's eyes.

"Why did I join you here Pandit Konrad? Why did I leave my calling in India?", Jhanda asked with kindly forbearance. "Was it not because I sensed a special need for my humble gifts, here with you and your daughter? A purpose that would justify departing from the needy of my own country? This same inner voice which directed me to you now says it is good to throw open the gate of knowledge to this Dr. Grier." Konrad drew in a long deep breath.

"You fear I may be mistaken Pandit Konrad," Jhanda went on. "It is possible it may be so. I cannot promise things will be as you wish if you heed my admonishment. Still, consider please that the counsel I give comes forth from long years in the service of Vishnu." If Jhanda's psychic powers were fading there was no slackening of his thrust to cut to the heart of the matter Konrad thought. What Jhanda was saying in his polite way was pretty much what Konrad had known but didn't want to face. Trust Jhanda's insights into the mysteries surrounding the find or forget the project entirely. Konrad realized he craved the surety of science, the comfort of the step by step knowledge gathering that was going on as a matter of routine in the labs all over his vessel. What Konrad wished for was for Jhanda to summon up on demand visions of all that ever happened at the temple site. Then the explanation of how Margo's powers, the carvings and what was still buried at the temple site were linked together would be forth coming. Jhanda was right of course. The old fellow was doing his best. Far more than Konrad had a right to expect. At any rate what was going on in the minds of Jhanda and Margo was beyond sciences penetrative techniques. Konrad understood that he'd be well advised to sit on his urge for quick and certain answers. He needed to put away his second guessing. There was little choice but to accept the hand Jhanda held out to him.

"Well Pandit Konrad what is it you decide? Do we proceed?" Jhanda asked expectantly.

"Of course, yes Maharsi," Konrad replied with a look of chagrin. "Forgive my vacillation." "I understand too well Pandit. You are frustrated. You are worried. This is natural when the life of a loved one is in question. When one is about to push aside the curtain that hides the unknown only the fool is without hesitation."

Konrad picked up the temple model being careful not to smudge the still wet paste circle. "I will talk to Margo in the morning Maharsi. If she is well enough and feels the time is right to receive the proteins we will proceed right away."

"Good Pandit Konrad. But concerning Dr. Grier. Do not wait. He must begin to understand the role that Brahma has ordained for him as soon as possible." Konrad opened his mouth in a half formed question then on reflection quickly shut it.

"As you say Maharsi. I will go to him now." Konrad gave a respectful bow, opened the door and headed down the corridor toward Colins's cabin.

"Hello?", Colin called out. The door to Jhanda's room had been left slightly ajar. There was no answer so he knocked softly not wanting to take liberties. "Anybody home?" Colin waited a moment and when there was no answer pushed open the door. Peeking into the sick room he saw that Jhanda's bed was empty. The bed covers were thrown back and there was a bottle of Nyquil with it's top off on the nightstand along with vials of various antibiotics. A glass of water with half melted cubes sat nearby. Wherever Jhanda had gone, Colin guessed he'd only been away a few minutes. He wondered whether he should wait or just leave the sketches and go. Colin walked out on the deck, looked up and down, then came back into the sick room. He considered beeping Tony then decided it was too late to disturb the young man over the question of where Jhanda might have gone. Colin laid the sketch on the bed and turned to leave. Then he smelled it, the faint but unmistakable odor of Legphene. Legphene was an old disinfectant Colin had often used to wash down autopsy room metal-ware. Colin followed his nose down a short hallway a few paces beyond Jhanda's bathroom. Unexpectedly he found a gray steel door at the end of the hall. Rather formidable for a linen closet Colin thought. He stood before it pondering for a moment.

Odd place for an autopsy lab. He was a guest and it would be impolite to go rooting into uninvited places. But curiosity got the better of him. The door was unlocked. Colin opened it. He was right. It was an autopsy room. But what was stretched out on the stainless table wasn't your average cadaver. Colin checked over his shoulder for any sign of Jhanda returning, then walked up close to the body. It had to be the corpse of the man Boka had mentioned. The one the microbe's had affected differently from all the others. The one who'd murdered his family. Only an empty bowl of a skull remained. Boka had done a clean job of excising the brain. The once seeing eyes were white, cancerous growths bulging out of their sockets. But what repelled Colin, who'd thought he was beyond repelling, was the rest of the body. There were terrible deep lesions everywhere, two to three inches apart. Craters filled with a mix of green pus and blood covered the cadaver totally, including the soles of the feet and palms. The oozing sores still dripped their sticky fluid onto the table even after the long hours since the man had died. Colin backed away. How infectious the lesions might be there was no way of telling. Dr. Boka hadn't sealed off the room. If there was the risk of an airborne threat he no doubt would have. Still the highest level of caution was in order. Colin realized that he'd frittered away the focus that should have been pinpointed on his number one job. With so much of his attention drawn to Margo and her sketches the epidemic had slipped into a waste bin at the back of his mind. Colin reflected with a pang of guilt that he'd nearly forgotten why he'd come to New Guinea in the first place.

The unpleasant thought that the dinner and wine had made him drop his guard angered him. Could Dr. Volger have set him up just to keep him from an investigation? Dr. Volger had said explicitly that all the epidemic data would be made available. If so, why would he keep the horror here hidden away? There was no question but that Konrad must know about this body. It was his job to keep on top of everything that happened on the ship. He would know too that keeping this corpse on board was an overt violation of his old agreement with McClure and Fratelli. There was only one conclusion to reach, although even now Colin resisted admitting it. Dr. Volger had purposefully mislead him.

He had gone out of his way to keep this cadaver from being discovered, but why exactly? The first and no doubt correct reason that came to mind was that Volger wanted to continue with Margo's work at the temple site. Chances were that he'd been working there all along in defiance of McClure and Fratelli's quarantine. He *hadn't* had his ship parked here for just the past few days. Probably he'd been here defying the quarantine order as soon as McClure had disappeared over the horizon two years ago. A new and catastrophic set of diseases had threatened to rampage for two long years yet Dr. Volger had cavalierly ignored the threat to pursue his selfish purpose. Colin closed the autopsy door and stood in the connecting hallway biting his nails. He needed to think. He'd been foolish for not consulting McClure's office before he stepped foot aboard the ERSEV. He should have insisted on going to the Barubi site as his first order of business. Instead he'd let himself be distracted by the twin tempters, wine and Margo. Instead of playing her guess the sculpture game, he'd allowed himself to be sucked into the arena of Hindu mythology while all the time he should have been attending to business.

Colin had let himself be bedazzled by the charms of Konrad's daughter when he should have been at his most professional. He'd been doing more self-indulgent wool gathering than objective analysis since he stepped off Ryan's plane. "Damn it" Colin muttered to himself. What was the old saying? "If it seems too good to be true..." There was only one thing to do. Roberto's sea-cat was probably still tied up alongside. He could take it and be on shore in a few minutes. Colin looked at his watch. It was past one A.M. If he left now he could get to the Barubi site by daybreak and do what he should have been doing while swimming among the coral. He would check out exactly what was going on at the temple site himself.

CHAPTER 8

APATCHY FOG LAY low around the ERSEV's hull as Colin clambered aboard the sea-cat. Luckily, with the light of a full moon he could just make out the north New Guinea shore. He remembered from the flight in, that Barubi was just off the ships midline beam. If he just kept the cat at the right angle to mid-ships he should land with the village directly at his front. Colin cast off the connecting line, fired up the motor and headed for shore at an easy eight knots.

Any faster would be to dangerous should the outboard ground on a hidden sandbar. The sea was glassy calm. The motor purred perfectly and in short order Colin could see his landing spot. Some thirty yards out he cut the engine. There was a clear sloping beach fringed with coconut palms. That was a natural spot to run the sea-cat up. Colin secured the boat, hopped down on to the wet sand and looked to his left and right. The luxuriant jungle foliage edged close to the lapping wavelets as far as he could see. Dr. Volger probably had used this same beach to evacuate the infected villagers. There didn't seem to be another clear beach along the rest of shoreline.

The New York office had always supplied a flashlight among the other paraphernalia in his bag that he thought a space waster, but he was happy to have it handy now. He walked along the arc of palms shining the light into the dense jungle until the beam caught a cleared path into the growth. Tire tracks, which looked like they were recent, led to a parked Land Rover about a hundred feet into the forest. Colin checked the SUV over. It had to be Volger's, of course, but the windows were the darkened type so there wasn't any looking inside. Two tire tracks of matted down foliage ran in front of the Land Rover further into the jungle, then stopped. Colin wondered whether Volger was using the vehicle to get to the temple or Barubi village. The trail, as indefinite as it was, should lead him to one or the other. Judging by the cooking smoke he'd seen from the ERSEV's deck, Colin guessed the village should be about a mile inland. With his flashlight probing before him Colin started down the path easily enough. The moon added it's bit of reflected light so he avoided stumbling over clumps of gnarled roots that networked here and there over the narrowing trail. Then suddenly the tracks ended abruptly. Why would Dr. Volger have stopped dead end here? Colin wondered. Maybe this trail was one that Konrad had abandoned. Squinting his eyes to avoid the tangle, Colin forged ahead into the thickening growth. If the trail didn't pick up in another few feet Colin decided he'd turn back. Ragged edges of thick leaved ground plants tore at his ankles. Colin held up his forearms to protect his face from the elastic vines. Colin stopped. He hadn't realized how much effort he was putting out. He was breathing heavily. The flashlight was wet with dripping sweat. He turned to look back, then realized his mistake. He'd been a pretty thoughtless fellow in thinking he'd just keep marching around. He was caught in a net of tangled greenery. It was as if the jungle had purposely folded in around him. "Shit," Colin growled. He wiped his soaked face with his sleeve. He reached for his cell phone and GPS. "Damn it," he spit. He'd left it on the ship. A three hundred and sixty from his flashlight showed nothing but a circle of oppressive verdant sameness. Reluctantly he absorbed the single fact that he was lost. "God damn it," he yelled out, loud enough to start a group of drowsy monkeys whopping overhead.

Colin's impulse was to barge through the dark foliage swinging and kicking at every vine that stood in his way. Then he thought better of it. Even if he'd had a machete he would wear himself out in a matter of minutes. Colin took a long breath of the moisture laden air then sat on the jungle floor. Not too long to sunrise. At least when the sun came up he could get an idea of how he was oriented east to west. Frustrated with his own stupidity in getting himself in this fix, Colin grabbed at a bundle of grassy plants and pulled them out by the roots. That's when he saw the galls. The stems of the larger plants to his right were laden with ugly grayish bubbles that reminded Colin of pictures of slime molds he'd seen in the old Botany textbooks. Colin didn't dare touch them. Some of the jelly balls had red ants stuck on their flypaper like sticky surface. He shone the flashlight on the stems of the surrounding plants. Nearly everyone was affected with at least a few of the repulsive bubbles.

Colin noticed too that the leaves on the most infested plants were wilting. There was no question but that the jelly globules were killing the plants. Images of the weeping lesions on the Boka cadaver and the crusted skin Colin had seen in Dr. McClure's photograph leaped up before him. What the hell was going on in this place? Canister poison designed to attack plants? Colin pushed through the growth to a stand of tall hardwoods. He was shocked at what he saw. The same clusters of noxious balls were infecting the heavier trunks. Only these were grapefruit size. Colin shone his flashlight into one of the globules. Hyphae like threads from the galls center penetrated into the hardwood, probably many centimeters deep. Did Dr. Volger know about these sucking parasites? He must Colin thought. Little matter that the rain forests were already under threat.

It looked like Konrad's failure to provide what the lawyers would call full disclosure was threatening not only people directly, but possibly, if the galls were infectious, the surrounding oxygen supply.

Colin understood he'd have to get a lot more help down here. A lot of questions needed answers and soon. For the moment however getting out of the claustrophobic jungle was priority number one. Colin tried to put his apprehensions aside. He pushed into the green maze in the direction his instinct told him was right. The possibility that he might spend his last moments walking around in circles was not far from his thinking. He pushed that thought back alongside the other reservoir of negatives and went onward- wherever onward might lead. The greenery seemed to be getting dense. Sweat dripped from the tip of his nose. Salt running into fresh insect bites made him want to scratch his skin off. He resisted the urge, not wanting to open up the bites to infection. There was nothing to do but plunge ahead. Hopefully he'd find the beach again, if not that, at least an open spot where he might get his bearings.

Colin's arms and legs were quivering but their ache helped him tamp down the panicky feeling that was starting to grow. The thought that the unseen beach might be but a few yards away was maddening. Colin groped ahead making about three feet a minute. At last the first glimmer of dawn shone a bit of light to his right. Colin turned in that direction. After only a few more paces his flashlight shone on a patch of gray among the vines. Colin approached hopefully. There was a natural stone cliff thrust up out of the jungle floor. It ran as far to his right and left as he could see. Colin took a couple of paces back into the green growth searching for the top. His flashlight beam just reached the upper edge maybe thirty, thirty-five feet up. Probably the wall was the remains of a violent earthquake up thrust in the long past. Colin guessed that it might run right down to the beach and then under the sea. Colin took a coin out of his pocket. Heads he'd go left, tails right. Fatigued as he was, his palm misjudged the tumbling nickel. It plopped to the forest floor and bounced tails up under a broad ground leaf. As he turned the leaf aside he was astonished. A buttercup sized flower glowed with streaks of pastel colors mixed with black. Just beginning to unfurl lower on the stem were curved white petals. Colin picked it up wonderingly twirling it slowly in his fingers. There was no question. It was a young specimen of the same flower Margo had held on the ship. A "one of a kind" that had taken years to develop. Isn't that what Volger had said? Colin squatted and began to search the ground. Momentarily he found a second, then a third flower growing against the cliff face. Curiously none of the little flowers showed any sign of the gall infection. What is it Dr. Volger? Colin thought. What do you want so badly to keep me from seeing that you'd lie to your daughter about hothouse rarities? And what other oddities of nature might you be keeping hidden away? Colin walked along the cliff face pulling down patches of vine. He surveyed the exposed rock and saw that even more of the young blossoms were growing out of crevices in the wall. Interesting that most were sprouting toward his right. Colin wondered if it was just a random growth pattern or the sign of a central source. He inched along the wall to his right. Soon he came across a virtual garden of the beautiful flowers, hanging like orchids from the cliff face. They decorated the gray wall in the hundreds.

Colin noticed too that the vine growth was becoming more sparse as he walked right. Within another minutes walk the indigenous rainforest plants had almost totally dissipated. The cliff face and the earth at it's base had turned into a blaze of pastel colors. The delicate blossoms competing for their space had surprisingly pushed aside the normally dominant rainforest growth. Colin searched the wall. There were natural hand and footholds he saw. If he were careful he should be able to make it to the top. Colin squatted then forced his tired legs to vault him high enough to grab a small ledge. After a few grunts and grimaces he managed to wriggle up onto the ledge. He paused for breath then began to pull himself up. Ignoring a bit of facial skin he was leaving on the rock he grabbed for a stringy cluster of vines overhead. He pulled hard to test them. Then ascended the final ten feet hand over hand. Shortly he stood satisfied on the cliff top. He brushed off the worst of the dirt. There was enough light now for him to faintly see the shoreline to his left. His guess about the cliff being an up thrust fault was correct. The little plateau he stood on angled slowly about four miles down under the seabed. To his right, about a mile on, he saw that the cliff face angled sharply inward, then out again forming a considerable inward cutout. At the tip of the wedge sat Margo's temple ruin. About twenty five feet below it on the rainforest floor there was a cave mouth.

From a distance Colin couldn't tell whether the opening was a man made or natural cave mouth.

Spread out in front of the opening there were many yards of Konrad's "one of a kind" flowers growing profusely. Oddly, the growth pattern formed fan-like streaks. It was as if the flower seed had been blown out of the cave opening shotgun style. Colin wondered if the temple might have been built in response to something inside the cave. But sitting up on a cliff plateau, as it was, there was the possibility that worshipers could have approached from the opposite side and never known the cave below was there. Colin shimmered down the rock face retracing the foot holds he'd used on the way up. The greenery to his left gave in a little to the rising sunlight. Soon he stood before the cave opening, ankle deep in a riotous shimmer of color. It was obvious now that the limestone cave was nature's work. But there was no time to waste at the flower show. Colin approached close to the cave mouth. There was light spilling out from deep inside the cave. Colin couldn't see the source. It reflected out from somewhere within a winding interior. He began to step into the entrance then stopped in his tracks.

From somewhere within the serpentine passageway a strange low humming sound faintly reached his ears. There was no doubt it came from some kind of non-natural source.

CHAPTER 9

D R. MCCLURE HALF drove, half skidded his olive green Volvo slowly down winding Melrose Way. He was looking for the house of his old second in command Dr. Fratelli. He had visited his deputies home in suburban Airmont once before and remembered it as a pleasant brick rancher with a flagstone walkway. Ms. VanWyck could have given him the exact address but he'd thought better of mentioning his visit to her. It would be best if no one knew he was using this Thursday afternoon to call on Fratelli's widow. McClure was sure the house number was one something, but it could be anything from 101 to 199. He twisted his head trying to scan both sides of the street. He hadn't figured on snowdrifts obscuring most of the numbers. A teenage girl in a yellow Hummer got on his tail and leaned on her horn. She had to be thinking what great fun it was to show off the Hummer's maneuverability on the half plowed street. Not much chance to do that within twenty miles of the city. Dr. McClure fishtailed toward the curb and the girl flipped him the bird as she roared past. "Little shit," McClure muttered between clenched teeth. Three houses on his left he spotted Fratelli's place. There was a snow cleared statue of the Blessed Virgin on the top step. It had to be the only house in town that had a religious icon so prominently displayed. Dr. McClure should have thought to look for it right off, but probably 'forgot' about the statue because he'd been embarrassed that Fratelli had the silliness to put it out front. McClure recalled that Fratelli had been active in the Knights of Columbus and had daughters at one of the girls Catholic colleges.

Might even be a member of that Catholic fringe group Opus something or other McClure mused. Dr. McClure walked to the door being careful to not step on the icy patches. There was no doorbell so McClure put on his best P.R. face and rapped the brass knocker. "Just a moment please" a tiny voice called out from inside. Dr. McClure saw a bit of the window curtain draw aside. Then the door opened a crack. "Excuse me Mrs. Fratelli for barging in on you like this. I'm Dr. McClure from your husband's office," he said expectantly.

"Oh yes, yes of course Doctor," Mrs. Fratelli countered opening the door wide. "Edwin isn't it?" "Edwin is correct," the chief answered, put off that the woman remembered his first name while he couldn't recall hers. Mrs. Fratelli, a sallow skinned lady who's small voice matched her five foot height, motioned for McClure to enter. A pleasant smile of anticipation lit her face. "Allow me to apologize for dropping in on you so unannounced Mrs. Fratelli. I was near by on other business and decided to take a chance on stopping." Dr. McClure forced a toothy smile. "How are you? How are the children?"

"Very well thank you." Mrs. Fratelli wondered if her husband's old boss had stopped in just to be sociable or had something important to say. "Won't you sit down?" she asked, offering a red leather wing chair. A kettle whistled shrilly from off in the kitchen. "I was just going to make myself a cup of hot chocolate. Would you care for some?"

"Oh no, thank you Mrs. Fratelli. Chocolate unfortunately gives me heart burn." Dr. McClure sat down running his fingers over the creases in his slacks. He felt unexpectantly awkward. He'd obviously cut into the woman's afternoon quiet time. She probably was looking forward to watching the afternoon soaps.

"I'll just be a second," she said, marching off to silence the wailing kettle. McClure looked around. The house, like so many Italian American homes, was even nicer inside than out. The old world style furnishings were expensive and scrupulously clean. With the kettle off Edwin could hear a tenor warbling some opera aria from an unseen CD player or TV. "Last month was the first anniversary of Anthony's passing you know," Mrs. Fratelli called from the kitchen. "It was such a shock his not making it through the bypass. For awhile I was afraid the girls and myself would never get over it." She appeared again in the living room and sat down, her chocolate and a tray of cookies on the coffee table. "With God's help we're all beginning to come to terms now with our loss." Dr. McClure reached for a macaroon.

"Well I can tell you he is still very much missed at the office," Dr. McClure lied. "He's left some big shoes to fill." Mrs. Fratelli dabbed at her eyes with a Kleenex. "I have to say he left everything in wonderful order too. All the initiatives he started up were picked up by Dr. Trimble." MCClure nibbled at the edge of his cookie. "You know Mrs. Fratelli we never lost a beat in the transition." McClure was laying it on rather thick. He'd judged Fratelli average at best. He didn't have that ruthlessness required to be a really top rate administrator. There was always a non-confrontational streak in Dr. Fratelli that McClure found infuriating. Never wanted to go nose to nose with the lazy staff the way a real leader should.

"My husband was always a conscientious man," Mrs. Fratelli nodded nostalgically. McClure choked down the last of the macaroon.

"As a matter of fact the reason I stopped by today is to pick up the one item that is missing from his office."

"Oh?" The little widow quivered with surprise. "Anthony was always so meticulous about the office documents."

"It's a very minor matter Mrs. Fratelli," Dr. McClure oozed. "You see we still keep a few of our records out of the computer system." McClure forced a phony chuckle. "Some of us still use fountain pens!"

"Oh," Mrs. Fratelli replied, not picking up on the attempt at humor. McClure cleared his throat. "I'm trying to locate a gray binder that's missing from his old office. It has some data on our personnel we need. Trivial things really. Being so conscientious, Anthony was probably bringing office work home and never got a chance to return it."

"I hope it's not terribly important," Mrs. Fratelli said with concern.

"Not at all," Dr. McClure assured. "A couple of people are retiring and I need to look at pension figures." McClure looked off toward Fratelli's study. "Would you mind if I make a quick check for it?"

"No not at all. After all they really are your records." Mrs. Fratelli led McClure into a book lined study that had been added as a new addition to the house. It still had an odor of new paint. A marble bust of Pasteur sat staring from Anthony's desk at the empty chair where he'd done the office's homework. "I haven't been in here very often since Anthony's passing. It's silly I know but I feel this space still belongs to him. Only the housekeeper comes in here to clean."

"I see," McClure said softly. Money enough too for domestic help.

"You know Dr. McClure we had a wonderful life together. Just before Anthony passed away we finally took the world cruise we'd always wanted. We spent the summer months touring Europe. We even got to spend a couple of weeks with my sister in Parma." Mrs. Fratelli sniffled. She turned away dabbing at her eyes again. "I think I'll make myself another cup of cocoa. You go ahead Dr. McClure. You're welcome to any of Anthony's personal books. He'd be glad to know they're being put to good use."

"Thank you Mrs. Fratelli." McClure laid a hypocritical hand on the woman's shoulder. "I'll be sure to leave everything just the way I find it."

Edwin stood in the center of the study surveying the volumes. Hopefully he'd find the binder quickly. Listening to Fratelli's widow whine was grating on his nerves. It had been McClure's practice to make after hour visits to his deputies Manhattan desks. Fratelli was stupid enough to keep the little key in his coffee mug. McClure understood full well that he had a good helping of paranoia in his own makeup. He'd long ago come to an understanding of that fact.

In any business it wasn't natural selection that weeded out the weak. It was cold calculation. And there were surely certain advantages a misanthropic streak could confer.

When the Barubi outbreak first occurred Fratelli had been assigned to handle it. The deputy had an irritating habit of stashing notes in binders labeled with the geographical locations of the outbreak.

Too keep them away from prying eyes, any outbreak memoranda should have been kept electronically filed and secured. But Fratelli insisted on having the original papers on a shelf within arms reach.

On one late afternoon before Fratelli's coronary, McClure had been looking for the "B" binder, which had the data on the Barubi outbreak. He recalled that when he plucked it from the shelf a little ring of paper had fallen from it. It was a money band.

A fifty thousand Swiss franc money band. Dr. McClure remembered standing there running the paper around his finger and wondering with rising fury if the band could mean what he thought it meant. McClure had forced himself to think analytically. He'd put Fratelli in charge at Barubi. The ERSEV chief, ostensibly doing archeological work, had resisted leaving his offshore anchorage. Fratelli was hard up for cash, yet he'd paid for his twin girls to go to expensive universities, funded a European tour, and bought an expensive Mercedes. ERSEV, McClure knew, was a Swiss based outfit. To think that the timid Dr. Fratelli would have the guts to take a payoff was hard to believe. But apparently the treasonous bastard had done just that. McClure ran his fingers slowly over the binders. Binder B was out of place stashed behind Pasteur's bust. A large bulldog clasp held the covers together. McClure decided against rifling through it with the widow near by.

"I found it Mrs. Fratelli," he called out in a cheery voice. Dr. McClure walked back into the living room holding out the gray book for the lady's inspection.

"I'm glad locating it wasn't too much trouble" Mrs. Fratelli said. "Are you sure there is nothing else you might need?"

"Not at all," McClure smiled. "This is all that I wanted." McClure edged toward the front door.

"Stopping here was a pleasant break from my usual routine. And the cookie was delicious." McClure thought of giving a good-bye hug but decided that would be too much schmooze. "If you would care to call me from time to time I'd love to know how you and the children are getting along," McClure said trying to sound sincere.

"Well thank you Dr. McClure," Mrs. Fratelli brightened.

"Maybe when we've fully accepted Anthony's passing. You do know how to get back to the city?" "Yes thank you," McClure grinned.

He started down the walkway careful to step into the snow prints he'd made coming in. As he opened the Volvo's door he turned to wave a big good-bye. Mrs. Fratelli stood waving back as the car slowly pulled away. Dr. McClure waited until he'd turned the corner then pulled into a Walgreen's lot. He parked in an isolated corner, shut off the motor and tore off the binder clasp. He propped the book between his legs and steering wheel. Quickly he flipped through the papers. There was a red string sealed enveloped scotch taped to one of the pages. Scrawled across the envelope flap was a date in Fratelli's sloppy cursive that said "August Payment." Greedily McClure tore it open. "Son of a bitch," McClure spit. Inside was a wad of violet and cream colored Swiss francs, twenty thousand dollars worth. Dr. McClure's blood pressure began to rise. He'd guessed right. That bastard Fratelli had been taking bribes from ERSEV all along. There was no other explanation for the cash. And at twenty thousand a month since the first outbreak two years ago that came to what? McClure was too infuriated to do the math. Fratelli had been living high off the hog, all the while risking a medical catastrophe. Fratelli of all people. Looks like he wasn't quite the no balls geek I thought he was Dr. McClure mused. "Damn it," he hissed slamming the binder down. Dr. McClure waited a few seconds to let his rage subside. After his breathing slowed he pulled out his cell phone and punched Dr. Trimble's office number. George answered on the first ring.

"George, listen up. I'm going to make this short. Are you alone in the office?"

"Yes," George answered, suddenly alert and alarmed.

"I just visited Fratelli's widow. The quarantine of Barubi I laid down two years ago was never enforced."

"What? Not enforced? Why?", George asked, half unbelieving. He mentally reviewed the history of the outbreak trying to figure out if *he* might have screwed up.

"Fratelli was taking a pay off from ERSEV. Almost for sure, probably right up to the time you took over. If you remember ERSEV requested a waiver so they could keep doing their archeological work. I told Fratelli to deny it. It looks like he crossed me. I found Swiss francs stuffed in an envelope in his study.

"The ERSEV outfit has been there all this time then?"

"George I don't think they paid Fratelli twenty thousand a month to stay for some weekend vacation," McClure snapped. "The outbreak stopped as quickly as it started. Fratelli probably thought it was safe again to let them dig near the village."

"So you think ERSEVs digging around has somehow exposed the disease agents again?"

"That's exactly what I'm thinking George. Have you had any communication from Grier?", McClure asked.

"No."

"How about Moresby's health worker, Lippincott?"

"Nothing from him either" George said, swallowing hard. "Dr. McClure there's something else. A call came in here from a small hospital somewhere off in the outback. A place called Kokoori. A Dr. Channer, one of Moresby's part-timers, called in to say he has a patient breaking out with bizarre chancres. The lesions seem to be associated with mental abnormalities. I can't get anything more specific. I thought the lesions might be a type of tetra chlorine case." George paused. "Just a second Dr. McClure." McClure heard inaudible background conversation from George's end. "That was Ms. VanWyck. A fax came in just now from Moresby. There is an ERSEV research ship off the coast. Colin is on board."

"Damn him," McClure shouted. He looked around sheepishly to see if anyone heard him curse.

Colin had been given clear instructions. Hooking up with ERSEV wasn't one of them.

He'd always known Mr. Colin Grier was something of a loose cannon. A little to independent minded for his own good. And mine too McClure thought. He wondered if Grier might be getting the same treatment as Fratelli. Look the other way for a wallet full of cash.

It wouldn't be beyond Konrad Volger, that interfering bastard, to give away a million to keep his own research programs going. Colin wouldn't be one to turn the loot down either. Probably Volger and his elitist little bunch of researchers wouldn't be beyond risking a catastrophe to get in a little treasure hunting.

"Sorry to keep you waiting George. Just doing some planning here," McClure said. "Listen up. We've been fishing around for nearly two days now. We have nothing from Colin. We need hard facts first hand. I want you to arrange it with Van Wyck to cover for us. She's at least one person I know I can trust. You and I are going down there ourselves."

"To New Guinea?", George asked incredulously. "But who's going to...?"

"Dr. Levy has been itching to sit at your desk since I appointed you. He'll be alright to mind the store for a couple of days.

"But Dr. McClure it will be so unusual for both of us to be gone."

"George pay attention. If I send a team down there suddenly there will be more grounds for rumor.

We'll call in sick. A coincidence. It happens." "Will we both be landing near Barubi?"

"No George. I'll get there first and go on board the ship directly. You're going to get yourself to Port Moresby. There you arrange to travel to Channer's hospital if you have to pedal there." A smirk spread across McClure's face. "I'm going to contact Major Hiller at the EMTRAN Unit. This is a situation that calls for more than polite political discussion." Dr. McClure disconnected. George filled a pipe nervously, dropping tobacco flakes on his desk. The EMTRAN Unit. George had forgotten the police squad did have a link with his agency. Tucked away in a corner of an army post somewhere, EMTRAN was the acronym for a classified Emergency Transport Unit. This in turn was a Washington euphemism for an ad hoc SWAT team. George wasn't privy to the particulars; only McClure had the power to call them in, but he'd learned EMTRAN was set up by the N.S.C. after the Korean "police action." Originally, it was designed as a mobile police unit to be put at the disposal of NATO officials. Over time it had devolved into an "as need" police unit, rarely used, but still on call to certain government agencies, McClure's office being one of them. On mulling it over George thought he understood McClure's line of thinking. The ERSEV people had defied a legitimate order to vacate Barubi. They'd convinced Fratelli to stay there probably going back and forth into international waters, and ending up putting all of New Guinea at risk. Or worse. Maybe a bit of prodding by friends of the military was what was needed to convince them to get the hell away from that coast. George flicked the tobacco flakes back into his pouch. The appointment to the Presidents Science Advisory Council was due to be announced in a few weeks. George knew Dr. McClure was desperate to get a chair at the table. Among the power brokers McClure was seen as a can do administrator who happened to belong to the right political party. But McClure did have his detractors George knew. Enemies he'd made who'd suffered from his heavy handed style. Should word get out that the Barubi business hadn't really been contained, as McClure had promised, the buzzing at the President's ear would be devastating for his chances. George got up and started toward Van Wyck's cubicle. He had convinced himself that Barubi's skin affliction was man made. Maybe he was wrong about the cause being a tetrachlorin-like compound. But if it wasn't that, it had to be some other related toxin. How could the kind of skin chancres Channer described be caused by anything else?

As for the hepatitis and small pox cases it had to boil down to germ warfare agents somehow getting into the environment accidentally. George hoped he was right. And he hoped ERSEV would be cooperative this time.

With his future on the line it wouldn't take much for McClure to do more with EMTRAN than threaten.

CHAPTER 10

"COLIN GRIER?" COLIN snapped his head around to see a red haired man standing off to the edge of the flower field.

He was in his forties, his khakis sweat soaked even more thoroughly than Colin's. "I'm Ed Lippincott from Moresby." The blue-eyed health department worker approached Colin with extended hand.

"Yes I'm Grier," Colin said, shaking Ed's. Colin felt a sense of relaxation due mainly to the fact he was suddenly not alone. "They told me you had gone back to Port Moresby," Colin said.

"They? You mean Dr. Volger's people on the ship?" "Yes," Colin said. Lippincott wore an ironic angry look.

"Things are not at all what they seem here Colin. I'm lucky as hell to be able to fill you in without Volger being around. First I need to know, were you told the outbreak here was caused by stuff from a sunken ship?"

"Yes. I swam down to see it."

"Did you? Then Dr. Volger is even more disingenuous than I thought. Not to put too fine a point on it, but Volger has been outright lying." Ed picked up a small flower and put it behind his ear. "I got here yesterday afternoon Colin. Before I could get into Barubi, Volger's people intercepted me. They invited me aboard the ship. Dr. Volger told me the infected villagers were being treated and that they'd found the source of the outbreak."

"Canisters on the YAHKA. That's what I saw," Colin replied.

"At least they're keeping their story consistent," Ed snorted. "I was due to report back to Moresby so I didn't take Dr. Volger up on his invitation to tour the ship. I was satisfied ERSEV had everything under control."

"But I saw the canisters," Colin said, still wanting desperately to believe he hadn't been fully taken in.

"What Volger showed you was staged," Ed said. He poked a finger into Colin's chest.

"Before I left the ship I got on the net. I found out some things. There wasn't any YAHKA. The ship that went down was the Esmeralda, a vessel carrying a load of raw rubber. I decided not to confront Volger. I came on shore to see what was really going on."

"So they even went to the trouble to repaint the ship's name? Set all this up to get us away?" "They're taking a chance on letting hell loose here and covering it up. Why I don't know," Ed said.

He bent over and rolled up a leg of his work pants. "This started this morning." Between Ed's knee and ankle there were hundreds of brown speckles. They looked like bites from fine grain buckshot. Colin recognized them as the same crusty lesions he'd seen on the photographs back at McClure's office. "This is how it started with the Barubi villagers," Ed said. "Small spots that within hours grows to cover the whole body. I was able at least to shoot myself up with antibiotics.......as if it's going to do any good. They had no protection at all."

"But antibiotics were shipped down here for the villagers two years ago," Colin protested.

"They got here all right. I found cartons of pharmaceuticals from your office left to rot. All unopened. Hidden outside the village where only the snakes could find them. Somebody didn't want the Barubi natives to survive." Ed looked quizzically at Colin. "You know who it might be?" Colin shook his head. He knew who had the motivation to do it. But would McClure really have done such a thing? And why would he? It was clear to Colin there was a lot going on that he needed time to think through. And right now wasn't real conducive to cool analysis. Ed gestured toward the cave entrance. "If we're going to find the real cause of all this we'll find it in there." As if in direct reply to Ed's words a low humming sound echoed out from the hidden recesses of the cave.

"First we should get you help Ed," Colin said. He tried to keep from staring at the brown lesions. "No. Maybe I'll make it. Maybe not. But whatever is simmering in there I'm going in to check it out. If I die I want to know what it is that killed me. You coming in with me?"

"Of course," Colin answered. He tried to imagine what could be making the hum. The low drone of whatever ERSEV had in there reverberated with threatening low overtones. Colin felt frightened but he had to go in. Overriding his fear was rage at what Dr. Volger had done and admiration for Lippincott's courage.

"Does Volger know you're on shore?", Ed asked. "No. I got here late last night."

"Good then. We'll have some time to check out the cave before he interferes."

"One other thing before we go in," Colin said. "Did you meet Dr. Volger's daughter on the ship?" "He has a daughter?" Obviously Dr. Volger hadn't made Ed privy to Margo's psychic feats. "Supposedly she's the reason he's down here. One beautiful woman. Sadly she's been paralyzed from the neck down." Colin raised his eyes to the crest above the cave. "She was the one who discovered the temple ruin up there."

"Did she now? So What?"

"Don't you think it's peculiar that the ruin sits right above the cave?" Colin asked.

"The only peculiar thing I've got time to worry about is how this outbreak started two years ago, stopped, then started up again. But if you want to conjecture about the temple being up there consider this. What if the temple is a diversion?" Colin gave Ed a quizzical look. "Maybe Volger is just using the daughter to force attention on the archeology while he's secretly up to some mischief in the cave. Hell, you can't even see the cave from up above us." Colin nodded agreement. Did Margo know anything at all about the cave here below? If so, what and how much? Colin felt oddly torn. He wanted to find out what was inside the cave, yet a part of him resisted. "You ready?", Ed asked, staring at Colin with irritation at his preoccupied expression.

"Yes Ed I am ready. Let's go in."

"It looks as if the ERSEV people have been busy in here," Lippincott said. Both men stood scanning the cave's interior. It was much bigger inside than the narrow mouth indicated. The walls and ceiling retained their natural contours in only a few places. Most of the wall was braced with beams still smelling of fresh pine. At regular intervals, for the first fifty or so feet, forty-watt bulbs were strung along the cave wall. The light was enough to keep Ed and Colin from groping but hardly enough to work by.

"Reminds me of the entrance to one of those old gold mines," Ed said, squinting to follow the path into the deeper recesses.

"Whatever Volger is digging for in here I doubt if it's gold," Colin replied. He shone his flashlight randomly along the damp wall. "ERSEV has plenty of money. Whatever he's been in here for is worth more than cash to him," Colin went on. "Ed, there has to be a switch in here that will give us more light. Volger can't be doing work in here with just these Christmas tree bulbs." Colin ran his flashlight beam shoulder high along the wall. "See if you can find a switch on your side Ed." Momentarily Lippincott saw a thick gray cable running along the inner edge of one of the beams. He followed it until it ended in a breaker box nearby.

"Here it is Colin." Ed pulled down the breaker switch. Instantly the cave was flooded with light. Colin covered his eyes to let them adjust to the sudden glare. Dr. Volger had installed a chain of flood lamps at strategic spots so that every square inch of the interior was covered. It was clear that the cave burrowed into the cliff face much further than they'd expected.

"This thing is at least four hundred yards deep," Ed said pointing his finger. "Look down to the end there. The cave doglegs off to the left." Ed started quickly toward the distant bend with Colin following a few steps behind. When Ed got to the tunnel turn he stopped abruptly. "Colin take a look at this." Ed waited for Colin to catch up.

"Surprise surprise," Colin said when he reached the turn. The line of the cave ran on for another seven to a thousand feet before it reached its end. The cul-de-sac end was lit even more brilliantly. The light shone down on a large rectangular pit dug into the cave floor. Colin judged it to be the size of a large swimming pool. He could see a wooden ladder leading to the pit floor. In the middle of the excavation the round top of a circular silvery object could be seen. Ed and Colin approached it cautiously. Standing at the edge of the pit they saw that the featureless metal ovoid was still buried up to its midline. When totally excavated, Colin guessed it would be about sixteen feet across. It was quiet now but both men unspokenly agreed it must be the source of the drone. "Reminds me of Swartkrans," Ed said.

"Swart what?"

"Swartkrans," Ed repeated emphasizing the T and K consonants. "A place in South Africa. In the forties a dozen or so bones of pre-man were found there in a limestone cave like this one. See the stuff on the table next to the ladder?" With his eyes fixed on the silvery ellipse Colin hadn't noticed the folding metal table in the pit. It was covered with opened gallon bottles, brushes, an old bellows camera and what looked like drafting tools. "This is a textbook dig site. Look there on the walls. See the little tags?", Ed asked. There was a patchwork of black and white numbered tags stuck onto various parts of the smoothly brushed walls.

"The tags are where Volger found fossils?" Colin asked. "Either that or where he thinks he'll find them."

"What's in the bottles?" "Probably acetic acid," Ed answered. "Limestone leaves most fossils covered by a kind of rock called breccia. They use the acid to dissolve it."

"You really know about this stuff?" Colin asked.

"A little bit. Summer reading for a paleontology course."

"So let's get to the elephant in the living room. What the hell do you think this metal thing is?", Colin asked.

"Have no clue Colin. But for sure it wasn't put here by ERSEV. That rock it's locked in is ancient.

He's done a pretty fair job of prying it out."

"Wait a minute Ed." Lippincott nodded his head emphatically.

"I know. I know," he said anticipating Colin's thought. "What's a piece of technology like this doing buried in rock with fossils that go back hundreds of thousands of years? How the hell should I know."

"It's running Ed. Some kind of electronic sound."

"Yeah. Mr. Java man didn't have quite the brights to build it but the rock strata shows it's from his time. Maybe it's being here will make sense with a closer look." Ed started down the wooden steps with Colin following. A mix of fear and excitement churned in Colin's belly. There had to be a sensible answer.

Somehow the diseases, Margo's paralysis, the temple carvings and this out of time machine were inter-connected Colin knew. Yet, what the rationale could be that would tie them together escaped even the beginnings of a reasonable thought. Colin found himself walking on tiptoe as he approached the shining object, almost as if heavy footsteps might stir some sleeping circuits. Oddly, the ellipse made Colin think of the back of a chromium whale frozen in mid dive. Ed squatted next to the machine, pulled out a ballpoint and gave a few tentative taps to the surface. A certain hollow echo issued, but clearly there was no way to tell what was inside using a pen for a probe. "Ed, I just thought of something." Colin was running his fingers over the surface looking for any little break in the tooled smoothness.

"What?", Ed groused, his nose inches from the metal surface. "This is off the wall, but what if these things aren't for real?" "What do you mean?"

"Well maybe they're making a film in here. This could be just a prop." Ed raised a dubious eyebrow. "Some movie company *could* have wanted a natural cave and put this together on the back lot. Hell it might be the top of a shell with no bottom under the floor. Maybe they got started in here then got scared off at the first sign of the outbreak." Colin knew he was stretching credibility in a try to construct a make sense scenario, at least in his own head.

"Wait a second. There's an easy way to tell." Ed said. "On the table there Colin. There's a hammer and chisel. Toss them over." Colin threw the chisel and a ball peen hammer to Ed. Ed brushed away sweat with his forearm and hammered the chisel where the metal met the pit floor. Splinters of rock flew in all directions. "You had an original idea I'll give you that," Ed said. "But no studio or anybody else put this here recently. This thing might as well be set in concrete. This floor is geriatric."

"So much for that," Colin said with a look of chagrin. "It was worth a shot," Ed smiled back.

"There has to be a way to get this open Colin. Let's check the top." Both men ran their hands over the upper curve reaching for some break in the uniformity. Colin was about to say he thought the ellipse was totally featureless when his fingers felt a rough area on the metal skin. About three quarters up the side there was a foot wide square that was etched in the surface. Inside the square were thousands of tiny dots scattered in a seemingly random fashion. In the middle of the square, evenly spaced were two large circles. They too were etched into the skin.

"Ed come over here," Colin said intrigued. "What do you make of this?" Ed put his pen back in his work shirt pocket and came over to Colin's side. He ran his fingers over the indentations then stepped back with folded arms.

"Braille for whoever is inside." Colin laughed. "Well it's as good a suggestion as your movie idea," Ed said. "Then again maybe an apprentice was practicing his etching," Colin quipped. Ed started a stifled laugh and in a second both men were howling. Ed and Colin sucked in fresh air, calmed down and looked at each other.

"Any other ideas?", Ed asked. Colin shook his head. The gravity of the situation fell on him anew. Impulsively Colin kicked the ellipse with his heel. Maybe it was in response to the blow (there was no way to be sure) but at that same instant the hum that had quieted began to grow louder again. Mingling ominously with the bass tone Colin could detect a hissing sound. Reflexively Ed and Colin stepped back.

"Look there *is* an opening!" Colin said. He pointed to the top of the ellipse. Millions of hair like white threads waved inches above the center of the ellipse. They swayed like new grown wheat blown by a gentle prairie breeze. The sound from inside began to grow. Now a new whining unpleasant dissonance joined in with the monotone hum.

"I don't like this," Ed said. "It gives me the creeps. Sounds like Auntie's tea kettle before it gets to full boil." Colin noticed the waving filaments were moving with much more energy, the breeze giving way to a gale. "Let's get out of the pit," Ed said. I think this thing is rolling toward a full orchestra finale and I don't think we want to be here for the cymbal crash." Colin and Ed scrambled up the steps. They stood with their backs against the cave wall. The ellipse might be perfectly harmless but they felt safer with some distance between the metal ovoid and themselves. From his look down view, Colin could see the filaments extended from an iris like opening, about a foot in diameter. The opening was not yet fully drawn back. "Is this thing stuffed with these hairs or what?", Ed asked. His face reflected total puzzlement. "What could the damn thing be for Colin?" As if in answer to his question, the swaying threads squeezed out of the ellipse another foot and began a rapid quiver. The sound glissandoed up to a near dog-ear whine that made both men clasp their hands to their ears. Colin thought he could see the metal skin vibrate. The hope that the machine was harmless turned around to surety that the thing was some kind of S.O.B. There was no question of being heard over the din. With their eyes Colin and Ed signaled their fear to one another. They started a brisk walk toward the cave entrance. They got to a few yards before the dogleg bend when the screaming sound suddenly stopped. They both looked back. There with the hiss of an engine blowing off steam they saw a fog like cloud blow out of the filament tips. The haze quickly filled the dig site. A second burst blew out even more of the atomized shiny spray. A large billowing mass began to tumble quickly in Colin and Ed's direction.

Instinctively they began a headlong run. With no time to formulate a coherent thought it was definitely a case of discretion over valor. Run now. Think later. Colin glanced back over his shoulder. Ed's eyes were wide with panic. The rolling cloud was gaining on them. Colin stepped up his run as fast as he could but his legs were fatigued from the cliff climb. He forced his aching thighs to go on, praying his legs wouldn't buckle. He was nearing the cave mouth. In an instant's realization he felt a fool in allowing himself to be sucked into Volger's story. And worse to be mesmerized by Margo's talk of Hindu Gods and psychic possibilities. He should have been at Barubi all along, the same as Ed, doing his job. Colin turned around again. Ed wasn't behind him. Then Colin saw him sprawled unmoving on the cave floor fifty yards from the dogleg. The leading edge of

The cloud was about to engulf his obviously unconscious body. Along the damp rock floor there were patches of slippery green algae. Ed must have slipped on one and gone down. For a moment Colin considered rushing back in. Instead he turned away forcing his legs to carry him out to the open air. If the talc-like particles in the cloud were the cause of the disease there was no sense in both of them getting infected. Colin burst out of the entrance bent over, gasping for air. His sides were aching fiercely. A voice from the edge of the flower field ahead jolted him upright. At a full run a figure dressed in a black latex-like suit was approaching him. Up close, through a plexi glass mask Colin saw it was Dr. Volger.

"Colin quick, put this on." Dr. Volger shouted through an in suit microphone. With outstretched arms Volger offered a suit identical to the one he was wearing. Colin pushed his outrage aside. He roughly snatched the suit from the ERSEV chief, quickly found the zippered front and jammed himself into it. Dr. Volger saw through Colin's mask that he was red with fury. Colin's mouth was moving in an avalanche of unheard words. Volger gestured toward a microphone button at a spot behind the ear and indicated for Colin to push it. Colin slapped it on with his palm.

"So what the fuck is really...," Colin got out when his accusatory question was preempted by the spectacle of the rolling shiny cloud reaching the cave mouth. As the cloud blew out it engulfed Colin and Dr. Volger leaving a glistening silvery residue on their safety suits. Slowly it spread over the trees dissipating in the heavy afternoon air. Colin stepped toward Volger with balled fists. With as much control as he could muster he decided he wouldn't punch the ERSEV chief first. Instead he'd settle for beginning a verbal assault. The question Colin had was whether to start with "you asshole" or not.

While this thought was running through his head he noticed Volger was looking intently toward the cave. A stricken look was in his eyes. Colin turned following Dr. Volger's line of sight, and sucked in his breath. Lippincott, or rather what was left of him, was at the cave entrance on his knees. Earlier there had been small crusty brown speckles on Ed's arms and legs. Now large blotches of dark crisp skin covered his entire face. In Ed's one partially clear eye Colin saw a look of bewilderment. The photographs of the desiccated villagers McClure had shown him didn't begin to convey the horror Colin felt. What kind of thing, man made or natural, could devastate flesh in mere minutes? Colin started toward Ed. He knew in his gut there was nothing he could do. Words of solace maybe, but it was too late even for that. Ed slumped forward. His face hit the ground with a heavy thud. A rush of sorrow washed over Colin. He'd known this man briefly, yet in that time he'd formed a bond tentative but true. Part of it had to do with the fact that they both did the same work, no doubt, but Colin would have liked to count Ed among his friends in any circumstances. Colin turned back to Dr. Volger. He waited for the plexiglas covered eyes to meet his own.

"You asshole. How dare you talk to me about niceties and graciousness. Lying isn't very nice is it? All your sweetness and light is allowing innocents to be exposed to agents of death." A pained expression crossed Dr. Volger's face, a tail between the legs look that seemed to register true anguish. But it could just be part of the ERSEV chief's act. "Konrad I want to know what the hell is really going on here, the truth and all of it." Colin walked closer just to the edge of Volger's personal space. "I think you ought to get yourself ready for a whole different lifestyle Konrad. The great chefs of Europe don't serve up gormet chow in prison." Dr. Volger stood with his head bowed. He began a stuttering reply but cut himself off with a shake of his head.

"Why all the bullshit about the YAHKEV? Why didn't you tell me the temple and that thing in there were fifty feet apart? What is it? What's the dig about? How did it get there? I need to know everything Konrad and now." Dr. Volger gathered himself.

"You have every reason to distrust me Colin. To despise me for what I've done. But before you condemn me completely please give me a chance to explain."

"I'm listening." It was going to be interesting to hear just how Dr. Volger would justify the horror he'd allowed to spread.

"Believe me Colin I was sure the machine was safe. I'd worked up probabilities that said it couldn't expel any more particles for another week at least. You see it runs on a kind of timing mechanism that..." Dr. Volger stopped abruptly. He was getting ahead of himself he knew. "Wait Colin let me go back to the beginning."

Colin sarcastically glanced at his soot covered wristwatch, then folded his arms across his chest. "Please. Look at these." Dr. Volger fumbled open a Velcro closed pocket on his thigh. He withdrew two objects wrapped in white medical gauze secured with masking tape. Carefully he uncovered the gauze to reveal two pieces of fossilized bone. He held them out for Colin's inspection. Colin turned them around in his fingers.

"They're jawbones. Two pieces of mandible." Colin stared back at Dr. Volger. "What's the point?" "Please, look at them more closely," Dr. Volger said, excitement coming into his voice. Colin laid both fossils across his palm so that the teeth were parallel. Now the differences jumped out at him. "You see Colin. One is a mandible of modern man. An angular chin. Thinner bone. The other is of Homo erectus. What was called Java Man in older days. The chin there is more rounded. The bone thicker."

"What do these have to do with what's back there in the pit?"

"Everything," Volger answered. The ERSEV chief rewrapped the bones tenderly as if they were holy relics, then pocketed them and pressed the Velcro closure shut. "When I told you we came here two years ago to excavate Margo's temple find I told you the truth. Then one evening after the others had gone back to the ship I stayed to explore the area more carefully. That's when I discovered there was a cave below the temple. Margo's visions had led me to it. The entrance was overgrown, hidden. The villagers told me about it. They considered it taboo to approach it themselves. For them the cave was sacred. Off limits to them for generations." "You were intrigued of course."

"Yes. I thought there might be a connection between the cave and the temple. Anyhow I'd decided to keep the cave's rediscovery to myself. If I did uncover something of value I thought I'd surprise Margo with it."

"How sweet. "Just like you surprised her with that one and only flower? Do you lie to your daughter often Dr. Volger?" A frown of regret wrinkled Volger's forehead.

"Please try to understand Colin. I had to keep what I found in there under wraps. There is a critical time line to try and make sense of the machines being here. With security concerns the way they are it would be automatic for them to first thing, close up the cave."

"Sounds like a pretty fair idea to me," Colin said. Dr. Volger shook his head no.

"What is in that machine may be of unimaginable value. But it's contents are disintegrating quickly and...." Colin cut Volger off again. He gestured to Ed's body.

"I'd call what's coming out of the machine the opposite of valuable. But go on. I'm curious to see where you're heading." Dr. Volger cleared his throat. "The first sign that this cave was used by ancient man was my discovery of charred embers from a meal probably cooked by Homo erectus. On digging further I uncovered the mandibles I just showed you. Then a most extraordinary thing. In the same stratum as the erectus jaw I dug out the jawbone of Homo sapiens. It could only mean one thing."

"What?", Colin asked. There was just the slightest tone in his question that hinted he might be open to Dr. Volger's apology.

"Well that both pre man and modern man once lived here side by side in this cave." Dr. Volger held out his hands in a gesture that begged for understanding. "Don't you see Colin. There's proof here that the evolution of man didn't inch by over the millennia. Modern man. Us. We burst forth in an instant. We were transformed at one stroke from chattering super apes into what we are now." Colin blinked. He tried to tie together all the threads of what he'd seen and heard in some kind of sensible construction, to jam the square peg of a machine that shouldn't be where it was into the cozy hole of understanding. If he could just elevate his thinking to consider more forest than trees maybe he could intuit the big picture here. But he couldn't.

"I'm sorry. I don't see. I don't see at all Dr. Volger. But do go on."

"I gave Dr. Fratelli money to let us work here. That's the fact of it. But after the initial outbreak the disease disappeared. We both believed the danger was over. It was wrong I know but I felt compelled to go on with the dig. Then I uncovered the machine. I only stumbled on it two weeks ago and I didn't realize it was the source of the disease until a few days ago." "So you knew the thing was the cause of all this misery and kept it exposed? You went to all the trouble of setting up the canister charade just to keep Ed and me away?" Colin cocked his head to one side. "Dr. Volger I think you made a terrible mistake. But I also think you're not stupid. After you dug out the machine what made you think the danger was over?"

"As I said Colin, it looked to me as if the machine worked on a timer of some kind," Dr. Volger sighed. "The bursts from the ellipse, the machine, came out at regularly spaced intervals, but these ran further and further apart. Based on this data I didn't think it would throw off the particles again until I had a chance to examine it's interior. Obviously I was terribly mistaken. I take full responsibility of course." Colin understood that Dr. Volger was a very vain man, a man highly jealous of his research priorities. It probably broke his egocentric heart to have to share ownership of a scientific discovery. But to be so craven as to deliberately put innocent villagers in harms way for some intellectual victory....no Colin didn't believe he could be that vicious.

"So then Dr. Volger. To return to the key questions. What is it? What's inside? Where did it come from?" Konrad's cheeks lifted into a Cheshire cat like smile.

"I have my own ideas about where it's from but I think it's best to keep silent on that score for now.

After I tell you what it seems to be I'll leave it to you to draw your own conclusions." "Go on."

"You saw the filaments come out of the top?" Volger asked. "Yes," Colin replied with impatience.

"I think those fibers are a kind of injection device Colin. The particles that are in the cloud that overtook Dr. Lippincott, that are glistening here on our suits, contain genetic fragments. I can't be sure but so far our labs show that the filaments are designed to inject genetic particles into the flesh. Probably at one time the flesh of Homo erectus." But that's impossible Colin wanted to say. A part of him wanted to brush Volger's assertion aside as not even worth considering. But the ellipse, as Konrad had called it, was there. Buried in brittle two million year old soil. Suddenly Colin wished he could be anywhere else. Anyplace where he wouldn't have to take the implications of Konrad's earnest words seriously.

"The mechanics of the ellipse are out of control Colin," Dr. Volger went on. "You've gotten a look inside?", Colin asked.

"No, the ellipse has opened for only seconds at a time. But we have reason to believe the inner workings are run by a computer. Not a normal computer Colin. A machine that uses DNA base pairs as it's binary zeros and ones. Slight quantum moves could trigger adenine and thiamine or guanine and cytosine to fire current on or off. But somehow the computer has malfunctioned."

"So what's the computer suppose to do when it's running right?", Colin asked with an increasing sense of unreality.

"Turn pre-man into Homo sapiens. I think if we could get inside the ellipse it's even possible we might find the remains of long dead Homo erectus who were meant to be transformed into a superior species of man." Colin searched Dr. Volger's eyes.

"Transformed? By whom?" Dr. Volger shrugged and continued.

"Colin, what if we are a flawed species? Flawed because of a simple error in the code that was to transform us. Maybe we were on the road from A to Z and due to some glitch two million years ago we never finished the journey. Only went from A to L to put it simplistically. In other words what if we are just a compromise with the possible?"

"Suppose that I grant that the ellipse, as you call it, is from some higher civilization. That's what you're implying isn't it?"

"Yes. It is."

"So why would a machine that was meant to change our ancestors be blasting out disease particles?"

"Colin keep in mind that we have technology on the ship that is generations ahead of anyone else. "A lot can be inferred from the particles we've been able to analyze. The splices of genetic material that are inside the particles have been cut improperly. They are causing the diseases. The one's we are familiar with here on earth and one's totally foreign to us."

"Like whatever killed Dr. Lippincott and infected Dr. Boka's cadaver?" "Yes. You saw what was in the autopsy room then."

"Seeing that horrible body was what convinced me to come ashore," Colin said. Again the urge to berate Dr. Volger welled up. Colin let it pass.

"Colin, we think there are trillion's of stored genes in the ellipse. Some of them I'm convinced have caused Margo's paralysis. But that's not all. I also believe some of the gene splices are responsible for giving my daughter her extra sensory powers."

"Sort of good gene, bad gene. All wrapped up in a shiny package," Colin sneered. "You could put it like that." Colin caught a hurtful look in Konrad's eyes and wished back the flip remark. Dr. Volger dearly loved his daughter . Being a wiseass about her condition wasn't in the best taste.

"I didn't mean to be insensitive," Colin offered.

"I understand the stress you are under Colin. Let me go on. Besides the disease particles in that cloud I believe there are some genes that can confer full psychic power. Genes that were meant to elevate pre man beyond us." Konrad put his hand on Colin's shoulder. "You saw Margo's abilities Colin. They are impressive. But they are weak now. The lab has found genes from these particles that are designed to create proteins in memory centers of her brain. Some of these genes have entered Margo and in trance like states she has seen glimpses of long ago events. The lab is synthesizing a complete set of proteins. We hope these will bring her broken visions into a meaningful picture of the past. Hopefully she will give us the answer to the events that took place here centuries ago." Colin felt a disquieting déjà vu like sense. A kind of light headed I'm here but not here at the same time. The feeling ran smack against that cold rational part of his mind he'd been struggling to hold onto since the fantastic assertions of Dr. Volger.

"Colin help us find the truth," Dr. Volger blurted with a hint of desperate urging. "You know very little of myself and Margo, so asking you to cooperate with us after all the deaths must seen arrogance at it's zenith. But I'm asking you to accept that you've stumbled on the impossible here, found the exception to the rule. Believe me, there's a whole complex here related in some way. The Temple, the ellipse, my daughters powers are all of a piece. Give me time to investigate." Colin slowly pointed his finger at Ed's body.

"What about his time?" Dr. Volger's eyes reddened ever so slightly.

"I can't communicate to you how sorry I am. I should have been absolutely sure I had the timing mechanism figured out before allowing anyone near the cave. I did not. And for that fatal misjudgment I'm willing to make amends." With deliberate slowness Dr. Volger reached for the zipper that attached his hood to the micro-stat suit. With a swift circular motion he separated the headpiece and threw it on the ground. "I always pay my debts."

"Dr. Volger you mustn't," Colin shouted.

"But I must Colin." Dr. Volger ran his finger across his chest picking up a sheen of particles that had settled there. With the studied formality of a samurai he slowly closed his eyes and rubbed the gene laden specks across his lips. "I can't bring Ed back but now the scales will be perhaps more in balance."

"You didn't have to do that."

"Oh yes young man. An eye for an eye you see." Dr. Volger took in a long deep breath. "I want you to understand that it is not for my ambition alone that I seek your help. It's true I paid for Dr. Fratelli's silence. To leave me here to excavate alone. But when I uncovered the ellipse I realized of course that I had made a monumental find. Now time is short. Outsiders who might come here will equivocate, argue, delay. The genes inside the ellipse will not remain long. In a few more days they will be rendered into a meaningless soup." Dr. Volger wiped the sweat from his forehead back into his thick white hair. "I want Margo to live Colin. I want her to receive the memory proteins, to give her the chance to open the door to the real meaning of this machine. Almost surely I've infected myself now. But my dying is not important if it convinces you of my motives to help all mankind."

Colin knew what he should answer. He should tell Volger.... It was his *duty* to tell Volger that he couldn't allow the ellipse to remain exposed. The fact was that the machine, no matter it's possibilities, was a killer. Stuff from inside was blowing out nasty little dots that did terrible things. Like first, spread your everyday diseases around, then follow up with an encore of chancre makers and the agent that killed poor Ed. The other fact, that some of the "good" genes brought on a combo of paralysis and ESP lead to who knows where? A new world order? Contact with creatures that inhabit some realm over the black hole rainbow? Actually it was simple Colin mused. He must weigh the present actual mayhem with the might be good stuff to come later. Any sane man wouldn't hesitate to draw the obvious conclusion. Real deaths versus illusions of the possible. I should just hang a sign on the cave entrance. "Closed until further notice," Colin thought. That's what George would do and McClure absolutely if they were in his place. The right thing to do would be to call in a platoon of cement mixers and have them fill the pit to the top. Then walk away, mission accomplished. Later in their whispering caucuses the movers and shakers could figure out what the ellipse was all about at their leisure. There would be no need to alarm Mr. and Mrs. Public. Sometimes innocence *is* bliss. Dr. McClure would be congratulated, sotto voce naturally, for keeping a potentially panic causing outbreak from getting in the news. The ancient vines would wind their way across the cave mouth once more and maybe after another generation had passed officialdom would send some "experts" down to jack hammer out the ellipse and decide whatever they'd decide. Rumors about the existence of the strange machine hidden in the New Guinea jungle might spread from time to time of course. Furtive gossip leaking out from the I believe in UFO's crowd. But the government would manage to pooh pooh the rumors like they did after the Roswell business. The public would be mollified as usual. Grateful to believe the pronouncement of the 'experts."

Colin went to scratch his itchy nose then hissed a quiet "shit" when his finger met with his facemask. "Just say no." That's what I should do Colin thought. Order Volger and the good ship ERSEV to steam into the sunset, call in the yellow bulldozers, then just walk away. Colin put his hands on his hips and looked up into the hot blue sky. For a moment he let the sun burn into his squinting eyes. Maybe it's rays would sear away the confusion. The logic arrows all pointed in one direction. Stay safe, do your job. Close the site now no matter what potential there might be in allowing the examination of an unknown (from a higher civilization?) piece of hardware.

The peoples safety had to come first. Yet from a place deep in his gut Colin felt an urge to throw the logic aside. There was a pernicious impulse banging around his brain to this time do the really dumb thing. What he was contemplating would probably end up in his sharing the same cell he'd had in mind for Dr. Volger. Could it be that before he'd gotten the suit on, he'd sniffed a few of the psycho stimulating particles and was just now on the border line of plain nuts? At least insanity would be a defense for the decision he was about to make.

"These proteins that will clear up Margo's memory. How long until they're ready?" "Once we're back on board an hour or two at the most." Colin grunted.

"I suppose there's a reason you haven't covered the excavation with a tarp at least." "It's no use Colin. The limestone below the ellipse is honey combed with fissures. The particles diffuse out of the cracks to the outside."

"You're sure all the villagers have been medevaced?" "To a facility we own near Darwin. Most of the ships personnel are standing by there too."

"Then here's the deal Dr. Volger." Colin swallowed hard knowing he might be making the mistake of his life. "I'm going to give you twenty four hours to figure this thing out. I'll work with you and Margo. Cooperate in any way you want." "Thank you Colin." Dr. Volger enthused. Colin held up his hand. "You understand" I'm laying my head on the block by allowing this. So if in a days time we don't know all there is to know about this machine and if you can't give me an iron clad argument for leaving it exposed, I'll call in the earth movers and this site will be covered by a mile wide concrete gumdrop."

"I can't tell you how much I appreciate this chance you're giving us Colin." Dr. Volger was close to fawning in gratitude.

"This might turn out to be the regret of my life Dr. Volger. But I have a knack for kicking common sense down the stairs now and then. Let's just say I'm taking a flyer on this and maybe I can help you save Margo's life." In his minds eye Colin recalled vividly sitting next to Margo on the ships patio as she so matter-of-factly told him she expected him to become a part of her life. Now in recollection

Colin pictured her again gloriously beautiful, an indescribable aura reaching out to him. A part of him hadn't wanted to take account of the possibility that her powers were real, or even more that her courageous personality had shaken him so deeply.

How much of his decision to give Dr. Volger time was based on the potential inside the ellipse, and how much on his desire to follow an enchantress, Colin didn't know.

Dr. Volger unclipped a cell phone from his waist and dialed.

"Roberto I'm at the entrance with Colin. We'll be coming aboard in a half hour. I want you to set up the protein synthesis program. And get Jhanda ready."

"One thing before we go Dr. Volger. About that pattern on the surface of the ellipse. It seems to be etched in. Any thoughts about what it is?"

"Only speculation. I brought a DVD of that patch back to the ship for examination. Roberto's best guess is that it's an identifying logo of some sort. Hopefully Margo will give us the meaning."

Colin walked over to Ed Lippincott's body. He stood there for a moment staring down at the ravaged corpse. It was hard to accept that this dry husk had been a vibrant human a short time ago. Taking in the full impact of the destruction the particles had inflected on this decent man, made Colin think of reversing his answer to Volger. That it was all too much to risk, too far a chance to take. But he'd sanctioned twenty-four hours. He would keep his agreement. Maybe in some way even Ed's death would be justified.

Colin squatted down next to Ed. He put his arms under the dead man and lifted the lifeless body to his chest. Thankfully the latex like suit kept him from feeling the touch of the dry crackling skin.

"What are you going to tell the Port Moresby health people?", Colin asked.

"The truth Colin. They've seen the same photos of this skin affliction that went to your New York office."

"Well no matter what the situation is by this time tomorrow I'm going back to Moresby with this body. His loved ones will want to learn what happened and I'll want to tell them."

"I understand of course Colin," Konrad said biting his lower lip.

"If I'm still alive myself after tomorrow I'll go with you." With Colin following a few steps behind, both men walked through the flower field to the waiting Land Rover. Among the tools piled in the back of the vehicle was a rolled up blanket. Seeing Colin eyeing it, Dr. Volger wordlessly spread it out on the grass. Colin placed Ed's body on it, folded it over him, then secured it with black electrical tape.

Dr. Volger got behind the wheel, buckled his seatbelt and started the Land Rover down a washboard trail. The path was on the opposite side of the place where Colin had first stepped onto the flower field.

"I got lost on the way here Konrad," Colin said.

"There are a couple of trails to the cave. I haven't used the one you took since Fratelli was here." Great, Colin thought. Busted my ass because I picked the wrong trail. He turned his head to see the receding Temple ruin beginning to fall into purple late noon shadow. Colin hoped the trail he was now on, more important by far than this physical one, would turn out to be the right choice.

"I have something else to tell you," Konrad said not taking his eyes from the winding path. "Something I was saving in case I needed to make one last argument to get you on our side."

"Saving the best for last were you?" Colin reached back to steady the rolled up blanket as the Rover hit a bad stretch of rut. "You asked me earlier where I thought the ellipse came from. I said I didn't know. That's true I don't, but you should know this."

Konrad down shifted into first as the four by four approached a steep drop. Colin could see the beach. The sea-cat was where he'd left it about a half mile away. "Remember much of your high school chemistry?" Colin gave Konrad a puzzled look.

"Most of it I hope. Is this a pop quiz?"

"Just one question Colin," Konrad said with a puckish grin. "Do you remember the atomic mass of Nitrogen?" Colin tried to picture the tattered periodic table that hung at the front of his junior year chemistry class. Often enough during boring stretches of Mr. Cobb's lectures he'd let his daydreaming eyes roam about it's squares and numbers. Nitrogen. Nitrogen. He strained his brain but couldn't see it.

"It's been a while since I've had my nose in a text Konrad but as I recall isn't it twelve?"

"Close," Konrad said. "It's a fraction over fourteen. Except, that is, for the nitrogen atoms from the ellipse." Colin's head bumped lightly against the door glass as Konrad jerked the wheel to avoid a deep pothole. "The nitrogen from the ellipse has an atomic mass of nineteen. Seven protons and twelve neutrons. Chemically it's just like any other nitrogen atoms of course but there's a question as to it's source.

"I don't follow," Colin said.

"The vast majority of nitrogen atoms have that fourteen plus mass number. Other isotopes are rare. But the atoms from inside the ellipse are all of the nineteen variety." The Land Rover scooted out of the jungle and onto the beach only yards from the sea-cat. He'd beached it only twelve hours ago but it seemed like a month. Konrad turned off the motor and jerked up the emergency handle. "All isotope nineteen Colin" Konrad said. "You wanted to know where the ellipse came from. I can tell you this.

The origin of the ellipse itself is open to investigation. But the molecules from the nitrogen inside definitely didn't come from this side of the galaxy."

CHAPTER 11

OLIN SAT ON a stainless steel metal stool in the middle of the ships dispensary. The room was spotlessly clean, a blue tiled antiseptic cubicle opposite Jhanda's sickroom. Nearby, Dr. Boka was just finishing up his post mortem autopsy of the chancre ridden corpse. On the way to the ship Colin had managed a ten minute power nap to the accompaniment of the sea-cats drone. He could have used some deep R.E.M. The rock face climb combined with the high emotional plateau he'd been on had drained his energy reserve to dry. "Roll up your sleeve." Bleary eyed, Colin looked up to see a grinning Konrad fishing around inside a refrigerator filled with capsules and vials. Konrad somehow had had time to change into fresh Kahkis. The older man looked irritatingly refreshed.

"All the stuff in there FDA approved?" Colin asked, suppressing a wide mouthed yawn. Konrad laughed. "Some of it Colin. But not what I'm going to give you."

"How about giving me something that will make me sleep for a week? Colin knew very well there wasn't time for a real rest. Konrad had said it would be necessary for him to begin his work with Jhanda and Margo right away. Still it didn't hurt to ask. Konrad held up a 10cc ampule to eye level and pushed the needle tip through its orange rubber cap. "This will give you a nice energy boost Colin. Run your metabolism up a notch without the usual later crash the amphetamines give." Konrad angled the needlepoint against Colin's triceps. "This will pinch a bit." Colin looked away. The thought of cold metal in his muscle stirred up old vaccination anxiety.

"No jitters with this stuff?", Colin asked.

"Nope. Just smooth energy." Konrad rubbed Colin's arm with a swab. Almost instantly he felt his weariness lift. No buzz. No sudden jolt of nervous jitters. Just a smooth transition into refreshing alertness.

"This stuff is great Konrad. What is it?"

"No name yet Colin. Right now it's just compound VK-274. It will be on the market in about two years. More like five years in the United States. Your country tends to go to extremes with their drug trials. Your lawyers I understand." Yes, the lawyers Colin thought. They'd made the FDA scared to death that one person in a hundred thousand might have a side effect like farting.

"A drug like this has to be worth billions to you," Colin said.

Konrad replaced the vial in the refrigerator. He turned to Colin with a look of mild reprisal. "You really haven't understood what the ERSEV Society is all about. We won't market this drug ourselves. We'll let some eager young molecular biologist from a corporation like Lilly or Astra-Zeneca discover it." Colin looked quizzically at Konrad. "Money we have Colin. What we're about is giving the benefits of new research to the whole world." Konrad put a finger to his lips. "We try to do that as unobtrusively as possible." Konrad pulled up another stool under his legs and sat close to Colin. "It works like this. After we're satisfied that the drug is a good one we'll submit a paper describing our newly synthesized molecule in one of the second tier Biochemical journals. There will be a picture of the molecule of course. But we'll have it shown with a purposefully misplaced functional group. A misplaced ester linkage perhaps."

"So then assuming the researcher who's reading your article is sharp enough he'll spot the "error" and fix it himself."

"Precisely." Konrad grinned. "He'll take the credit for perfecting the new drug. He or she will wonder how our people could have been so dense as not to have seen how a bit of tinkering with the molecule's structure wouldn't have made it work much better. The proud chemist will get the credit for the discovery. The stockholders will make money. Mankind will have a new or better drug." Konrad patted Colin's knee. "Time to get up to the MAX containment lab."

The small window in the door of the Maximum Containment Lab was covered with brown paper. Colin had assumed on his earlier tour that there was a P4 lab somewhere on the ship and that the room with the blocked window was it. He was pleased to have guessed right. Dr. Volger pushed a keypad code next to the door knob. The knob clicked itself open. Konrad led Colin into a small antechamber with a second door in front. Colin knew that this lab, like all labs designed to contain the most deadly pathogens, was fitted with a positive pressure ventilation system. This assured that outside air would always be flowing in. Konrad lifted a clear plastic cover over the wall switch and flicked it on. "Happily these fans are reversible" Konrad said. Colin heard the pressure fans turn on. With particles from the ellipse settling randomly it was more important to keep pathogens out of the lab rather than the normal setup of protection for the outside world. After several seconds the inner door opened.

"Welcome to our M.C.L." Konrad said with a sweep of his arm. The lab was larger than usual and filled with hardware much of which was foreign to Colin. Roberto sat at a semicircular console in the middle of the room intent on a variety of computer screens. He turned briefly with a smile and wave to acknowledge Colin and Konrad's entrance, then promptly went back to his rapid keyboarding.

Off to the side in a hospital bed cranked up to a comfortable angle, Margo appeared to be sleeping. Konrad walked to her side and checked an I.V. drip. Colin assumed this was the experimental drug Konrad had mentioned. "Any change?" Konrad called back to Roberto without taking his eyes from his daughter's face.

"For the moment her signs are good. I've increased the dosage .25 milligrams."

Colin walked over to Margo's bedside. Her skin still glowed with the same healthy pink undertone he'd admired on the patio deck. To look at her from a layman's perspective it would be hard to believe she wasn't at the peak of health. "Her numbers look fine Konrad," Colin said, as his eyes followed the blinking green lights.

"Right now thank God. She's had a few episodes of heart arrhythmia since the paralysis set in. One of the drugs you saw in the refrigerator has been able to stabilize her. But she's building up a tolerance to the drug very quickly. You just heard Roberto. There's a limit to how much we can give her," Konrad sighed. "Come on over Colin.

Let me show you what we've been working on these last few years." Konrad motioned for Roberto to shift chairs, took his place at the central monitors and gestured for Colin to sit on his right. In the center of the console a large screen showed a dozen or so threadlike objects tumbling slowly as in free space. At first Colin thought it was just the screen saver. The threads were braided in the unmistakable double helix shape. "We're a generation ahead of the scientific pack Colin. We've managed the feat of imaging down to near the quantum level," Konrad grinned. "You're looking at the real thing. Actual DNA strands."

"But the colors, red, green, yellow, blue. I assume they're the four nucleotides." Colin said.

"They are adenine, thymine, quanine, cytosine in living color," Konrad nodded. "The atoms of course have no real colors. We have doctored up the bases with cosmetics. Any tenth grade biology student would be able to read the sequence." Dr. Volger punched a series of beige keys on the panel. Three of the lazily tumbling braids were magnified to take up the entire screen.

"The genes in one of these fragments are the ones that will synthesize the proteins needed to complete Margo's memories," Konrad said. Colin stared nearly hypnotized by the gently rotating splices. Now it was clear just how far into the future the ERSEV society had forged. "How have you managed to do this?" Colin asked.

"Improved on pioneering work done at IBM and Stanford years ago," Konrad said. "Physicists there developed the first atomic force microscope in about '85. For the first time individual atoms could be seen, but the images were fuzzy. We built on their groundwork and came up with a machine capable of the crystal clear pictures you're looking at now." Konrad turned to Roberto. "You're the expert here. Show Colin what else our equipment can do."

Roberto wordlessly ran his fingers over the computers keys. The magnification zoomed to a resolution high enough for Colin to see the election clouds buzzing around the atoms' nuclei. "Unbelievable," Colin mumbled. "To think of the chemists toiling away in the nineteenth century" Colin went on, shaking his head in admiration. "Men like Bunsen or Wohler. They would have given anything to see this."

"It was their fundamental labor that made this possible after all. Their grinding away with mortar and pestle that step by step led to this development.", Dr. Volger reflected.

Earlier computer images of DNA Colin had seen gave no inkling of the molecules vitality. The actual splices here seemed to vibrate with a subtle energy, stretching and contracting as if in a nano level mimicry of breathing itself. "Roberto, show Colin the base sequences in letter form please." Roberto again clattered a computer command. Instantly the image of the three splices was replaced by their equivalent letter columns.

ALPHA	BETA	GAMMA
A-T	G-C	A-T
T-A	T-A	GC
G-C	G-C	G-C
A-T	G-C	G-C
A-T	G-C	T-A
C-G	A-T	A-T
C-G	T-A	C-G
G-C	A-T	C-G
T-A	T-A	G-C
A-T	G-C	T-A
T-A	A-T	A-T
A-T	T-A	C-G
C-G	T-A	G-C
C-G	T-A	A-T
A-T	C-G	A-T
T-A	C-G	T-A
G-C	C-G	T-A
G-C	G-C	T-A
T-A	A-T	A-T
G-C	A-T	A-T
A-T	T-A	C-G
C-G	A-T	C-G
G-C	G-C	T-A

"Bear with us a bit Colin," Konrad said. Roberto go to the neurotransmitter search." Roberto typed:

DATA BANK RETREIVAL/NEUROTRANSMITTERS

① SEARCH: CONFIG. MOLECULES:
   ADENYLATE CYCLASE
   PROTEIN(S) KINASE
   GLUTAMATE RECEPTORS (ALL)
② SEARCH: AMINO ACID SEQUENCE SAME
③ DISPLAY: DNA SEQUENCES ALPHA,BETA, GAMMA
④ COMPUTE: SPLICES MOST PROBABLE FOR TRANSCRIBING

"What are we looking for?", Colin asked.

"We've named our three splices alpha beta and gamma. Not real original I know, but naming things isn't where our expertise lies," Konrad quipped. What we're looking for are the sections of these three splices that code for memory molecules. We gave the computer the molecules in box ① as a take off point for the search. We're convinced the proteins made by these splices will be structurally related to those already documented."

The screen shut down for a moment as if the computer was having an electric hiccup. Then it flashed what Dr. Volger was searching for.

ALPHA	BETA		GAMMA V	
A-T	GC		T-A C-G C-G	⑨ SERINE
T-A				
G-C	T-A G-C G-C	② THREONINE		
A-T			G-C G-C T-A	⑩ PROLINE
A-T				
C-G	G-C G-C T-A	① LEUCINE		
C-G				
G-C			A-T C-G C-G	⑧ TRYPTOPHAN
T-A	A-T T-A A-C	③ TYROSINE		
A-T				
T-A				
A-T	A-T		G-C A-T T-A	⑦ HISTIDINE
C-G	T-A			
C-G	T-A			
A-T				
T-A	T-A C-G C-G	⑤ ARGININE		
G-C				
C-G				
T-A	T-A C-G C-G	④ ALANINE		
G-C				
A-T				
C-G	A-T T-A G-C	⑥ TYROSINE		
G-C				
	CG			
	GC			
	AT			
	TA			

Konrad noted a look of confusion on Colin's face. "I forgot Roberto and I know where this trail is leading, but that you weren't in on the original plans Colin. So just to clear this up. The ten boxed sections will link together the ten amino acids that will become the memory protein."

"Not to be academic, but properly speaking, it's a peptide. Too small to be called a protein," Roberto corrected.

"Always has to be one smart ass," Konrad said, rolling his eyes to the ceiling. "Peptide, protein whatever you want to call it, the computer says it should fold into a shape that closely mimics the cyclases and the other memory stimulators.

Everything points to the cause of Margo's trance memories being the action of specific molecules she absorbed from the ellipse particles. If we can produce them in a high enough concentration she should be able to remember much more of the past."

Colin thought for a moment about Dr. Volger's "if." He'd agreed to let Konrad pursue the puzzle for twenty four hours. Still, he could revoke that agreement. Officially he was derelict in his duty in allowing Dr. Volger to carry on with what amounted to a hunch. A hunch (backed by sophisticated computer analysis to be sure), that beside letting loose a cluster of deadly virus fragments, had entered his daughter and rustled up a hodge podge of psychic powers that might explain WHAT?

While Konrad brewed his concoction of chemicals that *maybe* would clear up Margo's memory visions Colin squirmed.

Do you really understand what you're doing?, Colin asked himself. Giving Konrad the okay to pour a dose of mystery molecules into his daughter wouldn't go down so good back in freezing New York City.

Colin's eyes roamed over Roberto's control panel. It would be easy just to reach out and shut off each switch. Stand up and just say I made the wrong decision. We're done. Point, set, match. Colin drew his fingers back from the consoles edge. "To build the memory molecules we're going to bypass the usual recombinant process Colin," Konrad said. He stretched his arm across Roberto and turned a key embedded in the console panel. A chromium contraption that looked like a three layer cake slid out. A binocular microscope angled out from the bottom layer. Roberto put his eyes to the lenses. He manipulated dials with both hands not taking his eyes away.

A new image of what looked like a plain white table surface appeared on the screen. The tabletop appeared to be tilted slightly toward the viewer. Roberto moved a small joystick and slowly a rough surfaced ball descended over the table and stopped. "Bring it down thirty more angstroms Roberto," Dr. Volger ordered. Roberto just touched the joystick with the faintest pressure. The ball moved down nearly touching the white surface. "Now you'll see true atomic force microscopy Colin," Konrad said. "The ball you see isn't a physical object at all," he went on. "Through computer slight of hand what looks like a sphere is really a mass of electrostatic charge." There were tiny spike like projections on the charged ball that brought to mind the nasty outer surface of a medieval mace."

"What are the spikes?", Colin asked.

"There are twenty of them," Roberto broke in. "Each spike is really a pyramid of one type of amino acid molecule." Simple enough Colin thought. Twenty acids. Twenty spikes.

"Because the amino acids are held on the ball with electrostatic charge they can be pulled off in the same way a comb lifts hairs on a dry day," Roberto explained. "The first acid of the peptide chain is leucine. We'll grab that one first," Konrad said. Roberto's skilled fingers set the ball slowly rotating until one spike was directly over the table. "The pyramid that's pointing down is composed of all leucines. Roberto will pick just one of them off." Colin watched in amazement as a green hair thin beam moved horizontally across the table. It's end stopped close to the tip of the leucine spike. Roberto fine tuned the beams position. When it nearly touched the tip of the amino acid spike a leucine molecule jumped like a magnetized paperclip onto the end of the beam. Roberto manipulated the beam back from the spike and deposited the dangling leucine on the table surface.

"The green laser is an advance on tractor beam technology started at University of California," Dr. Volger said. "The beams were first used to poke cell organelles around. We've refined them down to be able to move molecules."

"What's the table surface?" Colin asked. Clearly the table couldn't be real. Actual tables were made of atoms too. At this magnification the surface should be lumpy with electrons poking in and out. "The white table is another electrostatic field made to look like a table."

"Just a modern day cobblers bench," Colin remarked.

"In a way, yes," Konrad replied. "Instead of nailing tacks to leather by hand, we're joining molecule to molecule."

"Threonine is next" Roberto spoke up. Colin watched the beam move to the threonine spike. The thin green line extracted one molecule and then deposited it on the table surface. Then Roberto turned the pyramid of tyrosine acids facing tip downward. Deftly, he pulled off one molecule and lined it up next to the waiting leucine and threonine. "When Roberto gets all of our ten amino acids in order he'll use the beam to nudge them together. When they're close enough they'll bond. In an instant we'll have our memory molecule." In living cells the DNA would go through a long process in order to join the amino acids into peptides. Messenger and transfer RNA's would have to operate in turn. Roberto and Konrad had made a lengthy process a one stepper.

"The computer measures the movements of the ball and beam as Roberto works" Konrad said. "Once the ten acids are linked the program will join sets of ten quickly and automatically."

"How many peptide chains will be needed?" Colin asked.

"Three hundred or so. The memory influencing molecules attach to specific brain receptors.

They're powerful memory triggers.", Konrad answered.

"Dr. Volger a question occurs to me," Colin said. "Out of the fifty or so people infected with the particle genes only Margo has absorbed the psychic stimulators and only she has suffered paralysis."

"Yes as far as we know," Konrad said.

"On the other end however you have the case of Dr. Boka's cadaver in the next room," he continued. "He's the only one with the chancre and the only one where a growth in his brains' emotional center has stimulated rage."

"It's a point that has puzzled both Roberto and myself." Konrad sat up straight in his chair. "Everyone who's absorbed genes from the particles should have come down with the same afflictions or, in a case like Margo's, enhanced mind powers. Only in my daughter have the genes expressed psychic abilities and only in

Dr. Boka's felon has violence resulted." Colin gazed at the ceiling absentmindedly for a moment.

"Dr. Boka said the man was a murderer right?", Colin questioned. "Killed his wife and children" Konrad affirmed.

"Dr. Volger and I have speculated on just this point. Let me show you the brain MRI comparisons," Roberto interjected. He wheeled his chair to a second screen and typed in a command. Nose to neck sagittal slices of two brains showed up on the monitor.

"Colin, the left section is of the killers brain. The right MRI is Margo. Notice the hypothalamus in both."

Roberto touched his pen to each of the interior brain structures in turn.

"You see the killer's hypothalamus is grossly enlarged just as Dr. Boka showed you yesterday. But Margo's has actually shrunk to half it's normal size. It's as if the invading genes have intensified the rage center in the killer."

"And lessened the primal centers in Margo's," Konrad said. "This is pure speculation at this point but the comparison between the two structures and subsequent behaviors is most curious don't you think?" Colin pondered the implications for a moment.

"So you're suggesting that the way these genes act depends on the structure of the brain cell DNA when the particles enter the body?" Colin asked.

"Maybe because the man was evil already the genes from the ellipse amplified his evil.", Konrad said.

"And in Margo the genes somehow act in an opposite way?", Colin questioned. "You're making a case for mind over matter," Colin said.

"Or matter over mind," Konrad answered.

"Don't we take it for granted that material DNA orders the growth of brain cells in babies? Sets up the conditions for thought?", Roberto interjected.

"Of course," Colin said.

"And isn't it possible that intentions might just as well alter certain DNA sections? Matter making mind. Mind making matter," Roberto continued.

"Theoretically, in a small percentage of persons at least, enough intent toward good or evil could determine how DNA would react. That puts it as simply as possible." "Then you're saying that minute by minute a mental attitude might be altering part of our genetic makeup?"

"And in turn DNA would be making new molecules that could make the next moments decisions that much easier or harder," Konrad continued. Roberto leaned back clasping his hands behind his head.

"You'd be looking at a kind of mind-matter loop Colin. Mind states subtly changing DNA. DNA in turn producing enzymes that further strengthen that particular mind state."

"Of course tracking such a process is still beyond even our capabilities," Konrad said.

Colin thought again of Margo and what she'd said on the patio about the Karmic idea, the ancient belief that you are what you create for yourself. Could there be a possibility that the genes in the particles acted in her body as they did because of her intentions good or bad? Hard to quantify. That would be translating any Karmic force into physical reality. Could Boka's murderer have become psychotically violent because of some undetectable mind matter loop; the rage altering the brains DNA and that DNA in turn producing proteins that made it that much easier to build up stronger primal emotions?

"Excuse me," Margo called out from her bed, jolting Colin from his thoughts. "From the furrowed brows I see the three of you seem to be into some heavy thinking. May I join in?" Dr. Volger wheeled Margo's bed close in to the console.

"Just three guys spinning idle thoughts," Colin said. Margo looked intently at the tractor beam image. The beam was on auto pilot stamping out the peptide chains like a bottling machine popping on tops.

"How do you feel Margo?", Konrad asked.

"I'll be fine," she said with a wrinkle of her pert nose. She turned her face toward Colin. "I owe an apology to you. Have you been to the cave?" Colin nodded. "Father, could I be alone with Colin for a few minutes?"

"Of course." Dr. Volger looked at his watch. "It's time for us to bring Jhanda here at any rate." Konrad motioned for Roberto to join him.

Near the pressurized doors a cabinet held the micro stat suits. Both men zippered a suit on and disappeared into the outer hallway. After the fans settled down to their normal hum Margo looked again at Colin, this time holding his eyes with her own. "I'm sorry I couldn't tell you about the ellipse, but father begged me not to mention it. He was afraid you would have had the machine destroyed outright."

"You're apology is accepted. But tell me something Margo. You foresaw that I'd be coming aboard before I'd made the decision to touch down here. You saw the future then. Couldn't you see Dr. Lippincott's coming death?"

"When we talked on the patio I was only sure that I'd seen you before. Since the ellipse was uncovered I've experienced these weird kind of trance states. In one of them I saw you just as you were on deck, sitting in the lounge chair sipping your drink and talking to dad and myself. That's the way it's been, little images of what's to come held up before my mind like flash cards. There for a moment then gone."

"And if one of these cards had shown you Ed losing his life what then?" Colin tried to keep any hint of accusation out or his voice.

Margo turned her pillowed head away. Her lips trembled softly.

"Colin I feel terribly sad about the villagers who were stricken. I was very upset when I learned about Dr. Lippincott. I'm still shaken. But you must believe that what happened to them was necessary to happen. It could not have been otherwise. How do I know this you're thinking. I can't explain it. No. I didn't foresee Dr. Lippincott's death." A look of pain and exasperation crossed Margo's face. "I don't know why the images that came to me are of one thing and not another. Why didn't I foresee that father would jeopardize his life for this work? I just don't know. But I *do* know my intuitions are true."

"True enough so that if you did know of Ed's death you would still want to go on?"

"Yes. I know that the molecules being made in that machine will help me put together all the bits and pieces I've already foreseen." Colin got up and began to pace at the foot of Margo's bed.

"You're sure of that?" "Yes Colin. I understand how much you've struggled with your conscience. I know you're torn about your decision to let the ellipse stay exposed. If I were in your place I'd be asking myself too, whether I'd made the right choice. You're worried that while you wait for me to untangle what's really happened here more innocents will die."

"I was sent here to put a stop to the terrible outbreak Margo. Something I know how to do. I didn't expect to be dropped into an abracadabra world out of my depth. As much as I fear what that machine can do I'm fascinated by it. Part of me too senses that good may come from it." Colin thrust his hands in his pockets and stood staring at the floor. Margo waited until Colin's gaze moved to her again.

"Trust me Colin. I know these words have lost some of their force in these times, but they're the most appropriate ones for now. Don't look back. Believe you've made the right decision." Colin laughed and felt his tenseness ease.

"You really are asking me to go with a woman's intuition you know."

"A woman's prerogative," Margo grinned back. Colin thought back to what Konrad had said about the nitrogen isotopes. Not from this galaxy he'd said. Amidst the excitement of his conversation, at the cave, Colin had somehow let that stunning remark blow by him. Colin placed his hand atop Margo's.

"Do you have any idea where the ellipse came from Margo?"

"Friends out there perhaps. Those who have the choice to travel through space and time." Before Colin could reply Dr. Volger came bounding into the lab with Roberto in tow. Jhanda shuffled behind in his saffron robes. He supported his aged frame on a thorny cane. Konrad waited until Roberto had settled the old man in a chair then held up a piece of metal that looked like a cars alternator. "It was a radio telescope," Konrad said, flush with enthusiasm. Colin looked confused. "I'm sorry Colin. I'm ahead of myself again." Konrad turned the dirt encrusted tube around in his hands. "You see, a fragment of a destroyed metal structure was discovered buried in front of the Temple. With Jhanda's help Roberto and I have been trying to figure out what it could have been. Nothing made sense until we just now uncovered this. It's a piece of antenna that was part of a telescope dish."

"They were trying to communicate Colin." Roberto interjected.

"Whoever left the ellipse here was trying to establish communication with someone very far away." Konrad said.

"It looks like a long ago quake brought the whole business down." Roberto said.

"You see Colin, it's just as I imagined. All falling into place," Margo joined in, eyes wide with the news. "Father, just as you came in Colin and I were talking about the ellipse's source." And very serendipitously too Colin thought. Almost as if the other three were waiting offstage for just the right moment. Colin walked over to Konrad who held out the object to him. Colin took the steel (if it *was* steel) telescope artifact in his hand. He looked the ten or twelve pound cylinder over as carefully as he had the jaw fossils.

"Mr. Grier. Be patient a little longer," a small voice piped out from within the folds of draped robes. "I am Jhanda. Advisor and friend to all who are here." The old mystic held out a bony hand to Colin in greeting. "You will excuse I hope my boldness in advising patience. Perhaps you wonder who is this stranger to be giving advice at first meeting?", Jahanda asked, his sagacious eyes quizzing Colin. Colin heartily shook the old man's hand. "Konrad has told me of your esteem of Margo." Jhanda pointed to the metal fragment in Colin's hand.

"You have been much challenged by your findings here young man. Overwhelmed by most unexpected events. Is this not so?" Colin caught a look of hopeful expectation on Margo's face.

"I have been torn as to what path to follow Jhanda." "It is understandable that as a man of science you should crave clear answers to the mysteries that unfold here," the wrinkled seer intoned. He drew his finger up to Colin's chest. "Do not give in to the doubts that assail you Colin Grier. Wait a time longer. This object you hold will be a key that can unlock all that is clouded."

Jhanda drew in a long weary breath. "I am old now. My powers wane. It is you who must aid Miss Margo now. It is you who will enter among her visions. Together you will discover how to open the gates to unheard of realms."

"Me?", Colin blurted, not quite absorbing the meaning of Jhanda's words. Was this Hindu wise man actually saying he was to take part in some psychic ritual with Margo?

He'd always assumed his latent psychic talents, if there were such things, would prove to be close to nil.

"Jhanda will be our guide Colin," Margo spoke up, sounding blithely assured. "When I've fallen into the trance state, I have not been able to speak. Jhanda's powers have allowed him to join with me in seeing the things I see."

"He is the bridge from Margo's mind to us." Konrad interjected.

"Yes pandit Konrad. But the bridge is broken now," Jhanda replied. "Your Mister Grier will rebuild it for us."

From the perplexed look on Colin's face Margo realized how difficult it must be for him to absorb the overload of information that had bombarded him in such a short time. He'd been swamped with new technical data besides being asked to deal with a way of viewing the world that was the opposite of his usual outlook.

"You will have the power to do as Jhanda says," Margo said matter of factly.

"I just have to wish hard enough. Be pure of heart. Is that it?", Colin asked somewhere between sarcasm and sincerity.

"That would be a good start Colin. Anyone who desires to see into the mind of another must come with an open heart," Margo said. So with the help of the wizened wizard Jhanda I'm to sally forth into Margo's dreams and vanquish the dragons of ignorance, Colin thought. He could still say no. Put a thousand ton cap on the Temple site and be done with it all. The odds of his turning into a Quixote instead of a Lancelot were about even he figured. But he'd gone over all the shoulds and should not's long enough. There would be no more waffling. He'd climb aboard the train into the visions of a most lovely damsel wherever it was headed. Colin handed back the broken antenna piece to Dr. Volger.

"Alright. Roberto thinks whoever was here two million years ago was trying to chat with somebody out there. So we're banking that when Margo gets the memory stimulating preparation she'll be able to tap into that communication. Is that where we're going?", Colin asked.

"We don't need to depend only on what Margo can recall Colin. We have at least a dozen radio telescopes under contract with us at sites worldwide," Konrad answered. He gestured to Roberto. "Roberto use the cell. Get a hold of the Coolabundi station." Roberto scrolled through a list of ERSEV installations to look up the Australian station's number. "Colin, there's a scope working under our sponsorship in Coolabundi right now. Maybe four, five hundred miles from here," Konrad said. "The astronomer we have working for us there is Walter Polski. He's researching Quasar clusters for us at present. I'm going to change his assignment immediately. I'll have him train his dish on the sky patch in front of the cave," Konrad continued.

"You think a transmission coming in back then would still be coming in?", Colin asked.

"If it was a one time message to those who were here ages ago, then of course it will be gone. But it might be an ongoing communication. A message broadcast not just to those who were then, but to the entire galaxy," Konrad said. "We just don't know Colin."

"But it will take only a short while for Polski to find out," Roberto said. Colin looked at his watch. It was 4:20 PM. Roughly twenty hours left for Konrad to find out the truth of what happened here or rather twenty hours for all of us now Colin thought. He wondered just what communication could be zipping past the stars all these years to little old earth, all though if anyone would be able to capture an interstellar message it would be this potent bunch. Konrad was working the problems from both ends. Using hard science on one hand along with a large helping of psychic exploration on the other. Sort of the yin and yang approach to getting puzzles solved.

And just maybe, with the help of the newly synthesized peptides, Margo's flashcard images would morph into full length features.

CHAPTER 12

OOLABUNDI WASN'T MUCH to look at. Stretched out on a low plateau far over the horizon south of Darwin, it looked like the ghost town it was, wind whipped with echoes of a more boisterous time. Topaz had been discovered here at the turn of the century, drawing some ten thousand rough and ready adventurers to squabble over the gem encrusted rocks.

By the nineteen eighteens, after all the treasure had been plundered, Coolabundi was left to the bristly bush and the dingoes. Now only a smattering of semi civilized aborigines lived here, some of them taking over the tarpaper shacks left over from the brief years of greedy digging.

It was an ideal location for an observatory, the ERSEV's leaders thought. And so they'd constructed two modern scopes, a large reflector and a state of the art radio telescope on the isolated plateau in 1995. Hardly anyone ever came to Coolabundi. Astronomical work could proceed there with independence far from the lights of the big city and the occasional electromagnetic spill that could easily skew the precise readings taken by the big disc. A tall cyclone fence surrounded the three acre observatory site, for what purpose Walter Polski could never figure. Except for one of the local aborigines stopping by to borrow a bit of tea or sugar, there wasn't anyone to keep out. Polski was the perfect choice for the Coolabundi site. Basically a loner, he valued the privacy assignment the observatory offered. He could have accepted positions at several other private or university facilities but had chosen the ERSEV appointment for two basic reasons. First, he was given near unlimited freedom to test his own hypotheses about the universes formation, and second, there was virtually no limit on the money he could spend. To label Walter a misanthrope would be going too far, but he preferred the warmth of human companionship in carefully measured doses. Two or three times a year Walter would take himself off to Canberra. There he'd squander his salary on booze and call girls. He would then return satiated, hold up in his little bungalow tucked cozily under the shadow of the big dish. There he'd remain until the itch to break out of himself again needed to be scratched once more.

Polski was about to wrap up his afternoon work at the radio scope's computers when the phone rang. He was surprised. Walter couldn't recall the last time anyone rang him up after noontime. He thought it could be Dr. Berg, his supervisor in Ulringen, but then again Berg like himself preferred emails.

"Hello, may I ask who's calling?", Polski inquired with an affected tone.

"This is Dr. Volger, Mr. Polski. I'm calling from our research ship north of New Guinea. I hope you can be of some assistance to us."

"Pardon?" Walter was caught off guard. Although he'd never personally met Dr. Volger he knew he was placed at the top of ERSEV's organization chart. Being on the Board of Directors made him a person who could, Walter recognized, screw up his research project with the stroke of a pen.

"Walter we've run into a rather unusual situation on board here." Polski tried to imagine what that could be. Maybe Volger had run his zillion-dollar ship aground on the barrier reef. "I realize you're probably immersed in very important studies at the observatory, but I must earnestly request that you put them on hold for a while," Konrad continued. "We would like you to help us with a critical problem that's come up here."

"Problem?" Polski parroted back.

"Yes Walter. We need the use of your radio telescope for a few days. Would that be too much of an inconvenience?"

"You're sending someone here?", Walter asked with rising apprehension.

"No, no Walter. I need you to search a small quadrant of the sky for us. I'd like you to send a printout of any transmissions you might receive. I'm not at liberty to tell you more at this time but I can assure you our need is urgent. Your cooperation will be greatly appreciated." Walter made no reply for the moment. He didn't want to interrupt his research for a short, long, or any time. He'd love to tell Volger to shove it, but doing that wasn't in his best interest. A request from a powerful ERSEV society board member for the use of their own facility was tantamount to an order. Polski fingered his pocket protector. He needed to keep his annoyance from being sensed. He was after all an employee.

"May I ask what it is you're currently investigating?", Dr. Volger inquired.

"Some star clusters," Walter nonchalantly responded. He wanted to be as unspecific about his work as possible. In fact Walter didn't want anyone to know where he had the radio telescope zeroed in until his work was ready for the publishers. Before he'd signed on to work under ERSEV's umbrella he had been part of a team that had predicted the presence of huge quasar clusters only eight to ten light years away. The predicted clusters were in fact found.

Polski agreed with the thinking that the quasars were the cores of ancient galaxies that harbored enormous black holes. If the holes proved to be swallowing up matter in big enough gulps it would mean the Big Bang Theory might be wrong. The so-called Big Bang Theory could never account for the presence of such huge and plentiful quasars. Polski needed only to find another cluster large enough to have his name be spoken of with the same respect as Hubble himself. The fact of the matter was that Walter had indeed found his second cluster. All his efforts of the past few months had been concentrated on defining its exact parameters.

Walter had judiciously sent data to ERSEV's Swiss headquarters all along. Carefully edited of course. He was a covetous fellow. He was determined not to give Volger the slightest clue as to what he really was up to.

"That would be no problem at all," Polski lied suavely. "The computer has files on just about everything the scope has mapped so far. If you can just give me the coordinates Dr. Volger, I'll set up the dish to do a search within that patch of sky. If anything new shows up I'll contact you right away." Polski listened to Konrad clear his throat.

"Ah, we don't have exact coordinates to give you Walter," Konrad said. Dr. Volger suddenly realized he hadn't thought the situation through from an astronomer's viewpoint. Walter expected to hear exact sky coordinates. After analyzing the layout of all the buried metal fragments found to date, the only thing Konrad could say was that when the scope was standing, it had been directed toward the Temple front. The cave would have been directly below the ancient disc's center. "Just a second Walter," Konrad said covering the phone with his hand. "Roberto we need directions for Polski to use the scope. How do we get them to him?" Roberto started to answer but Colin interrupted.

"Wait a second. I know next to nothing about astronomy but don't you have compass markings for the Temple grounds?"

"Sure we do Colin," Roberto said. He plopped down at the computer again and quickly brought up a map grid of the grounds. In the bottom left hand corner was a finely graded compass rosette. Roberto called out the compass headings along with precise latitude and longitude figures to Konrad. Konrad repeated them back to Polski.

"Walter sorry for the delay here in getting you some numbers. These ought to eliminate a lot of sky for your search. If you can fix on an arc using these coordinates will that be okay?"

"No problem at all. That narrows things down considerably," Polski lied again. "My computer has files on everything the radio telescope has mapped so far. I'll have the dish do a random pattern search in that arc and will see if we come up with anything new." Obviously the best way to deal with Dr. Volger was to string him along, Walter thought. Volger was under the mistaken impression that allowing his big dish to sweep a sky arc would be enough to lock in any new transmission. It hadn't occurred to the bozo that in just one degree of the heavens there were a near uncountable number of radio sources to explore. Without pinpoint coordinates finding anything specific in an arc sweep would be like hunting down a single starfish on the ocean bottom.

"You can't tell me anything else about what you want me to look for?", Polski asked. He tried to sound sincerely interested.

"I'm sorry I can't be more specific Walter. Just put it down as an eccentric need of your ERSEV society. If you can scan that arc for us tonight you might go back to your own research tomorrow."

"Understood. Fine then," Polski said with feigned good cheer. "I'll realign the scope right away." "Very good," Konrad said, pleased that Walter's cooperation was so forthcoming. "Hopefully in the morning you'll have something for us."

"I'll call your ship as soon as I check my AM readout. If there is anything unusual I'll fax you a pen graph right away. There's just one thing. I need to know what wavelength you want me to set up for."

"Oh of course," Konrad chuckled, mildly embarrassed. Coolabundi's desk could pick up incoming frequencies along a very wide electromagnetic range. Anywhere from high-energy 1014 gamma and x- ray wavelengths down to the long undulating 102 meter power waves typical of radio and TV transmissions.

"We'll need you to search on twenty one centimeters Walter," Konrad said after another pause to confer with Roberto. "Twenty one it is then," Walter confirmed.

"Keep in mind Dr. Volger that there's a hell of a lot of hot hydrogen radiating to us from all over the sky. But if I get any oddball burst along your arc it will certainly show up by morning."

"Thanks again for the scope time Walter," Konrad said with gratitude. "I appreciate your going along with us without a full briefing regarding our purpose."

"Happy to assist," Walter jauntily replied. Although Polski hadn't the slightest intention of nudging his scope one inch out of it's preprogrammed track, Volger's request to search along the twenty one centimeter wavelength sparked his curiosity. That wavelength was the frequency most kook astronomers believed would be used should any alien intelligence attempt to contact us. Polski wondered if Dr. Volger was having him fish around for big eyed hairless ET's. Of course the SETI crowd had been searching for signs of alien life for years. And it was an unwritten ERSEV law that duplication of the work of other research groups be avoided. Copying what SETI was doing would be a redundancy Volger wouldn't allow.

Polski flipped on his computer and called up the last hundred radio source tracings his dish had gathered in the past few months. Most of the line graphs showed radiation spikes coming in from his freshly discovered quasar clusters. Walter wasn't interested in those right now. Instead he plucked out a few flat liners that had come through when his aim wandered outside the cluster's edges. Polski selected the flattest tracing line of those few then clicked on print. The graph came out looking nearly ruler straight. Polski smirked as he lifted the tracing from the printer. He would keep his scope mapping the clusters exactly as he'd planned and in the morning he'd fax the flat liner to Volger along with his condolences. "Awfully sorry old chap but I did try mightily. Seems the slice of the universe you asked me to hunt in went into hibernation." Polski's smirk swelled into a loud derisive laugh. The nerve of the man. Expecting him to abandon critical work at a moments notice. To go chasing willy- nilly through the nighttime sky. Of course, how could Dr. Volger know the work he wanted to interrupt might prove to be as stunning as Kepler's. But Volger would find out in due time. They all would.

Walter stuffed a copy of the tracing in his pants pocket. He shut the control room door and started out to his cottage nearby. He took only a few steps when a dark musty smell assaulted his nostrils. Polski stopped, sniffing the air with upturned head. The smell was vaguely familiar but Polski couldn't quite place it. Then suddenly it hit him. The stench was like the odor of skunk cabbage that grew in the dells near his West Virginia home. Only this was much stronger. Fetid, decayed smelling. It was odd Polski thought. The sandy Coolabundi soil was far more hospitable to desert xerophytes than to water loving species like the cabbage. The smell was coming from the north end of the perimeter. Polski stood undecided on the gravel path between his cottage and the control room. He wasn't sure if he wanted to walk the one hundred yards to the perimeter fence. His dinner was already a half hour behind schedule. Thinking that his roast could wait another ten minutes he ambled half heartedly along the cyclone fence. As he passed under the giant disc, he noticed that the sparse grass growing at the end of the compound seemed to be shinning. Strange, since the dew point wasn't right for condensation. With a mix of curiosity and apprehension Polski strode to the edge of the property. He squinted in the dimming light trying to locate the source of the glitter and the stench. Twenty yards, give or take a couple of feet, there was a weird patch of ugly vines spread over the ground. Walter had never seen anything like them. There were pencil sized tendrils mixed in with dark green cable thick vines. They spread from a central growing point radiating out nearly to the fence. There were odd bubbles too, bulging out on the larger vines. The light from the rising moon fell on a number of the pustules that had been pricked open by thorns of the indigenous prickly pear cacti. A nauseating grayish jelly dripped from them, molasses like onto the ground. The alarming thought that the plants might actually overrun the compound occurred to Polski. But then he calmed himself. In the boondocks of Australia there were any number of strange plants in the wonderful world of life. It wasn't beyond a continent that produced the platypus to concoct a stinking wart encrusted vine. Polski's eye caught a few runners, that he'd swear weren't there a minute ago, creeping under the wire fence. It had to be eye fatigue from too much computer screen he thought. Polski held a handkerchief under his nose and walked over to the strange plants. Warily he stopped to get a closer look. The vines seemed normal except for the nauseating blisters. Walter held his breath. He poked several holes in the blisters with the lead end of his number two pencil. Grayish liquid spattered on his hands with surprising force. Polski fell back on his ass chuckling at his startled reaction. His hands began to burn so he wiped away the gook and threw the handkerchief in the weeds. Walter's stomach began to growl as he walked back to the cottage. His dinnertime was over due by now and he hoped the rib roast wouldn't be overdone. Polski hated well done meat. He was convinced that anyone who ate well done meat had deformed taste buds.

Before he opened the cottage door Polski paused attentively on his concrete stoop. He listened here everyday for any indication – whine, grind, or other unusual sound from the motors that drove the big dish. Walter prided himself on maintaining the motors in tip top shape. This spot at the cottage door was acoustically ideal for listening. Walter smiled again. The delicate bearings and gears were moving as smoothly as a Ferrari V-12. The scope was imperceptibly following its preprogrammed path without a hitch. It would be another weekend before the quasar cluster was completely mapped. He could hardly wait. Finally getting the respect that would come when he published filled him with anticipatory glee.

If only he'd known. Sitting ten degrees to the right of his quasar covey was the constellation Centaurus. Somewhere within the mythological sky creature waited a discovery that would make his cluster find pale by comparison.

Polski threw open the cottage door and made a beeline to the oven. In a frenzy of clatter he yanked open all the cupboard doors searching for his potholders. When he'd found them he still scorched his fingers in his haste to pull out the oven rack. Polski breathed a satisfied sigh. His expensive roast (flown in with an assortment of otherwise unavailable foods) was perfectly done. Pink and plump with just a touch of warm blood at the center. Walter set the roast pan tenderly on the kitchen table to cool, then darted to the bathroom to freshen up. He reached up for the soap then stopped, his left arm hovering between mirror and basin where the jelly from the vine blisters had touched his skin. There now were little scales, little brown scales that tingled. The old TV ad 'heartbreak of psoriasis' dashed laughingly through Polski's head. But this was something else. The scales weren't more than a quarter inch across but they were as crispy as if they'd been drying out for years. Polski ran the cold water over the spots, dried his hands and put a dab of mercurochrome on the crusts. He considered whether they were worth a worry then decided they'd probably be no worse than the poison ivy he was allergic to. Just to be extra careful Walter slapped a couple of band-aids over the ugly spots. Back in his cozy kitchen he affectionately stroked the top of the rib roast with his fingertips. Impulsively he sliced off a slab, plopped it down on the butcher block and began to eat it off the wooden surface. He gulped down large chunks with eyes closed in culinary contentment. Juices ran down his forearm but no matter. When he opened his eyes again his gaze fell on the flowerbox under the sill of his kitchen window. The box had been full of scarlet sage and ox eye daises that he'd planted for a burst of color among the monotonous browns and beiges of the outback. Now a few inches from his nose were flowers such as he'd never seen. He'd have thought some prankster had switched boxes but the locked gate ruled that out. Beside it wasn't the sort of thing his aboriginal neighbors would do. Polski opened the window and stretched out his hand.

Tiny blossoms had elbowed aside the native flowers. Their petals were a swath of pastels, blues, pinks, and greens richly aglow with intense colors. At the base of each blossom the petals were a deep velvet black. Curious. The vines and now these. Polski stood looking out of the window for a while. His eyes shifted from the box to the distant vines and back again, Beauties and the Beasts. Polski decided he'd go to the internet in the morning and search for a botanical expert who could tell him what the plants were. That would be right after he'd sent Volger the flat line pen graph. Walter stretched his arms out of the kitchen window to pick a few of the remarkable blossoms. Just a few months before he could easily reach the flower box without standing tiptoe. He realized with chagrin how much his expanding pot belly had shortened his reach. With his fingers stretched out to the fullest he managed to pluck two of the petunia sized flowers. As he drew his arms back he left out a frightened yelp. The underside of his arms had erupted in the crusty plaque's all the way to his elbows. Defensively, Polski crossed his arms over his chest. He swallowed hard, panic stealing over him. He must remain calm he told himself. Aside from the burning, he felt fine. No nausea or chill. The brown husks had to have come from the oozing vines Walter was convinced. Nothing could have raged through his bloodstream so fast. The thought of finishing his meal was totally out of mind. Polski stalked to the bathroom. He grabbed an ancient bar of lava soap and lathered to the neck. The burning seemed to subside a bit he noted with satisfaction. As an after thought he gathered an assortment of salves, ointments and a tube of zinc oxide from the medicine cabinet. Polski proceeded to make a paste of the combination, rub it over his arms then wrap both limbs with rolls of ace bandage. He giggled when he saw the finished product in the mirror. At least he hadn't totally lost his sense of humor. He thought he looked like a half finished Tut. Walter held up his angular chin and looked there. Nothing. No sign of the brown scales between the thinning hairs of his head either.

Calmer now, and satisfied that the eruptions was due to the weird plant juice, Walter felt his stomach growl again. He went back to the half chewed meat, plopped the remains on a plate and set the microwave for three minutes. He began to hum a bawdy ditty he'd heard in Canberra letting the obscene rhyme lift his mood. By the time the microwave bell rang he was feeling a swing toward jolly.

It was probably a good thing that he couldn't see what was happening under the bandages. Not that he could have stopped the diseases rapid progress. Unseen by Walter the crusts were already marching across his back.

CHAPTER 13

WITH ONE HAND holding down his wispy hair Edwin McClure watched the helicopter circle up and away from the ERSEV's patio deck. Being lowered by the copter's sling hadn't been so bad after all. He congratulated himself that even at age sixty-six he could still muster the courage to be dangled between ship and sky.

The unusual helicopter winch touchdown had been necessary, he judged, given the time constraints.

The loss of even an hour was crucial if he were to regain his authority over the outbreaks spread.

Whatever had been going on at Barubi since his quarantine had been so disdainfully ignored McClure was determined to get to the bottom of. He had discovered from Fratelli's papers just how influential Dr. Konrad Volger was in the ERSEV societies hierarchy. This Dr. Volger obviously had access to vast sums of cash. He had been more than willing to shower Dr. Fratelli with whatever it took to keep him quiet. McClure could almost understand it. Fratelli did have kids to see through expensive schools and his salary as assistant director was modest. Then there were the Mercedes and the cruises to provide for. The son of a bitch had probably rationalized that the outbreak was in a village so remote that it had little chance of spreading, especially with ERSEV's own resources to stop it if it showed signs of a second spread.

McClure tucked in his starched shirt and scanned the nighttime patio deck. He could make out folded table umbrellas around the semi circular deck, but it was hard to see more. With the moon behind a band of clouds everything was suffused in tones of black and gray. Dr. McClure spotted a row of cream colored elevator lights. He walked over, pressed one and the doors opened shinning enough warm light out for him to see. He hit the hold button, turned around and was surprised to see a profusion of plants surrounding the deck. They were much more than the monochrome hedges they'd appeared to be in the dark. The warm light from the open elevator pointed out dozens of flowers that were a feast for the eye. A weekend gardener himself, McClure took considerable pride in his knowledge of thousands of flower species. There was one flower intertwined among the trellises he'd never seen, even in the reference books he regularly thumbed through. There were thirty or forty of the odd chrysanthemum sized blossoms in the entire garden. Dr. McClure decided he could spare a moment for a closer inspection. He broke one of the flowers off at the stem. He was sure the multicolored beauty wasn't classified in any genus he knew and he was certain he knew them all. The six-inch long petals were an impossible midnight black. And the slashing vivid pastel streaks. It was as if a Vlaminck or Derain had gone berserk with his wild colors. "Breathtaking" McClure muttered under his breath. Intrigued, he stooped down to search for some of the glowing flowers that might still be in the bud stage. He poked his hand blindly deep into the greenery pushing the heavier stems aside. A warm viscous liquid ran over his hand. Reflexively he drew back his arm. A wave of revulsion swept through him as he watched foul smelling gel drip from his fingers. McClure wiped the gray stuff off on his slacks. There was a burning left on his skin after most of the goo was off, but he was sure it was just a particular strong plant alkaloid stinging him. McClure pushed the stems apart more carefully this time to peer into the fulsome tangle. He was shocked to see that the entire inside of the floral bank was as repellant as its outer surface was attractive.

Rivulets of malignant looking jelly were spread out over every branch. Each leaf was rotting even while still attached to its stem. Dr. McClure saw what his hand had punctured. Viscous tennis ball sized galls parasitic on the largest branches filled to bursting with the odorous juices.

It was as if the entire garden was stricken with a rampant cancer. McClure screwed out a canopy umbrella from the center of a nearby table. He poked the trestles carefully aside from a safer distance. The life sucking jelly had a force of its own he saw, moving against gravity up some of the stems. In another few hours he reckoned every cell would be invaded. The whole garden would be reduced to a reeking mass of slime.

Suddenly, a fluttering sound from inside the growth startled McClure. On tip toe McClure warily again pushed the branches aside. Four tiny humming birds too weak to fly skittered out frantically flapping their wings. Their beaks were opened wide as they gasped for breath. McClure knelt down to examine them. In trying to escape they pathetically spun in circles like out of control toys. Dr. McClure stayed motionless until their futile struggling quieted down. Not daring to touch them, McClure gently placed his foot on the tiny wing of one bird with just enough pressure to keep it in place. The animals were clearly near death. Their feathers normally so metallically shiny had faded to dull shades of grayish brown. Dr. McClure was worried and very angry. He'd hoped the outbreak would stay confined to Barubi. Or at an extreme, not extend beyond the base of the Owen Stanley Range. He could see now that not only had the diseases spread offshore, but also the mysterious agent that had caused the skin desiccation had apparently mutated and begun to attack other animal and plant life as well. An out of nowhere nightmare had literally laid itself right at his feet. Smallpox and hepatitis at lease were known entities. Here was something ominous and totally unknown, caused by something so virulent it destroyed living tissue in minutes rather than days. Dr. McClure licked his lips with a tongue dry from anxiety. Damn Fratelli and damn Colin Grier. McClure's rage against Fratelli was futile now that the undermining bastard was dead. Grier was another matter. If he'd carried out his orders, the outbreak wouldn't have gotten out of hand. The chances were Grier had succumbed to Volger's lure of hard cash too, McClure thought. Everything had been going so well. Word had gotten around that Dr. McClure was the man who had squelched the first outbreak without getting CNN's and Fox's stations attention. He'd kept the muckrakers noses out of the picture and stopped the spread virtually before it started. The gossip was that Dr. McClure would be a fine choice for the next seat on the president's council of science advisors. Now this. Grier disobeying orders and risking both a catastrophe and more importantly, McClure's own reputation. Dr. McClure's insides began to seethe. One way or the other he'd stop this outbreak again before the media got wind of it.

McClure threw the umbrella down and walked resolutely to the open elevator. Dropping in uninvited as it were would mean there would be no time for Volger to cook up lies about what had gone on between him and Fratelli two years ago. Dr. McClure stepped in and pressed the button for the max containment lab. The elevator doors opened onto a long hallway, dark except for a lit room in the ships center. McClure strolled down the lab-lined hallway. Except for the sound of the P4 fans, the ship was eerily quiet. It occurred to McClure that Dr. Volger might not yet know that the diseases had spread to his garden and worse, far enough to reach Channer's patients in the little Kokoori hospital. Dr. McClure leaned on the labs buzzer for several seconds. Through the double windows he saw a good looking woman asleep on a hospital bed. An I.V. drip was inserted in her left arm. In the middle was a semi circular console with an array of controls. The rest of the lab was out of view. McClure smacked the bell again with the heel of his hand. Momentarily, a startled face with a shock of white hair appeared at the inner window. It was the damnable interfering Konrad Volger. Edwin held up his identity card with its wreathed world symbol and motioned to be admitted. After the fans had completed a cycle Konrad buzzed the doors open. McClure walked straight to Konrad stopping inches short of his nose. Edwin started to speak but stopped short when he saw Colin off to the side. Colin took his supervisor in with a frozen look of surprise. "You know one another?", Dr. Volger asked breaking the obvious tension.

"Dr. Volger, this is my supervisor Dr. McClure from our New York office." Colin felt discomfortingly awkward. He searched for something pleasant to say to smooth over the confrontation he knew was coming. For McClure to leave his office and intervene in a field agents mission was unprecedented. McClure would want precise no nonsense answers especially about how ERSEV was involved for a second go round. McClure would have wanted him to have a tight grip on the outbreak by now. The thought of explaining how the outbreak was tied in with the ellipse, the Temple and Margo's memory visions made Colin's head throb.

"How did you...?" "The base at Darwin got me here by helicopter Colin," Dr. McClure interrupted before Colin could finish. "I expected to hear from you." McClure folded his arms across his chest. "I don't have to remind you that keeping your supervisor informed is of utmost importance," he went on. "You were to call Dr. Trimble or myself as soon as you arrived. Not hearing from you has put us in a very tenuous situation." McClure's eyebrows shot up. "You have an explanation?" The skin on Dr. McClure's gaunt face was tight with anger, the look of a martinet schoolmaster threatening to use the switch. Colin felt a hot flash of anger well up but managed to hold his tongue. McClure could have no idea of the churning ambivalence he'd been wrestling with since first coming aboard. To burst in here and address him like a recalcitrant lackey was arrogant and demeaning.

"It was my fault that Dr. Grier didn't contact you," Konrad spoke up apologetically. "Due to the extraordinary circumstances surrounding the outbreak I thought it best for Colin to wait before reporting in. Developments were ongoing rapidly Dr. McClure. We wanted to be in contact with Port Moresby's health department first. I took the initiative to divert Dr. Grier's plane to our ship." McClure's face flushed crimson.

"You had no right. No right at all Dr. Volger." McClure pressed his lips with a tick like gesture that overcame him whenever his temper flared. "I know a few things about your ERSEV organization. I know it's not uncommon for you people to meddle in the work of others. When you can profit by it that is. A little money spread here, a little there has gotten your tentacles into places where it has no business." McClure licked a fleck of spittle from the corner of his mouth. "I can't imagine how your so called research relates to the abomination I just saw on deck." Dr. McClure pointed a quivering finger. "You are an unwanted guest Dr. Volger. The responsibility for managing this outbreak is in my hands." McClure paused to

144

take a breath. He was on the verge of shouting. "I know for a fact Dr. Volger that you bribed Dr. Fratelli into letting you remain here two years ago in spite of your pledge to me to abide by my quarantine." Dr. Volger said nothing. Colin knew the ERSEV chief must be calculating how to begin to explain the unexplainable. "You haven't been out on your garden deck lately have you?", McClure asked with an acid voice. "Your plants are being eaten alive by whatever it is you've suppressed here. Your garden has degenerated into a bouquet of malignancy."

"Just a moment Dr. McClure," Colin broke in. We didn't know about the plant infections until yesterday."

"Oh I see. So it's *we* now is it?", McClure hissed. "You should have notified me immediately that you'd made contact with this ship." Dr. McClure's eyes darted around the room. "Who's that?" he demanded, looking over to Margo.

"The young lady is my daughter Margo, Dr. McClure. And the young man here is my advisor Roberto Valdes. Jhanda is also an aide." McClure's eyes passed coldly from one person to the next. He made no attempt to offer his hand.

"What's wrong with your daughter?" McClure asked, thrusting his chin toward the bed.

"Margo has an unknown condition. Dr. McClure," Konrad replied. "It mimics palsy somewhat. She's been sick since shortly after the Temple discovery. It is non contagious." Konrad looked lovingly over at Margo. "I believe the answer to this outbreak lies very much with her," Konrad continued. "With Jhanda's psychic gifts she should be able to lead us to understand it." Dr. McClure's mouth folded down at its edges.

"Psychic gifts? Do I hear you correctly?", he asked, while his gaze fell on the silent, robe-swathed Jhanda. "Now it all makes sense" McClure said with mock appreciation. "The reason for the ERSEV societies research success is that you've been employing mind readers." McClure held up a finger seeming to suddenly recall an important fact. "Now that you mention it I did come across a note in Dr. Fratelli's papers that you have on occasion used psychic's in your work. How old fashioned of the rest of we plodders to insist on proven research protocols. Maybe if we all had seers in our labs we'd be as successful as ERSEV."

"You don't understand Dr. McClure," Colin interjected. "Until yesterday I felt the same as you about psychic phenomena but I've seen things here that have changed my mind." The words had slipped out of Colin's mouth automatically. He had a momentary impulse to bring them back. In saying this he realized his attitude had moved across the threshold from skepticism to belief. He was defending Konrad and by implication the ERSEV society and all that it stood for.

"ESP is nonsense," McClure shouted. His eyes flashed accusingly around the lab. "This paranormal garbage has been put to the test repeatedly. Every time it's proven to be bogus." McClure looked derisively at Margo. "I'm not interested in hearing about how your daughter's mind is entangled in the mess here. The reality of what I saw in your garden is proof enough to me that ESP has no place here or anywhere else for that matter." What is it about this man that makes him bristle so at the mention of psychic possibility? Colin thought. His reaction bordered on the paranoid. That McClure was ruthless in his ambitious cravings there was no doubt. But this barely contained rage was close to pushing the man over the edge of control.

"If you'll allow me to explain the events leading up to what you've seen Dr. McClure, I think you'll understand why I chose to use my daughter's and Jhanda's powers from the start." Before McClure could reply Dr. Volger cut him off.

"Dr. McClure I'm a practical man much like yourself. A realist. A scientist. I was reluctant also to consider the possibility of paranormal phenomena. But that was only until Margo predicted the existence of a cave nearby Barubi village. The cave she foresaw is there, one she never could have known about." McClure cocked his head aside in a quick avian motion. "Let me go on Dr. McClure."

"I'm listening," McClure allowed.

"I came here originally to help Margo with her archeological research. I'll spare you the details but just tell you she has also discovered the remains of a Twelfth Century Khmer Temple here..."
"And?", McClure interrupted impatiently.

"It was during the excavation process that she first showed the palsy like symptoms. Then within hours her trance states began. We didn't know what to make of the episodes. Margo would mumble a few incoherent words that seemed to be just ramblings of a hallucinatory state. I suspected a connection between her increasing paralysis and the mental oddities when one of the staff suggested she might be bringing up genetic memories."

"Where is this person?", McClure demanded.

"In our European headquarters now," Konrad answered.

"And then you toddled in this little sage here to give an assist. Do I guess correctly?", McClure asked, while staring contemptuously at Jhanda.

"With the help of this little sage Margo was able to see an undiscovered cave Dr. McClure. There is no disputing that," Colin fired back. McClure's righteousness was becoming hard to bear.

"In one of the memory trances my daughter foresaw the presence of a large metal vessel buried in the cave. The object was found recently by myself. For want of a better label we call it the ellipse."

"Do go on," McClure said putting a finger to his chin.

"The ellipse is at the center of everything that has happened here. All the phenomena you see is somehow tied in with it," Konrad urged.

"You do understand there is a question of obstruction of an official investigation here. But that can be thrashed out later in the courts," McClure said. "I'm interested in being amused however." McClure glanced at his watch. "I'll take a moment to entertain a short version of this ellipse story." Colin could sense the wheels turning in Konrad's head. It was imperative that McClure be convinced of the wisdom of keeping the cave open in spite of the outbreak's havoc. Unless Konrad could engineer a total turnaround in McClure's closed brained attitude, any chance of further access to the ellipse would go to zero.

"The ellipse foreseen by Margo is made of an unknown alloy. The disease agents we've encountered are issuing forth from the machine," Konrad said. McClure's lip quivered sporadically.

"You mean you *know* the point source of the disease and...,"

"Please allow me," Konrad cut in to McClure's bluster. Colin noticed that Konrad's earlier courteous tone was gone. In it's place was one of steely determination. "After the first release of the disease particles I was guided to the cave by Margo's vision. It wasn't until later that I uncovered the ellipse in a dig inside the cave." Dr. Volger motioned for McClure to move to the console. "Stay where you are Roberto, I'll do this myself," Konrad directed. He typed in a new command leaning over Roberto's shoulder. McClure looked on half-heartedly. Photographs of the pit wall that Colin had seen earlier flashed on to the monitor.

"What's this about?", Dr. McClure grunted.

"It's about a fantastic possibility Dr. McClure...No. I should rather say a high probability. This photo is from a series I took of the dig site in the cave. If you look carefully you'll see two small objects protruding from the dig site wall. The objects are pieces of primate mandible." McClure squinted for a moment before spotting the aged bones. "As you know Homo sapiens have been on earth a relatively short while Dr. McClure. We always find the remains of pre-man deeper in the earth than Homo sapiens."

"I've heard talk of that," McClure said. Konrad ignored the sarcasm and went on. "The jaw section you see on the left belonged to Homo erectus, the one on the right to us, Homo sapiens. Overwhelming evidence that at one time pre-man and our own species coexisted. At least at this place." Colin watched Konrad's face blush red with enthusiasm. "You see the implication of course Dr. McClure," Konrad said. McClure only stared back at Dr. Volger with blank hard eyes. "The signs are right there Dr. McClure. We didn't evolve slowly as we've assumed. Particles from the ellipse were almost surely used to transform erectus into Homo sapiens instantly, Dr. Volger continued. "What we're seeing now is a mechanism out of order. Working properly it may unlock knowledge to a realm of existence we can only dream about." Be careful Dr. Volger Colin thought. With McClure you had to marshall facts step by step. McClure is a man who dreams very little. Whose sense of the possible is feeble. With this man cool and dispassionate is the key.

"Seeing the DNA splices might help Dr. McClure understand the reason behind your assurance," Colin interjected.

"Of course. The gene strands inside the particles that have come from the ellipse are the key," Dr. Volger chirped.

"Stop," McClure demanded. "Who could possibly have put the kind of machine you're talking about in the cave two or three million years ago? The claim is ridiculous on it's face. For one thing, you've obviously made an erroneous assumption about the jaw section. This area is highly prone to earthquakes. If you had looked into it more thoroughly no doubt you would have discovered that the lower stratum holding the erectus mandible was uplifted. Uplifted to make it *appear* to be contemporary with the sapiens piece."

"Forget the fossils then Dr. McClure," Colin broke in. "Dr. Volger has shown me compelling evidence that the particles from the ellipse have great possibilities. Some of them contain genes that stimulate our memory centers. The DNA splices absorbed by Margo have given inklings of events at the cave eons ago. This is why Jhanda is here to help Margo bring up these past memories so an overall picture of the past can fall into place." Colin felt his exasperation growing. If McClure would only really listen to Konrad's argument, that the ellipse was more than a horror machine.

"Have you had access to this machines interior?", McClure questioned.

"Not actual access, no," Dr. Volger said. "But from examination of the particles we believe the genes are arranged in a kind of phylogenetic order. Perhaps breaking off a spool like mechanism, the more primitive genes on the outside and those with potential for paranormal abilities further in." McClure's face was stone rigid. "Whatever else it is, it contains some kind of computerized gene splicing mechanism" Konrad went on. "Somehow the apparatus has been distorted."

"What is distorted is your speculation," McClure snapped. "You'd have me believe that some superior race roamed these parts ages ago and decided to plant this machine here? Maybe the thing was left behind by technological cracker jacks from the lost island of Atlantis," McClure sneered. His eyes flashed from Konrad to Colin with an icy contempt. "I'm not privy to whatever neurotic need you have for fantasy building Dr. Volger, but you've clearly given it free rein. Consider this simple fact. Your ERSEV society is not the worlds only privately funded research organization. Some other foundation has obviously been experimenting here with a splicing machine. A team like your own wanted to conduct their research away from probing eyes. Let's assume their project went away. They'd abandoned it. Then you stumble on it and concoct a wild scenario replete with psychic powers, memory genes and all the rest."

"You're mistaken," Dr. Volger answered with gentle serenity. "The ellipse was placed here by an intelligence with far more understanding than yours or mine. In fact by beings from another galaxy."

"That's preposterous," McClure bellowed.

"There's one thing I haven't yet told you Dr. McClure," Konrad added. "The nitrogen atoms in the DNA bases from the ellipse. They're isotopes found rarely on earth. Nitrogen with an atomic mass of nineteen." For a moment McClure was caught off balance, his mouth working soundlessly.

"Alright. Let's assume you haven't made an error in testing the nitrogen. And even that you have come across a previously unknown isotope. That means nothing. There *are* reactors where nitrogen nineteen could be synthesized in a dozen countries."

"But what would be the reason for it?", Konrad questioned.

"For Christ sake man, it's more reasonable that a lab has put it together than to think that the atoms are from the other side of the universe," McClure spat.

"There are strong indications that an attempt to assemble a radio telescope was made by the people who placed the ellipse here Dr. McClure.", Colin said. He offered the broken antenna piece to McClure. McClure glared at the ancient object and Colin with a disdainful leer.

"Jhanda's insights, like my daughter's own, lead us to the telescope fragment. This piece was found at the forefront of the Temple grounds. We know in what area of the sky the scope was aimed. Signals may yet be coming from that section of the heavens."

"Dr. Volger only needs a few hours to determine if signals are still being transmitted Dr. McClure," Colin said. "A radio scope at Coolabundi Australia is set up right now probing for intelligent signals." Dr. McClure looked at Colin with a have you taken leave of your senses stare.

"Are you out of your mind Dr. Grier?", McClure whined. "This man has bulldozed you into thinking the solution to this plague will be arriving from outer space. You can't be that gullible. And I'm not so stupid as to believe that you're freely going along with all this nonsense." McClure stepped within an inch of Colin's face. "He's paid you off hasn't he? What was it, some bank notes from the Swiss franc fund? A cushy job with the ERSEV organization?" A bolt of rage welled up in Colin at McClure's hateful arrogance. In an instant the mounting stress of the past day overwhelmed his frayed nerves. Colin grabbed McClure by the collar. His trembling fists lifted his supervisors chin toward the ceiling. McClure suspended on tiptoe could only sputter in helpless protest.

"Now listen to me McClure," Colin hissed through clenched teeth. "You've done nothing since you walked in except piss on every attempt we're made to make this outbreak make sense. You are an extremely vain man. Dr. Volger's daughter is a few heartbeats away from death over there. If he's wrong about the ellipse her life is finished. And he's laid his own life on the line in order to convince me to try to save hers." Colin shook McClure so hard the man's cheeks quivered. "Do you think our telling you all this is just some fucking intellectual exercise?" Colin let McClure down with a lurch. "My instincts when I first met you was that you were a sanctimonious prig, a self-centered blowhard who would plow over anyone who didn't kowtow to your every whim. My instincts were right on."

"You've no right to talk to me like this," McClure shouted through a fit of coughing. "You're an ungrateful son of a bitch Dr. Grier," McClure barked, his cheeks twitching in fury. He dabbed a handkerchief at the drool spotting his lips.

"You never did squat for me McClure", Colin said. "You don't give two shits for the sick. For you, your job is just a stepping stone to a seat at some White House soiree."

"I make no apologies for wanting a place on the president's advisory panel. I deserve a seat" McClure said. "If you think I'm going to jeopardize my chances by giving the slightest credence to these bizarre theories you're mistaken." Dr. McClure smoothed down his collar in an attempt to reestablish his battered dignity. "All you've got here are a series of half baked coincidences," McClure laughed hollowly. "You've manufactured a whole set of relationships that are pure fabrication." McClure tilted his head toward Margo's bed. "As I see it Dr. Volger your daughter has been laid low by whatever genetic material rival researchers have put in their tecky but surely earth made device. The piece has malfunctioned. Loose material has, along with creating havoc generally, rendered your daughter's mind unbalanced. You have constructed some connection with ESP and alien worlds. Even if the slightest chance existed that you were correct I could never allow you further access to what is in the cave."

"It seems you've made up your mind then," Konrad said.

"Of course. It's the only sane option to a man with common sense," McClure answered contemptuously. He started to the air lock then stopped mid-stride. "By the way, this man Lippincott... Moresby is concerned about him. Technically his welfare is my responsibility now. Do either one of you know his whereabouts?" A sly twist of McClure's mouth told Colin that McClure suspected the truth. Lying about the death would do no good. It would only give McClure another legal reason to nail them, Colin thought.

"Lippincott is dead Dr. McClure. We brought his body back from the cave site," Colin said. "Particles from the machine?", McClure guessed.

"Yes," Konrad acknowledged. "I take the responsibility for his death. My foolish error in trying to predict the times the ellipse would be active was part of the reason he's gone. I should have thought things through more thoroughly."

"There is much you have not thought through Dr. Volger," McClure cooed. He looked up at the clock on the wall. "It's 2:20 now. The helicopter will pick me up in ten minutes. I'll get to Darwin around six. As soon as I do I'm going to call in a police unit to cordon off Barubi. Any unauthorized persons who attempt to go near the cave will put themselves in serious danger. By this time tomorrow the machine will no longer exist." McClure suddenly made a grimace of pain. A bracelet of what looked like bee sting welts had erupted on his forearm. Each little welt exuded a droplet of gray- green pus. He patted down the tiny lesions with his handkerchief.

"I see I have a souvenir to take with me from your garden Dr. Volger. Don't apologize. Just another confirmation that I arrived here just in time." Dr. McClure held up his arm for a closer inspection. There were none of the dry brown crusts he'd seen on the desiccated corpses of the villagers. Satisfied that he hadn't contracted *that* bizarre ailment, he moved on to the double doors. "You are confined to this lab until further notice. You are all to consider yourselves under arrest. Now open the air lock."

"Before you go out you should put on one of our protective suits Dr. McClure," Konrad advised. McClure's eyes darted around the lab with the quickness of a cornered ferret. In the fraction of a second it had taken McClure to order them arrested a sudden but unmistakable change had come over the man. He began to laugh. But it wasn't a normal laugh. It was more of a howl, wild and piercingly high pitched. Instinctively Colin and Konrad drew back. McClure stared with icy hardness. He began to sniff the air.

Like a predator sensing nearby food his head moved in quick jerky motions. "I don't need anything of yours," he shrieked. Colin watched revolted as McClure brought his oozing arm to his mouth. He licked the pus from his arm, cat like slow and tenderly as if it were the most natural thing to do. Colin and Konrad exchanged quick acknowledging looks but dared not speak. With a mixture of horror and fascination Colin realized he was watching a mind slip deeper into insanity second by second. Profuse sweat dripped from McClure's transformed face. His chest heaved with deep guttural breaths. He bent forward at the waist swaying from side to side. Then he began to giggle, a high falsetto uncanny sound. "You will make amends. You will make amends," he screeched over and over in an out of control tantrum of will. McClure thrust a finger at the glass case holding the micro stat suits. "I'll see to it that you *cannot* leave," he screamed.

The image of Boka's brainless cadaver popped into Colin's head, the body with the dripping chancres that had housed a criminally insane mind. A mind warped, Boka had suggested, by that swollen orange brain tremor. Was the same malignancy growing in McClure's head now? Colin wondered.

McClure snatched the broken antenna from the console and heaved it with all his might through the glass front closet. He reached the suits and hurled them throughout the lab. "Damn you. You dare defy me," McClure bellowed. He hammered the antenna deafeningly against the air lock windows. After several powerful blows the reinforced glass shattered. Yelping like a deranged animal, McClure (or what had been McClure) vaulted into the hall. In an instant he was up the far stairwell, his mad man's talking to himself echoing back.

Roberto, who had eased his chair to the wall quietly went over to the now useless air lock. He peered down the hallway. A faint remnant of McClure's unnerving giggle filtered down from an upper deck. Roberto let out a relieved sigh.

"That was like seeing Jekyll do his switch right before us." He walked back to his console seat and plopped down. "Those green abscesses. Only Boka's cadaver had them out of all of Barubi's villagers who got any of the disease. And that was the one who slaughtered his wife and kids," Roberto said.

"So is what we just saw a rerun of what happened to him? An eruption of the most base instincts?", Colin asked. He eyed the shattered door lock warily as if McClure might decide to make a fresh appearance.

"A case for the mind matter loop we spoke of?", Konrad asked.

"Wait a second," Colin said. "McClure's a miserable sample of a human being, but he didn't do anything like slaughter his family."

"Are you sure of that?" Konrad responded as if positing a philosophical query.

"What do you mean?" Colin asked with a touch of surprise. Roberto wrapped his arm around his shin and pulled his knee up close to his face. Jhanda sat impassively as he'd been doing throughout all the bedlam. Listening, absorbing.

"Just some facts you may want to ponder Colin," Konrad said. "When we were anchored here during the earlier outbreak I saw something I was almost sure was Dr. McClure's doing, something cruel and heartless. I couldn't be positive of his responsibility for the deed so I said nothing at the time." Konrad shut off the now useless fans, then took a seat next to Roberto at the console. "Port Moresby sent a shipment of supplies up here when the hepatitis first showed up. When this looked like a normal outbreak. There were enough medicines for a village twice the size of Barubi. Then McClure and Fratelli took charge. Before Dr. McClure decided I was the enemy he had Fratelli ask if I'd help move the medicines inland to the village. Of course we were happy to help. Along with a few of the crew we carted the medicines to the edge of the village. We wanted to be careful about getting too close as we didn't yet have the suits. Then the first brown skin crusts showed up on one of the villagers. McClure panicked. He ordered all of us, Fratelli included, back to the ship. He warned us not to talk to the media should they get wind of what was happening. Dr. McClure said he'd take care of the villagers himself."

"Did he?", Colin asked.

"Depends on how you define 'take care of' Colin. There were twenty four deaths altogether. Two died the way Dr. Lippincott did. There was nothing we could have done to help those two. But the others might have been saved. I'm convinced that McClure saw to it that they were not."

"Your saying he let them die on purpose?", Roberto broke in.

"I think so my friends," Konrad replied. "I didn't want to deal with that possibility at first," Konrad said turning to Colin. "Colin you do remember Dr. Boka's speaking of his assistant Bill Rutledge?" Colin nodded.

"Bill autopsied the villagers who died from hepatitis and smallpox. He does his post mortems with close attention to detail. He called me down to look at some unusual skin markings.

"The start of the crusts?", Colin asked.

"No, not that. Rutledge wanted to show me the holes where the I.V. needles had been inserted into the villager's arms." Dr. Volger tapped his inner forearm with his fingers. "The holes where the needles had put in were still fresh. Dr. Rutledge estimated that the I.V.'s had been pulled out within hours of being placed. It had to be McClure's doing."

"Why?", Roberto asked.

"Because McClure is more paranoid than I realized Roberto," Colin cut in. He caught the appalled look on Roberto's face. The unspoken understanding of what McClure had done was registered plainly. "Keep in mind Roberto that McClure heads up an office that even most security council members don't know they've authorized. Created in the jittery fifties and intended to be buried so far under paperwork that only a few top people are still aware it exists. Our office operates as much to save diplomatic face as it does to stop epidemics. P.R. comes first for McClure. Saving lives second. McClure wants fires put out before anyone else knows they've even flared up," Colin said. He nodded his understanding of McClure's deed to Konrad. "If all those who were infected and died were buried, nobody would be left to tell the truth," Colin said.

"The couple of villagers who were left alive, what happened to them?", Roberto asked. "McClure had them removed. Where I don't know," Konrad answered.

"Sure, if reporters came sniffing around later McClure could deny any outbreak. He would just adlib a story that they died of cholera or some other third world disease and how it was such a shame but so sorry. They'd have been cremated already. So he could just tell them to take their cameras and go back home." Colin recalled the crazy look on McClure's face as he hurled the antenna piece at the glass. Was there enough subterranean rage in the man for some gene splice to tip it over into madness? "Let's go with the assumption that McClure did pull out the I.V.'s," Roberto said. "We all just saw him go over the edge. If we could see into his brain would there be the same bulging orange tumor Boka's cadaver had?"

"If there is we can still only guess that it was caused by a splice that somehow recognizes evil," Konrad replied.

"We're talking a lot of conjecture here. A lot of 'ifs'", Colin added. Suddenly a green light flashed at the edge of the console. "The memory proteins are synthesized," Konrad said. He shut off the atomic force microscope and turned to Colin. "You're right. There are a lot of ifs. If Margo receives these proteins will she be able to glue the flitting shards of her memory into a picture of the past clear enough for us to understand?" Konrad placed his hand on Colin's shoulder. "Before McClure's police unit gets here it's not too late to change your mind Colin. It was my lie to you about the canisters that kept you from going to the village in the first place. Doing what McClure wanted."

Konrad searched Colin's eyes. "If you want to leave now I'll understand." Colin shook his head. "I made my decision. I said twenty-four hours. Twenty four hours stands."

"Thank you," Konrad said softly. McClure had probably called in the police unit before he'd left New York Colin figured. Made his decision to have all those still aboard apprehended as soon as he found out the ship was back off the coast. Konrad was wrong. There was no chance of leaving. Once put in motion the Emtran unit would do as ordered. Arrest them all if not worse. It was just as well. He'd already juggled the balls of common sense versus intuition up on deck when they wheeled Margo away. Any option of getting out even if he wanted to was academic now.

"What do you know about this police group Colin? How long before they get here?", Konrad asked. "Six, eight hours I would guess," Colin replied. "Emtran is the name of the force. I don't know much about it except that a lot of men who can't stand peacetime are in it.

It's a secret regiment kept under the table by the government. Like Blackwater was in the Iraq invasion. Say a coke kingpin needs to be eliminated. Emtran is always on call to politicians with the right connections."

"Then they'll come at McClure's request?", Konrad asked.

"If not his request then somebody who owes him a favor higher up can put them in motion."

"Well then, lets hope Margo can help us find what we need to know before they get here," Konrad said. He walked over to the vial that held the finished proteins in solution. Colin watched him unthread the ten-milliliter tube from a niche next to the atomic force scope. It held a clear pale green liquid that could have been a child's toy filled with vegetable coloring. What did I expect, Colin thought. That the memory proteins would be throwing off rays of radiation? They're just protein in solution like any other, too small to be seen. There would be no way to measure their power until they were connected to their other half. The half that hopefully waited to be completed in Margo's brain. "Easy," Konrad admonished himself as he carefully capped the vial. "No time to build these proteins again if this should spill." Konrad put the vial in a test tube rack and started toward the sleeping Margo when the beeper on the lab's fax sounded. Konrad wheeled round in mid step to the console deck.

"That has to be coming from Polski," Roberto called, joining Colin at Konrad's side.

"If Polski's telescope has picked up a transmission how will you be able to tell from the readout if there's intelligence behind it?", Colin asked.

"We'll be looking for a periodic pattern," Roberto put in. "If the Coolabundi scope is just getting generalized noise we'll get a fuzzy graph line. A strongly focused source will come in like a stock market graph." "But a repetitive one I'm sure" Konrad added. "We want to see a tracing that shows a regular pattern. As orderly as a healthy EKG readout." An EKG readout Colin thought. That made two places then where a healthy pattern was wanted.

Jhanda, who'd been mouse quiet since McClure's appearance, had quietly slipped over to a chair next to Margo's bed. His face showed little concern but Colin caught his glance up to the monitors hanging above Margo's bed. Colin guessed he was checking for any sign of the heart arrhythmia that unpredictably struck Margo. He recalled Konrad saying that her entering the trance state drew so much on her energy bank that staying under it too long was dangerous. No doubt Jhanda was being watchful that her heart stayed steady before the memory proteins were given.

Konrad impatiently snatched the fax from the machine and put it on the console desk. He looked at it intently for a few moments then his face slackened with a look of disappointment. "Nothing" Konrad sighed. "This readout is nearly ruler straight." Konrad tapped the fax thoughtfully. "Well, no need to worry" he chirped, his mood seeming to change instantly. "We have no right to expect that Dr. Polski will be successful so soon. This is probably just one of the first faxes of any number he'll be sending us."

"I'm afraid the chances of his finding anything intelligent out there are not good," Roberto said, while he furiously typed another command. "While you were on the phone with Poliski I made some rough calculations." Roberto slid his stool to the console desk and brought up a white on black onto the monitor screen. To Colin it looked like an image of a dark lake with a scattering of bright concentric ringed ovals on it's surface as if some kids had thrown in handfuls of stones. "This is a radio map of known electromagnetic sources that face the Temple's front. The map only shows sources in that small band of beams where we asked Polski to search. Each set of rings shows an x- ray source, quasar or whatever hasn't been picked up by a light telescope."

"Will Polski have access to this map?", Colin asked.

"For sure," Roberto said. "And let's assume he programs his scope to track around these sources looking for a new source." Roberto drew in a long breath. "To allow his scope to weave and wander around the already plotted sections will take him days rather than hours even with a cursory search. Even more, we're making the assumption that an intelligent signal will be on the twenty one centimeter wave length." Somewhere lodged among his facts on file Colin knew that hydrogen's radio signature was supposed to be the best choice for someone out there to broadcast messages. "If it *is* there but coming in on some other wavelength the game us up," Roberto said. "Just searching that little ribbon of sky, we are trying to catch a signal that could come in anywhere from a few light years away to the edge of the universe. We'd better hope it's on twenty one." Konrad stared straight ahead concentrated in thought.

"Let's think about this. If we're right that superior beings implanted memories into our genome long ago wouldn't they also have encoded their source, the place from which the signals come? I think so. And I think that once Margo assimilates the memory proteins she'll be able to tell us exactly where the Temple scope was aimed and where the signal was coming from." Jhanda rose up from his seat at Konrad's words. He smoothed his robes and walked to the pale green vial.

"She *will* tell you this," Jhanda proclaimed, lifting the glass vessel with both hands. He held it at eye level, scrutinizing as if the proteins themselves might have a message for him. Jhanda tapped it gently with a long thin finger, then he caught the eyes of the other three men. "You may doubt that within this glass are the answers to what you seek. I understand your fear. It has been given me by the grace of the Gods to turn aside the clock that hides a truer reality. My powers recede now, but all has not yet been taken from me." Jhanda pointed to Margo who seemed to rest easily in her sleep. "Margo will open the way for you to see all that is necessary." Colin thought for a moment to question Jhanda but smiling, the old man anticipated this and with a polite wave of his hand dismissed any query. He bowed his head and glided back to his seat next to Margo's bed.

"That's it then I suppose," Roberto quipped, with a facetious glint. Konrad shot him a disapproving look. "Remember Roberto, Jhanda's guidance has never led us astray. It was his insight that led to the telescope antenna. It was his vision that helped Margo first see the cave. I trust those abilities will not desert him now."

CHAPTER 14

I

T WAS MIDNIGHT when-George Trimble shut off the engine of his rental Kia. He opened the sedans door slowly, cautiously. Port Moresby was no hustle bustle burg by any means, but compared to the little town he was in right now Moresby was N.Y.C. The name on the weathered wooden sign on the outskirts said the town was Kokoori. After getting sidetracked, on a half dirt road coming in for three hours, George was finally parked in front of its hospital. He hadn't envisioned much of a facility, the place being out in the New Guinea netherlands, but taking in the building all in all he saw it for what it was, a dump of a converted old grammar school. Probably had been put up a few months after Booth shot Lincoln George mused. The hamlet and hospital sat in a natural bowl like depression. There were several boarded up homes and stores that sat forlorn and forgotten at its bottom. George had been told that the long vacant sites were once occupied by missionaries bent on bringing Jesus and McGuffey's reader to the native New Guineans.

George leaned back against the Kia's fender. He ran his finger between his sweaty neck and collar and thought his situation over. It was well past midnight. No surprise that the lights were out in the few shacks he'd passed on the long way in. But Kokoori's hospital was dark too. Even in these boondocks and with a handful of patients there should be some light from inside, but the little schoolhouse cum hospital showed no signs of being occupied. George reviewed his earlier talk with Dr. Channer from Manhattan. He was sure Channer had said he'd stay in the hospital. At least the basement operating room should be lit. That's where Channer said he'd watch over the duct-taped ex- convict with the strange green skin lesions. George hesitated before taking his first steps up the hospitals walkway. A pair of heavy old Victorian doors sealed the entrance. George realized he was no pup anymore. Twinges of sciatica pain flicked down his leg. It was from the long bumpy ride from Moresby he knew. When he got back to the city Dr. McClure was going to have to understand that this was the last time he'd be fit to go out on a case. Images of himself sitting contentedly in his Lay-Z- Boy with a bowl of microwave popcorn balanced on his ample belly drifted through his head. If he'd had a choice he would have spent the night at the comfortable Port Moresby Quality Inn and headed here in the morning. But McClure had insisted on warp speed and McClure wasn't one to be crossed.

George rubbed the sore spot at the top of his left buttock and approached the oaken doors. With a start he halted. He hadn't seen them from the car but there were vines of some kind spread ivy like over the buildings lower brickwork. George had never seen anything like them, gray instead of green. At six inch intervals there were half transparent tumor like globules along the stems. George took out his fountain pen. He warily pierced one of the ugly balls. A repugnant swelling juice squirted out spraying his slacks and shoes. Startled, George bolted back to the walkway as fast as his overweight body would allow. He knew instinctively these plants were foreign. Even in New guinea where evolution had freehand to come up with some oddities these vines were aliens. Channer's description of his chancre-ridden madman came to George's mind. He played with the notion that the globules might somehow be related to the awful open sores Channer had described.

George had been convinced up until now that the skin afflictions and the bizarre psychopathic behavior Channer told him about were caused by synthetic toxins, an isomeric form of Tetrachlorin 5 to be specific. He'd pictured himself coming to Kokoori and in short order uncovering a toxic dump nearby like the infamous one in Texas. But Tet-5 didn't cause pus balls to sprout on vines. For the first time since his phone chat with Dr. Channer, George's assurance that the diseases were poison caused began to crumble. This was not good. A toxin could be isolated, cleaned up. If a microbial agent was behind the loathsome galls and able to change a normal man into a howling maniac, then the problem here and at Barubi was of a different order of magnitude. George ran a tacky tongue over his dry lips, but not to conjecture he thought. He reminded himself that his business at hand was to make contact with Dr. Channer. One way or another he had to talk to the man.

George stared at the little darkened building with apprehension. The worn structure with it's encroaching vines brought an image of forgotten tombs to mind. Then there were the patients inside, if they were indeed still locked up. The sickening felon with the suppurating sores and the woman whose skin, according to Channer was a brittle brown husk. I don't *have* to go inside George thought. As dark and silent as it was he couldn't be blamed for driving right back out of town. Dr. Channer might be dead. Even if he'd only been infected, still he might be in no condition to give particulars. But he was the only person who'd watched the diseases wreaking their havoc. George needed to talk to him. And if there was only one person still inside who needed help, the oath George once took that said "I shall enter any house" had never been just lip service. Then again old Hippocrates never had to tend to patients with three-inch lesions or extra crispy skin.

George gathered his courage and started up the walkway. When he was close to the entrance he stopped. There was a flash of light from behind a curtained window on the second floor, then a high but gentle cry of a newborn after that. There was no mistaking that universal sound. The baby had to be less than a week old. In a rush to evacuate could an infant somehow have been left behind? And was it's crying a sign of distress or just a call for it's mother's warmth?

With a renewed ration of pluck George marched decisively through the double doors and into the pitch black of the lobby. Georges' eyes were useless. It was like barging through the swinging doors of an amusement park ride. Sudden blindness. After a moment of hard squinting George became aware of a feeble shaft of moon light dully washing a small reception desk. To his right and left the hallways were still dark tunnels. George groped for an emergency generator. If the laws in New Guinea were the same as in the U.S. there would have to be an emergency generator. Probably there was one in Channers O.R. but often there'd be another in the administrators office. George followed the contours of the desk until his knee banged painfully against the arm of a swivel chair. He cursed under his breath as the chair spun up against a wall with a hollow echo. As if in protest to the noise the babies cry came again. Odd George thought. It seemed to emanate from one of the first floor rooms, but he was sure the sound had come from the upstairs window. George rubbed his aching knee. There'd be a fat bruise tomorrow, but beside that no real damage done. George ran his hand over the desktop, feeling pens and pencils, a ledger of some kind and an old land line phone. He picked up the receiver and listened. Dead. Why should the phone be out? George squatted and ran his fingers along the inside edge of the desk. Then he felt it. A cool metal box with a rubber handle attached. "Good guess" George thought congratulating himself on his luck. He pulled the handle and machinery began to whirr from somewhere downstairs. Lights flickered, then came on full. George had been right about the place being converted from a little school. It was apparent that the classrooms had been partitioned down to smaller patient rooms. The desk that hid the light breaker still had a dull brass plaque screwed into it with the names of three long forgotten Kokoori school board members inscribed. George fingered a bit of tobacco into his meerschaum. Except for the intermittent sound of the infants cry from down the hall the place was eerily quiet. No respirator or monitor beeps. Only the heart breaking crying. But now the child's sounds seemed to be coming from a room directly around the corner to the right. George walked down the hallway a few paces and drew him self up with a gasp. The walls and floor were spattered with goblets of bloody green mucus. What could possibly have passed by here that would leave such a God-awful mess? George wondered.

It looked like the leftovers from an infernal version of a sophomoric food fight. Tiptoeing carefully between the droppings George came to the first patient door. There were four rooms in each wing. Oddly this first one like all the others had shut doors. George couldn't recall a hospital where all the patient room doors were closed. Closed by Dr. Channer perhaps as a desperate attempt to keep a microbe source away from the sick? Or rather were the rooms shut to keep what might be in them from spilling out? With rising apprehension George turned the knob on the two closest doors.

Both were locked. Then floating out into the hallway the whimpering sound came again. It was definitely from the second room on the right. The door was flecked with droplets of still moist blood. George wrapped his handkerchief around his trembling hands hoping it would be enough to protect him at least a little. This room was unlocked. George opened the door a crack. Warily he peeked in. It was a hospital room right out of the forties complete with an enameled cream-colored metal bed. In the bed was an adult figure completely covered by a cotton blanket. George swallowed hard. He forced himself to walk to the bedside. With one quick sweeping motion he flung back the covering. What lay there jolted him with a shock of horror. A mother and her newborn lay nestled together, the mother on her side, the child cradled in her arms. A wonderful picture of maternal love that except for the gore would have been heartwarming. George fought back the stomach spasm that tried to bring up his lunch. The heads were missing from both of the bodies. Two billows of very fresh blood mushroomed out on the pillow's from raggedly torn stumps. The heads had clearly been wrenched off with brutal force. George put his hands on his knees to quiet his quivering legs. He pulled the blanket quickly back over the pair as if hiding it from his eyes would make it less real. From behind him he heard a dull thumping sound. Rhythmic. Steady. Ominous. A sickening noise like a fish fresh from the sea slapping its tail against a wooden deck.

The infant cry wailed again. George was afraid to turn his head around. His instinct told him that someone was at the door just over his shoulder.

George did not care to make eye contact with whoever or whatever it might be. He wished he could just cover his eyes the way he did at the scary part of the movies when he was a kid. George ordered himself to turn around. What stood there blocking the doorway was as awful as anything he could have nightmared up. A man, if that's what it still could be called, stood grinning a hellish grin through a lipless bloody mouth. Large white globules filled its eye sockets. Still George felt a malevolent stare burn through him from the sightless spheres. Deep gouges pocked his body. Drying blood and a foul swelling green mucus dripped over tattered bandages onto the floor. The man-thing stepped toward George. From between long yellowed teeth came a perfect imitative sound of a crying infant. The heads of the mother and baby dangled by the hair from the things fingers. George wanted to look away but couldn't. Part of him wanted to believe he was hallucinating, but deeper down he knew he was facing a kind of reality that shouldn't be but was. With a howling insane laugh the aberration swung and smashed the severed heads against the wall. Sprays of blood and beige colored brain tissue spattered against the wall with a flat tacky sound. George dug deep into the depths of self- control. His own brain, for the moment intact, was pulsing with alarm.

George squeezed the bed frame willing himself to stand still. Any sudden move might provoke the creature into instant attack. What stood before him whimpering its mock infant cry he understood was human no longer. George's eyes searched for some way out. There was nowhere to go. The things high pitched baby cry had changed to a throaty growl. The demented man stood directly blocking the door. George backpedaled slowly. He held his hand out behind him praying to feel the window sill. After seconds that seemed like hours his fingers sensed cooler nighttime air. He let his hand reach outside the just open window. A spark of hope bouyed him up. He just might (pray God the frame wasn't warped) be able to throw up the window with a sudden thrust and scramble out before he was mutilated. George grabbed a bloody pillow. With a quick flick of his arm he flung it at the oozing malevolent face. He made a quicker move than he thought possible. George managed to get his fingers under the sill. He threw up the window with all his force. Thankfully, it ratcheted up with buttery smoothness, smashing the windowpanes into splinters. Just one more second and I'll be out George thought. He got one aching knee on to the window but still he wasn't fast enough. Two steel strong hands slapped down on his shoulders. A manic roar bellowed out from the man-things throat. Fingers dug into George's flesh so hard he lost the feeling in his fingers. The monstrous creature pulled him back then held him up like a dangling puppet. George kicked ferociously. In spite of the pain and fear George wasn't ready to cash it in. A surge of indignant rage rushed through him. He'd seen his share of spilled guts and torn limbs in combat and he wasn't going to surrender now without a fight. With the remaining power in his legs George kicked backward as hard as he could. His heel caught his tormentors groin perfectly. The thing let go with an ungodly scream. George dropped, then scuttled on all fours around the base of the bed. He tried to stand and run to the door but only made two strides before his bad leg buckled. He sprawled halfway into the hall. The thing was on him in an instant.

The incredibly strong hands came pounding down again on George's back. This time he found himself lifted by belt and shirt collar. The mutant, once human thing, swung him like a ten pound sack of flour headed for the back of a flat bed. George held his hands over his head. With a long swing the thing tossed him down the hallway floor like a piece of old luggage. George skidded into a metal cart at the halls end. He cracked into it with a resounding clatter that echoed throughout the hospital. Peeking out from between his fingers George watched the slobbering bug eyed face pant and measure him like a cat wondering how best to torture a mouse. The mutant was weighing the possibilities for play. As it quickly closed the space to George it began to giggle, a silly yet high pitched twitter of delight. George saw a downstairs staircase was only a few feet away. He tried to stand but couldn't work his leg. His sense of balance was gone. He wobbled drunkenly then collapsed. With a banshee like howl the mutant grabbed George by the hair and with the heel of his other hand twisted Georges head sideways. The mutants knee pressed into Georges chest pinning him to the floor like a bug in a glass case. Globs of slimy mucus dropped onto George's face. He felt his head twisting close to the breaking point. Through the sightless cancerous eyes George sensed the thing was gloating. The mutant was keen on snapping every vertebra in his neck.

The next twist wouldn't stop at the angle that now was inflicting such penetrating pain. Of that George was sure. The mutant started the corkscrew rotation again. George groped and slapped frantically with his one free arm for anything that might have fallen from the cart. His fingers felt bandages, syringes and a stethoscope but nothing to help him. Then with darkness crowding his consciousness his fingers lucked on a power saw. It was the kind used to cut open a sternum. Maybe Ms. Fortune was looking his way. George fumbled with the switch, then managed to flick it on with his thumb. The blade jumped to whirring life vibrating with fluid energy.

Suddenly a voice rang out from the direction of the far end stairwell. The mutant's hands flew back from George's head in a gesture of startled surprise. The pressing knee rose up so that for a moment the creature was in a crouching position. Quickly George caught sight of the voices source. A young man between twenty and twenty-five stood at the top of the stairwell. The man was stark naked and beautifully proportioned. The mutant's blinded eyes seemed transfixed on the youth. The naked figure silently pointed an accusing finger at George's tormentor like a master commanding a misbehaving pet. Some type of unspoken communication vibrated between the two, George realized. George grabbed at his chance. He smacked the spinning blade onto the mutant's breastbone. The lipless mouth screamed out in pained astonishment. George pressed the saw deep. It gave him sweet satisfaction to run it like a butcher in a carcass-carving contest deep into the monsters sternum. The mutant's arm swung back to clamp George's wrists, but before they could the blade was deep into its chest. George heard the saws sound quiet as it moved from bone into the mutant's heart. Bright red blood gushed down Georges arm. He felt a vengeful glow of satisfaction as the heart quivered it's last beats against the blade. The mutant's macabre mouth worked up and down managing only a few protesting squeaks. The vice like hands let go their grip. The mutant belched a last drowned gurgle, shuddered then fell to the blood-covered floor.

George had an angry impulse to sever the dead mutant's head as it had done to the young mother and child. What's good for the goose...but George held back. It would be easy to release the controls that bound him within the unseen borders of the civilized, but best to cut his indulgence of anger to the level he'd already been tolerating. George laid back on the floor. He let calmness slowly ease his trembling. His butt where he'd hit the wall throbbed with pain but it was fat enough, he thought, to recover in a few weeks.

George sat up resting on his good half ass for a moment, then finding nothing broken he stood up. He looked down to the far stairwell where he'd seen the naked figure. Was he a psychiatric patient inadvertently left behind in the evacuation George wondered. If he was sane why would he wander the halls naked?

Probably the man had been deranged by the same agent that had transformed the thing at his feet. Maybe the sculpted figure was in the first stage of a disease that shortly would morph him into another mutant. But why did his attacker cower at the naked man? George took out his tobacco pouch and tamped down some dark Latakia into his old meerschaum. Was it just a coincidence that the man had appeared precisely at the moment when his head was about to be separated from his body? Probably, but whoever he was, it was one lucky moment of distraction for grabbing the saw. George supported his battered body on the staircase banister for a moment. Then he limped along toward the far stairwell where he'd seen the naked man. "Hello?", George called out. His voice echoed hollowly throughout the silent building. No answer. George started wincingly down the steps. There was an operating room sign on the wall with a painted finger pointing to the basement.

"Please come in Dr. Trimble," a resonant voice called out. George stepped dead in his tracks.

Since leaving Manhattan he'd used an alias. He'd been careful not to use his credit card.

Dr. Channer had never seen him. The idea of going back up to get the power saw crossed George's mind. If whatever was attached to the pleasant voice turned out to be another hideous mimic he'd want to be prepared. With his back pressed to the wall George inched down the hallway. The voice had come from the O.R. It's doors were open spilling out a pale yellow light.

"It's all right George Trimble. You have no need to fear", the voice called out again. George peeked around the door joint with rising trepidation. On the edge of the operating table sat a naked man. He seemed utterly tranquil, legs dangling, lips smiling pleasantly in a room that looked like it had taken a mortar hit. Medical equipment was scattered everywhere. The wall cabinets were knocked askew. Even the out of date kettledrum operating table lights lie scattered on the floor. A dead woman sat taped into a chair. Her head was tilted so grotesquely that George knew instantly her neck had been snapped. Into the far right corner another chancre ridden mutant huddled. It was hardly distinguishable from the creature whose heart he'd just opened. The same lipless bloody mouth. The same bulbous white blinded eyes. Only there was no howling from this one. No hint of aggression. It cowered, lamb like, as if it's only wish was to become invisible.

The naked figure turned his fair-haired head toward the cowering creature. Just that motion evoked a fearful whimper as if the glance alone had power to crush its once aggressive nature. George needed to make up his mind about the nude man quickly. He hoped to be able to assure himself that the Olympian figure was in fact, whacko.

Yet the young man's whole demeanor was somehow too serenely at ease to mesh with a chaotic mind. Except for a slight scar over the left eyebrow the mans body was classically perfect. The nude figure gestured for George to enter. George did so with a curious combination of gravity and silliness. "How do you know my name? Who are you?", George demanded, amazed by the steadiness of his own voice. The naked man waved the question away. "You are looking for Dr. Channer are you not?"

The man sat with the nonchalance of a cowhand on a prairie fence as if disconnected from the destruction around the room. Could he be a physicians assistant to Channer?

George could play a let's pretend I don't notice you're naked game and pursue a conversation as if all was normal or, he could mention the obvious right up front. George opted for the second choice. "You know my name. Could you tell me how? And also, who are you and why are you undressed?"

The fair young man smiled a slow warm smile.

"It is not important how I know. There is little time for explanation. To understand how it is I know you and why you see me as you do, is best not answered now." George's everyday ruddy complexion deepened a shade.

"Look, I'm in no mood for riddles mister, whatever your name is. That thing huddled in the corner there and you and I might be the only one's alive within twenty miles. I have to know what happened here. Is Dr. Channer dead?"

"Yes and No", the naked man answered maddeningly. What kind of game is this joker playing, George thought. Is he nuts? And if he is sane, why the verbal dance? George decided on another tack. "The diseased man there in the corner, he's afraid of you, why?"

"You have many questions George Trimble. I am not here to answer them but rather to tell you what must be done if you wish to stop the spread of these afflictions." George looked intently into the naked mans face. The man met his own eyes placidly welcoming George's stare as if in understanding of George's confusion. George assumed, had been hoping, that the nude sphinx was certifiable. That would make him just another victim of the mysterious stuff that had been loosed. But the man seemed so self contained, so untroubled. Still George wanted to control the conversation. He couldn't allow this oddly bewitching fellow to distract him from getting specific answers.

"Who are you?", George asked again but softly this time. The naked man put a finger to his lips. "You will understand shortly after I have gone George Trimble. For now I cannot answer further.

You must trust in what I say." "But...," George began to object. The man shook his head from side to side.

"The diseases you have encountered are not caused by the viruses of nature. They have their origin in a vessel left by others before man began his stay on earth." A smirk spread over George's face. "Hear what I say." There was a hint of annoyance now in the naked man's tone. "This is not the first time you have stood here before me George Trimble. Nor is it the first time I ask you to fulfill a deed that needs be done. You have forgotten much. That is how it must be." The man swept his arm dramatically in a wide arc above his head. "In the Great Circle there are universes untold. Galaxies more than the drops of rain that fall. Within the great turning God sleeps and again awakens. Past becomes future then past again. The

Great Circle carries us, you and I, where it will. Within it's turning is our living, our dying, our forgetting and our remembering." A flutter of annoying embarrassment quivered in George's chest. This melodramatic man could not be cooking on all burners. Whenever he did dress, George figured the first thing he'd put on would be his Napoleon hat. George clapped his hands slowly in mock applause.

"Heavy stuff. But I am not here to listen to a philosophy lecture."

"Quite so", the man agreed. George was finding the complacent smile increasingly irritating.

"I understand your derision George Trimble. It was to be expected. But your cynicism is of little consequence. Shortly you will know of the truth I tell. Now put aside your doubts and listen to me."

The naked man's eyes again followed an arc his fingers traced above his head. "There are honored ones within times turning who, unlike you and I, have overcome their destiny. Through their noble works they have become able to enter the windows of time where they will. To them is given the power to begin a new wheels turning." The young man turned his head to the malignant figure cowering in the corner. "See this creature here. Fragments of matter from the vessel I spoke of entered him. They were waiting to be commanded. It was his evil intent that distorted their pathway. These fragments absorbed the hideous energy of his spirit. Inexorably they molded his body itself into a reflection of his poisoned will." For a moment George thought he saw the man's eyes change color. Like a prism angled at the sun his eyes seemed to flash the spectrum. The first inkling that this enigmatic man might not be a man at all creped into George's awareness. " Know this my friend. Just as the vessels molecules have nourished evil, so they will obey goodness." The mans eyes flashed again. This time there was no mistaking the glint of colors that passed through them. George felt his lower lip tremble.

"You have a coworker, a friend who was sent before you to the place from which the disease spread. Do you not?"

"I do. Yes" George said. There was no doubt that the naked figure was referring to Colin. But how could he know? If he dared to press the man for facts and names George suspected this man could come up with all the personnel data in his office computer. "You must go to the place where a vessel lies embedded. Join your coworker there. You will find a woman. She has also absorbed the vessel's fragments. Unlike this degraded one here she does not harbor the canker of evil. The matter of life must reach its end in her so she may take her place among the honored ones."

"But"...George sputtered confusedly, a welter of questions to be answered swirling in his head. "Be silent George Trimble", the naked man commanded. "Only listen and do. Go to the place where your friend has gone. There you will find the ruins of an Ancient Temple. Within a cave below this temple the vessel rests. It is necessary that the vessel be opened once again. There are sounds that must be spoken. These you will find inscribed on the temple altar. A woman will be with your friend. It is she who must speak the temple writing." George felt his pulse thumping in his ear. He knew intuitively that he'd arrived at one of those diverging paths on life's road. The decision to go this way or that would be critical to his future. Maybe even all futures. A prompt from somewhere in his innards nudged him to take this high on his horse fellow seriously. Somehow the man with the rainbow eyes knew stuff he couldn't possibly know. There was always the option of turning on his heel and marching back to the world of normality. But was there an assumption that the reading of this altar writing would end the disease spread? The naked man didn't care to be quizzed. That was clear. "Listen and do," he'd said. With an inner grin George pictured himself telling Colin he'd arrived with a message from the oracle of Kokoori.

"You have made the right decision", the man said as if reading George's thoughts. The steady Mona Lisa smile broadened ever so slightly showing a hint of pearl perfect teeth. "The time I am able to remain here is coming to a close. Naturally you have been alarmed by the events that have befallen you here. I would have wished to allay your fears with a fuller explanation of my command. This is not possible. However, I do not ask you to follow my requests because of my words only. I have been given the power to show myself in my crossing so that you may understand." The man pointed a finger over George's shoulder. "Turn and look." In the second that it took

George to swivel around he wondered what other surprise he might
have missed when he'd walked into the operating room. Something
tied up with a pink bow or something he'd overlooked just tied up?
Lying propped up against the wall behind him was a dead man.
The chin rested on the corpse's chest so that George could only see
the top of its straw colored head. The body was clothed in a white
doctor's coat. A stethoscope tumbled half way out of a pocket onto
the floor. George's hand trembled as he reached to tilt up the chin.
Somehow he knew the face he was about to see was an impossibility.
But it was exactly the impossible the man wanted to assure him
with. George slowly lifted the dead mans chin. It was. The exact
same face even down to the forehead scar. George felt a clutch in
his throat. In cursive red script across the pocket of the white coat
was written the name Dr. Channer. George turned back to the O.R.
table. The naked man was gone.

George eyed the doorway. He looked around the room again for
an exit he might have missed. There was none. What were the odds
the naked man had an identical twin? Pretty long George thought,
but a zillion to one that the twin would have an identical scar.
George tossed around the possibility that he'd actually witnessed
the apparition the man had said happened during the crossing over.
An ability to show one's what...spirit, soul whatever, during the
interval after death. Body less entities didn't have to go out exits.
Would he find Colin if he got himself over to Barubi like the naked
man said? What about the vessel? And the woman? Would they be
there? George wondered.

George stared down at Channer's body for a few long seconds.
He stooped down and gently closed the lids over Channer's still
spectrum eyes.

George decided to do what the magical mystery man said. He'd
go to the source of the outbreak, find Colin and check it all out. If
he'd absorbed a dose of mind altering virus there was nothing to be
done about it anyhow. George looked across the O.R. to the comatose
mutant and the woman with the broken neck. Oddly the fact that
they were still in place gave him some feeling of reassurance. Still if
the chemicals in his brain had been reshuffled how would he know

that his reality now wasn't unreality, a most ingenious paradox. Real. Not real. Sane. Not Sane.

If he didn't make a decision soon George realized he could debate himself right into a rubber room. He knocked out tobacco from his un-smoked meerschaum on the metal edge of the operating table. He stuck the empty pipe between his teeth. No more of this mental ping-pong George firmly resolved. A giddy sense of adventure he hadn't felt in years began to replace his worry. With the definite decision to do what Channer said in place, George felt a kind of invigorating irresponsibility. Bold. Even carefree. George plucked an expensive fountain pen from Dr. Channer's breast pocket. He jotted down the words "read altar writings" on the back of one of his business cards. Not that he was likely to forget the directive. Still, physically writing down Channer's instructions somehow made his mission seem clean cut. George looked about the wrecked O.R. once more to satisfy himself there truly was no other way out. So where is he now George wondered. Do the constructs of here and there extensions hold for the being that was (is) Dr. Channer? George refilled his pipe. He walked up the stairwell and into the entrance alcove. It seemed he'd been in the O.R. just a short time but already the little hospital was being lit with the first glimmering of dawn. George expected to be super sore by now because of the fight but actually he felt rather limber. The electric pain in his sciatic leg had gone. Inexplicably he suddenly felt closer to thirty than sixty. George started down the entrance path then came up short. He slapped his hand over his mouth. The vines that earlier were creeping over the lower brick walk had spread across the whole front hospital grounds. They reeked of a stench George hadn't smelled since he stood beside The rotting bodies of the fallen in battle. Incredibly the vines had spread all the way to George's car. Tendrils covered the driver's side tires with slime and slithered into the window crevices. The steering wheel was covered. There wasn't another car in sight. But Dr. Channer must have had one. George went around to the rear of the hospital tiptoeing through the goo. There was a black Volvo in the lot.

There was an oval sticker on the rear license plate with a caduceus symbol. It had to be Channer's car. George walked quickly past the reeking vines. He walked down the blood splattered hallway again and back into the O.R. Reverentially, he patted down Channer's body. A roll of life savers, a comb but no keys in the coat pockets. George pulled a wallet from Channer's slacks. Forty three bucks and his drivers license. Where there's a license there should be keys. And there were. A Buxton key case with a Volvo ignition key was in the left pocket. George left out an audible sigh of relief. If he had in fact entered the land of the loonies at least he was still capable of simple logic. George pocketed the keys and went back to the car. His shoulders drooped in disappointment when he opened the door. The Volvo was a five-speed manual. For George, handling a stick shift would be like driving the space shuttle. Images of the vines nauseating him to death popped into his imagination so he knew he'd have to learn the marriage of gear shift and clutch in one solo lesson. So what if I buck and jerk the car all the way back to Port Moresby George thought. There wouldn't be much traffic anyhow. George buckled up and managed to grind the transmission into reverse. Finally after a string of curses he managed to get moving. He found second gear and redlined the Volvo in squirrel like hops toward Moresby's general direction.

He got as far as the edge of the hamlet then stalled to a shuddering stop. A wad of papers that Channer had stuck behind the visor came raining down. An open envelope plopped on his lap. With time pressing, George ordinarily would have tossed it aside but there were photographs spilling out and a curious impulse to look at them made him pause. He pulled out three small headshots of children, probably school photos he thought. George guessed their ages were in the eight to eleven year old range. They were of two boys and a girl. All had dark lively eyes and beaming smiles. Channer's kids? George didn't think so. They would have probably inherited a little of his blond hair and blue eyes. Each of these three imps had glossy dark hair. With a little guilt, George pulled out a letter from the envelope. It was written in long hand with a flowery feminine hand. A stylized logo of a pair of arms cuddling a child was embossed at the top of the page. Beneath the logo were the words Child Hope. George had never heard of the organization but assumed it was along the same lines as Save The Children. George read the letter.

Dear Doctor Channer:

I cannot thank you enough for the kindness you've shown to Juan, Pedro and Alicia. The children wanted you to have their latest pictures (which were taken in Mexico City during the shopping trip your contributions made possible), so you can see for yourself how happy they are now.

The boys are doing well in school. They no longer must go to class hungry or be ashamed of their shabby clothes. All three look forward with great anticipation to the visit you have promised them.

The photo you sent of yourself we have framed. The children keep it on the kitchen table which is where they spend more time than they used to now that there is plentiful food.

As to Alicia. She says to tell you she is not afraid of the operation. (The money for her plane ticket arrived just yesterday. Thank you).

She is excited and a little anxious. I helped her find New Guinea on the globe. She says you are the best doctor in the world and will trust you with her heart that (her words) "will love you even more after the little hole in it is fixed."

Love from all at Child Hope
Juanita Gonzalez

George eased the letter back into its envelope and put it above the visor. So you are one of those George thought. From the letter's tone it looked like Dr. Channer was the real deal. A man who didn't just wish for a better world but one who dug deep into his own pockets to make it a reality. Probably Channer would be embarrassed to know a stranger had discovered the evidence of his kindness George mused. If it was Channer who had actually done the little girls surgery he had probably just returned here when the diseases broke out. George sat for a bit absent-mindedly running this thumb back and forth over the steering wheel. An interesting line of thinking began to string together. Dr. Channer's double or spirit or whatever it was had said that the demented half human had become the way it was because of it's evil intent. How he could know its moral track record was a mighty question but given the good doctor's knack for the now you see it now you don't trick George accepted that Channer did in fact know. What exactly was it that a person had to do to be enrolled on the list of the evil ones? Savage killing done in a moment? Or perhaps simmering evil will parceled out in small steady segments over the years. A grudge nursed too long here, a resentment allowed to simmer there. On the other side, do good and ...What? George managed to find first gear again. He got the car rolling toward Port Moresby without wrecking the transmission and hoped he wouldn't have to downshift again until he was in town.

He turned on the radio. The newscaster was giving the weather report. Hot and humid coming up into the high nineties. To think it had been seventeen degrees when he left New York. George gave a little more pedal. After he was satisfied he wouldn't stall the car again he thought over Channer's words. Were they the truth? Could they be? And how was it possible he'd seen the apparitions he had? He could have sat and puzzled for hours if he'd had the time. But he promised himself to go and do as the good doctor ordered. In a few hours he should be in Moresby. On impulse he opened the envelope again, put the snapshots in his shirt pocket and patted them with a strange satisfaction.

178

CHAPTER 15

I
T WAS FIFTEEN minutes since the pale green vial of memory proteins had started their slow drip into Margo's arm. After it was certain she had slipped into a trance like state Colin laid back in a lounger next to her bed and listened as Jhanda began his Hindu word ritual. Jhanda had told Colin to concentrate on his voice as if he were under the direction of a hypnotist. Colin did so and slowly let the repetitive chant sink him into a place that made him the center of his body. He felt as if his ego had crystallized somehow. His skin surfaces felt ten feet away. The last thing Colin had seen before dropping into alpha II was Jhanda sitting rigidly on his wooden stool at the lounger's foot, with eyes raised to heaven. Roberto and Konrad looked on from seats next to the console. Now Colin heard their voices echoing unintelligibly as if the sound source was everywhere but nowhere. Still, when Jhanda spoke his words were crystal clear.

"Are you at ease Mister. Colin?", Jhanda asked solicitously. Why the old fellow had taken to calling him Mister Colin, Colin guessed had it's answer in tradition from his youth in colonial India.

"I'm fine Jhanda", Colin answered. He wasn't sure in his darkening crystalline center if his words were coming from his lips or his mind. It was the strangest sensation. Under other circumstances he could feel anxious but the disconnectedness was pleasantly mellow.

"Mister Colin I'm going to put your hand in Margo's.", Jhanda said. Colin felt Jhanda's bony fingers grip his far away wrist. He placed Colin's palm softly across Margo's. Colin's fingers, as if they had a mind of their own, closed gently around hers. An immediate sensation of soothing warmth flooded Colin's consciousness. The

179

tactile receptors in his fingers seemed to have multiplied. His head was filled with the presence of her touch. Colin smiled aware of the subtle exotic stirring. He let himself bathe in the dreamy sensation before Jhanda's words cut in again.

"You will be going on a journey with Margo now Mister Colin. You will go where she goes and see what she sees. Please to trust in the truth of what you will be shown."

"I will" Colin answered, conscious that he was purposefully sitting on the tattered remnants of doubt still rattling around in the common sense department of his brain.

Jhanda had assured him that he had the psychic ability to bridge the gap between his own mind and Margo's. It would be easy for him to verbally transfer fragments of the past she'd be seeing anew.

"Trust me," the old sage had paraphrased. So with the touch of Margo's hand saturating his senses Colin slipped further into himself.

"Colin?" With a start Colin's eyes opened. Except he understood it wasn't his physical eyes anymore but the eyes that open in a dream. It was Margo's soft voice calling to him. Her sound reverberated around him. Each time she called his name waves of blue green color washed across his vision.

"Mister Colin tell me what you see", Jhanda broke in. In contrast to Margo's, Jhanda's voice seemed more hollow than a moment before.

"I'm in some kind of tube or hollow Jhanda. I can hear Margo calling. Her voice seems to be from the far end. If this thing you talked me into has an end that is." Colin heard Jhanda's light laugh waft over him.

"Be at peace with this experience Mister Colin. All will be well. Margo's memories have been strengthened now. Let us hope to see a full picture instead of the fragments she has seen. When you hear Margo call you must think, I wish to go where she is. You will find her." Colin squeezed Margo's hand tightly. He watched the colors swirl around him blending into a whirlpool of vibrant blues. In her trance was Margo seeing the same display? he wondered. Did she know who held her hand? She was already deep into her trance when he laid next to her. With her chestnut hair framing her flawless face against the white pillow she made Colin think of some medieval princess in one of Grimm's Tales. She *was* beautiful.

"Colin come to another place with me," Margo's voice whispered. Colin raised his head to see what was at the tunnels end. Except that he couldn't be sure if the head he raised was his own or a dream one. Then suddenly he realized he'd lost tactile contact with the lounger. He felt himself suspended, floating toward a disc of glowing creamy white color at the tunnels end. The tunnel walls seemed to expand and contract in long lazy waves. He was headed slowly toward the glowing disc.

"What is happening now Mister Colin?" Jhandas words repeated down the tube like an echo off alpine peaks.

"I heard Margo tell me to come to another place Jhanda. There's a vibrant white circle at the end of the line. It gets brighter as I get closer."

"It will open for you if you wish it Mister Colin...and only for you." The old mans words crackled with emotion. "The space you are in I have seen too Mister Colin. The unknown place with its shifting colors, I have traveled before you toward the lands Margo will reveal. But it was my lot that I should be a guide only. To go so far and no farther. The disc you see protects most who should not see what fate has decided for them."

As Jhanda's voice reverberated Colin watched the passageways colors cease their blending dance. Suddenly the walls gelled into solidity. From somewhere outside Jhanda shifted his chair. Colin could hear the rustle of his robes sounding off the now more solid circumference with amplified clarity. "The circle at the end. How far is it now Mister Colin?"

"If my judgment is still okay, I would say fifty yards."

"Very well. Margo is in a time among times Mister Colin. If you wish to be with her you have only to will it or rather, if you wish to keep past and future unseen you may choose that also. You must decide now. What is it you wish?"

"Should I tap my ruby shoes Jhanda?", Colin asked glibly. It was comforting to know he hadn't lost his sense of humor.

"Ruby shoes Mister Colin? Please explain."

"Forget it Jhanda. Just a story about a little girl and her dog trying to get home." The cream colored disc loomed larger now. The surrounding colors had faded leaving the circle in blackness. Colin imagined the lab as it must be right now. Jhanda sitting on his stool, Roberto and Konrad leaning forward in their chairs in anticipation, inches away and yet far beyond Colin's horizon.

From somewhere beyond the translucent disc Margo's voice whispered with beguiling sweetness.

"Come with me into our other time." Other time. Other time? Colin thought. What was it Margo had said in the ships garden? Colin tried hard to remember her exact words but couldn't. Something about kindred spirits choosing their destinies through various times. Colin stared hard at the glowing circle then began to walk toward it. Up close it wasn't as solid as it seemed. It looked rather like a series of sheer back lit veils. Cautiously, Colin reached his finger out and touched the disc. Instantly it erupted in a blinding flash of light. Colin reflexively covered his eyes. With the image of the disc seared on his retinas he heard and felt a rushing sound of wind pass over him. He stood stock still waiting for whatever forces he'd disturbed to recede. Colin blinked then looked around him. Astonished he found himself standing in a field of grass and wild flowers. An afternoon sun hanging over a line of distant snow capped peaks cast a golden glow over the plain. Colin turned around. Faintly he could see a far off village dotted with a few small white stucco homes. A tiny figure leading a flock of sheep or goats ambled past the village perhaps a mile off.

Colin turned back. In front of him were two copses of olive trees. Between them a path wandered out of sight down the far side of a hill. Just visible across the hilltop was the roof of a gleaming white marble building. Colin felt his blood race. He'd indeed stumbled on the impossible. All he was seeing he'd seen before. He was sure of it. In some uncanny way he was remembering too. To ask himself how this was happening wasn't really as pressing as the fact that it *was* happening.

The memory enzymes Margo had absorbed somehow had transferred their power to him. From a side path Colin hadn't noticed, a male figure dressed in a white belted tunic and sandals stepped out from behind the trees. The figure turned and looked directly at Colin with a curious gaze as if an unseen person had

182

called out his name. The figure paused, gave an I guess not shrug, then started down the hillside toward the temple's rear. Colin felt a wave of excitement clutch him. The young man was himself.

"Jhanda I see myself here", Colin said. "I've been transported to somewhere in ancient Greece I think. I've been reduced to a pair of invisible eyes. I don't think I can be seen."

"Follow the man who once you were Mister Colin," Jhanda's voice instructed. Colin floated to the ridge at the top of the glen. He looked down to see a magnificent Doric Temple close to a Sea. A long crescent shaped beach curved away to the horizon. Fading sunlight shone through the fluted columns casting orderly shadows on the surrounding grounds. Colin watched his sandal footed self walk down a stone path toward the front portico, and with only the desire to follow, found himself walking along side his past persona.

"Some part of me is allowing me to move wherever I want Jhanda. In some way I'm seeing a part from a perspective outside of what my eyes could have taken in. a kind of enhanced recollection. I remember this place. It was real." Colin's normal sense of what was now and what was then had melded into a feeling of eternal present. It was as if past and present existed simultaneously here. Colin watched himself turn the corner of the temple's porch. He hesitated for a moment before willing his eyes to follow. Somehow he knew what he would see. A semicircle of dancers and musicians waited for him. Along the edges of the Temple's sides, flowers, the same pastel streaked blooms he'd first seen Margo hold in the ERSEVs deck grew in orderly rows. At the Temple's front stood a group of young women playing on double flutes and lyres some ancient melody Colin could not hear. There were dancers too, a dozen in all, swaying gracefully to the soundless song. Colin watched himself walk with measured steps to the center of the performers. He turned in a formal gesture to face them.

"Mister Colin what is happening now," Jhanda's voice sounded in his head.

"It's the same as in the painting Jhanda. I'm at the steps of the same Temple. The celebrants are facing me for some sort of ritual."

"So then Margo was painting the past, hers and yours Mister Colin. Please go on."

"Two young women are approaching now from among the dancers. One is carrying a woven basket.

The other has a scarlet toga." "What is in the basket?"

"I can't see Jhanda...and for the moment I can't remember. My eyes are closed. The girl with the toga is removing my tunic. She takes my dusty sandals and puts new ones on my feet. I'm standing still, nude. My arms are at my side. Now the toga is being pinned at my shoulders with a bronze clasp...I open my eyes and bow my head...Another young woman is handing me the basket."

"And what is within it?"

"A glass flask holding some liquid." From somewhere far behind, Jhanda's muddled words filtered through to Colin. There was a pause.

"Mister Colin Roberto says the Ancient Greeks did not have glass."

"Well tell Roberto that this bunch has at least one bottle. It's inches from my nose and what's more it has metric marks on it. Okay, now I'm turning with the vial toward the steps. The musicians are playing. Of course I can't hear."

"In Margo's painting a man holds something out to her we cannot see. Is there any doubt that it is the basket?"

"No Jhanda. It is the same event." Jhanda began to speak but Colin hushed him. "Wait, Margo is coming from within the Temple. She is stopping at the top step speaking to me." Colin felt a breathless charge of recognition flood through him. "It's the same. Exactly the same Jhanda."

"Go on Mister Colin."

"Margo is dressed just as in the painting. I'm following her now into the Temple interior. The others have fallen into a double line behind me."

"Mister Colin can you describe..." was all that Colin heard before Jhanda's voice trailed off into silence. Suddenly his vision deteriorated into an impenetrable gray fog. Colin could see nothing. "Jhanda I don't know what happened" Colin spoke inside his head.

"It's Margo." Jhanda's voice was a bare whisper. "There was a moment here of heart change. Dr. Volger says it's correcting itself now but the mental effort she is using saps her energy. We must complete the remembrance soon." Colin thought back to his conversation with Konrad on the ERSEV's deck. How he'd learned that each psychic episode was linked with a weakening of her health. She'd been in a metabolic see-saw ever since absorbing the ellipse particles. As the molecules in the particles gave, they also took away. Psychic power paid for in paralysis and heart arrhythmia.

"Mister Colin, Dr. Volger says you should not be anxious. Margo is stabilized for now." No sooner had Jhanda's words faded then Colin felt the reassuring squeeze of Margo's hand. Her way of telling him that in spite of her fragile state she wanted him to go on with their centuries old remembrance. She had been totally confident, even blasé in her conviction their journey into the past would help answer the questions of the ellipse's source. But would her powers be up to seeing him through this recurrence before her health shattered completely?

And how did this vision from the past connect with the reality of the machine that even now was threatening to sow more violence?

Colin slammed the common sense questions back into the deep of his mind. His penchant for hardnosed thinking was a tough habit to break. He reminded himself that he'd made the decision to go with the can't be true and he would stick with it even if getting his mind wrapped around the everyday world he'd be going back to became problematic.

The sensation of Margo's hand in his began to strengthen. The opaque gray surrounding Colin began to evaporate like morning mist over a warming lake. With his inner sight clear again he saw the procession had ended with the dancers and singers flanking the staircase into the Temple's interior. The steps, made of pink tinged marble, rose up to well above Colin's line of sight. At the top Margo stood before a pair of gleaming tall bronze doors.

"Jhanda I'm back again inside the Temple. I'm walking up a staircase to an inner chamber. I'm holding the vial basket in front of me. Margo is waiting at the top of the chamber."

"We can go on for only a few more moments Mister Colin. Quickly. Tell all you can please."

"I'm at the top of the steps. Margo is smiling at me." What Margo did next was unexpected but exhilarating.

She took the basket, stepped forward and kissed Colin gently. Was this some part of theTemple ritual he wondered? Whether it was or not made no difference. Colin felt a rush of warmth, familiar and tinged with the erotic. In that moment Colin felt he knew Margo totally. The only time he spent with her had been those couple of hours in the garden, yet with the touch of her lips he felt he fathomed her uniqueness. It was if in one concentrated burst he knew her ways, could predict her whims as only those in love for a very long time are able to do. Colin's heart began to race. Vaguely, he could sense the touch of her body on his own. His impulse was to break the Temple protocol, take her hand and rush away to someplace where he could just be with her, away from the demands of whatever ancient rite he was a part of. But how could he, even if the ritual would permit? He wasn't really there at all. He was just a floating pair of eyes watching, following his old self like some wisp of a ghost. Still Colin's urge to talk with her, be with her was overwhelming. He ached to break into this unfolding past, to make it present again and fill himself with her.

"Mister Colin, only five more minutes. We must bring Margo out." Jhanda's words seized Colin with an icy grip he angrily wanted to cast away.

He struggled to reconnect with his physical place in the lab.

"Jhanda, there are two attendants, guards maybe, approaching. Margo nods to them. They are bringing torches to light two large stone kraters that stand next to the inner chamber doors. Now the doors are opening.

The others remain outside turning their eyes away. It's as if this part of the ceremony is not allowed for them. Margo is entering the chamber. I follow. There is an altar...Jhanda this is incredible."

"What is it Mister Colin?"

"It's the same Jhanda. The carvings on this altar are the same as those on Margo's sketches. The same mountain and underneath the two sun symbols." Colin began to ask himself how it was possible when Jhanda broke in again.

"What is at the mountaintop Mister Colin?"

"The figure is changed here Jhanda. In the sketch she has Brahma at the top of the peak. Here I'm almost sure it is a carving of Zeus. One hand holds thunderbolts and the other a cup. Maybe it symbolizes the same potion Brahma is offering in Margo's drawing. There is even a time circle surrounding the mountain."

Colin watched Margo place the vial with its pale blue liquid on the altar. His other self walked over and stood next to her. She closed her eyes and spoke brief soundless words. Slowly the marble floor behind the altar parted. Colin was astonished to see a silver ellipse rise fluidly from a hidden space below the Temple foundation. The top opened with the same eerie motion he'd seen in the cave. This time there were no quivering threads to be seen. Instead the inside of the machine glowed with several rows of lights. There was no doubt it was a duplicate of the Barubi device. Colin recalled how Konrad had told him of the isotope nitrogen atoms in the machines DNA atoms not from earth but some light years away galaxy. How did this all hold together Colin wondered? The ellipse, her powers, the radio scope? Before he had time to ponder what was before him, Jhanda's high pitched voice cut in.

"Pandit Konrad says it is too dangerous for Margo to remain in her trance state. We are bringing her out now." No sooner had Jhanda's words sounded in Colin's head than the clean colors of the inner chamber began to washout. The gathering gray mist that had earlier blocked Colin's vision returned again. In a few seconds the entire chamber was hidden. Still one part of the altar remained in clear view. The altar sun symbols were unobscured by the gathering fog. The two spheres stood out in Colin's inner eyes as if purposefully spotlighted. Had Margo saved the last of her psychic energy to pinpoint the two discs? Instinctively Colin felt she wanted him to concentrate on the carvings above all he'd recalled. With a slow acceleration the discs began to spin about each other. Gradually they gathered speed until they fused into a single blinding ball of fire. The roaring flames engulfed Colin yet he had no fear. In a moment he was at the center of the cauldron but remained unscathed.

He realized he was in another time now, far removed from the Arcadian groves of ancient Hellas . Then, like being violently prodded from a profound sleep, Colin abruptly was back in the P4 lab, his hand still folded around Margo's. She had wanted him to see further into their Temple ritual he knew but her flagging energy had made it necessary for Konrad to cut the session short. Colin pressed his fingers lightly on his eyelids. He waited until his eyes adjusted to the labs lights.

"It seems Margo took you on quite a journey" Konrad said.

Konrad was standing with Roberto along the other side of Margo's bed. She was breathing slowly in what looked for now like a restful sleep. Jhanda still sat next to Colin, the same serene look spread across his face.

"I was there. We knew each other over two thousand years ago," Colin half mumbled to no one in particular.

"We're stunned of course. The implications of a prior existence are tremendous," Roberto spoke up. His hands were thrust sheepishly in his pockets. "But we need to get at the source of the ellipse, what happened two million years ago. What the telescope was all about. We didn't get any info on that."

"What Margo has shown us will reveal these things in time.", Jhanda intoned with an unperturbed assurance.

"But how Jhanda? We were hoping for solid information", Roberto implied with more than a hint of disappointment. Konrad remained silent. Roberto was right of course, Colin thought. The whole reason for the protein synthesis had been to stimulate Margo's memory. To get a picture of what had gone on at the cave site ages ago. Still what filled Colin's head was his affection for Margo. Colin had half a motion to tell Roberto to go to hell. That what was most significant was the discovery of their intimacy.

A door opening to another existence had unexpectedly been unlocked. That's what he wanted to explore. The rest be damned.

"Look Roberto, before you brought Margo out of her memory, she had me see a concentrated image of the sun symbols on the altar. I was locked onto them. They began to rotate around each other. There's a reason she had me break away from the Temple ceremony to fix on that. The concrete facts we all want have to come out of that image. Roberto, let's take a look at your drawings again. The sun symbols, if that's what they are, are both on the Barubi altar and the Greek Temple,"

"Sure, but what about the machine?" Konrad waved Roberto's question away.

"We must trust that the ellipse was there in ancient Greece Roberto," Konrad said. "The Greeks hardly put it in the Temple. If we follow all the lines of speculation we could be guessing for days. I think it best to follow Colin's instinct. Concentrate on the altar carvings." Konrad gestured for Colin to take a chair next to his and Roberto's. Jhanda remained solicitously close to Margo. Roberto plopped the easel among them with the sketch showing the altar carving. Colin glanced at Margo's vital sign monitors. Gratefully he saw all were holding safely at least for the moment.

"Roberto, Margo said that anything in black here shows the cave altar as it looks now and the blue is your interpretation of what has been eroded. Is that right?" Colin asked.

"Yes. Margo asked me to make a reasonable estimation of what I thought would have finished the original. I compared it with hundreds of Khmer carvings before I took my shot at it."

"Colin you said the Greek Temple altar had two sun symbols on it," Konrad put in. Colin nodded. He'd told Jhanda that the altars were identical. Strange that the sketch clearly showed the cave altar with one sun symbol. Roberto had added his small blue dots around it.

"You've put in these points around the sun symbol Roberto. Just decoration?", Konrad asked.

"I don't know if the points already in place had any meaning or not." Roberto stood and run his fingers around the edge of the sun sign. "You can see from where I put in the black that only the right hand quadrant around the sun hadn't been eroded. I put in the blue dots in the other three sections for mainly aesthetic reasons. The Khmer artists wouldn't have left the carving unbalanced."

"You mean with the dot symbols all in one corner and not surrounding the sun," Konrad said.

"Sure. Whether they signify anything real or not, the original would have the points completely around."

"Balance" Colin mumbled under his breath. He stared intently at the sketch. He stepped up next to Roberto. "In the Greek Temple there were two suns where the right side of the Barubi altar is broken off. There could have been another sun right Roberto?"

"Probably. I was going to get Margo's view about adding one as a matter of fact."

"Let's assume before the earthquake cracked off the end that there were two suns on the Khmer altar."

"So Colin you're saying this one and the Greek Temples were the same?" Konrad urged. "Well, the mountain image was the same I'm sure of that."

"Were there any points bordering the suns on the Greek altar?", Roberto queried. Colin shook his head. He was tired. Finding it hard to think clearly.

"I don't know Roberto. The suns spinning overwhelmed me. There may have been."

"If we accept that the symbols have been eroded from our memories and that they came up from the subconscious of the Greeks and later the Khmers, it would be surprising if they were remembered in detail," Konrad said.

"Roberto sketch in a second sun with the points around it too," Colin ordered. Roberto considered the directive momentarily then with deft strokes drew in the circumference of a twin sun. In a moment he had the area surrounding a second sun covered with blue dots. Konrad bounded from his chair.

"I see it. How could we have missed it?" Roberto stood perplexed twirling his pencil between his fingers. "Your identifying logo Roberto. You called it a flag of origin." Roberto's face registered confusion. "The etching on the cave ellipse Roberto. You said it was some kind of identifying logo. "It is. Here it is," Konrad continued.

"Oh shit," Roberto muttered. "I was too close to the forest to see the trees."

"Please. What is it," Jhanda asked. He'd been so still Colin had forgotten he was still in the lab. "Jhanda hasn't seen the etching Colin," Konrad explained. "Jhanda, the sun symbols Colin described in the Greek Temple. There is an etching nearly identical. Two spheres surrounded by a field of points."

"And the Barubi Temple. The same image here" Roberto said, tapping the sketch with his pencil. "So then" Jhanda intoned. "We see why Margo has chosen to bring forth this image of the past. She has shown us that which links both past and future. Now we must find the meaning of this symbol." "Thank you." Konrad placed his hand on the old seer's shoulder. "I believe we may have unlocked it's meaning.

There is a critical connection with the telescope your insight has led us to find." Konrad caught Colin's and Roberto's eyes as he spoke. Colin understood that the three younger men got the linkage.

"Jhanda we think the Temple symbols and the etching are the same. The symbols represent real suns somewhere in the heavens. The other points must be background stars. The telescope remnant that you guided me to was probably aimed at that part of the sky." Colin said.

"It's a good guess that visitors from those stars gave us symbols carved in metal and stone so that we might contact them" Konrad added.

"Then when the Khmers carved this sun pair they hadn't seen the etching on the ellipse buried beneath their altar," Roberto theorized. The image must have come to them through subconscious memory."

"One wonders how much of creativity has its source in forgotten worlds...but that's a thought for another day," Konrad remarked. "The task at hand is to search for a habitable planet near to a set of double stars," he continued. "Roberto bring the camcorder photos up on the monitor."

"What photos?", Colin asked.

"I only chopped off the breccia rock covering the etching two days ago. We should see the sphere in a moment" Konrad replied. Colin felt a strange combination of rage and hopefulness as the photos popped onto the screen. The gruesome image of Ed Lippincott lying at the cave entrance played tug of war with the entrancing vistas Margo's recollection had opened up. The photos were of the entire upper half of the cave's ellipse. Roberto zoomed in so that the etching filled the monitors screen.

"Do we have the means to match the etchings star field with ones already mapped?", Colin asked. That would be like nailing down a specific pattern of sand grains among all the world's beaches he thought.

"Not quite," Roberto chirped. "If we had to scan for a match in all the double star systems we'd be in trouble. But we're going to eliminate ninety percent of the sky. We'll have the computer analyze only the binary star systems in the sky sector facing the cave front."

"Where the telescope was aimed," Colin said.

"Right, but we have to hope the stars have already been photographed and cataloged through an optical scope."

"Roberto we're assuming the etching stars are laid out the way they'd look through a reflector or refractor correct?", Konrad asked.

"Yes. So what we'll do is search through old photos from observatories like Lick and Palomar to find our match" Roberto answered. Colin looked up at Margo's readouts. They still were in safe zones. Assured that she wasn't worsening he focused back on the monitor. "First thing is we'll find out how many binary stars are on record," Roberto said. His fingers ran deftly over the keyboard. In a second the number 53,146 jumped up on the screen. "Now we make another assumption," Roberto added.

"What?", Colin asked.

"Well, that this bunch, take or leave a few pairs, are dispersed around evenly more or less. If that's the case in just the sector in front of the cave we should have a rough figure of about 1500 binaries. One could be our match. That's taking the earth's seasonal orientation into account of course."

"Of course," Colin repeated. Fifteen hundred down from 53,000, not a bad start he thought.

"Now I need some ascension and declination numbers for stars in the Centaurus box. The constellation is in front of the cave entrance right now. We need to make this as easy as possible," Roberto said. Colin knew that Roberto was looking for the numbers that would give star positions like latitude and longitude numbers for earth. Right ascension numbers told an astronomer where in the heavens an object was located right to left. Declination gave the position from the horizon to ninety degrees overhead. By fixing the R.A. and declination figures any of the fifteen hundred binaries outside those coordinates in Centaurus could be ignored. Almost instantly the figures were on the computer screen.

Recommemded	50,85° to 52,04°
Ranges =	8 hr 32m to 8 hr 77m

"Good Roberto. Now how many binaries within those boundaries?", Konrad asked. Roberto typed. The number 1306 came up.

"1306," Colin whistled. "Not far off your estimate." Roberto and Konrad grinned.

"The last step in our interrogation now", Konrad said. "Of the 1306 can we find out how many had their photos published in the older journals?" The screen stayed blank for a moment. Then flashed 387. "Hell of a lot easier to work with than 53,000" Konrad said. He patted the computer as if it were a dutiful pooch bringing in the morning paper. "Here's the tricky part. Asking the computer to match my jiggling camera shots with the photos of the 387," Konrad said. "Then again the digitals are flat and the etching is on a rounded surface. Can we get around that Roberto?"

"I think so," Roberto said assuringly. He brought the etching photographs back up on the screen again. Colin watched as Roberto divided the pictures into subdivisions, his fingers tacking rapidly over the keyboard. "I'm telling the computer to lay the photo's 387 pieces over the etching pattern in quick sequences. "Hopefully we'll find a match." Colin and Konrad watched intently.

"Come on baby" Colin thought to himself urging the computer on as if it had a life of its own. Then, after what seemed like forever the screen lit up with:

MATCH - PROBABILITY . 9802
BINARY SYSTEM – CONSTELLATION CENTAURUS
COORDINATES Dec. 51.17° R.A. 8h 46m

Colin could feel the tension in the lab subside. "Wait. There's more," Roberto said.

IDENTITY - PSR 175 + 08
KULGARA AUSTRILIA
NOV. 18, 1940

"It's a pulsar. Two stars are orbiting each other out there and one is sending out a radiation beacon with every revolution. Hold on a second." Roberto click clacked away. "Damn. Look at this.

When NASA sent up the Rossi explorer a frame dragger was found out beyond PSR 175 + 08. Way, way out." Colin and Konrad looked quizzically at Roberto. "A frame dragger is a tremendous gravity puller. It's so strong it distorts the space time next to it. It's almost as if the pulsar was placed there to guide the eye toward it." Roberto caught the looks of incredulity on the men's faces. "Just a wild thought" Roberto said. Colin felt a confident surge. His eyes rested on the match probability number. So the etching on the ellipse was a copy of a star system many light years away. The double suns Margo had burned into his mind were actually out there, circling one another as they'd been for eons.

What would McClure have said to this? Colin thought, a definite correspondence between the etching and the stars. How about a hearty dose of the not possible Dr. McClure? Or, are you not up to a brain stretcher of quite this size?

"Roberto, wasn't Mt. Simpson's refractor one of the smaller ones set up in the Margrave Range?", Konrad questioned. There had been two reflecting telescopes set up in the low Central Australian hills in the forties he knew. Whether the Kulgara scope had been one of them he wasn't sure.

"Yes Simpson's and Mt. Skeel. The war stopped work on both. Their domes were never completed."

"Then the pulsar photo could be one of only a few taken before they closed down. The pictures could have sat in some file until long after the war," Konrad suggested.

"But even so if an intelligent signal was in the pulsar's beacon shouldn't the scopes have caught it?" Colin put in.

"Probably not Colin," Roberto said. "Remember we're assuming another intelligence out there would radiate on the twenty one centimeter hydrogen wavelength. A wave of that frequency would be swallowed up by the x-ray energies the pulsar throws out. It wasn't as easy to separate those bands in prewar days as it us now," Roberto said.

"Well if a meaningful signal is still coming we'll catch it this time," Konrad replied. "Polski has the stuff to sort through any wavelength the pulsar is sending out, from miles long down to the size of an atom's nucleus," he continued.

"Can you bring up the old black and white pulsar picture?", Colin asked.

"Oh of course. I overlooked the obvious," Roberto said. In a moment the pulsar was on the screen.

The Simpson photograph was of excellent quality, crisp and sharp.

"Can we see them side by side?", Colin asked. Again Roberto clacked away. A screen came up divided in half. On the left was Konrad's still shot of the ellipse's etching, on the right the Mt. Simpson's photograph. Roberto overlapped them. The match was near perfect.

Colin thought the photograph could have been one of any number of patches of the heavens, each one holding multitudes of monstrous blazes of power. But this picture before him was not of just any random wedge of the cosmos. This one was special. Somewhere among these stars was a planet where beings of surpassing intelligence had built a culture so evolved they'd been able to travel here at a time when man was just starting to descend from the trees. They had left a machine behind intended to bestow enormous gifts. Somehow it had become flawed, capable of pouring out hideous diseases as well. Was there a message from PSR 175 +08? And if there was would it encode the remedy to the flawed machine? Colin's minds eye wandered back to Margo leading him down toward the ellipse again, the steps inviting them to climb up then into the machine. Had they gone inside it then? If so, what then?

Colin turned his head to the lady who'd captured him, who had lived another life with him. He would take her to *this* ellipse soon, as Jhanda had instructed.

This time he would enter it with Margo. And there would be... what?

CHAPTER 16

WALTER POLSKI LEANED back in his chair. His legs were crossed and up on his desk. Rhythmically, he kneaded his aching thighs.

The control room that ran the radio telescope was small, on the order of a road stop restroom. For Walter it was a cozy retreat he felt very much at home in. Except tonight it seemed oppressive. Ever since finishing dinner, a nauseous pain had settled in his stomach. The roast had tasted like cardboard. Maybe he was getting the flu. There was a sweaty film on his skin and his legs throbbed. Polski wrenched the door open of a small Kenmore refrigerator next to his desk. He always kept it stocked with an assortment of twinkies, doughnuts and other assorted junk food. He picked a half finished bag of nachos, grabbed a fistful and stuffed them in his mouth. His face screwed up at the unexpected bitter taste. Polski spit the wad into a wastebasket. As he was leaning over his eye caught a balled up fax he'd tossed in the wastebasket earlier. He hesitated a moment then picked up the soiled paper with two fingers. He plopped his feet up on his desk and for a few moments played toss and catch against the wall with the coordinates fax. He'd finished his map of his quasar field sooner than he'd expected. For the first time in weeks the radio telescope was idle. It wouldn't take too long to crank the big disc over the ten degrees into Centaurus. Not that there would be anything significant at Volgers' target of course. He'd heard the rumors about psychics on the ERSEV payroll. Just what the mind readers were supposed to do Walter wasn't clear about. But anyone who'd listen to those phonies in the first place wouldn't be past listening for messages from space.

Polski flattened out the balled up memo on his desk. Declination 51.17°, right ascension 8 hours 46 minutes. "These are the exact coordinates" Volger had scribbled at the top of the star map fax. The object was supposed to be a pulsar. Somebody aboard the research ship must have clued Volger in that it wasn't smart to ask a radio scope astronomer to do a random search, even one that eliminated ninety nine percent of sky arc. But, if there *was* anything to see at Volger's coordinates and another scope picked it up first, Walter knew he'd have some explaining to do. Dr. Volger might be strange but he wasn't stupid. He'd suspect rightly that Polski and his Coolabundi scope had never bothered to search at 51.17 – 8.46. Polski felt a chill. He grabbed a warm cardigan from a clothes tree next to his desk. The control room was a perfect seventy two degrees but it felt nearer to forty. A suspicion that his shivering might have a connection with the jelly globules outside passed through his head but he decided he was only alarming himself. There were probably flu viruses in Australia as odd as the animals. That was all it was he felt sure. Walter punched a series of keys on the telescope's control panel. Outside the scope's motors hummed softly. The move to lock in Volgers coordinates took less than a minute. Polski flicked on the audio switch.

If there were spikes of radiations from a pulsar he would hear a burst of bass sound with every star revolution. He didn't much care if the supposed pulsar was five light years away or five thousand. Polski had never locked on to a pulsar, but knew its radiation should be coming in on the x-ray band. If there was any kind of intelligent signal, whoever or whatever was sending it would be using hydrogen's twenty one cm. wavelength. Polski adjusted his receiver to sort out the x-ray energy from the wimpy Hydrogen 21 and shut the control room door behind him. As he started back to his cottage, he looked back at the telescope dish and was stunned. Viscous vines had overgrown the control room walls almost to the roof. Polski stood open mouthed at the profusion of them. They clung like gray leafless ivy, intent it seemed on engulfing his little blockhouse. The skunk cabbage smell assaulted Walter's nostrils with a sharp edge that stirred up the queasiness he'd been feeling since dinner. The vines had been little runners a few hours ago. How could any plant grow this fast? Polski side stepped the ballooning jelly globules and walked the couple hundred feet to the telescope. Vines had netted their way from the disc's base up to the bowl itself. Some of them were entangled around the amplifier straining at the disc's center as if determined to pull it down. Walter had an urge to pull them down with his own hands.

Along with the psychic dabbling, Walter had heard about edgy genetics experiments the ERSEV chief had going on. Were the plants a result of something let loose from the ship?

Whatever the explanation it didn't take away Walters fright. He tried to force himself to stay calm. A wrenching metal against metal sound overhead blew his try away. A tearing shear on the scopes metal lattice sent a jolt of pain through his head.

"Get off. Get off my scope!", Walter screamed at the creeping slimy vines. His outrage at the effrontery of the plants to attack *his* scope trumped his fear. At least a dozen cross girders at the disc bowl were shrieking their shrill metallic protest as the vines pulled at them. Polski clenched his jaw in fury. It was *his* scope the vines were punishing. On paper the telescope belonged to ERSEV. But Polski had lived with the big disc for over fifteen years. It had been his to use or abuse in his lonely outpost. His to talk to (as he sometimes did). The telescope had become an extension of himself, almost like another hand. Whatever the scope achieved he achieved. When it failed he failed. Walter Polski took any threat to its functioning very personally. Whatever the vines were or wherever they came from he didn't care. He wanted to rip them out by the roots. They'd grown much too large for that...but there was gasoline in the shed. He'd burn the hell out of them and then put out the embers with his fire extinguisher. Polski's heart felt suddenly cheery at the thought. Burn Baby Burn. He could already hear the crack and pop of the stinging blisters as their juices turned to vapor. Walter forced a jog back to the shed. His legs were trembling now but he could ignore that. He grabbed four ten gallon cans, plunked them in a wheelbarrow and ran them back to the scope. He was panting from the exertion but walked around the base of the scope searching for the roots of the thickest vines. There were three. A trio of thick stems rose up from gnarled clumps along the ground. All of the branches that were attacking his dish radiated out from those three. Walter hurriedly untwisted the gas can caps and splashed the eighty-nine octane all over the thick stems. He soaked them with two cans full, all he needed for a complete drenching. Walter reveled in the wonderful gassy smell. He poured the contents of the other two in a circle around the scopes concrete base. He gave extra splashes to any nodules that were fruiting new runners. Five minutes of burning should do it. Satisfied he hadn't left any spots dry, Walter pushed through the web of tendrils that hung over the control room door. He went inside and picked the fire extinguisher from the wall. He grabbed a pack of wooden blue tips from the shelf, limped out again, then stood for a moment glaring at the stinking vines. A devilish smirk played over Walter's face. This was going to be fun. He held one of the matches in front of his eyes. He twirled it slowly between his fingers. "Are we ready for a little excitement? Hmmm," he spoke aloud to the vines. "Hot time in the old town?" Walter threw his head back and laughed. "Wherever you came from the jokes on you, you mothers." Walter stepped back a few feet and struck the match. He tossed it into a puddle of high octane. A loud swoosh sounded like a dozen charcoal burners lighting at once. In seconds the vines were ablaze, their dripping skins quickly turning black. The flames soared well above the control rooms roof thirty feet into the night sky. Billows of thick black smoke blew off tops of the orange flames, wafting through the metal webbing before disintegrating into the Australian evening. "Beautiful" Walter muttered. "Chop them off at the knees." Walter stepped in as close as the heat would allow. The ugly globules were swelled to pumpkin size. He clapped his hands gleefully as the balls burst like pricked water balloons. The rank juices inside sizzled as the flames continued their work.

Walter looked up at the vines pulling at the metal lattice. He could see them slowly unwind one by one and drop defeated onto the steaming ground. He felt positively smug. Scorching the plants had worked even better than he'd expected. Walter would let the fire burn a while longer, put it out then clean up the debris after a good nights sleep.

He'd do a body count on the big vines in the morning. Walter walked around the circle where he'd splashed the gas. The vines were just glowing red embers now with only a few dying campfire flames left struggling among the last holdouts. Walter pulled the safety ring on the fire extinguisher. He aimed the nozzle at the closest bonfire and squeezed the handle. Nothing. He squeezed again, then again. "Shit." No rush of CO_2 was forth coming. Walter worked the handle feverishly until his hand froze up. He looked at the green inspection tag. Due for recharging in February 2009 it said. "You mother." Since nobody would hike out to Coolabundi just to recharge the extinguisher he was supposed to have done it himself. He hadn't. Walter's smug attitude withered like the dying vines. Basics, Walter basics. He hadn't attended to them. And more alarmingly, smoke was drifting up from the control room roof. In his rage he had failed to take into account one elemental fact. Although the walls of the control room were concrete, the roof and floor were made of wood. Old wood. Walter watched in rising panic as ember snowflakes from the fried vines wafted down onto the bone-dry roof. Stunned he let the useless extinguisher slip from his fingers. The first small flickers of flame were breaking out on the roof. "The Quasar data," Walter thought. All the stuff I've worked on is in there. All my proof! His tongue flicked over his suddenly dry lips in high tech panic. Walter had to think of something fast, but what? There was the garden hose on the side of the cottage. What was it, thirty feet long maybe? He couldn't remember the last time he'd used it. Its stream wouldn't hit the control room walls let alone the roof. Walter felt a commanding urge to do *something*. Then, from inside the speakers blared. Low bass tones thudded against the control room doors. The volume was at its highest setting. Something was coming in from the Centarus coordinates and it was not your normal pulsar signal. It sounded like a heavy metal drummer going berserk on twin bass drums. There was a definite pattern in the pulses. Walter managed to sit on his growing panic. He must think clearly now. He needed to get inside but the roof was nearly half engulfed in flames. There would be no saving his precious quasar data Walter understood. How foolhardy would it be to go inside? There was no smoke coming from the crack under the door. If he could get in for just a moment he could salvage some records and get a look at the pulsar wave pattern. Losing his galaxy data might not be all that bad. Not if he turned out to be the first astronomer to nail down an E.T. contact. Walter pushed through the blackened tendrils overhanging the door. The doorknob was still cool. He pushed the door open and stood back lest a rush of flame should greet him. But inside there was as yet only a haze of light smoke. Nothing so thick he couldn't manage. He put his handkerchief over his face and went inside. He guessed he'd have three minutes before he'd have to get out. The steady sound from the amplifier was deafening. Walter could feel the tattoo beat vibrate in his chest. He waved a free arm around to clear his view. His eyes were already teared up, but there was no mistaking what he could still see on the readouts. The computer graph showed a long series of spikes all in the twenty one centimeter range. The spikes were in alternating bands very close, spread out, then close again. "Son of a bitch they've done it," Walter thought. Below the wave pattern the screen read.

> Distortion Zero — Polarized.

Those words told him he was in fact receiving a communication from a cosmic intelligence. Suddenly Walter felt terribly responsible. The scope was reeling in a twenty one centimeter signal with no distortion. Whoever was sending the signal obviously had the technology to push twenty-one through all the interstellar free electron fuzz. And the frequencies were marching in like arrows through a picket fence.

Like a slot player numbed at a million dollar jackpot he was having trouble taking it all in. He only wished he'd have the time to translate the signal.

A ripping sound above Walter's head jolted him. Heavy smoke poured through a jagged crack in the plastered ceiling. Through burning eyes he saw the wooden roof slats roiling in flames. Choking and coughing, Walter managed to fumble to the fax. His fingers were trembling. Along with the instinctive fire fear, they quivered because he knew he'd be the first to transmit a message from outside the solar system. Shakily he managed to get the computer screen image onto the fax. He jammed at the send button, then glanced at the phone. Already he'd stayed too long. Did he dare call ERSEV? Heat from the red hot timbers pressed down scalding his head. He reached for the phone then the question was decided for him. A glowing chunk of two by four cracked across his forearm. The phone tumbled into the blinding smoke. Walter screamed in pain. His forearm was shattered. He could see the white tip of one of the bones ripped through his skin. He grabbed the fracture with his good arm squeezing hard to try and force out the hurt. A deep fear took possession of him. He'd certainly stayed too long at the fair. The thick choking smoke shut his eyes completely. The control room door was only paces away, but now he was totally disoriented. He got down on all fours. That's what they said to do he remembered. The heat and smoke would be lighter here. But it wasn't like they'd said. Walter coughed heavily. His lungs burned with a searing pain. As if in sheer defiance of the flames the speakers continued to pulsate their thunderous bass beat knocking chips off the burnt timbers. Frantically Walter groped with his good arm. Orange hot chips fell on him burning through his clothes branding his skin. His desire to be a scientific somebody evaporated as quickly as the juices in the vines. Along with the pain his mind was full of only survival. He hoped he could make contact with anything that would lead him to the door. His fingers stuck a metal post. The smoke was gravy thick and his eyes swollen shut, but he'd located his desk. The door that seemed a mile away a moment ago he knew was just feet in front of him.

Desperately he tilted his swivel chair over his head for protection. Chunks of hot plaster fell in showers. Walter knew any second the entire ceiling would buckle. His good arm ached with the effort to keep the chair balanced over his head. He thrust himself to his knees then lunged for the place where the door must be. Fiery ember flakes seared his lungs. Walter almost made it. The ache in his legs became a sudden paralyzed jolt of electric pain. He sprawled across a jumble of broken steaming timbers. He tried to rise but with mounting terror found his legs were useless ridged stilts. Walter did not want to die. Dying was for aged and inconsequential folk. Lying on the smoking floor he felt oddly betrayed. It wasn't fair that he should be sacrificed just as fame was so near. Walter stretched his fingers toward the door. It was there only inches away. He gritted his teeth. He managed to prop himself up on his broken arm. Walter flung his good hand toward where the doorknob must be. He had it in his grip briefly. He screamed a terrible scream of hurt and frustration. The flames had heated the knob to a radiant red hot bulb. Skin peeled from his hand like long cooked beef ribs sloughing off the bone. Then mercifully he passed out. With a roar that drowned out the still thumping amps, the roof beams split smashing Walter's electronics to smoking junk. One of the broken hot lances implanted itself in Walter's midsection piercing more of his organs than was necessary to ensure a rapid last gasp. The speakers continued their drumbeat for awhile after Walter died. Then at last their hardy wires crisped through.

If Walter had lived to study their wave pattern more closely he probably still wouldn't have guessed their message. He was a physical scientist and not attuned to the biological. As it would turn out the message in those spiked lines was, in a manner of speaking, a living one.

CHAPTER 17

COLIN, ROBERTO AND Dr. Volger gathered around the fax machine like predators waiting for a rabbit to pop out of its hole. It was 4:10 in the morning. Over two hours since they'd faxed new coordinates to Polski. Colin tried to ignore the knot of anxiety in his chest. He knew McClure's Emtran Team would be making an appearance soon. If Roberto and Konrad feared McClure's enforcers they were keeping it to themselves. Then the fax machines beep startled the three. Dr. Volger snatched the transmission away then purposefully kept his eyes from reading it.

"Who wants the honor?", he asked, tongue in cheek. He switched his gaze between Colin and Roberto. Colin thrust his chin toward the paper.

"You look at it Roberto. You know what a pulsar readout looks like," he said. The truth was that Colin was afraid to look at Polski's second attempt. He was afraid it would be another crushing flat line. Had there been enough time for Polski to find it? Polski would be aiming at a target in Centaurus that had been there two million years ago. The stars would have changed position ever so slightly since the etching was engraved. Enough for Polski's telescope to miss it? Colin looked on as Roberto flattened out the fax on the console desk. He flicked on an overhead lamp. His eyes scanned the paper intently. Roberto, with a quizzical grin signaled Colin and Dr. Volger to take a look.

"This is the damndest transmission I've ever seen," Roberto said. "See what you think." Colin and Konrad hovered close around the all important fax.

"Looks like a six or seven on the Richter scale" Colin joked in an attempt to keep the mood light.

Dr. Volger's fingers ran over the pen line.

"I was hoping for something like this" he said. "I knew it wouldn't be a normal pulsar tracing. Now it's up to us to interpret these lines."

"They look like a meaningless jumble" Colin said.

"But see here Colin. Right on the twenty centimeter wavelength," Konrad answered. Of course all three knew a normal tracing would bear no message at all. That would show a regular order of spikes not unlike the squiggles passing across Margo's heart monitor. But Colin had imagined an extraterrestrial intelligence would send a code that was somehow neat and clean. If there was a message in these spikes it was well hidden.

"Why the furrowed brow Colin?", Konrad asked seeming to read Colin's mood. "This is it Colin. What we've waited for," Konrad smiled reassuringly. "You expected the communication to come in English perhaps?" Colin laughed.

"It's just so...well, messy looking," Colin said.

"Order in disorder. That's what we need to look for here," Konrad replied in a confident tone. He brought over a large desk magnifier and adjusted it over the pulsar's spikes. "Now maybe we see something," Konrad said. At eighteen times magnification Colin saw the bunched together lines take on a clear definition. The closer packed spikes alternated in an apparently random way with those that were spread. "Roberto look at this," Konrad directed. Colin stepped back.

"Yes...uh huh." Roberto made knowing noises. What he might be gleaning from the fax, Colin couldn't imagine. "Roberto what are you thinking?" Colin asked.

"You'll see. I'm going to pull up a normal pulsar transmission so you can compare it."

Roberto typed in ASTRONOMY/PULSAR/READOUT/LIST. A selection of pulsar tracings appeared on the screen. Roberto clicked on the Vela pulsar, a remnant of the largest supernova in the sky.

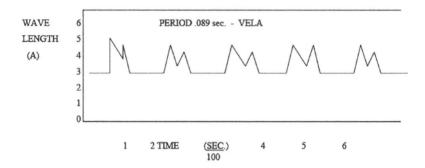

"This is pulsing slower than Polski's right?", Colin asked.

"No. You're reading hundredths of a second here. But forget the time," Roberto answered. "Notice that alongside every tall spike there's a smaller one on the down slope." Colin nodded. "Rotating pulsars have a north and south magnetic pole just like the earth, so every time the pulsar spins we get two pulses. Because one pole is more aligned with the earth we get the highest spike from that one. Understand Colin?"

"Sure, two spikes per spin. Strong and weak."

"Good. But now look at PSR 175 +08." Roberto clicked up Polski's tracing.

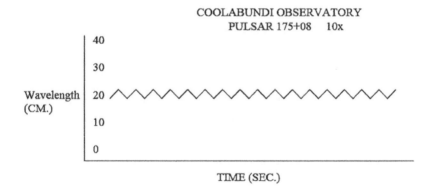

"Each spike has no secondary pulse Colin. PSR175+08 spins with only one pole," Roberto said. "Which means what?", Colin queried.

"It means this pulsar has been aligned somehow."

"Purposefully manipulated," Konrad broke in. Colin stared open mouth at the ERSEV chief. "We're dealing with visitors from another galaxy Colin. Beings with unsurpassed intellectual ability. If they've chosen a spinning star to be their mode of communication I don't think it's beyond their powers to make that star their tool." The idea staggered. Colin had assumed an extra galactic intelligence would have sent out signals by some kind of souped up transmitter. To be able to tame a pair of stars was nearly beyond comprehension. The thought left Colin a little lightheaded at the awesomeness - and a little fearful. Why would the trail begun with Margo's insight end with this? A star pattern carved unbeknownst in the twelfth century and earlier again in the age of Greece's glory? How could it be feasible?

Roberto's eyes registered a far away preoccupied look.

"A piece of pulsar the size of your fingernail weighs some hundred million tons and the average star is the size of Manhattan. The temperatures can be 108 Kelvin. How can you approach it let alone maneuver it?"

"Maybe they will teach us. But first we must find the language in these lines," Konrad replied.

"But how do we begin to look for meaning in this scribble?", Colin asked. "If we had months to search we might do it, but we have hours before Emtran gets here."

"Well I think we can eliminate any "greetings from your celestial neighbors" stuff. These beings wouldn't have rigged a star just to say hello," Roberto said.

"And we look for clarity Colin. They'll know their signal has to be as clear as possible. So we think in terms of the concise," Konrad added. Just then the phone rang. Dr. Volger moved to the end of the desk and picked it up.

"Polski?" Colin asked. Konrad shook his head.

"It's for you Colin, Dr. McClure." Reluctantly Colin took the phone.

"What is it McClure? We're busy here." Colin didn't try to hide the edge of contempt in his voice. "You are?", McClure giggled. "Are you working on an antidote? Trying to make amends? I think it's too late for that." McClure laughed. At first, a piping sarcastic titter, then a full blown whooping yelp that Roberto and Konrad could hear.

"Colin!", McClure shouted. "You best listen to me. It is not polite to disrespect your supervisor."

Had the particles finished their work on McClure? Colin wondered. He recalled what Boka had said about rage in that tumor infected brain.

"I meant no disrespect Dr. McClure." Appeasing McClure was a better tack than going nose to nose right now Colin thought. He understood, as head of section McClure had control of Emtran. Those enforcers would operate as his personal directees. They'd dole out sanctions from traffic citations to executions with equal disinterestedness.

"The Barubi natives your Dr. Volger evacuated to Darwin, nasty looking specimens, crusty scales head to toe. Certainly not what we want the public to see." Colin covered the phone.

"He's gotten a look at the infected villagers you evacuated to Darwin Konrad."

"You and Mister Volger could have neutralized this disease. Stopped it at its source," McClure screamed. "You let ERSEVs voodoo experimenting interfere with saving lives! Your first job Mister Grier was to stop the spread. Stop it! Do you hear me?" Colin pulled the phone away from his ringing eardrum. There would be no use telling McClure about 175+08. Colin knew the disease was amplifying his usual belligerence toward manic level. To ask now for more time to analyze a pulsar fax wasn't the correct move. "You're going to pay for the deaths of these villagers Mr. Grier. All of you have been most reprehensible. Irresponsibly criminal I would say." McClure tried to stifle a bubbling manic giggle. "I have been in contact with the appropriate authorities you should know. Sub Rosa of course. They agree there are a multiple of charges to be brought."

"Wait a second," Colin interrupted.

"How dare you" McClure shouted, in a shrill falsetto. "How dare you ask for one more moment! You have frittered away precious time. You have deliberately undermined my authority. Deny it, I want to hear you deny it!"

"I don't deny it McClure," Colin shouted back. He felt his own control slipping in response to McClure's harangue. "There are reasons for keeping the dig site open. Reasons you've dismissed out of hand. You talk about the villagers. You don't give a damn about the villagers. Did you help them by pulling I.V. lines out of their arms?" Colin listened to the silence on the other end of the line. "We know what you did McClure. You're a murdering control freak. You'd stop at nothing to protect your so called reputation." Colin bit his lip. He hadn't wanted to say that. The words spilled out in an overflow of anger and frustration.

"It was necessary to protect the others from contagion," McClure said in a quiet whisper. "One must call the weak from the strong. That's natures way. Beside Mr. Grier no one knows about this except you and your friends and I'm seeing to it that you're not available to tell on me." McClure roared with wild laughter, then switched abruptly to an ominous hiss. "I have my duty. I told the Emtran people this is code five. Can you guess what that means?" McClure tittered. "That designation is for the rarest of emergencies. I have ordered Emtran personnel to board your ship. They will be visiting quite soon. Bon Voyage." The phone disconnected with the echo of McClure's manic howling ringing in Colin's ears. He looked grimly at Konrad and Roberto.

"The little time we thought we had to work this fax out. We can forget it. McClure's gone round the bend. He's ordered Emtran aboard." Roberto and Konrad stared in disbelief. "We're a threat to his authority. He was paranoid already about getting the honors he thinks is his right. Now it's paranoid with a vengeance." Konrad sat shakily.

"It's unthinkable, the research here. A lifetime's work. All to be ended?" Konrad gripped the armrests to still his trembling.

"He's got us nailed," Colin said. "McClure's free to carry out whatever mayhem rattles around in his bent mind."

"Maybe we can get some help from headquarters in Switzerland," Konrad said. "They can't physically stop Emtran but we have influential people there with connections to national power players. Get them on the phone Roberto." Colin watched Roberto dial several sets of numbers in turn then shake his head. He tried his email contacts.

"Nothing Konrad. Our communications to the outside are down."

"They're probably already aboard then," Colin said. He walked to the lab door and pressed his cheek to a crack between the plywood boards. His eyes strained to angle down the hallway. "Empty?", Roberto asked. Colin nodded.

"They may not come down here. They know we can't go anywhere." "They'll spot us if we try to get off," Roberto added. Konrad's eyes caught Colin's.

"They mean to...eliminate us?"

"I think so," Colin said, trying to sound matter of fact.

"Think of it," Roberto said. "If he gets rid of us there are no witnesses to the outbreak. Except for us everyone else who knows what happened here is under his control. McClure will order the dig site sealed and get all the kudos for seeing to it that the media never got it's teeth into this." Konrad apprehensively looked up at Margo's readouts. Her cardiograph showed warning quivers of another arrhythmic episode. Colin thought he detected a hint of defeat on Konrads face.

"If we promise these Emtran people we'll be silent about our findings might they not relent?...at least see to it that Margo is helped?", Konrad asked.

"These people don't negotiate," Colin answered. "McClure ordered them to get rid of us. They'll do just that. If they have conscience troubles they don't become Emtran agents. Roberto, McClure knows about this lab. Can we transfer to one of the lower deck labs?" Konrad looked up with a glint of hope.

"We could go down to the molecular bio lab on J deck. It's not microbe safe though. We'll have to take our chances. At least we have the advantage of knowing the ships layout. We can use the freight elevator to get down there." Colin peeked through the plywood slats again. Still nobody.

"How many rooms on the ship Konrad?", Colin asked. "Up in the thousands."

"Good. They'll have to search one by one."

"How many agents do you think they have aboard?", Roberto questioned.

"Three or four," Colin guessed. "Do you have any weapons Roberto?" "A .45, a .38, a rifle, and a concussion grenade locked in the supply closet."

"Get them out Roberto. We may need them." Colin said.

"Roberto get Jhanda in a suit. You'll all go to J lab then. When they find me here I'll be able to buy some time," Konrad said.

"You can't. They'll kill you," Colin said. "Are you going to give up now? Throw away the chance to learn the pulsar message? You've believed all along that Margo's survival turned on following every avenue of exploration."

Konrad had seen Margo through her memories. Allowed her to risk her health in order to enter them again, Colin thought. Now when an extraordinary revelation was at hand had Konrad lost heart? Konrad held out his arms.

"It's over I'm afraid." Crusty brown scabs ran like bracelets around his wrists. Colin felt a catch in his throat. He'd come to regard this man as a friend.

"You have to come with us. We'll beat Emtran somehow."

"It's all right Colin. I knew the risk when I took off the mask. It was necessary to convince you of my sincerity. I gambled that the ellipse would remain dormant. I was wrong and innocent villagers died. Didn't I have an obligation to put myself at risk the same as they?" Konrad didn't wait for Colin's answer. "The important thing is for you to interpret the pulsar's communication and to carry out Jhanda's instructions to take Margo into the ellipse.

It pains me that I won't see the fulfillment of Margo's vision. But this is how it was meant to be... so no more talk of me. Go to J level with Roberto and interpret this message. You will find a way." Konrad moved to Margo. He looked down lovingly. He pushed her thick brown hair away from her sleeping eyes. He didn't need to look a the monitors to know she was failing. He color had gone from a healthy pink to the color of parchment. As Konrad had feared, the Corcid was losing its effectiveness. He turned the stopcock to let the last ten cc's drip more quickly into Margo's arm. "This is the last of it," Konrad said. Almost instantly Margo's heart beat steadied and her color brightened. "A few hours more is all she has. You have to get her into the ellipse before then Colin," Konrad said.

"I will," Colin heard himself say. And then what? In another time he'd entered the machine with Margo. The vision at the Greek Temple was a vision of what had happened long ago. Colin wouldn't...couldn't allow himself to question that. But then what? He'd recalled a slice of his long ago past with Margo. If only he could remember what the impending moments would bring.

"Once this wears off she'll be left with no energy reserve Colin," Konrad said.

"I understand" Colin nodded. "All or nothing." Konrad unhooked Margo's lines. He stood intently looking down at his daughter.

"I didn't imagine it would be so hard," he said. "I had hoped to see her healthy again Colin." Konrad's eyes followed the last drops of the drug down the I.V. tube. "Well we hardly have time for long farewells now do we?" He ran a finger under his moist eyes.

There was a sudden hiss as the lab doors opened. Colin grinned as Roberto and Jhanda came in dressed in micro stat suits. With the tiny Jhanda at his side, the pair looked like a couple of banditos from Pancho Villas gang. Roberto had a 30-06 slung over his shoulder, the grenade and a .38 revolver hung from his hip. Some extra ammo belts hung around Jhanda's neck threatened to buckle his rickety knees.

"I think we'll be able to get off without Emtran seeing us," Roberto said. "How?" Konrad asked.

"Whoever was suppose to haul the sea cat aboard after the dive forgot to do it. We can thank them for that. It's still tied up under the stern. The ladder down to it is close to J level lab. I doubt if our friends will have noticed it."

"Then we must hurry," Konrad said.

"Colin get out two more suits. While you're getting into yours I'll dress Margo." Colin tossed one of the protective suits to Konrad and stripped to his underwear. The suit was surprisingly light and thin with a smooth silky liner. In a moment Colin was comfortably buttoned up. "She won't be too much for you to carry?", Konrad asked.

"Not at all," Colin said. He put his arms under Margo and lifted her to his chest. Colin looked down through the clear mask at her lovely face. "She just seems to be sleeping peacefully Doctor Volger."

212

"Thank God for now at least," Konrad said. "There is so much more I would like to say to her but time is running out Colin. Allow me a simple goodbye to the four of you." Konrad struggled to keep his composure. "Thank you for believing in her visions" Konrad went on. "You'll overcome these Emtran people Colin. The communication from Centaurus will prove to be the key to all we've searched for." Colin thought of what to reply in turn. But whatever he could say would be too much or too little.

"Goodbye my friend," he said, then signaled for Roberto and Jhanda to follow in the hallway. The freight elevator was out of view tucked in an alcove at the hall's far end.

"Roberto cover our backs until we get down there. Emtran could pop out of the passenger elevator at any second," Colin said. Roberto nodded. Roberto walked backward, his 30-06 facing the passenger elevator as the others hurried toward the alcove. When he saw them make the left into the cubicle he ran down quickly to join them. In seconds the freight elevator dropped down to J deck.

"The molecular bio lab is just around the corner," Roberto said. He took a peek down J level's long hallway. "All quiet. Let's get in the lab before it's not." With Jhanda at his elbow Colin followed Roberto to the lab. "Damn. It's locked," Roberto said. He fumbled with a ring, of what looked to Colin, like a hundred keys.

"Do you know which one?", Colin timidly asked, knowing it would take forever for Roberto to try each one."

"A silver Yale. I think this is it." Roberto held his rifle under his arm and turned the key. "Damn it." As Roberto found another candidate the elevator doors opened at the far end. Colin froze. An Emtran agent stood at the elevators open doors, a figure dressed in a bulky olive drab protective suit. He held an automatic rifle in his hands. Colin weighed the chances of getting back to the alcove. The odds were not good. The agent began a steady walk toward the little group. "Last Yale," Roberto whispered holding the key up to Colin. With a quick jab he thrust it into the lock. The door opened. Quickly, he pulled Colin and Margo inside. "Jhanda get in," Roberto shouted, but the old man stood transfixed, blinking in the center of the hall. Roberto lunged for him.

"Halt I say!" echoed down the hall. The agent fired a warning shot over Jhanda's and Roberto's heads. The round ricoched off the far wall, came back and hit Jhanda dead center in his back. Jhanda pitched forward in a heap. Blood pulsed out soaking his orange gown. Roberto rushed out to Jhanda and turned him over. The old mans eyes were already rolled back. In a few more heartbeats he was gone. The Emtran agent began a slow tread toward Roberto. He held his automatic at port arms. Colin watched Roberto's lips thin into a rageful grimace. Roberto flicked off the rifles safety. When the agent was a few yards away he fired the 30-06 from his hip. The shell smacked the olive clad agent in the throat. The man staggered a few steps and looked at Roberto with astonishment from behind his Plexiglas facemask. His last few breaths produced an odd gurgle as the air found the route to his lungs shorter through the bullets new hole. Colin laid Margo down on a couch in the molecular lab then went into the hall. Roberto ran back to the passenger elevator.

"I'm hitting the emergency stop. When their friend doesn't show up in a couple of minutes they'll follow down."

"I'll hold the freight elevator too," Colin shouted. He jogged into the elevator alcove and pushed the stop button. "They'll have to use the stairs to get down here Roberto."

"Good, I can cover the fore and aft stairwells a lot easier without worrying about them coming out of the elevators." Roberto stooped down, took off Jhanda's mask and closed the old mans eyes. "You know Colin I never gave credence to any of the ESP stuff until I met this little man. He got me taking what was happening to Margo seriously." Roberto looked hard into Colin's eyes. "This has got to be worth it. Jhanda's and all the other deaths I mean. Wherever this communication is from, the pulsar has to justify the sacrifices. Understand what I'm saying?" A rerun of Lippincott's dying at the cave's entrance flew quickly through Colin's mind.

"We've put all our eggs in one hell of a basket, haven't we?", Colin said.

"We have to go on to the finish," Roberto answered. He unraveled Jhanda's ammo belts and slid them to the lab door. "Colin if you work on the pulsar readout I'll keep watch at the door." For a moment Colin wondered what to do with Jhanda's body. A quirky image of a burial at sea, military style occurred to him. Strange the picture your brain cobbled together when stress came calling. There was no way anything respectful could be done. He picked the frail body up from its pool of blood and carried it into the lab. He wanted to avoid Margo seeing Jhanda when she awoke. He'd break the news to her as gently as possible when the right moment came – as if there was ever a right moment for saying a beloved friend had died.

Colin looked around the lab. There was a walk-in supply closet with its door ajar. It was the only option he realized. Better than leaving Jhanda sprawled in the hallway. Colin lay the body in the closet and called out to Roberto.

"What's happening?"

"No sign of them yet. You start on the readout?"

"I'm starting now." Colin fished through his pockets for the pulsar readout then remembered he'd put it in his shirt pocket. Stupid. He cursed himself for not thinking to transfer it to one of the protective suits first. There was nothing to be done except to unzip the suit. What were the chances a stray disease particle would get inside in the second it would take to unzip and zip back up? No matter, Colin had no choice. With a quick pull he unzipped the suit, reached in, and pulled the graph out. He'd been exposed maybe three seconds. The odds were long that anything would have gotten inside he thought. Colin checked on Margo. He couldn't detect any change in breathing and her pulse was okay. The last of the CORCID had gone into her veins an hour ago. Ordinarily she'd be given another dose in six hours, so five more to go. Colin laid out the pulsar readout on a lab table. He weighed it's ends down with a couple of thousand milliliter beakers. There was a ten-power desk magnifier in a nearby cabinet. Colin placed it over the graph and flicked on its light. He hadn't looked at the pulsar readout critically back in the P4 lab.

Now, he began by drawing vertical lines through the graphs peaks and valleys. Separating them might begin to show at least the start of the pattern. For a few seconds the spikes looked just as before, a tangled series of random mountain tops. Then it jumped out quite clearly. Colin grabbed a metric ruler and cut his pencil lines closer to .5 centimeters apart.

"Yes!" he shouted.

"What is it?" Roberto asked from his guard post at the door.

"The readout. Where it looks like just a jumble there's organization." Colin erased his first pencil lines and filled in all half-centimeter marks. Then he marked numbers, one through four over the hundred pulsar graph peaks.

"Roberto listen to this. I've marked the peaks in groups of one to four. They're compressed most where four are crowded together; least compressed where there's one."

"And?"

"What do you mean and?" "There's a definite pattern."

"We figured on that Colin. So what's it mean?" Maybe I should insist on Roberto's figuring out the graph Colin thought sourly. Except that Roberto being a better shot was best to guard the lab door.

"Let me look a little more Roberto. What's happening at the elevator?"

"Nothing for the moment. You say you've got the peak clusters marked from one to four?" "Yes."

"More threes with fours or ones with twos?"

"I don't know Roberto. Wait." Colin scrutinized the peaks again. After every one peak there was a three. After every two a four.

"Colin instead of one to four use letters ABCD..."

"I know the damn alphabet Roberto," Colin started. And then like a two-ton weight it hit him. How obvious, how God Damn obvious! "Roberto we got it. Not ABCD, ATGC" It's the DNA bases. Has to be. We should have expected this from the first." Colin recalled Konrads guess that the ellipse, whatever else it might be, was an encyclopedia of genes, holding a collection of every possible pair of nucleotides from the most primitive to those with potential for unimaginable abilities. And Konrad had toyed with the idea that a piece of that collection might have genes that acted as a molecular computer, a governor for any electronics inside. Was it possible that something went wrong with the ellipse when it was put here? Could the computer be run by DNA sequences gone wrong? Could it be, Colin wondered, that a critical error releasing the deadly particles was even now trying to be corrected by the pulsar flashes?

"Another agent is going to show up pretty quick," Roberto said interrupting Colin's theorizing. "A sequencer machine is in the rear of the lab Colin, so go string the genes together." String the genes. Put them in the ellipse Colin thought.

"I only used a sequencer once," Colin shouted to the doorway. "It was an old applied Biosystems model. This one here doesn't have the same look."

"The one here is a thousand times faster. Made by ourselves. You just need to type out the DNA base pairs you want. The sequences will link them all automatically as fast as you can hit the keys. The key pad is on your right under a little dust cover. See it?"

"Yes." Colin lifted off the cover. Thankfully there were just four letters on it, ATGC.

"Colin all you need to do is read off the peak clusters. Like you said, one peak is always followed by a three peak and a two by a four.

"But we don't know if one and three are A with T or G with C. Same for the two and four peaks." The proteins to be made, and maybe the ellipse computer commands, depended on the order of the base pairs. Would beings from another galaxy have anticipated the problem and taken it into account? Set up the works inside the machine to accept the various combinations. There was no way to know and no time now to experiment.

"Roberto I'll run this through both ways. Once through with the one and three peaks being A and T and a second time making the G and C. I'll have to put both DNA chains in the ellipse and hope the machine recognizes one of them."

"Maybe it will choose one from column A and one from column B, menu style," Roberto quipped. "Seriously Colin it's the best we can do." Colin looked over the graph again. He had to relax. He darkened the vertical lines that separated the peak groupings. It would have to do.

"I'm typing in the base pairs possibilities now Roberto."

"I can hear faint talking Colin. It seems to be coming from the bow. I hear doors shutting. They must be searching every lab. I don't think they know one of their pals is dead yet." Okay. Can't worry about Emtran, Colin thought. They're going to do what they're going to do no matter what. Just punch the keys.

Colin grabbed a roll of scotch tape then taped the pen readout across the face of the sequencer. He pressed the 'on' switch and waited. When the green ready light came on he started hitting the ATGC keys. Colin estimated there were four to five hundred base pairs to put in and he was knocking out two or three a second. When he was nearly finished Roberto called from the hallway "Done yet?"

"A few more seconds, Roberto."

"Well I can hear them now at the top of the stairwell. When they start to come down I'm going to fire a shot up there. Hold them for a bit anyhow. We have to get the freight elevator down to the bottom deck. The ladder to the sea cat is there."

"Coming." Colin punched in the last of the base pairs then hit the "end" key. There was a green EJECT SEQUENCE button on the left. He pushed it and waited. After a few usual than stronger heart beats a stoppered fifty milliliter glass vial rolled out from a slot in the panel facing. Amazingly fast, just like Roberto said. Colin held the vial up to the light. The DNA sequence was tiny, a white streak that could easily be mistaken for a throwaway thread. Big things in small packages Colin mused. Is this what Brahma offered to those who climbed the mountain? Those who would become the Muktas Margo had spoken of, the same milky DNA in the Greek Temple vial? Colin put the vial in his breast pocket careful to press down on its Velcro closure.

"I'm finished Roberto."

"Be quiet when you bring out Margo," Roberto whispered. "They're right above us now." Colin cradled Margo securely in his arms. She seemed to be sleeping a child's peaceful sleep, all serenity and calm. A slight smile circled up at her lips edge. But Colin was only too aware how fragile her hold was on life. Only the CORCID was keeping her alive.

Colin carried her to the doorway.

"When I fire up the stairwell they'll instinctively jump back," Roberto whispered. He pulled a fistful of shells from his ammo belt and loaded them. "There's only a few steps to the freight alcove. Just follow quick Colin. With luck we'll be heading down just as they realize we were on this floor."

"Luck?" Colin thought. Is there such a thing? Or rather call it by its other name, Karma, Fate, Destiny, for that matter. He'd had his life intertwined with the lady in his arms once before. Of that he had no doubt. So then it was all laid out for them. He didn't know what these next moments would bring. These seconds, among infinite others had happened once before. But for Margo and himself "right now" was new again, as fresh for them as any other newly created now.

Roberto gestured for Colin to follow to the base of the staircase. He held a finger to his mask warning for quiet, then waved Colin toward the elevators closed doors. Quick chatter echoed down the stairwell followed by the sound of hurrying feet. Colin held Margo tightly and rushed into the elevator. Roberto raised his rifle to the stairwell and fired two shots. The bullets pinged and ricochet off the metal banister. Startled yells and curses mingled with the reverberations. Roberto ran to the elevator and pushed the button for K deck.

"Come on, come on," Roberto hissed at the all too slow closing doors. Colin gritted his teeth. He half expected to see a rifle muzzle thrust between the doors before they closed. Gratefully, he savored the slight tremor in his feet as the elevator began its descent. Margo stirred in his arms, her large brown eyes dreamily opening for a second, catching his own. Then with a contented sigh she dropped back into that mysterious place somewhere between trance and waking. Colin had an impulse to call her fully awake but her coming back to consciousness was a process that was best left to its own schedule.

"Roberto, where to when the doors open?", Colin asked.

"Run down the hallway as fast as you can. We should beat them down by a few seconds. You'll see a green hatchway door at the end on your right. It should be unlocked. Go in and you'll see a walkway to a second hatch that opens to the outside. We want to get Margo into the sea cat as fast as we can, I'll be a few steps behind." Colin nodded his understanding. But then what? That Emtran would take the elevator back up to the patio and start shooting from there was what. Colin didn't need to be a West Point grad to see that move coming, unless of course, they hadn't spotted the sea cat bobbing under the stern. "Ready?" Roberto whispered. Colin nodded again. When the elevator doors opened on K deck Colin sprinted down the hall as fast as he could with his arms full of Margo. Roberto followed closely on his heels. Echoes of shouts and footsteps sounded menacingly down the stairwell.

Colin approached the green door and looked back in time to see an Emtran agent leaping down the last dozen steps to K deck. Colin was panting from running with Margo's added weight. Without aiming, Roberto squeezed off two more shots in the agents general direction, then grasped the green door's handle. It opened. Thank you, thank you Colin thought as he squeezed through the hatch onto a narrow catwalk. Roberto followed and spun the wheel lock fast.

"This hatch is thick enough to hold off any firepower they have" Roberto said. Colin expected to hear the thud of machine gun bullets testing that statement, but apparently the agents realized too it would be useless to try to penetrate the hatch door.

"How many do you think are outside?", Colin asked.

"Minus the one we left in the hallway, maybe three or four." Yes, and that dead one was going to make Emtran's mission personal, Colin thought. Emtran agents might be ask no questions types up to a certain point. But killing one of their own was bound to make this mission very personal. Colin looked down the length of the narrow catwalk perforated metal walkway that seemed designed for elves.

There was no handrail. Below, the monstrous silver smooth knuckles and knobs of the engine thrust upward, silent now, but waiting to come to pounding life. Roberto started down the catwalk then stepped a few steps on with a quizzical backward look to Colin.

"Acrophobia," Colin muttered. "It gets me sometimes." Colin felt sheepish. "Isn't there some other way?"

"Hell no," Roberto shouted. He looked intently at Colin's flushed face. "You're serious." Colin shook his head. He could feel the shaking start in his arms weakening his grip on Margo. He fought a wave of lightheadedness. The couple hundred feet across the high wire catwalk looked like the last mile. The notion that he wouldn't get to the ellipse because of his primeval fear made him want to laugh and cry at the same time.

"Let me take her." Roberto laid the rifle on the catwalk.

"No. I have to do this," Colin insisted. The safer way would be to let Roberto carry Margo. That was clear. But an instinct (memory?) rising from his gut told him he had to be the one. "Go ahead Roberto. If I keep my eyes glued to your shoulders I think I'll be okay."

"Just keep in step with me" Roberto said. They began the long march across the high catwalk. Colin used the clock like thudding in his chest to keep his steps in time. The precision of the march like steps helped calm him. After all, he had a message from the stars in his pocket. In the grand scheme his personal phobia counted as nothing. "That wasn't so bad Colin was it." Suddenly he'd arrived at the other side of the catwalk. He stood on the platform that opened to the outside exhilarated that he'd made it across. Roberto unlocked the stern door. He opened the hatch slowly. Rays of the morning sun streamed into the engine room. Bright sparkles reflected off the silver machinery. There was no sign of Emtran below.

"The overhang of the stern is above us Colin. Unless they've already spotted the ladder they won't be able to see us from the patio rail."

"Let's hope," Colin said. Of course if Emtran had scouted around enough they could just wait for easy pickings when the sea cat pulled out from under the stern. Roberto pushed the hatch open all the way. He was careful not to let the heavy door slam against the hull. He looked around, satisfied himself that they were under cover so far, and gestured for Colin to carry Margo out. There was barely enough room on the steel ledge for the three of them. Colin saw the sea cat rocking gently below the ladder thirty feet down. Roberto scampered down and steadied the boat. Colin followed. With Margo secure in his lap, he sat in the starboard seat close to the controls. That excursion to the cave was about thirty six hours ago, but it seemed like forever. Colin smiled inwardly at the thought of Konrad's ruse to get him off the case.

Yesterday, the scam seemed the epitome of treachery. Now all his outrage dissolved in light of the wonders he'd encountered. Roberto loosened the securing lines then steadied the sea cat to keep it from drifting into Emtrans line of vision.

"I'm going to run the boat full out Colin. Keep a tight grip on Margo. When we get to the beach we're going to run right up on it. Run as fast as you can into the trees." Roberto started the sea cats engine. The rumble spread out over the cove startling a flock of beach birds into the air. If Emtran was on the patio they'd be fully alert now. Roberto jammed the vessels throttle to the wall. Colin slumped down. He braced his feet against the rail. The boat reared up like a nitro burner, then shot across the tops of the gentle swells so fast Colin could feel back pressure against his mask. The cat must be doing seventy knots. "Okay?", Roberto yelled over.

"Fine." Colin thought about turning to see if Emtran was on deck, but no need. If the agents were on the patio rifle shots would already be adding to the roar of the cat. White breakers loomed close. Colin picked out a spot he would run to, a clump of palms that fingered out to the sand just where the sea cat should beach. Roberto cut the engine back. The boat would still grind across the beach fast enough to throw them all out so Colin hunkered down nearly lying flat on the deck. He held Margo tightly.

"Get ready," Roberto warned. Colin closed his eyes reflexively, then heard the throb of the sea cat's props glissando from a deep hum to a screaming whine as they left the water. Colin strained to hold his place as the boat launched itself up the beach with jarring hops and thuds. At last the cat came to a skidding stop midway between the water and the trees. Without waiting he scrambled over the side squeezing Margo's body to his own. Roberto was already at the tree line urging Colin in. Colin half ran, half stumbled up the beach. He'd just stepped into the palm grove when he heard bullets banging against the sea cat. He watched as plumes of sand erupted along the path he'd just walked.

Chapter 18

"THAT MUST BE the ship there" George Trimble said, pointing a finger toward a white speck still some ten miles distant.

"Got to be. The cruise lines never come by these parts," Lieutenant Kullberg answered. The pilot dropped the old PBY seaplane down to twelve hundred feet. From the co-pilots seat George watched the Lt. flick a couple of switches on the World War II planes instrument panel.

"Never thought I'd be flying in one of these," George said. He struggled to get his legs into a supposedly germ proof suit. The Moresby Health Agency had given him the dusty suit, probably as old as the Catalina he was flying in. George calculated that the number of disease outbreaks requiring the use of the suit in the agencies history was exactly zero. But then again that was a good thing.

"You might want to go to the rear to get that on. More room to maneuver there," Kullberg said. "Thanks," George said, with a hint of irritation. He walked back into the fuselage and plopped down next to the large Plexiglas bubble that blistered out of the planes waist. The view was terrific. No wonder the Catalina had been so good for reconnaissance. Kullberg had said the twin-engine craft was one of only a handful still operational. The Papua Defense Service still had the spare parts so they'd decided to use the plane for air searches until they were gone.

"What's going on down there?" Kullberg shouted back. "Ebola or something?"

"Not suppose to say Lieutenant. Really just routine precaution. You know how everything gets blown out of proportion nowadays. The suit is just can't be too careful stuff," George lied. He wondered what Kullberg would think if he'd seen the retro-human that had stalked him in Kokoori hospital. On the flip side what might he say to the entity that could show itself between existences. Kullberg dropped the plane down close enough for George to see any movements on the deck of the big vessel. The ship clearly seemed deserted but George knew McClure's swat team must be on board or maybe at Barubi Village.

The PBY lowered close to the water. It's two old radial engines pushed pressure waves across the cove's clear blue water. Kullberg made a wide bank around the ERSEV's stern.

"Dr. Trimble look at that. It's not one of ours." Kullberg pointed to the ships patio deck. A helicopter with no identifying insignia sat on the deck. It was either an Apache or Blackhawk. George couldn't tell them apart. He leaned over Kullberg's shoulder to get a better look. "Know who's copters those are?", Kullberg queried.

"No, no", George blustered..."Maybe a call was put in for them while we were in the air." Kullberg made a second circuit around the big ship.

"I'll slide you up about a hundred feet off the beach. You should be able to wade in."

"Lieutenant it will be a chancy proposition if I have to swim in this suit." George made exaggerated swimming motions with his arms, bringing a laugh from Kullberg. George gripped the co-pilots chair anticipating the bounce of the PBY as it hit the water but there was no need to brace himself. Kullberg set the plane down deftly, hardly disturbing the surface.

"When you open the blister look for a foot hold on the fuselage. A few steps in and you'll be on the sand."

"Thanks." George shook Kullberg's hand then touched a gloved finger to his lips.

"A routine training flight is all this was," Kullberg winked. George patted the lieutenants shoulder and returned to the blister. He slipped into the surf and quickly closed the glass bubble. It was improbable that the disease agents would enter the aircraft in the few seconds the blister was open, but best to minimize the risk. Kullberg waited until George had waded safely to the beach then roared off trailing chains of silver droplets from the PBY's underbelly. George watched the seaplane until it disappeared behind a palm covered knoll. He stood for a while listening to the sounds of its engines drone into silence. Up to now he had been intent on getting to Barubi, scurrying to make the flight arrangements. He sat on the sand to consider his best course. He was the enemy now, certainly from the viewpoint of Emtran. George knew, as far as McClure was concerned, he was still at Kokoori hospital. He winced at what McClure's reaction would be when he discovered he'd commandeered a Catalina. George picked up a handful of sand and let it sift through his gloved fingers. None of the people back at the New York office had seen what he'd seen. Maybe only a couple of people in the last five thousand years had seen what he'd seen. An out of body entity knowing what couldn't be known manifest itself. A spirit creature that directed him to (George recalled the exact words) "allow the honored ones to pass through the portals of time." A shiver ran through George as visualized the nude figure gesture with that wide sweep of the arm that signified all of space-time. In spite of the stifling heat George had to bite down hard to keep his teeth from chattering. Dr. Channer's spirit, or whatever manifestation he saw, had told him to find a Temple here. There would be an altar with words that must be spoken. It made terribly little sense. And now to find Colin and the woman he was supposed to accompany was going to be a problem. All very strange. Still there was a needful sense in him, a must do feeling, that overrode his caution. He was on this beach blind as to where to go or what next to do. But it was of little real concern. George knew somehow he'd find his way. He brushed the sand from his hands and then spotted the beached sea cat. He walked up to the little powerboat. Whoever had been driving had been in one damned hurry to get out of the water. It was high and dry with skid marks in the sand thirty yards in. It seemed to be in good shape, until George took a walk around its front. Five or six fist sized chunks had been blasted out of the fiberglass. Bullet rounds had shattered the gauges. Two more rounds marked where gunfire had gone through the windshield. Little wonder that the craft had been running up the beach at top speed. George knew little about the Emtran team except what McClure had offhandedly mentioned.

They did what they were told no questions asked. So McClure had sent them here to secretly enforce ERSEV's compliance with the quarantine order. That shouldn't mean opening fire on civilians. Unless? Unless what? Unless they tried to escape the perimeter McClure had established. In that case McClure would have ordered them to use all force necessary. He could always claim stopping the spread of extraordinary diseases called for extraordinary means. George searched the sea cats hull for blood but saw none. It looked like whoever was aboard had been very lucky. Very frightened no doubt but very lucky. George needed to jigsaw together what might have happened here. Further up the beach was a cluster of palms crowded around a dark oasis of shade. George dragged himself into the shadow and sat among some cooler sand. When he had stood before the Dr. Channer entity in the operating room he'd been too overwhelmed to think about asking any specifics. Did he somehow imagine he'd show up here and run into Colin like Stanley bumping into Livingston? And Channer hadn't said anything about there being a connection between the altar he was to find and the ship.

Unexpectedly, a roar broke across the cove snapping George to attention. The copter on the ERSEV's stern had started up. George hid himself behind a thick trunked palm. The black helicopter rose above the ship then did a slow pivot, checking out sea and beach George guessed. Then it lowered its nose, hesitated and headed directly toward George's spot. If they've seen me I'm in big trouble George thought. The hot suit might be helping me now he hoped. White on white sand, like a snow rabbit in the snow. For sure Emtran must have seen the Catalina but maybe not his own splash to the beach. George crawled behind a thicket of vines and held his breath. For an instant George thought they'd fire one of those rockets that would scatter his crumbs all the way back to Port Moresby. He closed his eyes. Waited. The rocket's swoosh didn't come. When he dared look up again the copter was touching down only fifty yards from where he'd been sitting. If they had seen him, and decided to eliminate him they probably wouldn't waste an expensive rocket to do it George thought. He watched anxiously as two figures in protective suits jumped out. They were armed with automatic weapons. Thankfully, they made no move that indicated they'd seen him.

The men talked animatedly, pointing fingers here and there, probably deciding what route to take into the rainforest.

Then they marched off along a sandy trail into the trees. George relaxed a little. He'd have to move soon. Somehow he had to find Colin. Suddenly, George flinched as something hit his shoulder. He looked on the ground expecting to find a piece of fruit fallen from the trees. Instead there was a rifle bullet lying at his heel. From the branch behind him he heard a low "psssst." He turned to see a figure on one knee holding a rifle aimed at him. The man was wearing a black protective suit.

"Who are you?", The man challenged. George watched his eyes dart suspiciously behind a clear mask. He was wary of the Emtran agents too, George intuited. Like himself one of the hunted.

"George Trimble. I work with Doctor Grier." "McClure sent you?"

"Yes...No," George blurted. "He sent me to check up on an outbreak near Port Moresby, but I came here on my own."

"Why?", Roberto demanded. George began an explanation then realized he'd better change it. Whoever this person was, would accept his hospital story up to the point where he'd entered the operating room. Selling him on the naked Channer episode would be something else again.

"I got concerned when Colin didn't contact me. I found out a tactical team was sent. I didn't agree with Doctor McClure's decision to send them here. I thought I might prevent a confrontation if I came." George waited for Roberto's decision. Then the man in black laid his rifle down.

"I'm Roberto Valdes." Roberto extended his hand. "What do you know about the ERSEV society or why we came here?"

"I'm aware of the scientific advances they've made. I know you have a reputation for independent work. I also know you were prohibited from these waters."

Roberto made a mini patrol, satisfying himself that the tac team had headed inland. He sat down close to George.

"Colin is with us. He's with Doctor Volger's daughter, Margo. We're sure McClure has been infected. Made psychotic by the disease agents. What you don't know is that beside the viral type diseases, and the skin abnormalities, psychic changes occur in a small percentage of the infected."

"Negative type changes?", George asked. A pulse of fear rose up as he recalled the deranged creature that had stalked him down the hospitals hallway.

"Not always. For some the opposite seems to be true. Doctor Volger's daughter was paralyzed but along with the paralysis some extra sensory abilities have occurred. A clairvoyance that shows itself from time to time."

"Like what?", George asked.

"Memories of things from long ago." . George thought of Doctor Channer or rather Channer's spirit who'd known what couldn't be known. "We suspect that the viral particles somehow interact with the mind in a small number of personalities Doctor Trimble."

"Call me George, please."

"Sorry. George." "If the psychic force is strong enough it seems to activate the persons DNA. Like a kind of circular loop the DNA in turn reacts on the psychic center, magnifying I suppose is the closest word, a persons nature." I believe I've experienced that very phenomenon, George thought. He wanted to tell Roberto about the hospital happenings but would that be going too far? Telling Roberto a demonic human being had savaged a mother and child might go down okay. But would Roberto believe him if told his tale about the kind man who fixed a little girls heart. How Channer too had displayed extra sensory abilities. Had in fact directed him to come here? Channer had said the vessel molecules could obey evil intent as well as good. Wasn't that what Roberto was saying too? In essence he'd seen that very thing going on before his own eyes in Kokoori's O.R. George determined to tell Roberto everything. Let Roberto make of it what he would.

"Is the source of the disease particles a vessel of some kind?", George asked. He watched Roberto's eyes visibly widen.

"You *have* talked to McClure since he came down here," Roberto said accusingly.

"Not at all." George cleared his throat. Out with the entire truth, fantastic as it was going to sound, was the only way to go. "I went to Kokoori hospital, in the outback west of Moresby on Doctor McClure's orders. I was to contact an M.D. there, a Doctor Channer who'd had a man come in with terrible skin lesions, frothing, mentally disturbed."

"Interesting," Roberto said, with a searching look.

"We have a body in autopsy the same as you describe. We thought at first it must be a toxin case but..." George caught himself. He was starting to tell everything but there was no time for details. Best to skip the attack by Jenkins he thought. "I did meet Doctor Channer there. There's a temple and a cave near here isn't there?" This time Roberto's reaction was a blend of amazement and wariness.

"The only one who could know about that are a handful of people who've been on the ship." Roberto's lips tightened into a thin line.

"Roberto, I saw something it's going to be hard for you to believe. I can hardly believe it even now." George thought of how he could make Kokoori matter of fact but there was no way. "I saw an entity of Doctor Channer in the hospital, a kind of out of body being that talked to me. It was he who directed me to come here. He said I'd find Colin with a woman here. And about the existence of a cave and temple with words that must be read." George swallowed hard. "I'm trembling now just telling you about it." George waited for a disdainful sneer or a kind of what do you take me for laugh but it didn't come. Instead a look of bemused understanding crossed Roberto's face.

"A friend we lost was called Jhanda. He worked with Doctor Volger's daughter when her psychic episodes began. He predicted that the words Colin would need to enter the ellipse would be brought here by you." George groped for a reply but Roberto's words kept him momentarily mute.

"You said I'd find it hard to believe the things you saw in Kokoori. Now when I tell you what has happened here you may have questions of your own." Roberto looked out at the horizon preoccupied it seemed with how to put his thoughts in order. "I was deputy administrator to Doctor Volger on the ERSEV. My job was to facilitate the flow of the experiments in progress. When Jhanda was brought aboard to probe into Margo's psychic changes I thought at first it was a waste of time. Then when he began working with her it turned out she had these memory fragments induced by particles from the vessel. We synthesized related particles that were then injected into Margo." Roberto fumbled with his words making a couple of false starts before he could continue. "The molecules led Margo to conjure up a recollection of an existence she'd had with Colin in the past. The vessel you were told about *is* here in the cave. It's made of an unknown metal. We call it the ellipse. It was put here a couple of million years ago." An automatic how and why started on George's lips but he pulled the obvious questions back when Roberto raised a there's more you should hear finger. "We have received a radio telescope communication from a civilization somewhere in the constellation Centaurus. It's fairly certain the signal gives a DNA sequence that is the master strand for a library of genomes in the machine. We think a techno glitch killed whoever brought the ellipse here." So that's what Channer must have meant about a needed correction, George thought, a signal from far space that went awry. One, that when corrected, had the power to transform a few into malignant monsters and another few into what Dr. Channer had called the honored ones. Channer had said the vessel he would find was placed here very long ago. George hadn't asked who'd done the placing but recalled thinking it must have been done before the invention of the wheel. "Emtran is out to put both the ellipse and us underground. Before they can get to the machine we have to help Colin and Margo get inside," Roberto said. "There's a line of ancient writing on the temple altar. Margo was puzzled about it because it seems to be nonsense writing. But maybe it made sense to a group of visitors from the neighborhood of Centaurus." Roberto held out his revolver to George. "You any good with one of these?"

"I was hoping using that wouldn't be necessary." George stared at the handgun.

"I had to kill an Emtran agent on the ship Doctor Trimble. It was self defense. They're going to want revenge." George reluctantly took the gun. How sadly ironic, he thought, if the search for a new horizon should be sullied by more death.

"One thing before we go on Roberto. This remembering of a time in the past, what can you tell me about it?" Roberto glanced at his watch. It was 1:30.

"I'll give you the short version," Roberto said. He slung the rifle back over his shoulder. "Margo's visions of another time before Colin came aboard were always in disconnected pieces. Then after the memory molecules were injected Jhanda was able to draw her latest memories into a smoother flow. She'd seen Colin in some of her previous recollections. Even though she'd never seen him before she had him present in a Greek Temple scene she'd painted. Jhanda guided Colin into Margo's trance memories. He saw himself at the same Temple as in the painting. There was an ellipse under the Temple floor just like the one here in the cave." For a moment George stared at Roberto with unseeing eyes. Instead the nude Channer figure sat before his minds vision again. "Universes recurring and being born anew", George could hear Channer saying. When Doctor Channer had first uttered those words they sounded so pompous George had wanted to laugh. What a pretentious fool the young man on the operating table had been, George remembered thinking. But then he'd turned to see Channer's body lying there on the floor behind him.

"Roberto, I suppose you've thought through the other possibility. The more realistic one I mean. That what Margo and Colin remembered wasn't a memory at all. Just another aberration caused by the ellipse particles."

"Testing me Doctor Trimble? Here we are about to risk our lives on the basis of some peoples' flights of fancy and you want to know how confident I am about all the weirdness. Isn't that right?" Roberto didn't wait for an answer. "After the Greek Temple memory I researched past memory phenomenon thoroughly. I was looking for confirmation. That at least a few respected scholars took the possibility of past existences seriously. I Goggled up the old papers from The Journal of Quantum Mechanics that were written in the fifties."

George grunted wondering where Roberto was going. He couldn't pretend to understand much about Heisenberg's or Schrödinger's work. He'd heard about the cat that supposedly could be alive and dead at the same time but the whole quantum business was mostly a quirky curiosity.

"If you read what the wave equations empirically say they tell us there are an infinity of existence that have led to this one where we're standing right now...and an infinity of futures that will lead from here. A number of physicists won't say publicly that this is the case because it sounds so anti common sense. But it's true."

"How can?..." George started.

"Look George we don't have time. I believe you talked to an out of body entity so we'll accept what the wave mechanics tell us and we'll let it go at that." George nodded agreement. He understood the fascination of what might be possible was carrying them both forward in spite of the danger.

"What do we do if Emtran gets to the Temple first?", George asked. "They won't." Roberto pointed down the beach to a spot a hundred feet away.

"They started down a trail that leads to a cliff face. Colin got lost there yesterday."

Roberto led George to a second trail so clear of growth it looked nearly landscaped. "I give Emtran a minimum of a half hour to find it. We'll be there in ten minutes if we hustle. Keep the safety off on the .38." George checked the pistol. It was loaded with six shiny rounds. Roberto started down the trail a few steps then stopped and turned back to George.

He pointed to a gray ruin off in the mist. "There's the Temple. The ellipse is in the cave right below."

CHAPTER 19

COLIN BRAKED THE Land Rover to handle an unexpected series of hair pin turns along the rain forest trail. After the last curve he felt a sense of relief. In front of him, only yards away, stood the rear of the Temple. He thought with chagrin of yesterday's struggle in the green maze, the infuriating groping about, then smacking up against the escarpment face. All the while there was this clear trail he could have wandered down. At least he hadn't needed to run the gauntlet a second time. On its high plateau the Temple quivered in the humid late noon air. Crumbled cobbled steps angled up the brooding ruin like the stairway at Tikal. Under normal circumstances Margo would be getting more of the CORCID soon. Her heart beat would smooth out for a while longer, then a new dose would be at hand. With none left it would not be long before her heart would begin to stutter into fatal arrhythmia. Getting her into the ellipse in time would fix that. Jhanda hadn't actually *said* that putting her in the machine would stabilize her but surely that was his meaning. What would happen inside the ellipse that could reverse the paralysis was another matter. It was just one of a long list of questions Colin could tally up on the topic of what would happen when they got inside. But he'd agreed with himself to trust rather than skepticize. He wasn't about to let the siren of beckoning caution make him lose his nerve at this far juncture.

"It's beautiful in the afternoon light." Margo's voice startled Colin. It seemed a long time since he'd heard her speak. "When dad brought me here it was only for a little while in the morning. The light was different then." Colin checked that Margo was belted into the SUV's seat securely. She turned her face toward him. Her eyes were wet with tears. "I hoped that Jhanda and father would be here to see us enter the ellipse." Margo bit her lip to keep from crying, then tossed off that little laugh that had charmed Colin so much at their first meeting. "I better watch out or I'll fog up this mask."

"You know then," Colin said. He intuited that Margo was aware the worst had happened.

"Yes I know," Margo sighed. "Like most of what I've seen, it was just a wisp of a picture. I saw both of them on the lower deck. Jhanda and dad. They turned to me long enough to make eye contact then they were gone. I had a terrible feeling of foreboding but I wanted not to think of it."

Colin groped for something to say that would ease Margo's sorrow. He hadn't anticipated her waking, already knowing the terrible truth. There was that awkward search for the right words to say when none were ever good enough. The bond between Margo, her father and Jhanda had been strong. It pained Colin to see Margo's unhappiness.

"They'd be glad to know we're going to finish the work they started," Colin said. Margo's smile brightened a bit.

"I know someday we will meet again." Margo looked down at the belt across her chest. "If we're going to get up there I think first you ought to get me unbuckled."

"Oh, sorry Colin said, glad for the hint of lightness in Margo's tone. He unfastened her belt and lifted her carefully out of the Rover. She seemed lighter than before. The half hour since he'd carried her into the sea cat had apparently been enough time for his muscles to recover. Colin looked around apprehensively. If the Emtran agents discovered the Rover's tracks they would only be fifteen minutes behind. They were professional stalkers and it wouldn't take them long to catch up. The three hundred feet to the top of the temple steps was totally exposed. Konrad's people had cleared away the jungle growth at the temple's base. There was nothing for Colin to do but make a dash from his covered position across the clearing and pray the Emtran pair hadn't sighted them.

"You're worried Colin, what's wrong?", Margo asked.

"Emtran. The swat team that killed..." Colin stopped abruptly. "Margo, you don't know how Jhanda died?", Colin asked. Then he understood. Of course she didn't. Margo's version of Jhanda and her father fading in her vision had told her they were gone, but she had assumed Jhanda had fallen victim to disease the same as her father had. She knew nothing of Emtran.

"Margo, Jhanda wasn't infected. He was killed by a police unit. McClure had a team sent here to arrest all of us. He used the excuse that your father is risking a catastrophe by violating the quarantine."

"And they killed Jhanda because of that?"

"He was shot while we were getting away. There was gunfire. An Emtran agent was killed too.

Senseless. I'm sorry it happened and sorrier I have to tell you."

"But couldn't you have talked to them?" Colin waved away Margo's question.

"There's no talking to them. They probably weren't told anything except what they had to do to prevent an epidemic. Anyway they can coerce, arrest, shoot they'll do it. They're not about to negotiate."

"But we can't let them keep us away from the ellipse," Margo said with a note of alarm.

"No we won't let that happen," Colin replied with more assurance than he felt. "We're going up there now." Colin felt the hair raise on his neck as he trotted across the clearing. He held Margo tightly, half expecting to hear gun shots break out. Thankfully there was only silence. He pushed himself up the mossy Temple steps two at a time, not daring to stop. A small portico extended out from the Temples rear, with a pillared supported overhang. Colin laid Margo down and rested momentarily in its shadow. He had the high ground view of any threat that might come across the clearing. With his breathing back to normal, he thought about how best to fill Margo in what he had discovered. Under other circumstances he would have told her the details of how her insight had led to finding the pulsar signal. But he only had time for the basics. The intimate questions he had about their time in ancient Greece would have to wait for a more peaceful time.

"Ready for some good news?", Colin asked. Margo searched his eyes with heightened curiosity. "We found the link between the altar carvings and the ellipse etchings. If we'd known what was carved on the broken altar end we would have seen it was...," "The same carving as on the altar we saw in Greece," Margo interrupted. Her eyes danced with excitement.

"The altar image kept returning to me while I was in my trance state," Margo went on. "There were the two circles at the ends of the altar table in the Greek Temple and one circle on this one. The broken end would have made this one a copy."

"Yes, and the circles turn out to be a double star in Centaurus. We picked up an intelligent signed from the pulsar."

"That says what?"

"That tells us what the DNA bases should be in the ellipse. Your father was right about that. The correct sequence is here in my pocket. We sequenced it before we left the ship" Colin opened his pocket carefully. He held up the little vial for Margo.

"Doesn't look like much does it. A little white thread in a few drops of ammonium hydroxide." "Not much except an opening to a new pathway. Jhanda was right. The vial I held in the Temple and this one hold the same substance," Margo said.

"And Brahma ? The potion he carries in the cave carving, do you think it's the same?", Colin asked. "Yes. Our visitors may have been here at other times, not just at my Temple or this cave. Other machines may have been left for other cultures too," Margo added. Colin put the vial back in his shirt pocket carefully. How easy it would be to let a seconds inattention splatter the precious code like a shattered egg. He grinned with the irony of it, the power that he held, the responsibility that was his all because of this fleck of thread floating in his pocket. Colin shifted Margo more comfortably in his arms.

"Tell me Margo, did you know from the start the painting was real...of you and I?" Margo smiled sheepishly.

"If I'd told you the robed man was you what would you have thought?", Margo asked. "That I was totally crazy," Margo answered herself. "I realized afterward that telling you I'd foreseen you coming aboard wasn't real smart. What would your reaction have been only knowing me over the space of a dinner time, if I'd said the man in the painting was you?"

"I was thinking about ditching the dinner and leaving, as it was. I guess I would have."

"The vision of the Greek Temple came to me the day before the paralysis happened. I had an urge to get it on canvas like I never had with any of my paintings. I finished it straight through."

"And the procession carrying the basket, had you seen that?"

"No. The first time I saw all that was when Jhanda guided us. It was only then I realized the man and woman foreseen were us."

"When I saw you at the top of the Greek temple staircase I wanted to tell you that we were the ones meant to enter the ellipse. But there were no sounds. Instead I had to watch myself walk into the altar chamber unheard." Margo looked lovingly at Colin.

"I was longing to talk to you. I realized we were embedded watching our past unfold." Even with knowing only that smallest glimpse of their life in the past, Colin felt connected to Margo in the way only lovers do. He hadn't been able to define that feeling in the moments just after the trance. He had felt an attraction that flowed from his fingers to hers, yet wasn't ready just then to call it love. He'd come away from the Temple of the Two Gods changed in a way he never could have imagined.

"We recalled only a few moments. But they were the most important," Margo said. "Zeus with his thunder bolt and cup and Brahma with his lotus and potion. Different Gods but the messages are the same, handed down to us from twenty five hundred years ago and again when this Temple was carved." Margo nestled her head deeper into the crook of Colin's arm. "Colin, are you afraid? I mean of what might happen inside the ellipse?"

"A little."

"Our visions into the past and all, you do believe in them don't you?" Colin squeezed Margo tightly.

"Yes. Mostly because I believe in you." Margo sighed with contentment.

"What do you think our life was like then Colin? Have you thought much about it?" Margo ran on not waiting for a reply. "I've pictured us together at the Temple at night. I imagine we might actually have lived there. I've spent sometime putting together different scenarios. You know we only saw a few moments of the temple clearly. A tiny bit of what must have been a fascinating life together." Colin paused before he replied. In the few quiet moments he'd had, he'd fantasized some about his life with Margo. Now, being asked to verbalize his musings, he felt hesitant and strangely shy. Almost as if speaking aloud about those fantasies would make them vanish. "Colin have you considered that the explosions of arts back then might have been caused by particles from the ellipse? There's never been a good explanation as to why that concentration of genius occurred just then."

"Yes, but if that's true, what about the other side. There's no record of unexplained diseases being spread. We don't hear about a Pericles having to pay for his genius with paralysis. Except for that little peek into the past we've forgotten so much."

"What's that sound?", Margo asked. She glanced toward the ruins interior. Colin leaned around the pillar. He heard it too. From deep below the Temple floor the ominous hum was starting up again.

"It's the ellipse. Your father thought the machine was on some type of timing mechanism that malfunctioned. We're lucky it hasn't blown since yesterday. But I guess it was too much to expect that it had settled down for good."

"We should be able to fix it when we get inside," Margo said with a note of surety Colin didn't quite share. Colin decided not to bring up the fact that they had no idea how to open the machine... let alone do whatever had to be done inside to make it right.

"We have to get down there now." Colin said. He tenderly put two fingers to his mask in front of his lips and touched them to hers. He inched Margo around to the backside of the pillar. He was pretty well blocked from Emtran's eyes. Colin took a first look at the Temples interior. "Spooky." The long ago earthquake hadn't done as much damage as he'd imagined. Only a few side pillars were collapsed but most of the roof was still intact. Except for the few sections where sunlight filtered through, the inside was in deep violet shadow. In the low light about fifty feet ahead was a stone block with a triangular shaped cap. The right corner had been broken off.

"That's it...the altar?", Colin asked.

"Yes. When I sketched it I came in from the front."

"Listen Margo, your father said there was a passage down to the cave below. Did you know about it?"

"No", Margo answered with a look of surprise.

"One of the things he didn't think you needed to know. It should be behind the altar here." Colin carefully stepped around the shards of stone that had fallen to the floor. In some places, a film of algae had grown up making the surface slick.

"There Colin," Margo shouted. "Sticking out of the floor." Her eyes led his to a small crusty ring in the floor. It was nearly invisible among the rest of the debris strewn about. He sat Margo down with her back leaning against the altar's side. He tugged at the ring. A man hole sized plate began to break free of its covering of molded growth.

With a final pull the metal plate came free. Colin's arm quivered as he set the cover aside careful not to let it clang on the stone floor.

"What can you see?", Margo asked.

"Black mostly, but I can make out some foot holds down a shaft. The passageway must spiral after that because it's totally dark." Colin turned to Margo. "There are cobwebs all over down there. God knows what else has made its home in this hole."

"Can we both fit?"

"If we go down chest to chest I think we'll just squeeze down. Let's get...," "Wait a second," Margo interrupted, her voice an intense whisper. "I hear something." Colin jerked his head up. There was someone at the entrance. He could hear the sound of sand crackling under foot. Colin motioned for Margo to be quiet. He pulled her out of view behind the altar. Then with his hand on the butt of the .45 he crept forward behind an entrance pillar.

"Colin. It's me. George. Are you in there?" What the hell? Colin thought. It was George Trimble's voice alright. No mistaking that resonant sound. But how could George be here? The last Colin had seen of him he was puffing on his pipe as the snow piled up on their Manhattan office windowsill. Colin stepped from behind the pillar. He waved the white suited George from behind a tumbled mass of stone into the open. Quickly, he hustled George into the shadows. Emtran couldn't be too close or they'd have seen George by now Colin thought. Once inside Colin threw his arms around George in an affectionate bear hug.

"I don't know what to ask you first," Colin said. "What's happened? How...why are you here?", Colin blurted in a tumble of words.

"Long story Colin and strange." George squinted into the Temple's interior. "I ran into Roberto. He should be here in a minute. I got the story about the pulsar and everything from him." George sucked in a deep breath. "He told me about the machine that shouldn't be here." George pulled his pipe out of a thigh pocket. He brought it nearly to his lips before realizing the impossibility of smoking through the Plexiglas mask. "You're with a woman called Margo?", George questioned. "Roberto told me about the psychic powers...and the paralysis. But here's the thing. I learned that she'd be with you here in an unusual way."

"How?", Colin asked intently.

"I bounced around how to tell you so it sounds believable but..."

"It's okay George. I'm listening," Colin calmly repeated. George related the Channer story, trying to be more matter of fact than he'd been with Roberto..."

"So then I turned around and there was Dr. Channer's body on the O.R. floor. What it was I'd been talking to I don't know. His soul, ghost or whatever. But whatever it was it left me sure that what it said was true." George watched Colin's lips curve into an enigmatic smile.

"Let me introduce you to Margo." Colin led George behind the broken altar. Margo looked up at the white suited figure with a hint of apprehension.

"Don't worry Margo. He's not from Emtran. This is George Trimble, a friend and fellow worker.

He's here to help. George, I think Margo would like to hear about your encounter with Channer." George stooped down close to Margo. He began to extend his hand to shake but pulled it back remembering her paralysis.

"I'm sorry," George flustered.

"Thank you George. No apology needed," Margo replied warmly. George recounted his meeting in the O.R., once more, emphasizing Channer's command to read the altar words. "There was one other thing he said, that you were chosen to change one thing in the past. Roberto said you saw back into an earlier time in ancient Greece." George made sure he had Colin and Margo's full attention before going on. "I have to ask. Do you both believe you lived that other life?"

"Yes we believe it George. But a lot of what we saw is still mysterious," Colin replied.

"Inside was a machine like this one below. But what we were to do in there we don't know," Margo continued. A noise from the Temple rear startled the three of them. Colin clicked off the safety on the colt. He waited.

"Just me," Roberto called out from the portico. "I wasn't sure if you were Emtran."

"You had me holding my breath Roberto. Now that we've all made it here I feel better," Colin said. "Good but we can't relax. Emtran can't be far behind." Colin nodded.

"Margo, I think it's time to have a shot at the altar script" Colin said. He carried Margo to the altar face and sat her down before it. He held her upright with his hands.

"Any clues Margo?", Roberto quizzed.

"I wish I could tell you I've figured it out but I haven't. The letters in Khmer are these,. ธᏕᏗᎿᎮᏗᏗᎿᏕ. There's no doubt about that. But strung together like this they form no words. They mean nothing." "George tell me again what Margo was supposed to read. Do you remember exactly what Channer said?", Colin asked.

"Well I was excited naturally," George answered with a defensive tone."

"I'm sure...well, almost sure he said what I already told you. The altar words must be read." "But you just heard Margo, George. This writing is meaningless."

"Channer said read the altar words or the writing or the inscription. What difference does it make?
It's all the same."

"No it's not," Colin said softly. "Could Channer have specifically said read the inscription instead of read the words?", Colin pressed. George shrugged.

"He might have. What's the point?"

"Just this, we've all been assuming that the text is carved here too with some regular word order.
Margo you've been approaching it that way haven't you?" "Yes."

"But if Dr. Channer said read the inscription he may have meant you need to sound out each letter." Colin squeezed Margo's hand. "Margo, think back to when you put the vial on the altar. You stepped back and said something while looking at the script. I thought it was an invocation. But what happened after that?"

"The floor opened and the ellipse rose up" Margo answered. "But I can't remember what I read Colin."

"No matter, I think you read the same sounds then that you're to read now. They were in ancient Greek. These are Khmer. Different symbols. Same sounds. What brought up the ellipse and what opens it are sounds not words. My guess is that the ellipse is set to open by voice activation. If I'm right when you sound out the Greek altar letters and these in Khmer the sounds will be identical."

"Colin, we have to get down there quick. There's fifty feet of rock between us and the ellipse. Even if Margo shouts out the sounds the machine won't pick up her voice from here," Roberto urged.

"Okay Margo you'll need to memorize these letters," Colin said.

"Way ahead of you, I'm doing it now," Margo answered. Her eyes burned into the altar script. "You found the passage?", Roberto asked. Colin lifted the edge of the metal plate.

"Roberto will you go down first? The passage needs a bit of housekeeping after five hundred years."

"I'll go down and out to where the cave makes the dogleg turn. It will be a good place to wait for the Emtran pair. Chances are they won't have discovered the back entrance."

"Thanks. Then George you go next. I'll follow with Margo." George nodded with a bit of hesitation.

"I'm not as sleek as I was. What if I get stuck in this rabbit hole?", George quipped. "Then Alice will come to your rescue," Margo answered lightheartedly.

"And the Dark Wood Margo, you'll lead us through that won't you?", Colin spoke up. He didn't want to turn the banter serious, but couldn't contain the emotion welling up in him.

"Dark Wood? Wasn't that the Wizard of Oz?", George asked.

"Through the Looking Glass, George. It's a forest where things have no names. Alice goes in and forgets her name until she comes out the other side," Colin answered. George hadn't needed to grapple with the mystery of who he was in some other time. What was Margo's name then. What was his? Colin thought. Surely they'd had names. But for him and Margo, all meaning had been forgotten, except for that encounter in the Temple of the Twin Gods. Colin felt himself aching to dip down into that riot of color and sound again, to make a connection with the past once more.

"Colin are you ready?" Roberto's voice jolted him from his mini reverie.

"Just a second of wool gathering Roberto. Sorry." Roberto's face peeked out from under the floor plate. He held up its edge with his palm, his eyes just peering over the edge.

"I gathered up about a pound of spider web down there. Otherwise the passage is clear."

"Go out to the dog leg Roberto. We'll be right behind," Colin said. Roberto tossed out a small flashlight.

"The white rabbit can lead the way with this," he said with a touch of whimsy. "I'm down to find the mad hatter," he added then disappeared into the shaft. George shone the light into the tunnel then stepped back.

"If the ellipse was buried when the Khmers built all this, why the passage down? They could have just walked in the cave entrance," George said.

"The Khmers would still have heard its hum," Margo broke in.

"There is evidence of a fifteenth century outbreak here George. A sound like that coming from an underground source could have been interpreted as Siva's voice," Colin added.

"If your right Colin, the priests would have probably sealed the cave entrance," Margo said. "Only they would have been allowed into the space below."

George sat with his legs dangling over the edge of the shaft. He ran the flashlight over the freshly cleared steps. He started down. Colin picked up Margo. When George's head had sunk below floor level he eased himself in. He felt carefully for the toe holds before trusting his full weight.

"I'm half way down. I can see light below," George called up. "There are some figures on the wall here."

"What are they like?", Margo asked.

"There are four little images at the compass points. Painted little critters. Ugly. They are holding swords and shields. They have their tongues stuck out."

"They're Asuras George. Hindu demons, put there as a warning not to descend any further," Margo explained.

"Just what I wanted to hear," George grumbled.

"Let me know when you reach bottom George," Colin ordered."

"Another minute." Colin listened to the echo of George's labored breathing become more faint.

Then the sound of even footsteps.

"I'm through. The steps lead down here to a ledge overlooking the ellipse. The ellipse is about sixty feet below in front of me. There's a stone staircase to my left hidden behind a rock outcrop. It leads down to the cave floor." Now that George was down, Colin felt more confident descending the twisted tunnel. Light from the cave below cast the passageway in increasing shades of lighter gray. When he was all the way down he felt George's hands around his legs guide him onto the ledge.

"Can we rest awhile?", George asked. Colin could see that behind his mask, George's face was wet with sweat.

"For a minute," Colin allowed. He sat Margo down at the back of the ledge. Both men sat at her sides.

"It's exactly the same", Margo said. "What?", Colin asked.

"The ellipse, just as we saw it in the Temple."

"Yes it is." Colin forgot that Margo had never been in the cave. All of her sketching had been of the ruins above. "Confirmation?", Colin asked.

"No, not really. I knew this machine would be the same." Colin made no reply. There it was again. That take it for granted mindset that had been consistent all along. Margo surely had to still be grieving for her father and Jhanda. In spite of that, there was that calm assurance that all was working toward some better purpose.

"I feel better now," George said, replacing his water bottle onto his belt.

"You stay here George. There's no need for you to put yourself in harms way," Colin said. He stood and lifted Margo to his chest.

"No way Colin. You'll need to protect Margo." "Thanks George. You're okay with the .38?"

"I know which end the bullets come out of, that good enough?"

"Sure. Let's hope you won't have to use it." George started down the stone staircase to the half buried ellipse. Colin carried Margo behind. He held her tightly and walked to the edge of the excavation pit. Colin felt so differently than when he'd been here yesterday afternoon.

"Margo, I hated this machine yesterday. I took what it did to Ed and the villagers personally. I still hate it for that. Is it crazy to have feelings about a machine?"

"Only human," Margo replied. Simultaneously with her answer Roberto came rushing into the excavation chamber.

"They're coming in Colin.

I tried to get to the breaker box to shut off the lights. I wasn't quick enough. They're halfway to the dog leg already."

"What are our options, Roberto?", Colin asked. There was no question of getting the ellipse open before the Emtran pair arrived.

"The two of them are together. Chances are they didn't find the tunnel otherwise they'd be heading down already. Let's hope they don't discover the passage to the upstairs altar. Then they'll have to come through this narrow pathway here to get in. We'll block them there.", Roberto said.

"Where do you want us?", Colin asked. Roberto scanned the chamber.

"It would have been better if one of us stayed up on that ledge. Too late now. You three get back to the stairs and stay behind the outcrop. I'll be on the wooden steps going into the pit."

"How are you doing?", Colin asked Margo. He had her leaning back against the steps hidden from the sight lines of the chamber entrance.

"I'm fine Colin. Don't worry about me." Actually she wasn't so fine Colin could see. The Corcid was wearing off. Dark smudges discolored her lower eyelids. Her lips had taken on a purplish hue.

"We can't change this Colin. You want to avoid the senseless hostility that will be happening now. I hate it too. But we don't have the power to change this. I wish it could be otherwise. What will happen now must be so," Margo said. Colin wasn't sure how he'd handle another death. Damn McClure and his like. All those hypocrites who put on their happy public faces and privately seethed with power hunger.

"Colin. Roberto is signaling", George whispered. Down in the excavation pit Roberto pointed to his rifle and then gestured emphatically to the entryway. Any second now the Emtran pair would be putting in an appearance. Colin felt a cold film of sweat break out under his gloved gun hand. A feeling of ambiguousness nagged. Part of him looked forward to the chance to avenge Konrad and Jhanda. He had little sympathy for these twenty first century editions of guns for hire. Anyone who could mindlessly head off to an unthinking assassination had to have serious social adjustment issues. Colin realized he might have to take the life of one or both of these individuals. The thought of actually aiming and squeezing the trigger left a lump in his throat. Colin strained his eyes. He searched for a sign of movement at the chamber entrance. Suddenly a burst of automatic fire resonated off the rock walls. Intuitively Colin pulled his head down. The Emtran pair sprayed the cave with random fire. Colin leaned back protectively across Margo, afraid a glancing round might catch her as it had Jhanda. George poked at Colin's elbow, directing him to look again at Roberto on the wooden stairs.

The Emtran pair walked slowly forward, their heads on a swivel.

They had body armor on. No doubt, extra protection in light of what had happened to their pal. Roberto motioned for George and Colin to hold their fire. They watched anxiously as Roberto did some finger work with the concusion grenade. The Emtran pair continued moving cautiously forward. Then a noisy clank.

"Damn I dropped it." Colin and Margo sucked in an audible breath as they watched George's .38 tumble down the stone steps. It stopped not more than thirty feet from the Emtran pair. Instantly a barrage blasted their stone protective wall. One of the shells tore through George's mask just missing his nose by millimeters. George put his hand to his face. His eyes grew wide with fear. Colin pulled his quivering friend down behind the wall.

"Am I hit, am I bleeding?", George stuttered. "No, but hold you breath," Colin demanded.

Colin groped for the metal catch that attached George's headpiece. He slipped it off and quickly replaced George's mask with his own.

"Colin you can't..."

"Shut up George. You got into this situation by the back door. If one of us is to suck in the particles it shouldn't be you. Anyhow, the fog has dispersed. I don't think there's much left to bother us."

"The machine is still running Colin," George said with a wary glance at the ellipse. Colin patted the vial in his pocket.

"I'm betting this will shut it down before it gets to its red line," Colin answered. Out of the corner of his eye Colin watched the two agents walk down the opposite side of the cave wall. They'd probably walk around the excavation pit and fire point blank. Fish in a barrel. Colin held the .45 in front of him. He waited for them to come into a better view. As they strolled around the far end, Colin saw Roberto's grenade arch up out of the pit. It took a high parabola and landed perfectly at Emtran's feet. One of the men crouched down. He swept his arm back as if to bat the grenade back at Roberto. He was too late. The weapon exploded with hammer force. Even from twenty yards away the concussion banged against Colin's chest like a heavy weight's punch. Roberto ran up the wooden steps.

"Wait there," he called to Colin's group. Colin watched Roberto walk to the fallen pair. He waved his arm to clear away the dust that was suspended over the pit. He raised his rifle to his shoulder.

"No Roberto. No more killing please," Margo cried out. Her eyes were heavy with fatigue. "Colin can't we just restrain them? We've seen enough of death."

"Wait Roberto," Colin called out. He carried Margo to the prostrate pair with George tailing behind. The grenade had stunned them badly. A trickle of blood seeped from the ear of one of the unconscious men.

"They'll be bruised as hell and woozy for a day, but they're just knocked out now. Do we take Margo's advice," Roberto questioned.

"Yes Roberto," Colin said emphatically.

"Okay then." Roberto pointed the rifle into the pit. "There's some duct tape on Konrad's work bench. That should do the job."

"I'll get it," George volunteered. As George waddled down the steps Roberto took two packets from the waists of the unconscious agents. He handed the clay like bricks to Colin.

"C-4. After they got rid of us, they'd slap these on the ellipse and boom," Roberto said. "Wouldn't have dented it" Colin answered.

"Yeh, but they didn't know that," Roberto answered with a wink. George puffed up the steps with several rolls of tape.

"Colin while I wrap these gentlemen up you and Margo go ahead and do what you come here to do.

Okay?", Roberto said.

"You're opening it now?" George asked.

"If it looks like we can't well use the C-4 to bring the roof down," Colin said.

"Colin, hurry please," Margo called out with a note of urgency. Quickly, Colin ran over to her. Her pallor had deepened in just the last few minutes. Her eyes were only half open. Colin rushed her down the wooden steps and stood before the machine. Colin lifted her face to his.

"Margo think of the sounds. Say them now." It was all she could do to nod an assent. Groggily she repeated each sound as distinctly as her weakened state would allow. Colin held his breath. A second passed, then two. Tiny fragments of time seemed to scroll by in Colin's head by the millionths. Then slowly with a liquid like flow the steps extruded out of the ellipse.

"We were right Margo." Colin kissed her mask. The whining hum wasn't far from the sound peak that triggered the earlier explosion. Colin estimated they had maybe five minutes before it blew again. George and Roberto stood riveted with attention as Colin stood on the excavation floor. What exactly he was to do with the pulsar DNA he had no idea. He recalled it was at just this point in the Greek Temple, where the steps slid out, that their memory ended.

Clearly, the molecule fragments in his pocket needed to be placed somewhere inside the ellipse. Colin sucked in a deep breath. He hoped there were no unseen disease particles lurking in the air.

As in the Greek Temple, there were the same twelve steps leading to the opening in the top of the ellipse. At Margo's sound key, the opening had expanded to double the circumference Colin had seen when he was here with Ed Lippincott. Even though the ominous hum was growing shriller, there was no sign of the hair like fibers whose appearance would signal an imminent explosion. Carefully, Colin walked Margo up the mirror like steps.

"The same inside as at the Temple?", Margo asked. Her eyelids fluttered as she struggled to hold on to consciousness.

"Yes, you'll see in a minute," Colin answered. He'd had only the briefest look into the ellipse interior in the Athens Temple. The inside flowed with the same soft light he'd noticed then. The blue green color emanated from the walls as if the light source was the very molecules of their surface.

Except for a few small toggles, the interior was free of clutter. A gently sloping ramp led down into the heart of the machine. There in the center were two comfortable looking reclining chairs. Comfortable that is if you're less than two years old Colin thought. Each chair was no longer than a baby's car seat.

"We're going in Margo," Colin said.

"Okay," Margo answered dreamily. As Colin walked down the ramp he noticed a faint smell of ozone. Maybe a sign of electrical problems in the circuitry he knew must be below his feet. Colin stood by the tiny seats surveying the interior with a jumble of apprehension and anticipation. What looked to be solid walls from outside were not solid at all. Every few seconds now they flowed into a gel like substance that defied Colin's comprehension.

"Colin, close your mouth and look at the chairs," Margo said. "I didn't know my mouth was open. What about the chairs?"

"Just look at them." Colin looked quizzically at Margo. But he focused his gaze obediently. "I'm looking Margo. Nothing is happening."

"Don't try so hard. Relax your attention." "How the hell do you relax your attention?"

"Just find the balance," Margo insisted. Colin fought a feeling of foolishness. As he was about to complain again, amazingly the miniature recliners morphed into adult size. Like pulled taffy the chairs stretched into adult configuration. "Now I hope you'll listen to me without the patronizing tone Mr. Colin Grier," Margo said.

"I wasn't patronizing Margo. Just clueless." Of course, the most sensible explanation for the transformation was that somewhere in the solid gel wall there were detectors that measured height and adjusted the seats accordingly. But Colin suspected that whoever placed the ellipse had gone the hard route and hooked up mental intent with physical change.

"The one on the left is a little smaller, so it must be meant for me," Margo chirped. She sounded like she was about to clamber aboard a carnival ride.

"You aren't the least bit afraid are you?", Colin asked.

"Hopeful, not afraid. We don't know what's going to happen it's true," Margo said. "We've seen a part of our past. But would it be wise to be able to see what happened to us here again? Maybe it's a good thing we can't. Now is the time to follow our instincts."

"Take no counsel of our fears. Alright," Colin agreed. It's easier for her than me Colin thought. He supposed being blessed (or burdened with) ESP abilities, Margo found sliding into belief a bit slicker than he did. Colin carefully lowered Margo into the smaller of the recliners. He placed her arms neatly at her sides. He looked around for safety straps then abruptly stopped. Why should there be any belts at all? Was the ellipse going anywhere? Would they be going anywhere?

He would be lying down next to Margo in a moment and didn't know what to expect. Colin rolled himself into the recliner, aware of each contact point his body made with the chair. As soon as he settled in there was a quiet steam like hiss followed by a noiseless closing in of the whole inner circumference. The contraction was so smooth Colin understood instinctively that the adjustment was specifically designed for both of them. He reached out his arm. In any direction he moved, his fingers came in perfect contact with the low glowing walls.

"It's like it's waiting just for us Colin," Margo said. Colin looked carefully around. Without his noticing, the walls had more than contracted. They'd changed shape. What had been an ellipse was now hemispheric. Above their heads ten inches away were a cluster of hexagonal objects imbedded in the pliable surface. When Colin focused on any group of four or five of the geometric shapes he found he could move them cursor like with just his eyes. There were odd symbols on some of the buttons, whether letters in an alien language Colin couldn't tell.

"Bring them close together," Margo said. With his eyes Colin drew the multicolored group into a square patch. Margo surveyed the square for a few seconds. "The white one. I think that's the one we need first." Feeling more confident using his eyes as a mouse, Colin placed the white hexagon at the center of the cluster. "You can turn the face if you want to," Margo said.

"You think so?"

"Uh-huh. Try it." Colin willed the white piece to turn. Slowly it did. There on the reverse face were drawn two intertwined threads.

"The double helix. Do we touch it do you think?", Colin asked.

"Wait a second Colin," Margo said weakly. Abruptly, the gel wall changed to a warm yellow. The white hexagon changed shape. It became somehow a clear quartz crystalline tube on the screen.

The finger long cylinder filled with clear liquid. Then the tube complete with gradations became real. It floated out from the screen. The tube hovered weightless in front of Colin's face.

"Margo, it would be too much to think the culture that put this machine together scored their lab glass in metric units wouldn't it?"

"The civilization that made this is capable of most anything Colin." A few inches behind the suspended cylinder an image was forming on the gel wall. First the glass cylinder appeared. Then another double helix began to blink on and off inside of it.

"Couldn't be much clearer could it? See and do," Colin said. Margo made no reply. Her eyes were closed.

Out of force of habit, Colin took her wrist but of course there was no pulse to be had through the suit. There was nothing he could do. Colin took the vial of pulsar DNA from his pocket. He forced his fingers to stop trembling, then removed the rubber stopper. Carefully he poured his pulsar DNA fragment into the hovering cylinder. Colin took Margo's hand again. He held it tightly wishing the force of his grip could transfer his strength to her. Feebly, her hand squeezed back. Margo mumbled incoherently. Colin strained to make out her words but they were too disconnected. He watched the filled tube glide silently back into the gel surface. Gradually it faded, then a blank screen. The hum that had been gaining in frequency for the last hour began to drop off to a less threatening level. Was it because he'd inserted the DNA splice just now, or was the timing mechanism correcting on its own? There was no way to know. Colin prayed the lowered sound meant the immediate threat of more disease particles was quashed. After the code had come in from Kokoori, Roberto had calculated it was fifty- fifty whether the splice controlled only the release of genes or if it also was a key component in running the machine computers. Colin thought back to the cave entry way and his face off with Konrad. Dr.Volger had argued then for a missing splice that was both master genetic controller and the keystone computer component. Colin was about to find out whether either or both.

"Margo, can you hear me?", Colin demanded. Margo gave no reply. Colin shook her arm hard. She laid waxen faced and still. Colin felt a wave of anxiety crest. They were where they should be, inside the ellipse. Still the machine was not doing anything to help. If something didn't happen right now, whatever change the machine was going to make in them didn't matter. Colin didn't want to go alone.

Without Margo alive at his side, he didn't care what was to happen now. If she died, whatever fate held in store was meaningless if he had to travel it's byways alone.

A tingling sensation on his skin refocused his attention back in the moment. It was mildly pleasant, lasting for ten seconds or so. There was another steam-like hiss from under the floor, then Colin felt himself lift up, suspended, just as the crystal vial had been. He floated inches from the recliner. Margo was hovering too. A static crackle sounded from beneath the chairs, like the far away beginnings of a lightening storm. The prickling sensation passed over his body again. For an instant the ellipse went dark. When the light glowed on again their suits had evaporated away. Colin and Margo were naked. She hovered next to him, some balanced force holding her perfectly motionless. Her body was perfect in its stillness. When he had first seen her on the ERSEV's patio, he'd marveled at how supple, how beautiful her face was in spite of the paralysis. Now seeing her unclothed, Colin was amazed that the affliction had left her so perfect. Margo's white skin was vibrant against her thick chestnut hair. A moment ago her lips were dull, washed out. Suddenly, they were full red, alive. Colin's heart throbbed in his ears. He reached for her bare wrist. A shock of joy swept through him. There was a beating there, regular, steady. Colin settled back onto his invisible recliner. He kept one finger on Margo's wrist. Silently, countless threads alight with firefly color reached out from the semi solid walls. Colin recognized them as the same fibers he'd seen vibrating wildly just before they had spewed out the infection genes. This time they moved with gentle purpose, arching out toward both of them. The threads made contact with their naked bodies, just resting on the skin. Colin guessed there were about ten per square inch. Except for their faces, the fibers totally covered their bodies. Colin watched them move along his arm. The fibers probed, like insect antennae, touching, drawing back, then touching again as if searching for the perfect spot. He realized they were lining themselves up over all the thinner arteries. With Ed Lippincott he'd seen them blow out their gene particles in a wild spew of chaos. Some had given Margo her powers. Others doled out death. Now the threads were working as intended. They were poised to insert the pulsar DNA fragment into his and Margo's bodies. Colin felt a slight kitten claw scratch over his skin. The fibers stiffened as the solution with the pulsar gene code began to flow. Colin looked over at Margo. He watched the liquid run down the fibers, first starting at her legs, then turning into a miniature cascade as it worked through to her upper body. He let out the long breath he'd been unconsciously holding. He tried to settle himself into a normal breathing rhythm. He waited to feel something. Except for the hammering of his heart there was only silence. Had the ellipse malfunctioned? Then, before his nervousness became too much, the interior again fell into deep darkness. A pinpoint of bright white light began to burn at Margo's navel. Except it wasn't glowing *on* her body, it was shining from within. The point grew acetylene bright, then expanded to fill her with a brilliant radiance. Colin watched it shimmer and pulsate like a radioactive core, throwing off streaks of overpowering energy. Colin was stunned, spellbound. He wondered why he hadn't been blinded. Margo's fingers began to move. Then her face, glowing vibrantly, turned toward him. She smiled and said something Colin couldn't hear. Incredibly, the paralysis was gone. She put her hand, soft and warm on his. The phosphorus white light bridged through her arm and into his with lightening quickness, then condensed into a roiling ball at the center of his sternum. Fear gripped him, and happiness. Colin felt an impossible stir of emotions. Lifetimes of happenings, faces, images, crowded and swept through his brain in an instant. He was bewildered and pleased all at once. Colin strained to hold onto some semblance of his identity but felt himself brushing against the edge of madness. He fought an urge to bolt, to get outside of the ellipse and of himself. But this was the way it was supposed to be. He tried to slip that thought in amongst the barrage of sensory overload. It was his memories, he knew. Reflections of other lives rocketing through his mind, their emotions concentrated, nearly too intense to bear. Then the anxiousness stopped. Margo had put her reassuring hand on his chest. The relieving gesture comforted Colin, drew him back to normality. The dizzying chain of visions slowed, faded and slipped out of his brain. It was over. Colin's eyelids ached. He'd been squeezing them so hard they didn't want to relax. Gradually his vision cleared. The walls had returned to their wider dimensions. The inside of the ellipse seemed the same. He was still in his recliner, except that next to him Margo was gone. And above his head the top of the ellipse had spread wide open. Colin looked up to see a midnight black sky, filled with glittering stars. Clearly the ellipse wasn't in the cave anymore. He laid quietly for a moment staring out into the midnight deep. The constellations Crux, Lupus, The Southern Cross, were all reassuringly in place. Oddly now, he felt as relaxed as he had after the patio dinner cabernet. The tensions of the last few minutes were gone. Colin expected he should feel a spike of worry that Margo wasn't at his side but he didn't. Maybe he should be alarmed that he wasn't alarmed. Colin laughed a little ripple of a laugh. He felt content as he listened to his laugh, echo off into the deep black vault.

"Colin come on out," Margo's voice piped from somewhere outside.

It had the good natural challenge of an oceanside, "come on in, the water's fine." Colin pushed up to a sitting position. Aside from the fact that the laser had left him hairless as well as naked, he was the same as when he'd entered the ellipse. He *seemed* to be anyhow. It wasn't at all clear what, if anything, the new DNA had done to him but he was happy to see, on the outside at least, he was the same. Colin walked up the angled steps to the outside. The ellipse had moved. It was in the little meadow about forty feet from the cave entrance. The pastel flowers that had dotted the ground were gone. So was any sign of the foul smelling galls. At the bottom of the silver steps Margo stood looking up at him. She spun around in a circle, her bare body supple. The paralysis that had frozen her muscles was gone. Colin began to speak but stopped in a stammer. He couldn't put the words together that would express his wonder and delight. Margo held out her arms. Colin hurried down the steps.

He rounded her shoulders with his hands and drew her close in a long embrace. He reveled in the feel of her breasts against his own. Collin buried his face in her lustrous hair. He kissed her deeply, tenderly, a feeling of forever pressed against his lips.

He drew her fragrance deep inside, letting it intoxicate him. Margo nestled her face against his chest. "You've been brave Colin," Margo whispered. She glided her fingers along his arm. "I had flashes of other worlds to guide me, Jhanda to encourage me. It was so much harder for you."

"And worth it all if only to have you whole again," Colin said.

Margo stepped back. She took Colin's fingers in hers. There was so much to explain to him she thought, all the Worlds, and all the Universes. Telling all would take so long and, she thought, it wasn't important. What he needed to know would come to him in good time, and of itself.

"You don't know why I've brought you here do you?", Margo asked. The teasing tone remained, but Colin saw deep purpose in her eyes.

"For whatever reason you've chosen I know it must be right." Colin trusted her completely. He guessed who she was. Who she had been. Beyond those shinning eyes were glimmers of the many worlds she'd traveled through.

"Why did you choose me Margo? Of all the others you might have reached out for?" Colin stroked Margo's cheek with a silken touch.

"For the simplest reason Colin Grier. I always loved you."

Colin looked up at the blue white stars. The air was clean and crisp. He let Margo's words roll around inside his head, let her meaning fill him. He wanted to press her for answers; go on like a fascinated three-year old who doesn't know there are limits to the knowable. Margo looked off across the treetops hesitant, thoughtful.

"There was here. There was Athens with you. There were many times, many places. For you, life was chosen by an inscrutable universe. Even I cannot know it all. Now you will be able to say yes or no. Now it will be your choice too, as mine has been." Margo could see the look of dawning understanding cross Colin's face. Before he could speak she hushed him with a gentle finger to his lips. "Be patient love. The answers will come. Even to questions you have hardly thought to ask." Margo raised her hand high above her head. She looked up directly at Centaurus' stars as if her eyes could penetrate through their glitter to the ancient light behind. Colin said nothing. He was capable now of speaking to her silently if he should choose to use that new power. But just now her fierce concentration told him to be silent. An easy breeze swept across the grasses of the meadow. It started at the edges of the field, grew stronger until it bent the blades inward, blowing in from all directions. The little winds met and whirl pooled up around first Margo then Colin.

"Look down Colin," Margo spoke into his head. Colin looked at his feet. The ground under them began to fade. The wind reversed itself and blew out from the place where they stood, toward the edges of the meadow. As it rolled in an ever expanding ring it unfolded into the blackness of space and a bottomless panorama of stars under their feet.

"Where are we Margo?", Colin asked.

"Everywhere and anywhere" she replied impishly. "Just look around Colin." Colin turned his head left, then right. Then he did a complete turn around. Magically, where there had been woodland moments before, a shimmering, endless procession of gleaming galaxies, nebulae, bursting novae, stretched out in every direction.

The world, their world, had vanished. There was Margo, standing before him happily as she'd been and himself, weightless in the middle of some unknown vastness.

"It's open to us Margo. All of it, isn't that so," Colin asked. The question blinked into Margo's mind. So naïve, so lovable, he was she thought. He'd said once before, when she was still rigid with paralysis, when he didn't know what was in him now to know, that he'd trust her, follow her. Margo wanted to bring all the knowing to him at once, the time when her friends had visited, the troubles with the ellipse and the terrible diseases. So much to tell.

"For us, all is open Colin. Uncountable pasts have lead to here. Infinite futures stretch away,"

Margo said. For a moment, Margo searched the dazzling parade of light that surrounded them. "We can begin again Colin. Anytime, anywhere." Time and place. Every time and no time. Every place somehow at once, Colin thought. Margo read his thinking.

"The world we knew, Dad and Jhanda's world. We could make the change there Margo. Make it different, better. That's what I want to do. Starting with the time in Athens and then all the rest."

"Yes. I guessed that you would want that first of all," Margo nodded. She held out her hands to him again, drew him to her and kissed him sweetly. She stepped back and pointed to a swirl of suns and planets light years away. Colin watched them gather together into a ball of surging power, concentrated, radiating, vibrating. Margo reached out her palm to the boiling mass. A planet, a star, Colin couldn't know what it was exactly, burst out from the fiery nucleus and hurtled directly toward them. In a heartbeat the blazing world grew huge bearing down, ready to annihilate everything in its path. When its mass filled his field of vision Colin's resolve wavered. The instinct to recoil from obliteration was still there. He heard Margo's mind whisper to be calm. Colin stood firm. The massive speeding sphere made contact. Colin felt nothing, heard nothing. In an instant the monstrous ball was through them and rocketing off behind. Colin turned to see it grow smaller and smaller until at last it dissolved into a cloud of star stuff in some far away universe. Margo's body was different now, still perfect. But she glowed. Colin looked at his arms. They were radiating light too. Every atom of their bodies seemed to have taken on a life of its own. Like a pointillist's painting rendered in three dimensions, the molecules of their bodies danced with vibrant color. Then there was darkness.

TEMPLE OF THE ELUSINIAN MYSTERIES

PLATO LOOKED ABOUT him with dry mouthed anticipation as he stood waiting in the center of the Temple's inner chamber. He watched nervously as, one by one, the chosen attendants hung heavy woolen curtains between the white pillars of the Anaktaron.

In a moment he would be alone, closed off from any prying eyes. The thousands of pilgrims who had come singing and dancing to Eleusis had been allowed only to approach the Temple's outer hall. No one in five hundred years had been permitted to witness the curtained ceremony that was about to take place within the sacred Anaktaron. It had even been said that some were put to death for daring to steal a look around the pillars once the curtains had been hung. Plato shivered at the thought. He had been summoned to Demeter's Temple by a most rare command. But why?

Plato absent mindedly rubbed his hand over the still vivid forearm scar he'd received in the Battles with Sparta. He stared at the carving of Zeus with his upraised thunderbolt on the altar before him. Could it be that somehow the Gods themselves might intervene?

He had tried every ploy his brilliant mind could think of to stay the Master's execution. But those of the highest standing in Athens had demanded the philosopher's death. And even if the authorities drew back the hemlock cup what matter? The Master himself had insisted that his death sentence be carried out. "When you go to Eleusis' Temple you will bring back to me the treasure that has been prophesized," The Master had said. The Oracle at Delphi had indeed promised gifts from this sanctuary. But what possible good, Plato thought, could outweigh the Master's death?

The sudden opening of the great bronze doors drew Plato from his thoughts. Firelight from the burning kraters at the chambers entrance sent flickering steamlets of light across the Anaktaron floor, and bathed the altar in a golden glow.

Momentarily, Eleusis' rich robed priest slowly entered the secluded chamber. Handsome and calm, he carried a basket before him. An offering to Demeter and her daughter? Meanwhile the Temple's priestess had taken her place at the center of the altar. She too was clothed in like scarlet robes. The great doors swung silently shut. Plato watched the high priest process slowly up the altar steps.

He offered the basket to the lustrous haired priestess. Gracefully she placed it on the marble slab. She withdrew a clear glass vial from the basket and placed that also on the altar. She turned to Plato.

"You who are known in Athens by the name of Plato, do not be anxious. You have been called here to receive a most rare gift." Plato nodded deferentially to the priest and priestess. Was he permitted to speak in this hallowed hall, he wondered.

"About your Master Socrates you have great concern. We understand fully your anguish at his coming death tomorrow," The high priest spoke. "Even the powers of the Goddesses we serve here cannot alter his chosen fate," the priest continued.

"Then there is nothing to be done?", Plato stuttered timidly.

"We are the keepers of Eleusis' secrets surely," the priestess replied. "We have great powers. Though we are mortal, it is given to us to begin a new wheels turning. One thing only, of the future we may change, but alas, not Socrates own wish." Plato's eyes filled with tears. "Lighten your spirit," the priestess said. "We have come from afar to give you our gift and our teaching. Your master Socrates will leave you with a joyful heart."

"From afar?", Plato inquired, surprised by his own boldness.

"You and Socrates have conjectured that souls may fly from body to body. We have come from a time and place far beyond Olympus' heights," the priest replied. "We have had many names," he continued.

"For this moment we have names that will sound most strange to your ears. I am called Colin." "And I am Margo," the priestess said. "Come forward to us Plato," Margo ordered. Reluctantly, Plato walked forward to the altar table. Colin gestured for the philosopher to stand between himself and Margo. "What you will witness now must never be spoken of. Do you promise this?", Margo asked.

"Yes," Plato answered with deep sincerity. Margo turned to a sunken pit behind the altar that had been hidden from Plato's sight. Plato watched the priestess point to the center of the deep cutout. Slowly, silently, a large metal sphere rose up until it was level with the chamber floor. Plato looked up wonderingly at the object. Was it made of silver, of gold? Plato had never seen such perfection of form. Even the sculptor Phidias could not have fashioned such a pristine sphere. What might it contain? Plato wondered. Could it hold Persephone returned from the underworld? Could it be true, as some maintained, that the Goddess herself appeared in this sanctuary each spring?

The sphere opened from top to bottom leaving a large wedge like slice open to Plato's view. There were twinkling varied colored lights inside. How was this possible? Plato could see no flame or feel no heat. It was if the stars themselves had been sprinkled into a multi colored world inside the gleaming sphere. And in the center were two small couches. In those were placed two babies unclothed and babbling happily. Plato guessed the boy and girl to be perhaps three months of age.

Colin spoke silently to Margo. "This man is of the highest intelligence. He has not traveled far from this place. We must remember he has not seen the wonders we have seen. What we say must be clear." Colin placed his hand on Plato's shoulder. "Democritus has written of the smallest particles that may be. You have read his writings. He has called them atoms. But long ago, the form these atoms took in man became distorted. How this happened we do not have time to speak of now. We have come to bring order to the chaos they have caused."

"The noble goals of which the Master has taught, these will be realized? And the great questions, they will be answered?", Plato asked eagerly.

"Not all," Colin replied. "And not without false pathways along the journey. The search must always be hard. But at the final time, we can promise more will be fulfilled than you can know."

Colin picked up the crystal vial from the altar. He held it up into a beam of slanting sunlight that arrowed down from above the curtain tops.

"The young men and maidens outside have come here to Eleusis with high spirits. They are now making sacrifice at the nearby sea, and they will soon drink the sacred Kykeon cups," Margo said. "They hope and believe that the vial they have brought us contains the magic to bring beautiful Persephone back from black and brooding Hades. I am the Persephone they have desired, but the vial they have brought does not hold the atoms that I must use." Colin reached into the folds of his robes and withdrew the vial he'd filled inside the cave's Ellipse. To Plato, both vials looked the same. Both might just as well have been filled with water from Athens wells as far as he could see. Democritus atoms must indeed be very small.

"Margo, destroy the other now," Colin ordered. As Plato stared with rapt attention, Margo picked up the vial that Colin had carried at the head of the long procession from Athens. With deliberateness, she held it out in front of her and slowly turned her wrist. She poured the contaminated DNA solution at her feet. Then she smashed the crystal vial on the marble steps. Plato watched the droplets trickle slowly to the chamber floor.

"We sacrifice to the Gods in hope they will smile upon us, Plato. But as you know too well they can be capricious with their gifts. Along with the power they have infused in the liquid I have destroyed, were atoms that caused disease and great distress. Dear friends and those we loved have died to our sorrow."

"You have not the power to bring them back?", Plato asked. "In good time we will see them again," Margo answered.

"It is time for us to leave you as you see us now Plato," Colin said. He turned to the open ellipse being careful not to spill the Pulsar DNA fragment. Colin walked down the ramp into the ellipse's glowing heart. The little ones looked at him and gurgled a greeting. Plato watched the priest run his finger over a number of strange buttons until it rested on a white polyhedron with an odd marking like two intertwined snakes. The priest pressed it and a second crystal vial came forward and hovered in the air.

"Careful now," Colin heard Margo say in his head. Colin caught Margo's eye then delicately ran the pure DNA solution into the suspended vial. The vial proceeded back into the wall somehow lit with no flame. Plato's mouth was agape.

"We do this to make your Master's dreams and our own come true," Colin said to Plato. "When all is done here, you will take these babies to Socrates. The Oracle has promised he will see them before he must drink the hemlock cup."

Margo turned and took a place close to the baby girl. Colin stood next to the boy. Plato watched the priest and priestess bend down and kiss the little ones on their foreheads.

"Are you ready for your adventure?", Margo asked them in a soft motherly voice. The children cooed happily kicking their tiny legs. Colin and Margo offered their index fingers to the babies. The boy and girl gripped them tightly.

"When all is done and you take these little ones to your Master he will understand," Colin said." "In a few days Academos will call on you. He will give you land on which to build a school. There, you will raise these babies as your own. When they come of age they will tell of many secrets. We can speak to you no more."

Silvery threads, thousands it seemed to Plato, arched out from the sphere's radiant walls. As if having a mind of their own he saw them curve around the priest and priestess and settle gently on the babies' bodies. Wordlessly Margo spoke to Colin. "We will be forgetting now."

"Among the oceans of futures that lie before us we have chosen well my love," Colin replied. Plato stole behind the altar to be closer to the machine. No matter what injury might befall him in approaching too near, his curiosity and excitement could not be contained. He watched the myriad threads stiffen. Then liquid course through them and into the babies. The children's eyes flashed briefly, all the colors of the rainbow passing through them in a moment. A minute passed, then two. The threads withdrew as silently as they appeared. Except for the prism of color passing through their eyes, to Plato they seemed as before. The little girl looked over at the baby boy. He sucked juicily on the back of his tiny hand. The girl let out a squeal of delight. The priest and priestess closed their free hands over the babies grip on their index fingers. It was important that the physical bond not be broken now. "Are you ready?", Margo asked.

"Yes," Colin answered. Plato backed up against the rear of the altar slab. He gripped its edges with back turned hands. A sound of swirling wind came from the machine, yet nothing stirred. He watched fascinated as the bodies of the priest and priestess began to radiate a creamy glow, as if the heat of their bodies had taken on visible form. The soft light hovered for only a moment. Then suddenly they were filled with blazing color, tiny jewel like points that pulsed and quivered. In a time too quick for Plato to register, the dancing points swept down the arms of the priest and priestess and flowed into the babies. Then the priest and priestess were gone. How could this be? Plato wondered. The little ones seemed content and happy as before. Then Plato understood what he'd seen. Socrates had been right. The Passing. The spirits of the priest and priestess had traveled into the children. He stood trembling for a moment. His heart raced. Yes, of course now he understood. These little ones would someday have children of their own. The magic atoms given by the Gods would spread slowly through their descendants. The hopes of all good men would come to pass.

Plato walked into the ellipse. The little girl held out her hand to him. It contained a tiny flower, foreign but beautiful with streaks of many colors. He bent over to savor its strange perfume. The baby girl pushed it into his broad nose and giggled at his sneeze. Plato tucked the flower behind his ear. He picked up the babies from their couch, held them in his arms and walked to the great bronze doors. The doors opened. Plato looked out to the sea where the thousands were winding their way back to Eleusis' temple from their seaside sacrifices.

When they arrived back at the Temple he would speak to them. Much of what he had seen he could not tell. But he would assure them that the smoke from their offerings would not rise to the Gods in vain. The chains that bound their minds, and the shadows they had taken for reality would vanish, if not for them, then for their progeny. In due time the Gods would give their blessing, and then new and unimagined vistas would become theirs.

Lightning Source UK Ltd.
Milton Keynes UK
UKHW011853070121
376641UK00007B/522/J